PRAISE FOR CATHERINE

Wife by Wednesday

"A fun and sizzling romance, great characters that trade verbal spars like fist punches, and the dream of your own royal wedding!"
—Sizzling Hot Book Reviews (5 stars)

"A good holiday, fireside or bedtime story."
—Manic Reviews (4½ stars)

"A great story that I hope is the start of a new series."
—The Romance Studio (4½ hearts)

Married by Monday

"If I hadn't already added Ms. Catherine Bybee to my list of favorite authors, after reading this book I would have been compelled to. This is a book *nobody* should miss, because the magic it contains is awesome."
—Booked Up Reviews (5 stars)

"Ms. Bybee writes authentic situations and expresses the good and the bad in such an equal way . . . Keeps the reader on the edge of her seat."
—Reading Between the Wines (5 stars)

"*Married by Monday* was a refreshing read and one I couldn't possibly put down."
—The Romance Studio (4½ hearts)

Fiancé by Friday

"Bybee knows exactly how to keep readers happy . . . A thrilling pursuit and enough passion to stuff in your back pocket to last for the next few lifetimes . . . The hero and heroine come to life with each flip of the page and will linger long after readers cross the finish line."
                                        —*RT Book Reviews* (4½ stars, top pick [hot])

"A tale full of danger and sexual tension . . . the intriguing characters add emotional depth, ensuring readers will race to the perfectly fitting finish."
                                                                    —*Publishers Weekly*

"Suspense, survival, and chemistry mix in this scintillating read."
                                                                    —*Booklist*

"Hot romance, a mystery assassin, British royalty, and an alpha Marine . . . this story has it all!"
                                                                    —*Harlequin Junkie*

Single by Saturday

"Captures readers' hearts and keeps them glued to the pages until the fascinating finish . . . romance lovers will feel the sparks fly . . . almost instantaneously."
                                                —*RT Book Reviews* (4½ stars, top pick)

"[A] wonderfully exciting plot, lots of desire, and some sassy attitude thrown in for good measure!"
                                                                    —*Harlequin Junkie*

Taken by Tuesday

"[Bybee] knows exactly how to get bookworms sucked into the perfect storyline; then she casts her spell upon them so they don't escape until they reach the 'Holy Cow!' ending."

—*RT Book Reviews* (4½ stars, top pick)

Seduced by Sunday

"You simply can't miss [this novel]. It contains everything a romance reader loves—clever dialogue, three-dimensional characters, and just the right amount of steam to go with that heartwarming love story."

—Brenda Novak, *New York Times* bestselling author

"Bybee hits the mark . . . providing readers with a smart, sophisticated romance between a spirited heroine and a prim hero . . . Passionate and intelligent characters [are] at the heart of this entertaining read."

—*Publishers Weekly*

Treasured by Thursday

"The Weekday Brides never disappoint and this final installment is by far Bybee's best work to date."

—*RT Book Reviews* (4½ stars, top pick)

"An exquisitely written and complex story brimming with pride, passion, and pulse-pounding danger . . . Readers will gladly make time to savor this winning finale to a wonderful series."

—*Publishers Weekly* (starred review)

"Bybee concludes her popular Weekday Brides series in a gratifying way with a passionate, troubled couple who may find a happy future if they can just survive and then learn to trust each other. A compelling and entertaining mix of sexy, complicated romance and menacing suspense."

—*Kirkus Reviews*

Not Quite Dating

"It's refreshing to read about a man who isn't afraid to fall in love . . . [Jack and Jessie] fit together as a couple and as a family."

—*RT Book Reviews* (3 stars [hot])

"*Not Quite Dating* offers a sweet and satisfying Cinderella fantasy that will keep you smiling long after you've finished reading."

—Kathy Altman, *USA Today, Happy Ever After* blog

"The perfect rags to riches romance . . . The dialogue is inventive and witty, the characters are well drawn out. The storyline is superb and really shines . . . I highly recommend this standout romance! Catherine Bybee is an automatic buy for me."

—*Harlequin Junkie* (4½ hearts)

Not Quite Enough

"Bybee's gift for creating unforgettable romances cannot be ignored. The third book in the Not Quite series will sweep readers away to a paradise, and they will be intrigued by the thrilling story that accompanies their literary vacation."

—*RT Book Reviews* (4½ stars, top pick)

Not Quite Forever

"Full of classic Bybee humor, steamy romance, and enough plot twists and turns to keep readers entertained all the way to the very last page."
—Tracy Brogan, bestselling author of the Bell Harbor series

"Magnetic . . . The love scenes are sizzling and the multi-dimensional characters make this a page-turner. Readers will look for earlier installments and eagerly anticipate new ones."
—*Publishers Weekly*

Not Quite Perfect

"This novel flows extremely well and readers will find themselves consuming the witty dialogue and strong imagery in one sitting."
—*RT Book Reviews*

"Don't let the title fool you. *Not Quite Perfect* [is] actually the perfect story to sweep you away and take you on a pleasant adventure. So sit back, relax, maybe pour a glass of wine, and let Catherine Bybee entertain you with Glen and Mary's playful East Coast–West Coast romance. You won't regret it for a moment."
—*Harlequin Junkie* (4½ stars)

Not Quite Crazy

"This fast-paced story features credible characters whose appealing relationship is built upon friendship, mutual respect, and sizzling chemistry."
—*Publishers Weekly*

"The plot is filled with twists and turns, but instead of feeling like a never-ending roller coaster, the story maintains a quiet flow. The slow buildup of a romance allows readers to get to know the main characters as individuals and makes the romantic element more organic."

—*RT Book Reviews*

Doing It Over

"The romance between fiercely independent Melanie and charming Wyatt heats up even as outsiders threaten to derail their newfound happiness. This novel will hook readers with its warm, inviting characters and the promise for similar future installments."

—*Publishers Weekly*

"This brand-new trilogy, Most Likely To, based on yearbook superlatives, kicks off with a novel that will encourage you to root for the incredibly likable Melanie. Her friends are hilarious and readers will swoon over Wyatt, who is charming and strong. Even Melanie's daughter, Hope, is a hoot! This romance is jam-packed with animated characters, and Bybee displays her creative writing talent wonderfully."

—*RT Book Reviews* (4 stars)

"With a dialogue full of energy and depth, and a twisting storyline that captured my attention, I would say that *Doing It Over* was a great way to start off a new series. (And look at that gorgeous book cover!) I can't wait to visit River Bend again and see who else gets to find their HEA."

—*Harlequin Junkie* (4½ stars)

Staying For Good

"Bybee's skillfully crafted second Most Likely To contemporary (after *Doing It Over*) brings together former sweethearts who have not forgotten each other in the eleven years since high school. A cast of multidimensional characters brings the story to life and promises enticing future installments."

—*Publishers Weekly*

"Romance fans will be sure to cheer on former high school sweethearts Zoe and Luke right away in *Staying For Good*. Just wait until you see what passion, laughter, reconciliations, and mischief (can you say Vegas?) awaits readers this time around. Highly recommended."

—*Harlequin Junkie* (4½ stars)

Making It Right

"Intense suspense heightens the scorching romance at the heart of Bybee's outstanding third Most Likely To contemporary (after *Staying For Good*). Sizzling sensual scenes are coupled with scary suspense in this winning novel."

—*Publishers Weekly* (starred review)

Fool Me Once

"A marvelous portrait of friendship among women who have been bonded by fire."

—*Library Journal* (best of the year 2017)

"Bybee still delivers a story that her die-hard readers will enjoy."

—*Publishers Weekly*

Half Empty

"Wade and Trina here in *Half Empty* just might be one of my favorite couples Catherine Bybee has gifted us fans with so far. Captivating, engaging, lively and dreamy, I simply could not get enough of this book."

—*Harlequin Junkie* (5 stars)

"Part rock star romance, part romantic thriller, I really enjoyed this book."

—*Romance Reader*

Faking Forever

"A charming contemporary with surprising depth . . . Bybee perfectly portrays a woman trying to hold out for Mr. Right despite the pressures of time. A pitch-perfect plot and a cast of sympathetic and lovable supporting characters make this book one to add to the keeper shelf."

—*Publishers Weekly*

"Catherine Bybee can do no wrong as far as I'm concerned . . . Passionate, sultry, and filled with genuine emotions that ran the gamut, *Faking Forever* was a journey of self-discovery and of a love that was truly meant to be. Highly recommended."

—*Harlequin Junkie*

Say It Again

"Steamy, fast-paced, and consistently surprising, with a large cast of feisty supporting characters, this suspenseful roller-coaster ride will keep both series fans and new readers on the edge of their seats."

—*Publishers Weekly*

My Way to You

"A fascinating novel that aptly balances disastrous circumstances."
—*Kirkus Reviews*

"*My Way to You* is an unforgettable book fueled by Catherine Bybee's own life, along with the dynamic cast she created that will capture your heart."
—*Harlequin Junkie*

Home to Me

"Bybee skillfully avoids both melodrama and melancholy by grounding her characters in genuine emotion . . . This is Bybee in top form."
—*Publishers Weekly* (starred review)

Everything Changes

"This sweet, sexy book is just the escapism many people are looking for right now."
—*Kirkus Reviews*

The Whole Time

"Adorable. Sweet. Sparky. Sexy. Full of good food and wine and family and friends and all the things! I so need to see this series on TV one day! *The Whole Time* was such an adorable + fun + sweet + sparky + just beautiful romance—I loved it! Run to your nearest book dealer for your own Ryan—this one is mine!"
—BJ's Book Blog

All Our Tomorrows

OTHER TITLES BY CATHERINE BYBEE

Contemporary Romance

Weekday Brides Series

Wife by Wednesday

Married by Monday

Fiancé by Friday

Single by Saturday

Taken by Tuesday

Seduced by Sunday

Treasured by Thursday

Not Quite Series

Not Quite Dating

Not Quite Mine

Not Quite Enough

Not Quite Forever

Not Quite Perfect

Not Quite Crazy

Most Likely To Series

Doing It Over

Paranormal Romance

MacCoinnich Time Travels

Binding Vows

Silent Vows

Redeeming Vows

Highland Shifter

Highland Protector

The Ritter Werewolves Series

Before the Moon Rises

Embracing the Wolf

Novellas

Soul Mate

Possessive

Erotica

Kilt Worthy

Kilt-A-Licious

All Our Tomorrows

CATHERINE BYBEE

 Montlake

Text copyright © 2024 by Catherine Bybee
All rights reserved.

Published by Montlake, Seattle

www.apub.com

Amazon, the Amazon logo, and Montlake are trademarks of Amazon.com, Inc., or its affiliates.

ISBN-13: 9781662517235 (paperback)
ISBN-13: 9781662517228 (digital)

Cover design by Caroline Teagle Johnson
Cover image: © alexfiodorov, © tainted, © Povareshka / Getty

Printed in the United States of America

This is to every woman who has ever had to make a choice.

Chapter One

The absolutely best part about attending a funeral of a close family member was the ability to wear sunglasses inside. Anyone looking assumed the shield was there to hide the expression of pain and sorrow. For Chase and Alex, it was all about disguising their shock and disbelief of the complete bullshit being spewed from the pulpit. It was one thing for the priest to deliver an appropriate sermon, but the line of people standing up to verbalize their love for Aaron Stone churned bile in Chase's stomach.

"Husband, father, philanthropist, the builder of an empire. Aaron was more than an employer, more than his gilded name that graces so many hotels and resorts all over the globe. Aaron Stone was my friend. Someone I could share a drink with after work or spend a weekend in Vegas with on a moment's notice . . ."

Chase leaned close to his sister's ear and whispered, "High-end escort service on speed dial, no doubt."

Alexandrea, or Alex, as she'd always been called, nudged his elbow and placed a handkerchief over her lips to hide her smile.

Exactly ninety grueling minutes of needless prayer and praise for the prick in the casket later, Chase escorted his father's latest wife behind the coffin while Alex and their mother followed behind.

Chase had been asked if he wanted to be one of the six carrying his dead father to his final resting place, to which Chase replied,

"Hell-to-the-no." He didn't trust himself not to "accidentally" drop his end just to see the man tumble out of his perfect funeral and hear people laugh.

A long line of limousines stacked up behind the hearse. Melissa Stone, wife number three and a woman two years younger than Chase, climbed into the back of the first car with her brother and parents.

Chase, Alex, and their mother, Vivian, closed themselves behind the darkened glass of the second limousine and released a collective sigh once the cameras of the media could no longer record their reaction.

"Damn, that was painful," Alex said as soon as the door closed.

"It's far from over." Their mother patted Alex's leg as if that would cure the agony they all felt.

Chase removed his sunglasses and looked at the both of them. They wore black, despite Alex's threat to wear a bright pink floral dress that screamed celebration and happiness.

"Philanthropist? Exactly what did Dad have to do with giving money to those in need?" Alex asked.

"Tax write-offs, I'm sure," Chase replied.

The limo started to move.

Chase knew from the plans he'd been shown that four uniformed motorcycle police officers were escorting the procession to the cemetery. From the cemetery they'd inch their way up the hills until they were safely behind the gates of their father's Beverly Hills estate, where a reception would host the fake smiles and insincere tears.

A man as wealthy as Aaron Stone was living his death the same way he lived his life. *Large.*

According to the head of the legal team representing Aaron Stone, the man had planned his funeral a good fifteen years before his death.

Considering Aaron was only in his early sixties and in relatively good health, the fact that he planned his own funeral because no one would be able to do it better put an exclamation point on his narcissism.

"Any idea if Melissa is staying in the house?" Alex asked.

Chase shook his head. "I don't have a clue."

"Knowing your father, he and Melissa had a prenup."

"If it's anything like yours, she'll be lucky to keep her jewelry."

Chase held his comments and listened to his sister vent. She wouldn't get much of a chance until the show was over and they could retreat to their mother's modest home in Santa Monica. There, they planned on catching their breath before the morning appointment with the lawyers.

If it wasn't for the fact that his sister's and mother's names were on the list of people requested, Chase would blow off the in-person drama altogether and find a dark bar so he could tell his dead father to fuck off one final time with a shot of whiskey.

They pulled into the cemetery, and sunglasses found their way back on noses.

Thankfully, the service at the gravesite was much shorter than that at the church.

Melissa's loud cries and overly animated tears were out of a scene from a soap opera. The cool breeze of the early spring skies pushed clouds overhead that threatened rain. Literally hundreds of people circled Aaron Stone's casket, most muttering among themselves, some averting their attention when Chase looked directly at them.

Finally, the priest ended his final prayer, asking God to accept the soul at his gate so Aaron's family could move on in peace.

It was only then that Chase stared over his father's casket and felt loss.

Loss for the father he never truly had.

Loss for the chance of redemption.

The man would never again have the opportunity to right the wrongs he had done to his family.

Death had a way of ending all possibility of reconciliation.

∽

A long line of funeral guests slowly sauntered up the steps of Aaron Stone's lavish estate.

Chase stood with Alex on one side and Melissa on the other. It took all of ten minutes before a woman with a cane blocked the parade, giving Chase the out he needed to stop shaking hands and smiling at strangers. "I need a drink," he said to his sister.

"Great idea," Alex chimed in.

They both stepped away from the door at the same time.

"You can't leave me here to face these people alone," Melissa whined.

"You want to shake the hand of every person that has ever kissed up to my father for the last forty years, be my guest." Chase smiled at his sister. "Chardonnay?"

"I'm thinking vodka."

Chase and Alex moved past the foyer and into the formal living room. Framed by pillars and hosting twenty-foot ceilings, the room was large enough to accommodate four separate conversation areas, complete with sofas and chairs. Wall to wall windows were outlined by arches standing side by side, giving the room a spectacular amount of light.

A bar had been set up at one corner of the room, and waitstaff was already circulating with trays of wine.

The table in the formal dining space was overburdened with food. The kind brought in by a caterer rather than thoughtfully made from the kitchen of loved ones overwhelmed with grief.

Alex avoided moving farther into the room when she stopped beside their mother and Nick.

She immediately grabbed whatever Nick was drinking and put it to her lips.

"Atta girl. It's about time you got hammered. That funeral was painful," Nick said to their small group.

"Don't encourage her," their mother responded.

Nick was Alex's best friend, who she often referred to as her gay husband. They'd known each other for years, and because of that, Chase often thought of him as an extension of the family.

"I'll get her her own," Chase told Nick as he walked away and toward the bar.

"Vodka martini and a double shot of whiskey." There was no need to specify a brand, the only liquor behind the bar was top shelf.

"Must be a rough day," someone said behind him.

Chase turned to the slightly familiar face. "There's certainly other places I'd rather be," he responded appropriately.

"I bet."

He had a slight southern accent that tickled the back of Chase's head as he tried to place the man.

"You don't remember me."

"I'm sorry. It's been a long day with a lot of people," Chase explained.

The other man extended a hand. "Jack Morrison."

The name clicked with the face. "Morrison hotels," Chase said.

Jack nodded. "One in the same. I believe we met right before you graduated high school."

"I can't say I remember, but I do know who you are." Hard not to, considering the name. The Morrison family made their way into the papers, just as the Stones did. Families of wealth and power had a way of flashing on the front page from time to time.

"My father would be here, but he's ahhh . . . not in good health," Jack said.

"He sent you."

"I volunteered."

Chase narrowed his gaze. "Why?"

Jack was slow to smile, but when he did, he started to laugh. "Polite thing to do."

"I take it you didn't know my dad."

"No. Not well anyway." Jack rocked back on his heels.

"That makes two of us."

Jack paused. "The tabloids had that right, then?"

Chase took in the other man's expression. "The part about my father being estranged from his kids? Yeah, that would be one hundred percent accurate."

"Damn. That makes today extra rough," Jack said.

"You have no idea."

The bartender placed both drinks on the bar.

"Can't pick your family."

Chase shook his head, grabbed the drinks. "The tabloids had the estranged part right, the rest is crap. Don't believe everything you read in the paper," he said.

"I don't read them. My wife does. In fact, it was Jessie that suggested I come. She said if there's an ounce of truth behind what the papers said, you and your sister might need a friendly face among the wolves that are bound to come out of the fields."

Chase regarded the man with a tilt of his head. Jack seemed genuine, but he didn't know him well enough to determine if kind words at a funeral put him in the trusted category. "We appreciate that," Chase spoke for Alex. "I should get this to my sister. We could both use some liquid courage today."

Jack nodded. "I'll leave you to it. I'm not hard to get a hold of if you need anything."

Chase smiled, took a couple of steps, then looked back. "What you said about your father being sick . . . is that true?"

Jack hesitated. "He thought your dad was an asshole. My father is a little hard to ignore in a room and didn't want to make a scene."

For the first time that day, Chase laughed. Any man as wealthy and influential as Jack Morrison who was willing to call a dead man an asshole . . . at his funeral, was good by Chase. "I'll be in touch," he said.

"I look forward to it."

Back at his sister's side, Chase handed Alex her drink.

"Who was that you were talking to?" she asked.

"Jack Morrison," their mother answered for him.

Nick peered over the rim of his cocktail. "He has some swagger working for him. Is he single?"

Alex swatted Nick's arm with her free hand. "You are not picking up dates at my dad's funeral."

Chase could always count on Nick for some comic relief. "Not only is he not single, he mentioned a *wife* . . . so not on your team," Chase clarified. "He seemed like a decent man."

"Do you know him, Mom?" Alex asked.

"I don't know Jack, but everyone in the hotel industry knows his father, Gaylord. I saw *him* at many dinners and events when I was married to your dad. Gaylord's love for his children . . ." Her voice trailed off, her gaze traveled to the floor. "I'm sorry."

Chase caught his sister's eyes.

Alex placed a hand on their mom's shoulder. "It's not your fault."

The "sorry" was a theme their mother used often. Sorry for every shortcoming their father had that she felt she needed to repent for.

"The man is dead," Chase said, lifting the whiskey to his lips. "Stop apologizing for him."

"If I had just been—"

"Mom."

Vivian sealed her lips and nodded once.

The subject was closed . . . at least for now.

Chapter Two

Piper shoved her hand into the sleeve of a clean shirt she was folding, right as her phone rang.

The number displayed from the caller twisted in her gut like a knife.

She reached down, her arms still engulfed in the shirt, and silenced her phone. "Go away," she said out loud.

With her shirt right-side out, she proceeded to fold it with short, angry movements. It was the middle of a workday. One that she shouldn't be home folding laundry and worrying about how she was going to pay her upcoming rent.

Her phone rang again, only seconds from when she silenced it.

Piper snatched it off the side of the sofa, ready to silence it again.

Only this time, Julia's name appeared.

Piper slid the answer button over, put the phone on speaker, and spoke without so much as a hello. "I told you not to call me from the office line."

"I know," her friend said in a voice that lifted a full octave above normal. "Sorry. I'm distracted."

Piper looked at her pile of laundry and huffed. "Me too. I'm *completely* overwhelmed."

"Turn on the news."

"I don't watch the—"

"Channel five. Hurry. They broke for a commercial but they're coming back."

Piper dropped her folded shirt on top of the pile and reached for the TV remote. "Is this about *him*?"

"The whole office is buzzing. Well, those of us that are here today."

The TV flashed to life, and the local news station was selected. "Let me guess, he didn't die of natural causes after all."

"You think someone killed him?" Julia asked with a short laugh.

The tail end of a commercial suggesting the latest antidepressant could be a life changer for you greeted Piper. "I think he pissed off plenty of people. I wouldn't be surprised if foul play is determined."

The afternoon news crew led in with a welcome and a smile.

"What am I looking for here?" Piper asked.

"They're covering his funeral."

That wasn't a surprise. "So."

"The camera's zeroed in on his kids."

Piper sat on the arm of her sofa and turned up the volume on the TV. "You mean his adult children."

"Still his kids."

Considering Piper had worked with Stone Enterprises for seven years, the last five as the executive secretary to Aaron Stone, and never seen the man's children, she was interested enough to watch the images on the screen.

The news anchor led into the story with a graphic of Stone's image overlaying a picture of the hotel's logo, along with the man's birth date and death date boldly placed at the bottom of the screen.

"Are you watching?" Julia asked.

"Yeah."

The news crew captured several people leaving the church where Aaron Stone's funeral had taken place.

Melissa, the trophy wife, was hard to miss. Perfect hair, perfect dress, and flanked by people Piper had never seen. Behind her followed a tall man with dark, almost wavy short hair, stern jaw, and a lifeless expression.

"Do you see him?"

"The guy behind Melissa?"

"Yeah."

"That's the son?" Piper asked.

"Chase Stone."

"He looks like an asshole."

"Oh my God. He's gorgeous. How can you say that?"

"If you like 'em tall, dark, and brooding."

"He just lost his father," Julia said.

Piper shrugged. If Ebenezer Scrooge had children, they wouldn't have been upset with his passing. "Who is he hovering over?" Chase had his arm around a woman, similar in age, and an older woman close by. He held out a free hand, pushing away the media.

"The sister and the first wife."

"Stone's first wife?"

"Yeah."

Piper tilted her head to the side. "She looks too normal to be married to Stone."

"They were divorced a long time ago."

"She's lucky she got out."

The news cut to the cemetery and scanned the faces of the guests before returning to the studio, where the anchor announced that the state of Stone Enterprises would be discussed on the evening edition of the news.

Piper turned off the TV, plunging the room into silence.

"Everyone here is worried."

"About?"

"Their jobs."

"That's ridiculous. That company is run by a hell of a lot more than one man."

Julia lowered her voice. "Yeah, but we both know things haven't been completely in the black for a while. There're whispers about a takeover."

Piper stood and grabbed a towel from her laundry basket. "He still owned sixty-three percent of the company. That isn't exactly ripe for a hostile takeover."

"That depends on who he left his shares to. If Melissa ends up with it, she'll sell to the highest bidder and walk."

"He didn't love her enough to do that."

Julia huffed. "You're probably right."

"I was his secretary, Julia. Trust me on this." Considering the amount of flowers she sent to other women on his behalf . . . Piper knew the man wasn't devoted to anyone but himself.

"He could have given his shares to his kids. I heard today that the daughter, Alexandrea, works for Regent Hotels. She could sell her shares to them."

Piper folded a towel and placed it to the side. "You're jumping to conclusions and getting all worked up over nothing. That company needs to run, and the executive floor isn't easily replaceable."

"You're right, you're right," Julia repeated as if she was talking to herself. "I can't afford to lose this job."

Piper huffed.

"Oh, God. I'm sorry. That was insensitive of me."

"It's okay."

"No, it's not. I suck. How are you doing? How is the job search?"

Piper picked up a sock, looked at it, and threw it back in the basket. "Considering my boss fired me a week before he died, it isn't like anyone can call him and get a reference."

"I didn't think about it like that."

Piper had. The moment the news broke of Aaron Stone's death, all the wheels in her head started to turn. She'd been terminated with two weeks' pay and notice that her health benefits would expire at the end of the month. Piper had applied for unemployment after she stopped feeling sorry for herself and was told not to expect a check until her employer verified that she hadn't quit or been let go because of misconduct. And even then, the earliest the check would arrive was four weeks. "I'll be fine," Piper told her friend.

"You have a savings, right?"

"I'll be fine."

"You don't sound fine."

"I'm still pissed. It's gonna take a while for that to wear off."

"I wish I could do something," Julia said. "If you don't want me to call you about the gossip, I can stop."

"No, it's okay. I'll let you know if you exceed my morbid curiosity about what's going on around there." And sadly, she had a truckload of curiosity, especially once her jerk of a boss had kicked the bucket.

"Good. I miss our lunches."

"I do, too. Tell everyone I said hi," Piper said with a sigh.

"I will."

"And don't call from the office phone."

Julia laughed, promised she wouldn't, and hung up.

Piper ended the call and looked up at her ceiling. She did have a savings, but only what she'd managed over the last eight months since she'd paid back her student loans. She lived in a one-bedroom guest house behind her seventy-three-year-old landlord that needed her rent money to pay his own bills. Much as the man liked her, he couldn't afford to float her if she didn't find a new job soon.

A familiar noise at her back door prompted her to get off her sofa and abandon the laundry.

"Damn it, Kitty . . . how did you get outside?" she muttered as she walked to the back of her house.

Chapter Three

The law offices of Cadry, Harrison and Cadry were located just south of Beverly Hills.

If the address itself didn't indicate the wealth of the law firm, the inside of the building would. The modern design with harsh edges and bright lights welcomed clients at the front desk with the name of the law firm in backlit black letters inscribed on the wall. While there were several potted plants in the space, not one had a dead leaf or wilted flower to be seen.

Stuart Cadry sat behind a desk with a floor to ceiling window behind him. The usual suspects of law books and framed accolades were perfectly positioned on the open shelves of the built-in bookcases surrounding the room. Cadry looked to be somewhere in his seventies. Chase had remembered him from his childhood on the rare occasion he'd been in his father's home when the lawyer was told to be there. Cadry's salt-and-pepper hair was much saltier now than it had been then, but the man himself hadn't seemed to age. His thousand-dollar suit and Rolex watch that glistened from his wrist flashed his nine-hundred-dollar-an-hour fee.

Chase sat beside his sister while Melissa nudged her chair a good foot away from the two of them before settling into it. Hiding behind large-rimmed sunglasses, Melissa held a handkerchief and dabbed it to her perfectly polished nose that sniffled from time to time.

Alex wore a pencil skirt and smart jacket while Chase had opted for a gray suit minus the tie. He was going to nix the jacket altogether, but his mother reminded him of the media that might be camping out nearby. The reading of Aaron Stone's last will and testament was likely to have someone with a camera close by.

And while Chase didn't give one thought to what he looked like as a reflection of his father's legacy, Chase's own business, and his employees, needed to see his professional side.

"Thank you all for coming. I know this is a hard time, but Aaron was very specific on his wishes after his passing," Stuart started.

An audible sniffle emitted from Melissa.

"I will do my best to keep your time here to a minimum."

Chase cleared his throat. "I'm sure whatever you have to say to us is short and sweet."

Neither Alex nor Chase had expected anything from their father after his death. Knowing the man, their presence at the reading of the will was probably requested so Aaron could tell his kids, one last time, that they should have sucked up to him more in life to collect a few more zeros upon his death.

Stuart offered a noncommittal smile and opened a drawer on his desk. From there, he pulled out three individually bound files. Two were equal in size, and one less than a quarter of the others.

Turning his attention to the widow, Stuart filled his lungs with air and slowly blew it out. "Mrs. Stone. The prenuptial agreement you signed before your marriage with Aaron is still in effect. Provisions were laid out for the unexpected event of his death. Because no foul play has been suspected and the medical examiner ruled Aaron's heart attack to be from natural causes, there is no reason to hold back what Aaron promised you."

"The prenuptial was in case of a divorce." Melissa looked between Chase, Alex, and the attorney.

"It is written for the time of the termination of your marriage, be that divorce or death."

"But—"

Stuart held up a hand. "There were additions to your husband's will after your marriage."

Melissa folded her hands in her lap and sat back quietly.

Stuart opened to a flagged page. "I'll paraphrase here to get us through this process. If you need more, I can explain things line by line."

"Paraphrasing is good," Chase told him. Line by line in what had to be, at minimum, five hundred pages would take weeks.

He took a breath and started reading. "At the time of my death, should my marriage still be intact, I bequeath my beautiful wife all the gifts I gave her in our marriage. The five-carat pink diamond wedding ring is hers. Any car she may be driving, if I was the one to purchase it for her, is hers. If I bought property in her name, she is entitled to it, as we negotiated at the time of our marriage. As is the five million dollars we agreed to. Her personal effects, clothing, shoes, handbags, furniture in her personal space within our home, limited to her bedroom and conservatory . . . are hers, as described below. At the time of the reading of this will, I request assessors to be in our home, taking inventory of Mrs. Stone's personal possessions."

Melissa sat taller, her eyes glued to the attorney.

Stuart paused, glanced over the glasses on his face, and went back to reading. "Should the personal items in Melissa Stone's possession exceed half a million dollars, including but not limited to cars, jewelry, art, designer bags and shoes . . . Jet Skis, boats, property, et alia . . . joint memberships to country clubs, social clubs, et cetera . . . and were purchased after the day of our marriage, these items will be considered part of my estate. If my loving Melissa wishes to keep these items, she may buy back said items from the trust at fifty percent of their estimated worth."

Chase closed his eyes and listened to the sharp inhale of his stepmother.

"I don't understand," she told the attorney.

"Which part?" Stuart asked.

"All of it."

Chase nearly rolled his eyes. His father was screwing over his wife in his death. No shocker there.

"Mr. Stone prepared a file of all the items he'd gifted to you during your marriage." Stuart tapped the papers on his desk. "It's all in here. The Range Rover, the jewelry he gave you for holidays and anniversaries."

"The house in Italy?" Melissa leaned forward.

"That is part of the estate."

"He took me there last summer, said it was mine."

"Not according to the deed."

Melissa slapped her handkerchief-filled palm on the armrest of the chair. "My Aston?"

"If it doesn't exceed the half a million—"

Chase could practically see the calculator running numbers in the woman's head. Knowing how Melissa dressed and how she shopped, he could only imagine what kind of bills she'd run up during her five-year marriage.

"This is ridiculous."

"Mr. Stone was very meticulous with his wishes."

"What about Stone Enterprises?"

Stuart folded his hands together. "You're not named."

"The house?"

"It belongs to the estate."

Melissa's gaze swung to Chase and Alex, her voice rose. "And what? They get the house?"

"Mrs. Stone . . ." the attorney said quietly.

"I live in that house. It's *my* home."

"Don't look at us," Alex spoke for the first time since Stuart had started reading. "We don't want it."

Chase shook his head, doubting the home was left to any of them. Yet when his eyes found Stuart's and then drifted to the larger files on his desk, Chase started to squirm.

What had his father done?

"They don't want it. You heard them." Melissa shifted her weight to the front of her chair, all pretense of tears and sorrow dropped from her face.

"That's not how it works, Mrs. Stone."

"But—"

"As stated in your prenuptial agreement, if you challenge any of Mr. Stone's wishes, or the agreement at the time of divorce or death, you'll be entitled to nothing."

"We were married for five years!" She was yelling now.

"And you're entitled to a million dollars for each year of marriage. Mr. Stone appreciated your companionship."

Alex winced at Chase's side. Even though there was no doubt that Melissa had married their father for the dollar signs, it hurt to hear their marriage summarized as a "companionship."

Melissa shot to her feet, her hands over the desk and on the file with her name on it. "I will have my attorney look at this."

"That is certainly within your rights. Any legal *action*, however, will void—"

"That son of a bitch."

On that, Chase would have to agree with the woman.

"You have seventy-two hours to vacate the house in Beverly Hills. A penthouse suite at the Stone Hotel on Wilshire is at your disposal until you acquire a new address."

"Oh, how generous of the bastard."

"Not to exceed ninety days."

A stream of obscenities flowed from Melissa's mouth as she pulled the strap of her purse up on her shoulder and juggled the pages of the will at the same time.

Pure venom strung from her eyes when she fixed her gaze on Chase and his sister.

"Does this make you happy?" she snapped.

"You're showing your age, Melissa," Alex said without malice.

"We were born the same year."

Alex pulled in a deep breath. "A fact that has always grossed me out."

"This isn't over." With that, Melissa stormed out of the office, a whiff of perfume followed her out.

Alex leaned back, crossed her legs. "Is there a particular reason we had to be a witness to that?"

Stuart smiled. "Your father's wishes. He wanted no misunderstanding or misinterpretation of his intentions. Mrs. Stone has more than enough to keep her comfortable for the rest of her life. Your father saw to that."

"Better than he did for our mother," Chase muttered.

Stuart cleared his throat, squared his shoulders. "If it helps, I advised him against that."

It did help, for reasons he couldn't name.

The room grew silent for a moment.

Stuart pulled the remaining two files in front of him. "The good news is you can right the wrongs of your father. Both of you. As the counsel to Aaron at the time this was written and as acting executor, I have reviewed this thoroughly. I can go over each line item"—he tapped his fingers on the files—"and will, if you want me to. Or I can summarize the highlights and let this digest. Perhaps schedule another meeting next week or whenever is convenient for you both."

"Why would we need that?" Alex asked. "We weren't exactly high on *Daddy's* list."

Chase let his sister do the talking, all while he watched the attorney's body language. The man looked tired, like *he should have retired five years ago* tired. At his age, shouldn't he be off playing golf somewhere right about now?

Alex waved her hand at the files. "If he thinks we're going to jump through a bunch of hoops to get a check from him, he underestimated how little we need his money."

"It's a lot of money."

"We know." Alex sat forward, waved a hand at the door. "We're well versed in how our father treats the people he's supposed to love when he walks out of the picture. Melissa may have been a gold digger, but that shouldn't have been a surprise to the man. Much as I don't like the woman, she shouldn't be forced out of her home less than a week from burying him."

Chase placed a hand over Alex's in an effort to calm her fiery temper. "Why don't we listen to what Mr. Cadry has to say. He's just the messenger, Alex."

The rapid rise and fall of Alex's chest continued after she stopped talking.

Stuart folded his fingers on top of the files. "Aaron may not have shown you in his life that he admired and respected the adults you both became, but he has in his death. With his actions." He paused.

"Tell us," Chase said, eyes drifting to the files, which seemed to grow while the attorney got to the point.

"Aaron Stone left his entire estate to his children."

Chase felt his body grow rigid. Money, he somewhat expected. Maybe an old photo with a note attached saying . . . *maybe you should have come around more.*

"Stone Enterprises, in its entirety. All the hotels, properties, undeveloped land. The holdings, stocks. Personal items, of course, cars, homes—"

"W-what?" Alex's hand was cold under Chase's. Her one-word question hung in the air.

"Everything, Alexandrea."

Chase stared past the attorney and out the window. His father ran a multibillion-dollar hotel empire with a half dozen arms reaching to all corners of the globe.

"Aaron watched your career at Regent. He knew that while you never wanted to work with him, you have this business in your blood." Stuart turned to Chase. "You reached your first eight-figure year eighteen months ago. Are slated for nine figures in the next two years should things continue. Aaron may have never said it to you, but he was proud . . . of both of you."

Not words Chase wanted, or needed, to hear.

Alex stood abruptly and walked to the window. "And if we don't want it?"

That was anger talking. "Think of Mom," Chase told his sister.

"You all will equally share in the responsibilities and votes on the board. There are people at Stone Enterprises ready to bring you in and up to speed."

Chase found his head tripping over Stuart's words, almost like a stutter. "You all?"

"Excuse me?"

"You said, 'you all.' You mean Alex and me."

Stuart shifted in his chair, his lips drew a flat line.

"Yes . . . except."

Anything that followed the word *except* couldn't be good.

"Except, what?"

A shiver ran up Chase's spine when the attorney hesitated.

Alexandrea turned to face him . . . slowly.

"Aaron has another son. You have a brother."

Chapter Four

Chase and Alex stepped out of Cadry's office, dazed. The California sun coupled with an unseasonably dry wind put an extra layer of dirt on a day that was already covered in filth.

Chase had intended to drop Alex off at her place so she could retrieve her car and follow him to their mother's home.

After one look at the outside of the condominium complex where she lived and the multitude of media vans parked along the curb, Chase changed plans.

"Do you think they know?" Alex asked as they both took in the sheer number of reporters trying to get a sound bite.

"Stuart said the information about the brother is private."

"That doesn't mean the information won't get leaked."

Chase turned the corner and headed back toward the freeway. "It's a little soon for that."

"We can expect a long line of Baby Stone candidates if this gets out," she mused.

Yeah, the thought had already crossed Chase's mind.

Stuart had told them what he knew.

"Your father came to me shortly after his divorce with your mother. He told me then that he'd fathered a son that is a year older than Alex. When I pressed him for details on the boy, he wouldn't tell me. Only that he planned on leaving his estate to his children. When he married Melissa, we revisited the will. I pressed again, he wouldn't talk. By then, he'd sold enough of his

shares of the company to put a three-way even split when he passed. This assured him that your two shares alone would work to pass any important issues with the board, but should one of you sell, it would put the other in jeopardy of losing controlling interest.”

“And if we both want to sell?” Alex asked.

“You need to find the brother first. My job as the executor is to follow Aaron's wishes to the letter. You have a year to find the brother. Only then can we revisit selling anything.”

“Why would he do this?” Alex asked.

“To keep us from making a rash decision,” Chase said.

“That's my guess,” Stuart agreed.

“And you don't have the name of the mother either?” Alex asked.

“Aaron believed you'd both be smart enough to figure it out.”

“Leave it to Dad to ignore us his entire life and then tangle us up in all his sins when he dies,” Chase mused out loud.

“We already knew he was a cheating, selfish asswipe. He didn't have to prove it from the grave.”

Alex's words should have been etched into the man's tombstone.

Chase wondered if he could make that happen.

Chase shook off the earlier conversation and said, "Text Mom. Let her know we're on our way." They needed to work through this as a family.

"You think Mom will know who this mistress is?" Alex removed her phone from her purse and started typing.

"I think she's tried hard to forget all of that time in her life."

Alex typed more and pressed send.

"I'm in shock."

"Me too," he said.

"What am I going to tell my boss?" Alex whispered. "Stone Enterprises is a direct competitor."

"We don't have to make a decision today."

"I know." His sister sighed. "My cheek hurts just thinking about the number of times we'll need to get swabbed for DNA testing once this gets out."

"I'm pretty sure we'd only have to do it once."

"That's not the point," she snapped, slapping a hand on the door of the car. "I don't get it. Why was he such a jackass . . . a cheap jackass all these years, and now he just hands everything over?"

Chase shook his head as they inched their way to their mother's house. "Unless he left a hidden note somewhere in his personal belongings, we may never know."

An hour later, huddled around the mass of papers that made up their father's will, Vivian offered a possible answer to Alex's question.

"Your father was all about appearances," their mother said.

"Dad didn't care what anyone thought," Alex countered.

"I know how it would seem that way to you, but he did."

Chase leaned against a wall, his arms folded in front of him. "It doesn't matter. What we need to do is concentrate on finding this brother . . . half brother," he corrected himself.

Alex placed a hand over Vivian's. "Did you know who he was having an affair with?"

Chase watched his mother as she shifted in her chair and patted Alex's arm. "It was a long time ago. I lived with his indiscretions until—"

"*Indiscretion* is not a word you use for a man who gets another woman pregnant while having a family at home." The edge in Chase's voice, and the way he spat his words, brought both his mother's and sister's eyes to him.

Vivian lifted her chin. "Maybe not. But I made a commitment a long time ago that I wouldn't bad-mouth your father to either of you."

"We're not children anymore," Chase said. "The man is dead. You don't have to make excuses for him, apologize for him, or lie about him anymore." The muscles in Chase's forearms tensed. He took a deep breath and willed his rapid pulse to slow. "No one is more aware of what a bastard the man was than Alex and I. So please, Mom . . . stop sugarcoating his behavior."

Chase visibly saw the shift in his mother's eyes. A combination of anger and pain was followed by her eyes swelling with unshed tears.

Guilt for his harsh words twisted in his gut. The last thing he wanted to do was lash out at her.

"I don't know exactly who he was seeing," she said, her back stiffened. "The better question would be who wasn't he sleeping with."

Chase pushed off the wall, crossed to the window. The backyard he'd grown up in instantly brought up memories of birthdays and hot summers. First kisses and first beers. "We need to find the mother."

"We need to find the brother," Alex argued.

Chase kept staring out the window. "If our brother knew who he was, he would have come forward the second the news of Dad's death hit the airways. We need to find the mom."

$$\infty$$

Chase had given himself three days.

The day before the funeral.

The day of the funeral.

And the day that changed his life forever.

It was after five, and Chase had closed all the curtains in his house to drown out the sound and light coming from the news vans that were parked on the street outside.

Up until dear ole Dad kicked it, none of his neighbors were the wiser about who Chase was.

He liked it that way.

A horn blasted outside his property.

He lifted the glass in his hand to his lips and let the whiskey burn down the back of his throat.

His cell phone rang, pulling his attention from the dust accumulating on his coffee table.

The words "possible spam" flashed.

It was as if his personal phone number was blasted on a billboard off the 405 freeway for everyone to see.

He silenced his phone and put it on vibrate.

In the space of a breath, the phone started to move around on the coffee table as if it were possessed.

He reached to turn it off, saw the name, and answered. "Is everything okay?"

"Not by the look of this shit show out here. Are you home?"

It was Busa, his friend and second in charge.

"I am. Where are you?"

The sound of a motorcycle revving blasted from both the phone and his driveway.

"Trying to get through this madhouse."

Chase pushed off the sofa and walked to the front window of his place. "That you?"

"Yeah."

Chase disconnected the call and crossed to his front door.

At least the media was happy to sit out on the street. Chances were they'd all be gone by the time the evening news was off the air.

He opened the front door and moved away from it.

Busa walked in seconds later. "Has that been going on every day?"

"Yeah." Chase topped off his glass and sat it back down with a little more force than he'd intended.

Chase moved away from the counter and back into his living room to resume his brooding position.

"How did today go?"

Chase leaned his head back and stared at the ceiling. "I didn't think I could despise my father more than I already did. I was wrong."

Busa circled to a chair that sat opposite Chase. "You didn't expect an inheritance. Don't let it get to you now that it's over."

He closed his eyes and shook his head as a slow, humorless laugh rumbled in his throat. "Oh, no . . . he gave us everything."

"W-what?"

"Stocks. The hotels he personally owned, all his properties, possessions, bank accounts. Everything."

Busa's pause had Chase opening his eyes.

"Holy fuck."

Chase took a drink and repeated Busa's words slowly. "Holy fuck!"

"So why the hatred?"

He blew out a breath. "Us. All of us. Me, Alex . . . and a brother."

"What?"

"A half brother. One he fathered while he was still married to my mother."

"Jesus."

"We don't have a name or location. Nothing. Alex and I can't sell or do anything other than manage the estate until this guy is found."

"What the hell?"

"First thought was to hire someone to find him."

Busa leaned back in his chair. "Sounds reasonable."

"If the board finds out there is another player, there is no telling what kind of havoc will ensue when things come to a vote. We have a year before everything has to wrap up, eighteen months if we need to push it."

"That's a long time."

"I know. And then there is that nut show . . . out there . . ." Chase nodded to the window. "They get a hold of this, and there won't be a moment's peace. Suddenly everybody becomes Aaron Stone's second son."

Busa chuckled. "I always wanted a brother."

Chase found a smile. Busa was born and raised in southern Louisiana and had the accent to show for it. The man's parents still lived close to the bayou and pulled out catfish and crawdads and ate them on the regular. Busa himself could look at his father and see exactly how he was going to appear in thirty years.

"I don't need you to be my brother, I need you to be me for a while." Chase sat forward, put his drink on the table, suddenly losing interest in consuming it.

"What do you mean?"

"I need you to run things. I can't be in two places at once, and I know I can trust you to take care of my business while I'm figuring out my father's."

"I got your back."

"Let's pull someone up to help carry the load and bring in an intern to take their place."

"Do you have someone in mind?"

At first Chase shook his head, then he nodded. "Shania."

"In sales?"

"She's smart, ambitious."

"And just out of college."

"I was in college when I started this business." He rubbed the bridge of his nose. "She's the right fit. Shuffle people, make it work."

Silence filled the room.

Chase reached for his glass.

"How much money are we talking?" Busa asked. "The news reported north of a few billion."

The amber liquid swirled around the ice cubes in the glass, giving something for Chase to focus on other than the reality of the answer to Busa's question. "Something like that."

Busa slapped both hands on his knees and stood. "In that case, I'll order dinner . . . and you can pay for it."

"You don't have to—"

"Yeah, yeah. Drinking alone is never a good habit to get into."

Chase met his friend's eyes and offered a quick nod.

☜

Parking an oversize truck in the underground parking lot of a high-rise was always like looking for a jigsaw puzzle piece that had fallen to the floor and slipped under the table. It wasn't until Chase found the lowest possible space that would accommodate his vehicle that it dawned on him that his father would have his own parking spot much more conveniently located.

Unlike some buildings where the office area of a company filled one small section, Stone Enterprises had its name on the building and thus used all of it.

Chase purposely kept his visit to himself.

Alex was clearing her calendar at Regent for the beginning of the following week. The two of them had talked about their next steps. Yes, finding the brother was a priority, one that would likely fall on Chase since Alex understood the corporate level of the hotel industry a hell of a lot better than he did.

Business was business, and thankfully, they both knew how to run one.

He stepped into the foyer and looked up at the massive ceiling with sleek, modern lights dangling from above.

It was after ten, and the lobby was relatively quiet.

Before the bank of elevators stood a set of double sensors, ones similar to those you'd see at an airport. These weren't for weapons but for identification via sensors on a key card. At first glance, anyone unfamiliar with the business of high-rise corporations would think the company wanted to know when their employees were coming and going. Chase knew this was more about identifying who was in the building at any time should there be a catastrophic emergency. In short, it was a way of knowing exactly how many bodies first responders were looking for in the case of an earthquake or terrorist attack.

Chase walked to the large reception desk and smiled at the man sitting under a wall holding massive backlit gold letters spelling out *Stone*.

"Good morning," the man greeted him with absolutely no recollection in his eyes. Not that Chase expected anyone to know who he was. Outside of the people he'd seen at the funeral.

"I need access to the executive floor."

The receptionist hovered his fingers over the keyboard in front of him. "Who is your appointment with?"

"I don't have an appointment."

"Is anyone expecting you?"

"No, I'm—"

"I'm sorry, but we can't let you in the building without someone here vouching for you." The man dropped his hand to the desk. "If there is someone I can call for you . . ."

Chase's gaze moved to the name on the wall behind the desk. "Stone," Chase said slowly, thinking briefly how pathetic it was that his own father's company had no way of knowing who Chase was. Not the fault of the man sitting there doing his job, but of the dead man who never thought it was necessary to bring his children around. "I'm Chase Stone." He reached in his back pocket and removed his wallet, not expecting the employee to take his word for it.

The man's smile dropped.

Chase removed his ID, handed it over.

"Oh."

Chase offered a smile. "What is your name?"

"Malcom, sir. No one told me you were coming."

"Nobody knows I'm here." Chase leaned on the counter. "It's my first day. I want to see who showed up to work."

Malcom huffed; his smile grew.

"If you can get me a badge and avoid picking up that phone and alerting all the brass that I'm here, that would be great."

"Absolutely, sir." The receptionist handed back his driver's license and quickly scanned a visitor card as he typed on his computer.

A few minutes later, Chase held the card in his hand, tapped it on the counter. "My sister, Alexandrea Stone, could show up at any time. Take a moment and google her so you know what she looks like."

"Of course, Mr. Stone. Will she be in today?"

Chase shrugged. "You never know. It's been a bumpy couple of weeks."

Malcom's smile fell slightly. "Oh, of course. I'm sorry about your father."

Instead of saying anything and risking a snarky remark, Chase nodded and headed to the elevators.

Minutes later, he walked out of the elevator bank on the top floor.

Another reception area greeted him. The woman behind the desk resembled a runway model. Perfectly etched makeup, not a blonde hair out of place, and a good twenty pounds underweight.

She smiled as a stranger would, and then her eyes opened wide. "Oh."

Apparently, the executive floor knew *exactly* who he was.

"Good morning."

She scrambled to her feet as she tugged on the hem of her tight skirt. "Mr. Stone. Were we expecting you?"

He motioned toward the interior of the offices. "No."

"Oh, uhm . . . what can I do for you?"

"It's been a while since I've been here. If you could point me in the direction of my father's . . . late father's office, I'd appreciate it."

The woman removed her headset and rushed around the desk. "Of course. Follow me."

Chatter from the employees in the few cubicles and surrounding open office doors slowly faded as they caught their first glimpse of Chase as he walked through. Open curiosity and hushed whispers were quickly replaced with rushing feet as people ran around to tell their bosses he was there.

"I'm Kira, by the way," the blonde told him.

"A pleasure to meet you, Kira."

Tight carpet kept the space much quieter than what Chase had in his office. Not hearing the click of a woman's heels or the echo of voices was somewhat of a relief. He wondered if it had been that way the last time he was there. Chase honestly couldn't remember.

They took a sharp left at the end of the room, then passed what looked like several conference rooms until they landed at a corner office. The double doors were closed, Aaron Stone's name was in back-lit gold letters, just like the one in the lobby. Only this one slightly less egregious.

The sound of someone nearly running caught Chase's attention as he stared at an empty secretary's desk.

"Mr. Stone?"

The voice belonged to another woman, this one slightly less runway modelish and more conservatively dressed.

"Hello."

She stuck her hand out. "Julia Escobar. I'm Mr. Gatlin's assistant."

Chase processed the name quickly. Gatlin, vice president. The man had gushed about his father at the funeral. He also made sure Chase knew he was keeping everything running smoothly in Aaron's absence at the company.

Julia's handshake was firm, her smile genuine.

"A pleasure. Where is your boss?"

She cleared her throat. "He's on his way up."

Chase turned to the empty desk. "My father's secretary?"

"Assistant," Julia corrected him. "All the executive secretaries here are called assistants."

Julia glanced at Kira.

"Okay, where are they?"

"She's ah . . . actually, we've been using temps. Since your father's death, ah, passing, we haven't brought one in."

"Why a temp?"

"Your father let his assistant go a couple weeks ago."

"Why?"

Julia and Kira both shifted their weight from one foot to the other.

Chase waited for an answer.

"I'm not really sure."

Chase didn't buy that. Office gossip spread faster than news of donuts in the break room.

Not that it mattered.

"I should get back to my desk," Kira blurted out. And she was gone.

He turned to the sleek doors, pushed them open, and stepped into his father's space.

Chase sucked in a breath and held it.

Nothing was the same from the last time he'd been there. The furniture, the layout, the paint on the walls.

The artwork comprised black-and-white photographs of some of their most recognized hotels and resorts.

Blinds were drawn, blocking the direct sun from entering the room and casting shadows throughout the space.

"Can I help you find anything?" Julia asked.

"Do you know where everything is in here?"

She shook her head. "No, but I helped the temps as much as I could. I probably know more than anyone else that's here today."

Chase stepped farther into the room. "How do we open these blinds?"

Julia scrambled around the desk to the wall. "There's a remote somewhere. And a wall switch here." One press of a button and the soft burr of a motor rolled the blinds up.

"Thank you."

Julia moved to the center of the room as he crossed behind the desk.

"I can call the temp agency and get someone," she offered.

Chase pulled out his father's chair. "Bringing someone in who isn't familiar with the needs of my father, without my father being here to direct them, is useless. I'd like to know why my father's assistant was let go."

Julia swallowed. "I'll have someone from HR bring up her file."

"That's a start."

He took a seat and slowly sat his arms on the desk. In front of him was a computer, a phone, and a leather-bound folder.

Not one picture of his wife or his children. Nothing that described the man who sat there.

Or maybe the absence of these things described Aaron Stone perfectly.

Julia cleared her throat, catching his attention. "I-is there anything else I can do for you?"

He started to shake his head and then changed his mind.

"I'd like your boss and Mr. Ripley to clear their schedules and be here in an hour. Is that possible?"

She nodded. "I'll inform them."

"Thank you."

Julia turned to leave, then stopped.

"Yes?" he asked.

"I'm . . . I'm sorry . . . for your loss."

The sentiment was starting to resemble fingernails on a chalkboard. One that made him cringe every time he heard it.

Instead of a retort that would carry in the office like wildfire, he nodded once, and Julia left, shutting the door behind her.

Chase closed his eyes and took a soul-cleansing breath.

Chapter Five

"Oh my God, he's here."

Piper listened to her excited friend over a bowl of cereal and a cup of herbal tea.

"Why is it you sound like you're talking about a potential Bumble date?"

Julia's whisper was so low Piper had to stop chewing her food to hear her. "He's so hot."

"You might want to get over that if you want to keep your job."

"A girl can fantasize."

Piper swallowed and swirled the colored bits of marshmallows around the equally sweet, but not as bright, Lucky Charms in her bowl. She hadn't eaten this much sugar in the morning since she was ten. But lately she couldn't get away from the crap. Who knew her depression food would be meant for a four-year-old? "I guess that means Daddy gave his company to his son."

"Nothing official has come through the pipeline, but that's my guess."

Piper filled her spoon, shoveled more sugar into her mouth.

"He wanted the HR file on you," Julia said.

"Why?" Piper asked around her food.

"He asked why you were fired."

"Ha! Tell him because his father was a misogynistic, womanizing asshole."

"I'm sure that would go over really well." Julia's sarcasm was crystal clear. "He probably needs to know what Stone was working on . . . his schedule, meetings . . . stuff like that."

Piper immediately found her mind listing off all the places for the newest Stone to find what he needed. Instead of voicing any of that, she shoved more food in her mouth. "Sounds like a problem . . . for him."

Julia cleared her throat. "You know, you could play this right and maybe get your job back."

"Not interested!"

"Why?"

She swallowed and set her spoon down. "The thought of sucking up to any Stone to get my job back makes me physically ill." Considering her stomach started to churn at that very moment, Piper stood firm on her convictions.

"I wish you would try . . . Oh, shit. Floyd's here. I gotta go."

"Talk to you—"

Julia disconnected the call on her end, leaving Piper staring at her phone.

She pushed aside the cereal and looked down at herself. It was after ten in the morning, and she hadn't yet gotten out of her pajamas and bathrobe.

Kitty sat at her side, eyes bright.

"I'm making a habit of this."

Taking Piper's attention as an invitation, Kit pushed his hundred-and-ten-pound rottweiler frame to his feet, his mouth open in a pant.

"I should probably take you for a walk."

Kit slapped his jaws shut with the word *walk* and tilted his head just enough to tell Piper he understood her.

"All right, Kitty . . . let me throw on some clothes."

His stub of a tail started to wag, and the panting began again.

∽

"Chase! I didn't expect you so soon." Floyd Gatlin walked into the office after a single knock.

Chase stood and moved around the desk with an extended hand. "No time like the present."

They shook hands as Arthur Ripley, Stone Enterprises' CFO, joined them.

"Thank you both for making room in your schedules today." Chase turned to Ripley, shook his hand, and then indicated for both men to sit in the chairs provided in front of the desk.

The men glanced at each other. "We've kept meetings outside of the office light since your father's passing. It wasn't uncommon for your father to be away a couple of days a week."

"I assume those meetings have been canceled or rescheduled for you."

"Without any direction, that was the plan," Floyd said.

Chase took his father's chair and placed his hands in front of him on the desk. "Probably for the best."

Ripley was a good twenty years older than Chase, bald, trim, his suit tailor-made. "We weren't sure who would be sitting in that chair."

"No one was more surprised than me."

Both men chuckled.

"And Alex. She couldn't be here today, but she will be in a day or two."

"Alex? Alexandrea?" Floyd asked.

"Yes," Chase answered.

"Your father left Stone Enterprises to both of you?"

"You sound surprised."

Floyd shrugged. "We haven't been told anything."

Chase leaned back. "Which is partly why I'm here today. Before the news of my father's will becomes public, we wanted you to hear it from us first."

They exchanged looks and stayed silent.

"He left it to us." Chase paused and then clarified, if only to himself, "His children."

Gatlin sighed. "What do you know about running this company?"

Instead of admitting he knew nothing, Chase said what he'd want to hear. "Business is business. Alex and I have both been in the corporate sector our entire adult lives. It will take a while to come up to speed, but we'll figure it out. I assume that we can depend on the both of you to provide whatever we need to do that."

Ripley's slow smile felt like support, whereas Gatlin's was guarded.

"What about your own business?" Gatlin asked.

"My second in charge is quite capable of running it while we figure this out."

"Wouldn't it be better to put someone else in this chair at Stone Enterprises while you're 'figuring this out'?"

"Who would you suggest?" Chase questioned. "You?"

"Well . . ."

Chase brought his hands together in front of him, fingertips touching. "All due respect, Mr. Gatlin, if my father wanted you to take over for him, he would have put it in his will. We all know that my father didn't do anything on accident. Now, that isn't to say that Alex and I won't conclude that the company would be better off with someone else running it. Which may or may not be you. But in the meantime, your cooperation with this transition is imperative. The employees out there need to know they all have jobs and that nothing is going to change."

Gatlin's shoulders started to relax, and so did his questions.

"We'll need to call an executive board meeting with the shareholders and put them at ease. Preferably before the media jumps. I'd ask my father's secretary . . . assistant to do this, but it appears he's without one."

"I'll have Julia get on that."

"Perfect." Chase relaxed his hands on the desk once again. "I certainly don't want to treat either of you like an assistant, but since

I don't . . ." He hesitated. "Why don't I have an assistant? Do any of you know why she was let go?"

"Your father didn't tell me," Arthur said.

"I'm not completely sure either. I know she was late a couple of times, according to the staff gossip," Floyd said.

Chase tapped a finger on the desk. "Regardless, we'll need all the numbers. Quarterly statements, profit and loss. Anything my father was currently working on. Anything pressing or pending."

Someone knocked on the office door.

"Come in."

Julia walked in, a file in her hand. "I'm sorry, I can come back later."

Chase unfolded from his chair. "No, we're done here. Gentlemen . . ."

Floyd and Arthur followed Chase's lead and stood.

Chase rounded the desk.

"We're here to help," Gatlin said before walking away.

"Thank you."

Arthur paused and patted Chase's back. "I am sorry for your loss. I'm not sure I had an opportunity to say that at the funeral."

Nails.

On.

Chalkboard!

"There were a lot of people there."

Another pat on his back, and Arthur dropped his hand. "I'll get those numbers for you."

Instead of thanking the man, Chase turned to Julia and accepted the file she handed him.

"Thank you, Julia."

He turned and headed back into the office without looking at her.

"If there is anything—"

"I'll let you know." Chase heard the door close behind him as he opened the employee file of the fired assistant.

"Piper Maddox." The first page in the file was the last correspondence. Her termination paperwork, which stated she had been chronically late without notifications and that her performance had declined in the months before she was let go. All of which were reported by Aaron Stone. Piper had signed her name with a giant *P* and a line.

The second evaluation was presented as a warning of the need for improvement for the eventual causes of her termination. It all seemed pretty straightforward . . . until Chase flipped the paper over and read a note by his father. That's when doubt crept in.

Chase chuckled as he moved on to a performance evaluation from six months before that didn't show any sign of problems. High praise from her colleagues and a satisfactory mark from Chase's father. The one before that was a year before the last . . . same results. The evaluations went back five years to when she'd been promoted to his father's assistant. She'd joined the company after what looked like an internship. His father's assistant at that time had hired Piper as her assistant. Those evaluations were off-the-charts perfect and given by her immediate boss, who wasn't Aaron Stone.

The last page in the file had a picture of her when she'd been hired. She looked like a young, enthusiastic intern. Brown hair and bright eyes with an infectious smile. Girl-next-door pretty with a hint of wisdom in her gaze. The fact that she had jumped through the ranks of her position so quickly, to end up as the assistant to the CEO in only a handful of years with the company, was impressive.

"This smells bad, Piper Maddox."

Going with his gut, the one that suggested that a conversation with her might give some insight into his father's actions, Chase picked up the office phone and dialed the number on the résumé.

On the third ring, she picked up. Instead of a hello or orderly greeting, she yelled into the phone. "Darn it, Julia. I told you not to call me from the office number!"

"I'm sorry . . . is this Piper Maddox?" he asked.

"Wait . . . what?"

"Miss Maddox? Who used to work with Aaron Stone."

Her voice pitched higher. "Who is this?"

"This is Chase Stone."

It sounded as if she'd pulled the phone away from her ear, the obscenity she used was muffled, but he still heard it.

"What do you want?" she finally asked.

"I am speaking with Miss Maddox, correct?"

"You called me, so yeah."

She did not sound happy.

"I'm wondering if I could have a conversation with you in regard to your employment."

"I don't work there anymore."

"Clearly. I'm looking over your termination paperwork, and something doesn't feel right." Chase lifted the picture of her and tried to imagine what her expression was right now. Not the smiling, happy-to-get-a-job one that was in his hand.

"That's because it's bullshit. Aaron Stone was a d—" Her words trailed off. "I can't do this."

Chase jumped. "Wait, don't hang up."

"You're the son, right?"

"I am."

"Then you know how your father was. I'm sure I don't have to explain it. And since I was raised to not talk ill of the dead, I see no point in this conversation. Goodbye, Mr. Stone."

The line went dead.

Chase stared at the receiver as a slow smile crept over his face.

Unlike every member of the office staff who had a vested interest in saying the right things and laying platitudes at Chase's feet . . . this woman did not. The fact that she cut him off and came short of calling his dad a dick showed she truly didn't have anything to hold back.

Which meant only one thing . . . he had to get her back in that assistant chair.

Chapter Six

Dressed in leggings and an oversize sweatshirt, Piper took her frustration from the unexpected phone call out on the weeds that were growing in a small planter on the side of her house.

Kit sat a few feet away, a massive bone set between his paws, his jaws making good time with whatever was tasty on the thing.

Her small vegetable garden had all gone to seed over the winter and had a huge amount of neglect calling her name. The pail she used to dump the weeds quickly filled, which meant frequent trips to the bigger garbage can. She considered digging up everything, but there were a few volunteer vegetables peeking through the mess, which made her take the extra time to be selective with what she tore out.

Besides, the work had calmed her down.

It was incredibly frustrating to be angry at a dead man.

Part of her really wanted to feel sorry about the situation. That would be the part of her that was raised by two midwestern parents that dragged her to church every Sunday of her life growing up. The other bits of her, though . . . they wanted to scream that karma was a bitch.

The sound of a car rolling down the driveway caught her attention.

It sounded bigger than the old Buick Mr. Armstrong drove, which probably meant it was a delivery truck. They made the mistake of driving onto the property all the time, not realizing that there was no way to turn around. And most were not as proficient as they believed they were in backing up all the way without running over a sprinkler or the lawn.

Piper pushed to her feet and slapped her gloved hands together to remove a layer of dirt.

Kit stopped chewing and looked up.

"Stay here," she told him with a point of a finger.

He got to his feet and then sat where he'd been told to hang out.

Satisfied that he wasn't going to try and chase off the delivery guy, Piper made her way around the house and opened the side gate.

Expecting to see a big brown truck or one in blue with a light blue smile, she was shocked to see a double-cab truck with a man in a business suit stepping out of it.

He grabbed papers from the inside of the truck before walking toward her front door.

All Piper could see was a solicitor, one ballsy enough to drive on her narrow driveway, right past the "No Solicitors" signs Mr. Armstrong posted everywhere.

"Can I help you?" She made herself known and, at the same time, opened the side gate wider and signaled to Kit to come.

For a big dog, he was at Piper's side before the man could respond.

He stopped and looked over at her.

"Miss Maddox?"

The hair on her neck stood up. How did he know her name? And why did he look familiar?

"Whatever you have to sell, I'm not interested," she told him.

A low noise came from somewhere deep inside of Kit.

The man took notice of her dog.

"I'm not here to sell you anything."

On closer inspection, he looked nothing like the average day solicitor. The truck was newish, and the suit wasn't your everyday variety, but more likely higher-end threads that weren't bought off the rack. His short brown hair had a little wave. He had a strong jaw, with a bit of a frown covering his face.

"We spoke on the phone earlier." His eyes left Kit and moved to her. "I'm Chase Stone."

And then it all clicked.

Yes, the face was the same one she'd seen on the news . . . minus the sunglasses.

"What are you doing here?"

The edge in her voice prompted Kit to growl.

Piper removed her garden gloves and motioned for Kit to hold his position.

"Does that dog bite?"

"Only when I tell him to. I said all I need to say on the phone."

"You hung up and didn't give me a chance to explain."

"So you drove all the way here to do that?" she asked.

"Face-to-face conversations are better than those over the phone." He tapped the folder in his hand against his leg. "Just a few minutes of your time."

She considered turning him away but heard her mother's voice in her head telling her it never hurt to know your options.

"Piper? You okay out there?"

She looked past Chase and saw her neighbor standing at his back door, watching them.

Her voice softened. "I'm fine, Mr. Armstrong. Thanks for checking." Piper sighed and started toward her door, signaling Kit to follow.

She opened the screen and held it. "Come on in." She'd listen to the guy, but she wasn't about to offer him coffee or tea.

Chase hesitated as he walked through the threshold, his eyes on Kit. "You sure?"

Piper pointed a couple of feet away. "Kitty, sit." The dog moved with a whine as he followed her command.

"Kitty? That dog's name is Kitty?"

"Don't let it fool you." Piper motioned toward her sofa and then moved to the armchair next to her dog.

Chase pushed aside his suit jacket and sat. "Thank you."

"Don't thank me yet. The only reason you're sitting here is because Mr. Armstrong is almost as protective as my dog. He knows I've been upset. You can tell by his age that he doesn't need to be worried about anything but himself."

"I'll be sure and thank him," Chase said with a sigh.

Piper looked at the papers in his hand. "What is that?"

He handed it to her. "Your HR file."

She opened it, saw the termination paperwork that she'd seen when they let her go, and felt her blood boil for the second time that day. The next page was new. She pulled it out and read it to herself.

It was the equivalent of a write-up. It stated that she had missed several deadlines and was exhibiting a bad attitude. Not only was the information crap, the entire write-up was bogus. The signature on the bottom, the one that should have been hers, wasn't. "This is simply a lie." She waved the paper in her hand. "I've never seen this. That isn't my signature."

"Did you read the back?" Chase asked.

She turned it over.

Written in Aaron Stone's handwriting, it stated:

Miss Maddox has made a handful of suggestive comments over the past couple of months that we should spend time outside of work together. When I turned her down, her performance as my assistant started to waver. I'm hoping this formal warning changes her behavior.

She squeezed her fist around the paper. "Suggestive comments," she whispered under her breath.

"I'm guessing that was a fabrication," Chase said.

"More like projection. And clearly, since he managed to slip this in my file, he was concerned I'd come back and point a finger at him."

"Was that why you were fired? You rejected him?"

"Repeatedly."

"Why didn't you go to HR?"

Piper stared him down. Was he that naive? "Accuse your billion-aire CEO boss of sexual misconduct, and you'll never have another billionaire boss to worry about again. You'll be starting from scratch in the mail room or, worse, a go-nowhere start-up that can't afford to pay you. No thanks."

"What did you do as my father's assistant?"

She rolled her eyes. "Everything. There wasn't a paper that passed his desk that I didn't have knowledge of. I knew his schedule better than he did. Meetings, the players at the meetings. I sat behind him when the board met, taking notes and shoveling him information if he needed facts he didn't remember. Not to mention sending *I'm sorry* flowers to his wife, and *it was nice to meet you* flowers to the women that caused him to send the *I'm sorry* flowers."

"You managed his personal life?"

She nodded. "The first few months on the job, I thought every assistant had that role. It wasn't until I became friends with the others that I realized your dad pushed the boundaries with my job description. Not that I pushed back."

Chase rubbed his jaw as he clearly thought something over in his head. "Did you like your job?"

"When I wasn't slapping your dad's hands off my butt . . . yes."

Chase's lips fell in a thin line. "Do you want it back? Minus the butt slapping," he quickly added.

Piper lifted her chin. "Why?"

He sat forward and folded his hands together. "The first reason is practical. My sister, Alexandrea, and I will be sharing the responsibility of taking over our father's position. Since he didn't bother with mentoring either of us on what he did to run Stone Enterprises before his death, we're coming in blind. We need to know what's going on, and we need to trust the person shoveling *us* the information. That would be you."

Piper felt her stance on saying no to his offer wane. Finding another executive secretary position wasn't the easiest task, and God knew she needed the money now more than ever.

"What was your second reason?" she asked.

"You might be the only person in that office that doesn't feel the need to kiss my ass or my sister's. When people are sucking up to you, you have to wonder what their motive is. You don't have one. I'm asking you to return, you didn't come to me."

Maybe this would work. "I won't kiss your ass."

His lips finally started to move into a grin. "I wouldn't ask you to. And Alex is the nice one, she won't either."

Two bosses, one job . . . and they needed her. "I have conditions."

His eyes lit up. "I'm listening."

"I want a raise."

"Fine."

"And a bonus for the weeks I've been out of a job."

"Sounds reasonable." He was smiling now, and with it, Piper felt her chest tighten. Chase Stone was a hell of a lot easier to look at than his father had been.

"If it doesn't work out for whatever reason, you don't like me, I don't like you . . . I get high letters of recommendation and this crap . . ." She waved the still-wadded-up paper she'd pulled from the HR folder in the air. "Goes away."

"Consider it done." Chase slapped his hands on his knees and stood. He took a step her way, and Kit immediately jumped to his feet and stood in front of her with a growl.

Chase pulled back.

"Kit!"

"Is he always so friendly?"

"He's been protective lately." She motioned for her dog to stand down, but that didn't stop Kit from giving Chase the death stare.

Chase put his hand out . . . slowly.

Piper put her hand in his, felt the warmth of his handshake.

"Thank you," he said.

She met his gaze. "You're welcome."

He smiled and let her hand go.

His eyes lingered.

Eyes that were nothing like his father's. It was then a twinge of guilt for talking ill of the dead man to his son slapped her upside the head. She'd been raised better than that, and if her parents were there, they'd remind her. "It can't be easy hearing negative things about your father so close to his passing. I am sorry . . . for your loss."

Chase physically winced and tilted his head. "Are you?"

Good manners and telling the truth collided in her head like a war between good and evil. "No," she squeezed out. "I mean, yes. He was your dad."

"He's been gone a long time for me, Miss Maddox."

That was even more sad, in her eyes.

She walked toward the door and opened it.

Chase stopped just outside, and she handed him the HR file, including the crinkled-up lies.

"You can keep this one," he handed her the wad of paper. "We won't be needing it."

She took it and crushed it even more. "I'll be in tomorrow morning."

He smiled. "I do have one request of you."

"Okay."

"Whatever Alex and I discuss with you, it stays with the three of us."

"Collaborating with the other office staff is—"

"I'm not talking about the work . . . well, unless there is something that requires confidentiality. I'm talking about the personal life of my father. The media would love to hang some juicy gossip on any of the facts they learn. That kind of stuff distracts the players and employees . . . makes people nervous. I don't want anyone thinking they're losing their job because Aaron Stone died."

"I can do that."

He offered a nod. "I'll see you tomorrow."

Piper smiled as she watched him climb into his truck.

Back in the house, she walked into her bathroom to wash her hands and glanced in the mirror.

There, on her forehead, was a smudge of dirt that went all the way across her brow. Her hair was a mess, and she was as pale as a ghost.

"Great first impression, Piper," she said to her reflection in the mirror.

Not that it mattered, she had her job back.

With a raise.

It was time to celebrate.

⌒

"How was it?" Alex asked over the phone as Chase drove home through LA traffic.

"No one knew I was coming. It's safe to assume there isn't a pipeline from Cadry to the office executives. Gatlin, the VP, thought he was going to take over . . . wasn't too happy to see me, and equally surprised that you are coming on board."

"How unhappy?"

"I think he was more annoyed than he let on. Time will tell. We should have the current financial stats tomorrow. And I rehired our secretary."

"Rehired? Did she quit after Dad died?"

"No. Dad fired her. Accused her of coming on to him."

Alex flat out laughed. "Let me guess, she's young and beautiful and didn't accept his advances."

Chase found a smile on his face as he envisioned Piper Maddox. Dirt smudged on her forehead with a rottweiler snapping at her side. Her fierce expression when she'd thought he was a solicitor made the garden makeup look like war paint. Even through all of that, Chase took close notice of her high cheekbones and hazel eyes that seemed to have a hint of gold in them. Five five at most, but she held herself as if she were six feet tall. Confident in her convictions and honest despite who she was talking to.

"Chase, did I lose you?"

Chase blinked a few times. "Sorry, yeah, she's all that. She also managed a lot of Dad's affairs . . . his personal affairs."

"That's gross."

"True, but we can use that to our advantage. She may know something about this brother of ours . . . or the mother."

"Oh! Good point," Alex said.

"How did your boss take it when you told him the news?"

Chase heard his sister groan. "I'm delusional if I think I can keep my job after so much as setting foot in Stone Enterprises. And even if I don't, everyone is watching me."

"You can't blame them."

"I know. It's a lot to adjust to."

Traffic slowly picked up to a whole thirty miles per hour, giving Chase a little hope that he'd be home within the hour. "I don't think we're going to get a lot of sympathy from anyone. We both became billionaires overnight."

Her next moan made Chase laugh.

"Did you know that the richer a woman is, the more her romantic prospects decrease?"

"That can't be true."

"Oh yeah? When was the last time you slept with a woman that made more money than you?" Alex asked.

"I don't think I should be talking to my sister about sex."

"Just answer the question, Chase."

Red lights glared as traffic slowed . . . again. He ran through the list of women . . . "I don't know," he said.

"The answer is *never*. You've never done the nasty with a CEO of her own shit."

Alex wasn't wrong.

"Since when are you worried about your next date? You never bring anyone around."

"Which proves my point," she shouted. "Just the link with the family name intimidates men. Even without the money. Or they'd see a golden ticket, and *baby this* and *baby that*, then realize I don't have that kind of bank account, and they split."

"So don't tell them."

She scoffed. "Have you googled your name this week? Our names, pictures, and profiles are everywhere just with the *speculation* of our inheritance. When the news breaks with the facts, you'd have to be living in a cave to avoid knowing who we are."

"I think you're overreacting. Besides, who googles their dates?" Traffic picked up once again.

"You don't?" she asked.

"No. You do?"

"Every time. Background checks, social media, school records to make sure they aren't lying about their education."

"Jesus, Alex . . . it's dinner and drinks, not an interview for an employee."

"Nice male perspective there, brother."

Chase reflected on her words. "Oh."

"It's going to make it harder, that's all I'm saying."

"Since when are you looking for a boyfriend anyway?"

"I'm not. I'm just bitching, and since you're the only one that can possibly understand, I'm crying to you." When she stopped talking, she started to laugh. With that laugh, Chase found himself chuckling along with her.

"You need more girlfriends."

"I know!"

Chase laughed harder. When they both settled down, he asked, "Are you coming in tomorrow?"

"Yeah, in the afternoon. I'm pretty sure there's going to be a box with all of my personal stuff on my desk waiting for me at Regent."

"Did they say that?"

"It was implied. Along with a reminder of confidentiality."

That was amusing. "Confidentiality to who? There isn't anyone higher on the food chain at Stone Enterprises than the two of us."

"Exactly. I guess a visit with the corporate lawyers is due sooner than later to make sure I don't inadvertently do something that gives Regent a reason to sue."

"That's smart."

"I know."

Chase shook his head, smiling. He loved his sister, respected the hell out of her. And even though he wasn't entirely comfortable talking with her about the men in her life, he would rather know who was around so he could step in if needed.

"I'll see you tomorrow."

"Sounds good."

Chase disconnected the call and hit the brakes as traffic came to a crushing halt.

Chapter Seven

Chase arrived early the next day, before most of the staff members on the executive floor were due to come in.

He informed the security desk that Miss Maddox had been reinstated and to give her access to the building as if she'd never left.

Unlike the day before, Chase took his time in the nearly empty offices and greeted the early employees in an effort to get to know them. He found a break room that housed a small kitchen with two coffeepots that were already percolating. In the cupboards, there were real plates, silverware, cups, and glasses. A dishwasher surprised him, but it made sense. A note attached to a clip on the refrigerator said: *Your mother doesn't work here, take care of your own dishes.* A second note said the refrigerator was emptied on Fridays by the cleaning staff. Everything except condiments would be thrown away. No exceptions.

He poured himself a cup of black coffee and made his way to his office.

A man smiled as he walked by and greeted him. "Good morning, Mr. Stone."

Chase hesitated. "Good morning. You are . . . ?"

"Miles. One of the junior accountants."

Chase skipped the handshake and offered a smile as he walked away.

Another "Good morning, Mr. Stone." This time from an older woman, maybe in her fifties. Instead of stopping to collect another name, he replied the same and kept walking. Three more people called him out, the last one jumping up from her cubical closest to his office.

"Mr. Stone. Hello. I'm Dee."

"Good morning."

"Sorry, yes. Good morning. Can I get you some coffee?"

Chase held up his cup.

It took a full three seconds for her to register that he held a cup of coffee in his hand.

"Oh, okay. Sorry."

"Not a problem." He turned toward the open door to the office.

Dee scrambled to his side. "I'm sorry I wasn't here yesterday when you came in. My son was sick, and the school won't let him come in with any cold symptoms. Not that I blame them. And my babysitter couldn't come early. It doesn't happen often."

Chase held up his free hand. "Dee, is it? I wouldn't know that you weren't here yesterday since this is my second day. What is it you do here?"

She pointed to the still-empty assistant desk. "I'm Piper's assistant. I mean, I was Piper's assistant. She was fired."

Now the conversation came into focus. "She's been reinstated and will be in today."

Dee's shoulders slumped with relief. "Oh, thank God. It's been crazy without her. First, she was fired. Then Mr. Stone dies. I didn't know if I . . ." Her words trailed off and her cheeks turned red. "Oh God, I'm so sorry." She covered her face with her hands. "He was your dad. I am so sorry."

It was almost comical how nervous and flustered the woman was. "Dee?"

She kept shaking her head, her palms covering her face. "I'm such an idiot."

"Dee?"

She finally looked at him.

"When children get sick, they need their mothers. I'm sure my father's death and the absence of the person you report to can't have been easy. That all changes today. Your apology is unnecessary."

"But I—"

"Completely unnecessary. Now, do you know who is in charge down in Human Resources?"

She nodded. "Ah-huh."

"Can you give them a call and explain that I'd like to meet with them early this morning? I won't take up much of their time."

Dee's head bobbed like a child's toy. "I can do that."

"Thank you." Chase escaped the nervous assistant and closed his office door halfway to block out anyone who passed by.

He'd had enough meet and greets before his first cup of coffee.

Ten minutes before the official start time of the workday, Chase heard his assistant arrive. Not because Piper made herself known but because of the surprise resonating from the staff outside his office welcoming her back.

Once the welcoming committee dissipated, he heard Piper start to bitch. "Who did you guys let take over for me? Is there a monthly report? Did anyone take notes from the board meeting? Where is the schedule?"

The sounds of drawers opening and closing followed her outburst.

Chase was on his way to the door when he heard Dee's reply. "We haven't had a schedule since . . ." Her voice lowered to a whisper. "Mr. Stone died."

"I suppose that makes sense," Piper replied.

Chase pulled his office door open and peered at his assistant's desk.

Piper stood there, no longer dirt smudged, with messy hair and a dog protecting her like a mother bear watching over her young. No, she was wearing a knee-length skirt and matching blazer, a white button-up shirt, and high heels. Her sun-kissed skin looked as if she'd been on vacation and not in her own garden. But he knew the truth about that. Her hair was pulled back in a loose bun on top of her head, and the dusting of makeup she wore amplified the sparkle in her hazel eyes. Gone was the girl-next-door vibe, and out came the teacher every heterosexual schoolboy wanted to be in detention with.

Chase blinked away his thoughts.

This was his assistant.

The one that didn't want to take her job back for fear he was just like his father.

Thinking about the color of her eyes or glow on her skin was *not* a step in the right direction.

"Good morning, Piper."

She looked up, offered a smile. "Hi."

"Is there a problem?"

She pulled back her chair, sat, and started typing on the computer.

He could tell by her face, and how she punched the keyboard, she wasn't happy.

"I can't get in."

"Dee . . . any response from HR?"

She shook her head. "They aren't here yet."

"Put a fire under them when they arrive." He signaled to Piper. "Let's check if my computer will find what you're looking for."

She shoved her purse into one of the drawers in her desk and followed him into his office.

Before she shut the door, he asked, "Did you want some coffee first?"

She turned and hesitated. "No. I'm okay."

"You sure? I can give you a few minutes to get settled."

She walked to his desk and twisted the keyboard her way without sitting. "I had some at home."

Chase moved around her and looked at the monitor while she clicked away.

"What are you looking for exactly?"

"Mr. Stone's schedule. It's probably the best way to walk you through his role here. Not that he spent a lot of time in the office."

Chase pushed his chair toward her, encouraging her to sit while he stood at her side, watching the monitor.

She sat without argument and pulled the chair closer. "Here it is." She clicked a few keys. "And none of it has been updated since I left."

"Was that your job?"

"Yeah, but they had to bring in someone to work with your dad." She scrolled back the calendar and pointed to the screen. "Like this. Your dad had a meeting with the head of Titus bank." She clicked on a link, which brought up another window. "Huh."

"What?"

"Looks like your father's objective for the meeting, along with follow-up calls and any action items I needed to make sure were accomplished." She moved down to the week before Aaron Stone died, clicked on a different meeting, and while there was an objective in the pop-up, there weren't any notes for the assistant. "Nothing. Either he didn't tell the temp what he needed, or they didn't know how to update this calendar. Your father would have insisted that this was done."

"Maybe there's a paper trail."

"I'll dig in my desk and look for one. Maybe Dee has something."

Chase narrowed his gaze. "She seems rather frazzled."

"If by frazzled you mean afraid of her own shadow, you'd be right. But she's good. She simply needs direction. And without an assistant or a boss, I'm surprised she's still here."

For the next ten minutes, Piper navigated the schedule that had been mapped out before his father's death and pointed to meetings—in person, Zoom, and ones he was scheduled to travel to.

"What I really need is my schedule. I hope they didn't delete anything, along with my passwords."

A knock on the door had them both looking up.

Dee poked her head in. "Human Resources is here."

"Perfect."

Dee walked away, and a man, somewhere in his forties, walked in. He first glanced at Piper, then took in Chase.

"Thank you for coming on such short notice."

"Absolutely. I'm Tate Lyell. Head of HR."

"Chase Stone."

"I knew that."

"And you know Piper."

Piper smiled. "Hi, Tate."

"Piper." Tate attempted to mask his confusion and failed.

"Mr. Lyell, I need you to reinstate Miss Maddox and inform payroll to retroactively pay her for the time she has been gone."

"Oh, okay."

"In addition, Miss Maddox will be receiving a six percent raise." Chase glanced at Piper, her expression hadn't changed. "And if she is still with us in two months, an additional three percent will be added on to that."

"I'll see it done."

"Great. Now, how long will it take to reinstate all of her computer and corporate access?"

Tate kept looking between the two of them. "An hour at the most."

Chase smiled and started walking toward the door. "Great. Call Dee when everything is ready."

Chase walked him out before turning to Piper. "I hope that meets your expectations," he said.

Her lack of emotion made him question if he should have given her more. Considering he had no idea what her pay was, he figured six percent should cover it. The extra three was there as an incentive for her to stick around.

"It will do," she told him, her poker face intact.

He stood with one hand on the doorknob. "While we're waiting for you to get your computer back, I need you to give me a tour of the building. Floor by floor."

"I don't know everyone on every floor," she said.

"I only need a rundown of the departments and who is in charge of them. I don't need introductions to everyone. Not at this time."

She stood. "That, I can do."

"We'll make it brief."

Chase held the door open and let her pass.

Piper set the pace on the executive floor, which he'd somewhat gotten a leg up on the day before. The conference room en route to his office didn't hold a candle to the one that took up a good portion of the south side. The one the board used when they gathered.

As requested, Piper took him down one floor at a time. There were more departments than Chase expected and so many employees his head spun. New Development, Customer Relations, Customer Service, Mergers and Acquisitions, Public Relations, Social Media Management, Accounting on what felt like every floor and in every department. Risk Management, Human Resources, Billing and Payroll. The list went on. There was a section of one floor dedicated entirely to computer specialists, not only on the corporate end but also those who responded to a mainframe for the hotels owned by Stone. Some empty offices . . . why was that?

The elevator doors opened on the third floor to a deserted space.

"What's going on here?" He stepped out while Piper stayed in the elevator.

"It's used for storage."

He kept walking. "Why?"

"I don't understand your question." Piper relinquished her place in the elevator and followed him.

"Why is it empty? What *was* here?"

"Marketing for a while. We had an international team, but that was restructured a few years ago. Many of our departments were tightened up when the economy slowed down, not to mention a fair number of employees that telecommute."

"Work from home," Chase clarified.

"Correct."

Chase ran his hand across an unused desk, one of many cluttering the space. "And this sits empty."

"Yup."

"Why not rent the space out?"

Piper crossed in front of him and ran a finger on the dust covering a file cabinet. "Your father didn't want anyone in the building who wasn't his. And he believed that he was going to need this again when he expanded."

He turned his attention from the dust on her finger to her eyes. "Is there a plan for expansion?"

"Nothing big enough to fill this space with employees."

Chase walked from one end of the space to the other. Several offices were closed off from the modular cubbies that filled every floor. Efficient but sterile.

"What are you looking for?" Piper asked.

"Nothing particular."

Piper stopped walking and quickly sneezed three times in a row. Tiny squeaks of sound that could have come from a child instead of a full-grown adult. "Excuse me."

"Let's keep moving," he suggested. "And have housekeeping spend some time in here."

"I'll call them."

After heading back to the elevator, they soon walked around the second floor, which was only half-filled and mainly used as the mail room and also housed giant printers. Boxes upon boxes of printed brochures and bound notebooks sat in corners.

Only a handful of employees occupied this space. Chase shook a couple of hands and followed Piper down to the first floor. Housekeeping, security, and a giant meeting hall.

The tour took a good hour and a half before they walked back onto the executive floor.

Julia intercepted them. She squealed and hugged Piper. "I'm so glad you're back."

"I am, too." Piper's gaze moved to Chase.

"I have welcome-back donuts in the break room," Julia said.

"You didn't have to do that."

Chase watched the two of them and saw the genuine friendship pour out.

He slipped away from their chatter and escaped to his office.

His father's schedule was still pulled up and staring at him. An unfamiliar vibration ran through his gut. Meetings and events that his father had planned, suddenly meaningless in the face of death. And what wasn't on this calendar? What about his personal life? The women? Chase knew there were more of them.

Stuart was currently working on getting Chase and Alex access to their father's bank accounts. Something he hoped would direct them to the third recipient of the estate. But these things took time.

His cell phone rang, dragging his attention away from his father.

Chase looked at the name on the screen and smiled at the familiar. "Hey, Busa . . . What's up?"

"Two questions."

"Shoot."

"Shania asked what pay came with her promotion."

Apparently, today was the day to give everyone a raise. "Three percent. Room for negotiations in three months."

"Cool. When do you want to schedule the team meeting? Doesn't have to be long. The people here need to know all is good."

Busa was right. Chase clicked around on his father's schedule, saw two open dates back to back, and gave them to Busa. "See which one is best."

"I can have Shania take care of this."

"Sounds good. How is the media there? Have they backed off?"

"Only one van this morning, but they're already gone," Busa said.

"Good."

Piper stepped into the office, papers in her hands.

"I gotta go. You know how to get ahold of me."

They said their goodbyes.

"Sorry to interrupt," Piper said from the door.

He shook his head. "If the door's open, you can interrupt. If it's closed, don't."

She walked in, handed him what she held in her hand. "Last board meeting and the P&L for the last three quarters."

Perfect, now he had a direction to move in.

He took the papers. "Are you logged in?"

"I am."

"Dissect my father's schedule from the day of his death to two weeks from now. I need to know who he was scheduled to see and why. Find out if anyone filled those obligations in his absence."

"Okay." She turned.

"And Piper?"

"Yeah?"

"Thank you."

She smiled. "Just doing my job, Mr. Stone."

Chapter Eight

Julia hadn't lied about the office chatter when it came to the new boss. There wasn't a recognizable face that didn't stop Piper and ask how she'd gotten her job back or if she had any knowledge of Chase and his sister selling their shares of the company.

Everyone was nervous. Especially the big bosses. Not that they came to her with questions, but she could tell by the way they interacted with Chase. They attempted to make small talk, which failed miserably.

Piper was starting to wonder if Chase had an aversion to smiling. He'd only done so a couple of times that she'd noticed and for such a brief period of time that if she'd been looking the other way, she'd have missed it completely.

And then Alex arrived.

Piper thought Chase was a force, but Alexandrea Stone was the tornado.

She entered like a politician, shaking hands and smiling. Piper heard her before she saw her. Her hair was pulled back at the nape of her neck and hung down her back. Her full lips and wide eyes belonged on the cover of a fashion magazine, and not in an office behind corporate doors. Her slim hand shot Piper's way as she hesitated by her desk. "I'm told you're Piper."

"I am. You must be Miss Stone."

"Alex, please. I know it took some convincing from Chase to talk you into coming back."

Piper hesitated. "Your father put a bitter taste in my mouth with my termination."

Alex huffed out a gasp of air that sounded a lot like a laugh. "He put a bitter taste in mine in third grade. I win. Thank you for being here. I hope Chase made it worth your while."

"I don't have any complaints."

Alex pointed toward his office. "Is he in there?"

"Yes."

And with that, she disappeared behind the massive double doors and closed them.

As soon as Alex was out of sight, the phone on Piper's desk rang.

"What do you think?" Julia asked.

"Powerhouse."

"Rumors are she is part of acquisitions and mergers at Regent."

"Is or was?" Piper asked.

"No idea."

Piper lowered her voice. "I think things are going to get very interesting around here."

"Going to get? Where have you been?" Julia asked with a laugh.

"At home eating Lucky Charms," she said, deadpan.

"Oh, that's just wrong. Do you know how much sugar is in that crap?"

Maybe so, but damn, they sounded really good right about now.

The door to Stone's office opened, and Chase poked his head out.

"That's perfect, thank you," Piper said in an effort to sound like she wasn't participating in the office gossip. Then she hung up.

Chase waved her into the office.

She grabbed a legal pad and a pen and followed him in.

"Close the door, please," Chase said.

"Am I fired already?" Piper asked, half joking.

Alex laughed from where she stood.

"No," Chase said without humor.

"That would have been the shortest reinstatement ever." Piper took a seat across the desk.

Alex moved from where she stared out the window to sit beside Piper. "I like you already. Chase said the three of us have something in common."

"What was that?" Piper asked, her eyes moving to Chase.

"None of us cared for our father."

It was Piper's turn to chuckle.

"And Chase said you're not an ass-kisser."

"I did that with your father, figuratively," she clarified. "And look how that turned out."

Alex crossed her legs and sat back in her chair. "We don't need that from you. We need your loyalty."

"Confidentiality," Chase added.

Piper narrowed her gaze. "Why do I get the feeling you're about to tell me something I shouldn't know."

Alex waved a hand in the air. "Oh, we'll wait until next week for the family secrets. Right now, we simply want to know what everyone in the office is chattering about."

Piper blinked several times. "I've only been back a few hours." It wasn't even noon.

Alex smiled and stayed silent.

Chase folded his hands together and waited.

Piper felt the need to confess a crime she didn't commit. "You two are really good at that."

"Silence is a great tool," Alex said.

Piper put the pad of paper and the pen on the edge of the desk since, clearly, she wasn't going to need it. "There's a general hum of worry about if the two of you are going to sell your shares of the company."

"Even management?"

"The big bosses are always the first to go in a takeover," Piper said.

Alex glanced at her brother.

"And?" Alex asked.

"There is a rumor about your employment with Regent."

"Told you," Alex said to Chase. She turned to Piper. "I resigned from Regent this morning. I was a part of their acquisitions and mergers, which can be determined by looking through their employee database. Feel free to clarify that to anyone asking over the water cooler."

"You want me to be a part of the gossip mill?"

"We want you to spread the facts," Chase said. "This one anyway."

"However, I signed a corporate confidentiality agreement with Regent long before my father's death. So, while we are in this office, if something slips that perhaps I shouldn't have shared, I . . . *we* expect that you uphold the same agreement to us."

"Us personally," Chase added. "Not only Stone Enterprises."

The intensity of both Stone children had the hair on Piper's neck standing on end. "I can't see any of that as an issue."

"Great. Now, how much of our father's personal life did you manage?"

Piper considered the question and wondered why they were interested. "I arranged his travel and booked accommodations for his *companions*."

"Women?" Chase asked.

"He had a lot of *nieces*." Piper smirked. "I sent flowers, messages, gifts . . ."

"You had access to a personal credit card."

"Yes."

"Is that in here?" Chase asked, pointing to the computer on the desk.

"It's on my computer."

"We'll need access."

"That should be simple enough," Piper said.

"Did you ever send money out to anyone on that account?" Alex asked.

"No."

The two of them exchanged glances again.

"Is there something specific you're looking for?" Piper asked.

It was in the moment of silence that followed that Piper knew there was something these two weren't revealing.

Alex recovered first with a smile and a shake of her head. "There's so much about our father that we didn't know. I'd personally like to know if we should expect a grieving lover to come out of nowhere making demands."

Piper sighed. "I guess that could happen."

"Were the women in his life local?" Chase asked.

"On occasion."

"How many were there?" Alex asked.

Piper shook her head. "I didn't count. I kept my head down and did my job."

Chase ran a hand through his hair.

"Why does it really matter?" Piper asked. "The man's dead. Any promises he made to the women in his life, unless it was documented, isn't going anywhere in court."

"There's no guarantee he didn't write something down that he didn't give to his estate attorney," Chase pointed out.

"Your father was an orderly man. Very cut and dry. I doubt he would have left anything out there to chance. If he bequeathed something that wasn't specified in the will, it will be written somewhere for you to find."

Chase pointed to the computer on his desk. "I haven't found anything personal in here."

"Oh, you won't. He gave me the charge of organizing his . . . indiscretions. If anyone looked at his computer, they wouldn't find it. Not that it mattered, I suppose, considering he owned the company. Maybe you'll find something different on his personal computer at home."

Alex rolled her head back. "Of course. I didn't think of a home computer."

Chase leaned forward. "Did he work from home a lot?"

"Oh, yeah. In fact, he really only came in here a couple of times a week."

That seemed to surprise them both.

"Did that make it difficult for you?" Chase asked.

Piper felt her body easing back in her chair, any discomfort in talking to her new bosses floated away as the conversation continued. "He had me come by his home on occasion . . . which I didn't think anything of until . . ."

"He got handsy," Alex finished Piper's thought.

"Yeah. I made my assistant come after that. Eventually your father gave up the idea of seducing me and didn't demand I come by the house that often. There have been circumstances that I was there. But only when he was meeting with other staff or a business associate."

"Safety in numbers."

Piper shrugged. "I never really felt unsafe . . . He made comments, made a pass, or three or five, until he let it go. That didn't stop him from looking."

Alex shook her head, disgust written on her face. "Very unacceptable."

"What do you think prompted him to fire you?" Chase asked.

Piper hesitated before shaking her head. "I don't really know."

Alex turned her attention to Chase. "We're going to have to go to the house."

"Not with Melissa there."

"I think she's supposed to be out by now," Alex said.

Piper felt a little like an outsider listening to a private conversation. Not that it stopped her from making a comment. "Wait, your dad didn't leave the house to his wife?"

Alex shook her head. "No."

"That's a crappy move."

Alex chuckled. "Yeah, and not public knowledge. Let's keep it that way a little longer."

Piper made a locking motion in front of her lips.

"I'm sure his computer is password protected," Alex said.

"Do we have a professional hacker on staff?" Chase asked with a tsk.

"You don't need a hacker," Piper said.

Both sets of eyes were on her.

"He constantly locked himself out of his computers. I put a fail-safe in both so I could get in."

Alex started to laugh, which put a smile on Piper's face.

"I'm really glad you hired her back," Alex said.

Piper met Chase's gaze. His eyes softened, and a slight, rare smile lifted the corners of his mouth.

∾

Julia stopped by Piper's desk thirty minutes before five. "Hey."

Piper smiled up at her. "What's up?"

"A couple of us are going to happy hour. You should come and celebrate."

"That sounds great." And it did . . . but.

"Perfect."

"I can't."

"What? Why?"

Piper's mind scrambled for every excuse but the truth and settled for a classic. "I have a lot of stuff here that needs to get squared away."

"You're not expected to work overtime," Julia said. "Bobbie is taking the kids to his mother's for dinner for her birthday. C'mon."

Julia and Bobbie had been divorced for four years. Leaving Julia to raise her now seven- and five-year-olds on her own. Bobbie stepped in on his scheduled weekends, but only when his current girlfriend didn't bitch. And she always bitched.

Piper moaned. "I really can't. Getting all this straightened out is only going to make my job easier."

"But—"

"Sorry, Julia."

"Then Saturday. It's his weekend."

Piper hesitated.

"What about that place on Sunset?" Julia said quickly.

Piper cringed. The last place she wanted to go was the nightclub on Sunset. "How about a rain check."

Julia shook her head. "No. You've been putting me off for weeks."

"I was fired."

"Even before then."

Piper knew her friend enough to understand she wasn't going to drop this. "Fine, but I'm the DD. And we're not going to Sunset."

Julia smiled ear to ear. "Perfect. You pick the place."

With that, her friend bounced away.

Piper watched her leave, knowing she'd dodged a bullet for another day.

"You don't have to stay late."

Glancing up, Piper realized that Alex had heard the conversation.

"I know, I just . . ." She glanced down the hall at Julia's retreating frame and then lowered her voice. "I really don't want to go. Truth is, I'm kinda tired. I've been lazing around for almost three weeks. I need to train my body to get up early again."

Alex smiled. "In that case . . ."

"Yeah . . . Oh, by the way. I scheduled a doctor's appointment for Monday. It's in the afternoon. I can try and change it, but you know how doctors are."

"Is everything okay?" Alex asked.

Piper waved a hand in the air. "Routine stuff. I was out of work. I figured I'd make all my appointments while I had the time."

"Makes sense. That's fine. I'll let Chase know."

"I can return for a couple of hours after."

"No. Take off at noon. I'll put more on Dee."

Dee was currently not at her desk and down in the copy room, personally making sure the board meeting agenda was getting printed.

"Thank you."

Alex stared down the hall for a moment, lost in thought.

Piper waited quietly for the other woman to move. Finally, she asked, "Are you okay?"

"Numb. I buried my father on Friday, and here I am five days later, scheduling an executive board meeting for *his* company before the weekend."

The empty tone of Aaron Stone's daughter put an actual ache in Piper's chest. Her first inclination was to apologize for Alex's loss, but then Piper remembered Chase's response and held back. "That can't be easy," Piper said instead.

"No," Alex said. "But it will get better." And with that, she turned, went back into Aaron Stone's office, and closed the door.

Piper sighed and whispered to herself, "We all have our crosses to bear."

Chapter Nine

News of Chase and Alexandrea Stone's inheritance made the airways late Thursday night when Melissa held a press conference.

The second Chase saw the sound bite for the evening news, he called Alex. "Are you watching this?"

"I'm taking a bath with my bottle of wine."

"Well, put the bottle down, dry off, and turn on the news."

"What is it now?"

Chase heard the sound of water splashing as, presumably, his sister was getting out of the tub.

"Melissa held a press conference."

"What? Why?"

"From the sounds of the headline, to make us look bad." Chase flipped to another newscast and saw a picture of him and Alex with the caption, *Stone Enterprises falls to disgruntled children.*

Melissa, perfectly polished and smiling for the snapping cameras, stood beside two men wearing suits. "It's the shareholders that need to worry. Chase and Alexandrea are in no way competent to run this company. They hated their father and all things Stone Enterprises. That hasn't changed. Their disapproval of my late husband crushed the man, and I'm sure that stress is what ultimately caused his heart attack." The evening news cut the clip and spliced into another sound bite. A reporter asked if she'd been given any portion of Stone Enterprises. "No.

I'm told the entirety of Aaron's shares went to his children. A surprise to me, to be honest."

"Will you contest?"

Melissa placed a hand on her chest. "I cannot so much as audit a copy of the will without voiding our prenuptial agreement."

Alex spoke up on the phone. "What channel?"

"Five," Chase told her.

"Mrs. Stone," another reporter interrupted. "Do you think there's a chance the will was altered?"

She smiled sweetly and made Chase's stomach turn. "That sounds a bit much, but in a world where you can't swipe a credit card at a gas pump without the risk of someone stealing your identity, you never can tell."

The reporter broke away from the conference and spoke to the camera. "We learned that earlier this week, Alexandrea Stone resigned from her position with Regent Hotel Group to help run her father's company. Chase Stone, Aaron Stone's only son, who owns a successful shipping company, has been seen entering Stone Enterprises' main headquarters here in Westwood all week. Clearly these newfound billionaires are quickly putting themselves in the shoes of their late father, even while the company is struggling to make up for a decreased revenue stream due to the economy. So far, Stone Enterprises has held the stance of 'No comment.'"

"Fuck," Alex cussed.

"This isn't good."

"No. She's bitter and vindictive."

"She can't audit the will, but what is stopping the other shareholders from asking questions?"

"You think that's why she did this?" Alex asked.

"What else can she do? You heard Cadry. If she files one piece of paper in any court, she's out of the prenuptial money." Chase flipped through the channels to see if there was any more coverage of Melissa's press circus.

"She's not trying to get any more money," Alex pointed out. "She's just playing her last bitch card to cause us havoc."

"That's what it looks like to me."

Alex moaned. "And here I was, trying to figure out a way to give her the house."

"Not after that. It will look like a payoff."

"You're right."

Chase turned off his TV. "We need to keep that will closed up until we find this brother."

"Cadry knows that."

"Thankfully we have the board meeting tomorrow and can nip this before it grows bigger," Alex said.

Chase sat on his sofa, switched his phone to his other ear. "It's a little convenient that she came out today, before tomorrow's meeting."

"I'm sure she has friends at the office."

"I don't know what's more important, figuring out how to run Stone Enterprises or finding our brother before the world learns about him." Both were overwhelming.

"Look at it this way," Alex started. "We have some time on our side, but eventually, the board is going to want a vote on something important. And the truth is . . . this unknown brother carries a twenty-one percent voice on those decisions. Things get sticky, are we committing corporate fraud if we vote on his behalf? And is there anything in the will about how this should be handled while we search for this guy?"

Chase ran a hand through his hair. Alex's questions were way outside of his wheelhouse. "We need to sit down with Cadry again."

"I agree."

"We also need to get over to the estate and get into Dad's computer."

"I vote that you do it."

He knew she was going to say that.

"Pick a day next week and have Piper meet you over there," Alex suggested.

He'd already considered that. "Yeah."

"Except for Monday. She's off in the afternoon for a doctor appointment."

Chase's focus switched from computer hacking to his assistant . . . his *sexy* assistant. "Is she sick?"

"Normal stuff. She scheduled it before you hired her back."

"Fair enough."

He heard his sister sigh. "So much for my relaxing evening."

"Don't drink all the wine. We need you sharp tomorrow."

"It's a single-serving bottle, Chase."

Chase laughed and wished his sister a good night.

He set his phone down, only to have it ring almost immediately.

He expected the media but saw Piper's name.

Warmth grew in his stomach that he tried to ignore. "Hello, Piper."

"Hi, uh, sorry to call you so late. But did you, by chance, see the news tonight?"

"We did."

"Oh, good. I thought if you hadn't that maybe you should before tomorrow."

"I just spoke with Alex. We'll draft a public statement after the board meeting. If you can get an entire copy of the press conference, that would be ideal."

"I'll get on it first thing in the morning."

Chase smiled. "I didn't expect you to do it tonight."

Piper laughed. "Good, because it's my bedtime."

Chase heard her dog bark. "Does that dog sleep with you?"

"Yes, and he's a bed hog. Aren't you, Kit?"

He imagined the dog cocking his head as she spoke to him. And that thought put a smile on Chase's face.

"Thank you for making sure I knew what was going on."

"I *am* your assistant."

He was sure this was the first time an employee called him to watch the evening news. "I'll do everything I can to keep that from eight to five."

"This is an unexpected situation. So long as you don't make me send flowers to your girlfriend, we're good."

Chase ran a hand along the stubble on his chin. "You have to have a girlfriend to send her flowers."

"Oh, ah . . . I wasn't really asking. It's none of my business."

Funny, he had a desire to know if someone was in her life. Only he held his tongue. He did not need her thinking he was coming on to her. Even though the thought had entered his mind more than once since they'd met.

"Get some sleep, Piper. See you tomorrow."

"Right . . . okay," she stuttered. "Good night."

Chase smiled and hung up the phone.

∽

Chase and Alex filed into the meeting room, with Piper trailing behind them, exactly one minute before the meeting was due to start.

The board members were already seated, some that Chase remembered from his father's funeral, some he didn't know at all. Most were dressed in suits, with ties and tight smiles. All but three of them were men.

Sitting in chairs behind the board members were secretaries and assistants, much more female dominated and culturally diverse. It did make Chase take notice and question what the ratio of men to women in the top positions within Stone Enterprises was.

The moment the three of them entered the room, everyone quieted.

There were two empty chairs at the head of the stark white table.

Chase moved in front of his sister and pulled out the chair at the very head for her to sit in.

She looked him in the eye, said nothing, and sat.

Piper took a seat behind her, and Chase settled on Alex's left.

"Thank you all for taking the time to get here on such short notice," Alex started off.

The two of them had rehearsed how they were going to run this first meeting, with each of them pausing long enough for the other to chime in. A show that they were both in charge and expected that they would be treated equally.

"We've invited Stuart Cadry to join us"—Chase indicated Stuart, who sat at his side—"our late father's private attorney, to assure you and answer any legal questions about this change on the board."

A few members glanced at each other but stayed silent.

"Our goal was to have this meeting before the media exposed our father's last wishes," Alex said.

Someone at the far end of the table chuckled. "That didn't work."

Chase met the older man's gaze. "No. It didn't."

"We're here now," someone else said.

"The purpose today is to set your minds at ease," Alex told them. "And answer any questions that we can."

Piper leaned forward at that moment and set a piece of paper between Alex and Chase with a seating map of those at the table. Starting with them, the name of each individual person was labeled, along with a share percentage under their name. All of which she'd managed in the short time they had been in the room.

Chase offered a brief nod to Piper before she sat back in her seat.

"The agenda in front of you has a brief description of my skill set as well as Chase's. It is true that I have worked with Regent in their Mergers and Acquisitions Department and have been in the corporate end of the hotel business since college." Alex went on to tell the board what Chase's background was, boasting on his behalf.

She'd barely finished her introduction when the man who'd spoken up earlier did so again. "What are your intentions? From the sounds of this"—he picked up the agenda and dropped it on the table—"you plan on running this company."

Chase glanced at the seating map and put a name with the face. Mr. Yarros.

"That's exactly what we're going to do," Alex told him.

Across from Chase sat Gatlin. And while he attempted to hold a poker face, the way he shifted his body in his seat and glanced down the row of the board members signaled his unease.

"We're not selling anything," Chase explained. *At least not now.*

The man on Gatlin's right looked at Stuart. "Aaron left everything to them?"

The attorney cleared his throat. "Aaron revisited his trust every year. His estate and business ventures were always slated for his children."

"Yet neither of you have ever been in this boardroom."

"True," Chase said. "Regardless, we're here now. Alex and I will be dividing up the responsibilities as we navigate this new challenge." Once the man looked away, Chase glanced at the paper, put a name to the face.

"Then who is in charge?"

Alex pointed at Chase. "We're partners. Equal say. It's that simple."

"Who are your advisers?"

"The entire executive floor has been generous with their time while we onboard. With the death of the CEO, we have a grace period to extend any changes that were pending, as well as any voting on new items. Any negotiations our father was dealing with in private are suspended until we have definitive information. Operations within Stone Enterprises will continue exactly as they were the day our father died," Chase said.

"What private negotiations?" Mr. Fergese asked.

"That's unclear," Chase replied. "According to our father's schedule, there were several trips to various locations and businesses that are not completely accounted for. We're unsure why he was going there. These could have been as simple as keeping in contact with valued customers, trades . . . or any number of new business line items. Anyone could come forward claiming unsigned promises."

"Has that happened?" someone new asked.

"No. But we're prepared if anyone should."

"If you have any concerns, now is the time to voice them," Alex told them.

A low hum came over the room as several people turned to each other and muttered.

Chase sat back in his chair and waited.

Alex did much the same, her lips sealed.

Gatlin captured the attention of the room. "Aaron's passing was a surprise to all of us. I think we should be thankful he didn't give this company to Melissa."

There were nods of approval with that observation.

"She could have sold her shares to us," Mr. Yarros said.

"Oh, please, Paul . . . You don't have the funds."

Yarros started to argue with the man across the table.

A debate on who at the table was in a position to buy additional shares ensued. And while that conversation went back and forth, Chase kept one eye on the people talking and the other on the seat map Piper had put in front of them.

He glanced over at Piper, who was typing into a laptop as fast as she could move her fingers. What was more impressive was the fact that she never once looked at the keyboard. Her eyes scanned those talking and her fingers clicked away.

With everyone talking at once, and no one addressing either of them, Chase glanced at Alex and shrugged.

They sat quietly listening.

While the constant stream of individual conversations continued, Chase couldn't help but think that the information about the unknown Stone son would result in complete anarchy.

Alex leaned forward, her lips close to his ear. "Should we put a stop to this?"

He lifted an index finger in her direction and cleared his throat.

"I hate to . . ." His voice trailed off as the room slowly pulled their attention his way. "I hate to disappoint any of you, but the debate on who would buy what is a complete waste of this board's time since

Alex and I are not selling. We opened the opportunity for you to ask *us* questions, not argue points that are irrelevant."

His words appeared to have sobered up the group and quieted them down.

One of the three women at the table raised her voice. "I have a question."

"Go ahead," Alex said.

"Is it true that Melissa Stone is not in a position to challenge Aaron's will?"

Chase gestured toward Stuart. "Go ahead."

"It would be highly unlikely that Mrs. Stone would file any grievance. We were extremely careful in how we constructed the verbiage in Aaron's trust to protect this company and his personal assets upon his death. While I can't speak for Mrs. Stone, I attest that any action she might attempt would be a complete waste of her time. Of anyone's time, to be fair," the attorney said.

Another murmur went through the board members, but they quickly settled.

It was then that Gatlin was given the floor, as previously planned, and briefly went over a few pending issues.

"When should we expect to vote on the acquisition of the Starfield hotels?" Yarros asked.

Chase looked to Alex, his pulse quickened. The one thing they had to push off was anything as big as buying or selling something without the vote of the missing brother.

"Starfield is a bad gamble," a voice at the end of the table spoke out.

"Aaron said it was solid," Yarros replied.

A debate ensued.

Alex raised a hand in an effort to silence the room. "Please . . . can I . . ."

Someone shushed the room.

Alex offered a thin smile. "This board, or any board, for that matter, cannot expect, nor want, the majority shareholders to vote on anything without thorough investigation."

"There are reports—" Yarros jumped in.

"That may be. But until we can digest the scope of what we're taking on, those reports can't be thoroughly understood. I'm sure you comprehend that," Alex said directly to the biggest voice in the room.

"How long until you catch up?"

"Dammit, Paul. They just lost their father," a woman at the end of the table spoke up.

Chase glanced at the seating map. Much as it hurt to say what he needed to say, Chase choked it out anyway. "Thank you for understanding that, Mrs. Monroe."

"Of course. I'm sure there are some kind of standards in place for the death of a CEO."

"Turmoil and uncertainty," Yarros muttered.

Alex placed a hand on the table and sat forward. "There will be no turmoil or uncertainty. Only thoughtful, educated, and intelligent decisions. The best thing now is no action. I think you would all agree with that."

Several people at the table nodded.

"Our office door is open to all of you," Chase told them. "We will do everything we can to be as transparent as possible without jeopardizing what our father has built." He didn't want this meeting to go down as the first place Alex and Chase lied to the board. Telling them about the missing brother would absolutely jeopardize Stone Enterprises. And based on what had gone down, it was ever apparent that they needed to find this man before anyone else or lose control of everything.

Chapter Ten

Piper left Chase and Alex to wade through the individuals that stopped them as they were exiting the boardroom.

Julia walked alongside her.

"That was painful," Julia said.

"You can't expect people to be enthusiastic that two strangers to the company now have complete control over it."

Julia lowered her voice. "Floyd's been on the phone with almost everyone in that room."

"Discussing what?"

"Hard to tell, but he isn't happy."

In Piper's opinion, Floyd Gatlin wasn't a jovial person in the first place. It was only when the late Mr. Stone was around that Floyd became more animated and accommodating. "Is he ever?"

Julia sighed. "I don't think he and his wife sleep in the same room."

The thought of Floyd doing anything with a woman had her stomach churning. "Would you if you were married to that?"

Julia physically shook.

It's not that Floyd wasn't a halfway-decent-looking man, it was the fact he was an asshole that made him so undesirable. He and Aaron spent a lot of extra time in cities that only required their attention for twenty-four hours.

Eyes open.

Mouth shut.

Do your job.

They were almost back to Julia's desk when she dropped reason 230 as to why Piper was nowhere close to being ready for kids.

"I have to cancel clubbing tomorrow."

"Oh?" Piper lifted her voice as if the intonation alone said she was disappointed.

She wasn't.

Julia rolled her eyes. "*Bobbie*"—she said her ex-husband's name with a whine in her voice—"is shirking his fatherly responsibilities . . . yet again."

Julia had started calling her ex *Bobbie* after the divorce. Before then, she referred to him as Robert. But with the return of the man's adolescent behaviors, *Bobbie* was meant to belittle the man. Julia was the proud parent of two children. Five-year-old Nina and almost-seven-year-old Robert Junior.

Piper met Julia when her position at Stone Enterprises elevated to the executive floor, right in the middle of Julia's divorce.

Brutal . . . absolutely everything Piper witnessed in her friend's divorce had been painful, needles-in-your-eyeballs brutal.

The two had married relatively young, had kids before they could afford their own home, and were filing for divorce before their fifth wedding anniversary. Bobbie wanted fifty-fifty custody of his children when he realized how much he'd have to pay in child support.

The man wanted Julia to pay him alimony because she made more money. That fight went on for a while until they negotiated a minimized amount of child support. Then Bobbie moved to Orange County, making the shared-custody part an absolute joke, and ultimately had them back in court and Julia fighting for more money since he now saw his children, at most, four or five days a month.

Happy hour after work consisted of watching Julia drink way too many vodka tonics and replaying all the scenes from divorce court.

Nope.

Nope.

And nope!

"What is his excuse this time?" Piper asked.

"Get this. He rolled his ankle while he was hiking up in Big Bear with his buddies, and the doctor put him on pain meds that he can't take and drive," Julia gasped. "And of course, he shouldn't be watching the kids if he's high on Vicodin. What am I supposed to do, argue with that?"

"No."

"Big Bear," Julia muttered. "Do you know how long it's been since I've done anything remotely close to hiking in Big Bear?"

They both stopped at Julia's desk. Piper offered a sympathetic smile. "I'm sorry."

"Me too. I was looking forward to getting out."

"Maybe your mom can—"

"No. She does enough. I can't afford a sitter. Besides, the kids get pretty moody when Daddy doesn't come around. I need to be there for them."

"If it gets too bad, let me know. I'll bring Kit over. He always cheers them up."

Julia smiled. "They'd love that."

Piper saw her new bosses out of the corner of her eye as they walked down the hall together.

She lifted her chin. "Let's not lose our jobs."

Julia glanced over her shoulder, grinned. "I'll call you this weekend."

∽

By four thirty, a trickling of staff started leaving the floor. By five, the noise level was reduced to only the hum of the fluorescent lights hanging in their enclosed spaces in the ceilings.

Chase walked out of his office at a quarter after five, expecting the office to be empty.

Instead, Piper sat behind her desk, typing quietly away on her computer.

"I'm pretty sure the five o'clock whistle blew," he said, interrupting her.

She lifted a hand in the air, index finger up, her eyes glued to her screen.

Then she typed for a few more seconds before lifting her hands as if she were saying *abracadabra* and made a whooshing noise. "And it's off."

"What was that?"

She clicked a few buttons before pushing her chair away from her desk. "Board meeting minutes. I need to get them done on the day, or I'll forget something that was said."

"You can always record them."

Piper opened a drawer in her desk and removed her purse. "Too many things are said off the record. If you're recording it, it's on the record."

"Destroy the recording."

Piper stood, grabbed a sweater that was on a hook on the wall. "Miss Maddox, have you ever destroyed documents from Stone Enterprises?" she said in a high-pitched voice. "No, Your Honor," she replied in her own voice. "What about the recording of your board meetings?"

She looked Chase in the eye as she swung her sweater over her arm and pushed her desk chair in.

"That makes perfect sense."

They both started toward the elevators at the same time. "I had a college professor that drilled into us habits that keep you out of a courtroom."

"I didn't take that class."

"Not a lot of people do. A lot of them end up in court."

"I've managed to avoid it so far."

They rounded the corner to the lobby. Chase pressed for the elevator.

"I'm not sure that track record is going to hold."

"Why do you say that?" he asked.

"Your dad dealt with a lot of litigation. Nearly all that was settled by the lawyers." The elevator doors opened; she kept talking after pressing the lower parking level of the garage. "I never understood the news when they'd talk about some famous person or businessperson not going into a courtroom during their trials. Then I saw your dad do it all the time. Too busy for a courtroom. Send the lawyer."

"I suppose that's to be expected with a company this big."

Inside the elevator, they stood a respectable two feet apart and stared at the closed doors.

Piper sighed. "It's been a long week."

"You've been back four days," he corrected her.

She looked him in the eye. "And in four days, I've caught up with three weeks."

"Oh."

"Yeah."

He stared at the closed doors once again. "I should probably pay you some overtime for the extra load."

"No *probably* about it," she said.

Chase fought back a smile.

The doors opened on the lowest floor in the parking garage.

Piper stepped out, and he followed.

"You don't have to walk me to my car. It's a safe lot."

"While my mother did teach me to be a chivalrous guy . . ." He pointed toward his loan truck opposite a white Kia. "This is where I'm parked."

She stood there, dumbfounded. Eyes moving between his truck and him.

Chase stepped away from the elevator and let the doors close behind him.

"What?" he asked.

They both started walking.

Piper said nothing.

"You don't like the truck?"

She shook her head. "No. It's nice. But you're all the way down here."

"The spots are tight. I'm not going to be the asshole who takes up two spots on the prime floors. Down here, there's less competition for space."

Piper stopped walking at the Kia and stared.

Chase took a few more steps, then turned and looked at her. "What?"

"You *own* the building."

"Yeah? So?"

"There's a space with your name on it right by the entrance."

"Still small. Besides, Alex uses that one."

Piper simply shook her head. "Then take Floyd's or Gatlin's . . . or both."

Chase was deeply amused at how vehemently she was advocating for him to flex the Stone name and demand a better parking space.

While he knew that he could just have the spaces reassigned and park higher in the lot, he kept purposely saying the wrong things to see how far Piper would go with her fight on his behalf. "Then where would they park?"

"You're kidding, right?"

Chase held back his grin for as long as he could.

Then Piper rolled her head back and started to laugh. "You have the best poker face," she told him before rounding her car and grasping the handle.

"No, really. Parking down here isn't a big deal."

"Whatever, Stone. You're the boss." She yanked her car door open.

He was still smiling. "Wait, Piper."

"Yeah?"

"Tuesday?"

"What about it?"

"Will Tuesday work to meet at my father's place to get into his computer?"

She tossed her purse and sweater into her car, looked at the ceiling of the garage. "Tuesday will work. Eight o'clock?"

"Let's do nine. It's a little out of the way." It wasn't, but an extra hour of sleep was a small token he could give her for doing this.

"Nine is even better," she said.

"Alex said you're leaving early on Monday. A doctor appointment?"

She pulled in her bottom lip briefly. "Yup. I can try and reschedule if you need me—"

"No, no. It's fine. Have a nice weekend, then."

Piper's smile wasn't as wide or as free as it had been only a moment before. "You guys did well this week. Considering everything."

It was strange to hear her praise, but soothing, nonetheless. "See you Monday," he offered as she stepped into her car.

In his truck, Chase turned it over to let it warm up and pulled his phone out of his pocket. He glanced in his rearview mirror and saw Piper grasping the wheel with her head lowered. When she didn't move for several breaths, he found himself watching and wondering what was going on in her mind.

Finally, the taillights in the car flashed as she started her car and looked over her shoulder.

Chase expected to see her smiling, still amused with their conversation.

Only that wasn't her expression.

A little sad, maybe annoyed . . . but not happy.

The second she realized he was still there and saw his eyes, she instantly put a smile on her face as she backed out of her spot.

∽

Piper sat on the exam table, still wearing the slacks and button-up shirt she left the office in, and waited for the doctor. This was, quite literally, the last place on the planet she wanted to be.

Just walking in the door forced Piper's mind to go where it didn't want to go.

Being unexpectedly stuck at home for three weeks put her mind on the rat wheel of reality so much that she had been paralyzed. Then Chase Stone walked into her life and gave her the distraction she needed.

Only now, she couldn't escape her reality any longer.

Piper stopped staring absently at the wall across from the exam table when the door to the room opened and in stepped Dr. Resnik.

The petite, curly-blonde-haired doctor wore a white lab coat and a smile.

"Hello, Piper," she greeted after closing the door. "I was looking at your chart. It's a little early for your exam. What's going on?"

The words stuck in the back of Piper's throat so much that she had to clear it to spit them out. "I'm late."

"Your period?"

Piper closed her eyes, nodded once.

"How late?"

"Four . . . five . . ."

"Days?"

"Weeks."

Dr. Resnik leaned her back against the wall. "Any chance that you could be pregnant?"

The question was almost comical. "Unless I ended up with five pregnancy tests that were all faulty. I know I'm pregnant." Just saying it out loud spiked Piper's pulse.

"I prescribed the pill for you."

"Yeah, well . . . that didn't work. To be fair, I missed a couple days. I didn't think much about it. There isn't anyone in my life. A couple of missed days wasn't going to . . ."

"Clearly, there is *someone* in your life."

Piper squeezed her eyes shut, tried to block out the images of the bad sex that created this mess. "No. Not really. I mean, yes. There was a guy." She actually laughed at how that sounded. "My name isn't Mary."

That made her laugh harder. "We even used a condom." Piper ran both of her hands down her face. "Fuck."

Dr. Resnik pulled a rolling stool close and sat. She placed a hand on Piper's knee. "It's okay, Piper. If your timing is right, then it's still early. You have options."

The back of Piper's throat started to constrict.

Dr. Resnik paused, and when Piper didn't say anything, she patted her knee. "Let's get a urine sample, do some blood work, and I'll do an exam. Let's get the facts."

Piper nodded, but still couldn't look at her.

Twenty minutes later, Dr. Resnik pushed away from the exam table and handed Piper a tissue to wipe the lubricating jelly from between her legs.

Not that Piper needed the doctor to confirm what she already knew, but the look on Dr. Resnik's face said it first. "You're definitely pregnant. The cervix is high and soft. Your urine test here confirmed it. The blood test will tell us a more exact date, but my estimate is ten weeks based on your last cycle."

Piper knew exactly when she had sex and didn't need a blood test to tell her anything.

She sat up on the table, holding the tissue paper, not wanting to touch herself in front of the doctor. Which was stupid, she thought to herself, considering the doctor put the damn jelly there to start with.

Still, she held the tissue.

"Why don't you get dressed. Let's talk in my office."

Once the doctor was gone, Piper frantically rid her body of the goopy mess before wadding up the paper modesty drape that covered her naked lower half and throwing it in the wastebasket.

She dressed quickly and seriously considered leaving the office without talking more.

Then she reminded herself that she could run if she wanted, but that would change absolutely nothing.

Dr. Resnik sat behind an overloaded desk while Piper took one of the two chairs on the other side.

"I know this is a hard time when it's unplanned."

Piper met her eyes. "I'm not in a position to be a mother."

"I understand."

Did she? All the women in the lobby were holding their stomachs and smiling, or they weren't pregnant and talking to the women that were and congratulating them.

She didn't want anyone congratulating her on a mistake.

"You have three options," Dr. Resnik started.

Piper blew out a breath. "Twice I've driven by a clinic," she told the doctor. "I grew up in Ohio. My parents still go to church twice a week. My mom sometimes three."

"If your religious beliefs are such that terminating the pregnancy is—"

"Not *my* beliefs," Piper interrupted. "*Theirs.* I couldn't wait to get out of Ohio. Haven't stepped inside a church since I moved. Unless I'm back home. But all that sin crap . . . is in here." She placed both of her hands on her head. "I know, intellectually, that the best thing for me is to just end this." She swallowed hard. "But I can't."

It hurt her to say what she already knew.

"I wish I could."

There was real sorrow in Dr. Resnik's eyes. "Adoption is always available."

Piper nodded several times.

"And you can always keep the baby."

That resulted in a quick shake of her head. "No. I can't." It would be a challenge keeping her parents out of her life for the next seven months . . . eight if she wanted to look even remotely normal . . . so they didn't know about any of this. Keeping it. She thought of Julia's life, how her mother was her rock. There would be none of that from her parents. And even though she had her job back, there was no telling if that security would be yanked out from under her again. She wanted children . . . one day, with the right man. Piper hated that her thoughts kept jumping from possibility to impossibility one moment to the next.

"Okay, Piper. You can always change your mind."

She nodded.

"What about the father?"

That made Piper laugh. A manic kind of laugh that said crazy and not happy.

"Tall, dark hair. Met him in a bar. He gave me two different names. It was a joke, but I, for the life of me, couldn't tell you which one was real, if any. The kicker is . . . I don't do this. The last time I had sex before him was over a year. I gave myself a pass." She moaned. "They call it a one-night stand for a reason. Pretty sure his parting words to me were, 'We're okay, right? If anything happens?'"

"Ouch."

"Yeah."

Dr. Resnik scooted back, opened a drawer in her desk, and pulled out several pamphlets. "I'm giving you everything. Options one, two, or three. If you choose two or three, we need to get you on the right vitamins, make all the appointments. Make sure you and the baby are getting what you need. Did you stop taking the birth control pills?"

"You mean the ones that didn't work? Yes. Right after the first test."

"Alcohol, recreational drugs?"

How was that even a question? "I don't take drugs."

"Marijuana?"

"No. I might have drank the night the double lines showed up, but not since. Cut out caffeine, too."

"Good." There was a small smile on the doctor's face. "Nausea?"

"A little. Couple mornings, I couldn't eat."

"You might be one of the lucky ones and avoid morning sickness. You're almost through your first trimester, when it's worse."

Piper had read that.

"I'll have the nurse give you all of the *what to expect* stuff on your way out. I want to see you in four weeks, sooner if you decide to terminate your pregnancy." She handed Piper all the papers in her hand, along with a business card. "I don't perform terminations in this office. This is who I refer my patients to when that's what they choose. They get you in quickly, and like the clinics, there will be an advocate there for you, to go over your options. Not for judgment, just so they know that you're informed."

"Thank you." This was all too real.

"Do you have any questions?"

Piper nodded. "But not right now."

The doctor stood and rounded her desk.

Once Piper moved to her side, she held her arms open.

Piper allowed the other woman to hug her.

"You're going to be okay. Call anytime."

Chapter Eleven

It was as if her body only needed the suggestion of morning sickness to decide that was the course she needed to be on.

Piper started her day off face-first in her toilet, with Kit staring at her from the bathroom door.

Getting sick when there was nothing in your stomach to bring up was awful. Thankfully, the extra hour she had before meeting Chase at the Stone Estate gave her the time she needed to pull it together.

The herbal tea she'd switched to wasn't possible to keep down. The Lucky Charms were out of the question. Which was probably for the best.

Dressed a little more casually than she was for the office, Piper bit off the edges of a saltine cracker as she drove through the celebrity mansions of Beverly Hills.

Piper pulled up to the security gates of Stone's home ten minutes before nine. She rolled down the window and pressed the button on the intercom.

A few seconds later, she reached over and pressed the button a second time and wondered if she'd beat Chase there.

The speaker crackled, and Chase's voice came through. "Hello?"

"I'm here," Piper told him.

"Sorry . . . yeah. Shit." His voice was frazzled.

"What's wrong?"

"I don't know how to open the gate."

"How did you get in?"

"The lawyer gave us a remote."

"Oh," Piper said. Gated homes were not something she was familiar with, but it struck her as odd that Chase wasn't familiar with opening the gate from the inside of his father's home.

"Wait."

The sound of a telephone tone sounded from the metal box, but the gate didn't open.

"Did that work?" he asked.

"No."

More tones beeped through in what Piper imagined was Chase pressing random numbers on a keypad.

When the intercom went silent, she said, "It's still not opening."

"Okay, hold on. I'm walking down."

The line went dead, and Piper sat in her idling car for several minutes until she saw Chase walking down the driveway.

Several yards from the gate, he lifted his hand, holding a remote control, and the double iron gate opened, letting her in.

Once inside, she stopped next to Chase, who had already turned around and started walking back toward the house. "Good old-fashioned remote controls."

"Sorry about that," he said.

Piper went ahead and parked behind Chase's truck in the driveway.

The home never ceased to amaze her.

Two stories with a turret as the front entrance. Massive stone walls and huge windows. She knew the inside was just as impressive as the outside, at least in what she'd had the opportunity to see.

With Aaron Stone, she saw the entrance; the main living room, which was hard to miss from the foyer; Stone's personal office; the kitchen; and one of the bathrooms. She'd seen the grounds from the living room windows but had never been out in the back of the house.

Piper brushed the crumbs from the two crackers she'd managed to keep down from her shirt and climbed out of her car.

It took a few moments for Chase to walk to her side.

"Getting your morning workout in?" she teased.

"I didn't think to ask how to open the gate when I picked this up." He waved the remote in the air.

"I could have sworn your dad had a housekeeper."

"Melissa fired her the day she moved out."

"Can she do that?"

"Apparently." Chase stared up the steps to the house, where he'd left the front door wide open.

"Do you need to hire her back?"

Chase hesitated as they approached the front door and looked up at the house. "I'm not cleaning it."

The image of him on his knees cleaning a bathtub amused her.

"Do you know her name . . . phone number?"

"Couldn't tell you." Chase lifted his hand to the door, suggesting she walk in first.

"Can you ask Melissa?"

One look at Chase's face and Piper said, "That's a *no.*"

"We're not exactly on speaking terms."

Inside the home, Piper blew out a breath. It truly was spectacular. Much as she hated to admit Aaron Stone had any taste, he had picked out a beautiful home. Or maybe that was Melissa. Although Piper doubted the latter. Melissa didn't seem to exhibit any real taste of her own. She dressed in whatever the high-end fashion was, regardless of if the style suited her. She'd suggested a couple of decorative office changes at Stone Enterprises, which Aaron nixed the second his wife was out of earshot. And since the woman didn't frequent the main office all that often, it was as if she'd forgotten her own requests.

Chase moved in front of her and, thankfully, led the way.

"It's been a while since I've been here," Piper told him. "This place always turns me around."

"I know what you mean."

Piper glanced over Chase's frame and noticed for the first time that the man was wearing jeans and a pullover shirt. His casual clothing sat in contrast to the house.

When she realized her eyes had settled on the man's ass, she snapped them away and looked past the bay windows. "Did you spend a lot of time here?"

"No."

"I should have guessed when you couldn't open the gate."

Chase stayed silent as they walked through the house and down a corridor to Aaron's personal office.

Unlike the man's office at Stone Enterprises, this one had a more traditional look, with big wood pieces, built-in bookshelves filled with actual books, and built-in filing cabinets that took up one entire wall. The desk sat in the center of the room with two massive high-back leather chairs.

The computer was a top-of-the-line Mac, which always surprised Piper when she saw it, considering the PCs they used at the office. And Aaron had never really grasped how the thing worked. Hence the reason she'd been summoned to his home to fix a computer problem or two. If the issue wasn't easily solved, she was the one on the phone with support, ticking away at the keys with a patience the senior Mr. Stone never had.

Chase stopped in front of the desk and lifted his hands to the computer. "Have at it."

Piper dropped her purse on the desk and settled into the chair. She removed her phone and opened a note page that would help guide her through the backdoor boot that would bypass Stone's password and allow her to change it. "This shouldn't take long."

Chase folded his arms across his chest and stared absently in her direction. It was as if he was looking at something but seeing nothing.

She reached for the button that would power down the computer completely since it was already opened to the password screen.

After the space of a few breaths, she waved a hand in the direction of Chase's stare.

He didn't flinch.

Eventually, the silence in the room seemed to snap him out of the trancelike state.

"Did you say something?" he asked.

She shook her head and placed both of her hands on the desk. "Are you okay?"

He nervously ran a hand over his jaw, their eyes met.

No, he wasn't okay. Piper didn't need him to say a word.

Instead of answering, he pivoted on his heel and started to leave the room. At the door, he asked, "Can I get you something? Coffee?"

Normally, yes.

Pregnant, no.

Nauseated . . . absolutely not.

"How about water?"

He exited the office about as fast as anyone could without running.

Palms on the desk, Piper looked around the room and wondered what it was that Chase saw. Did he see his father in this room? Was the reality of his passing hitting a cord in his brain . . . heart?

She shook off her questions and read the sequence of keys she needed to press to open the computer on an admin screen.

The process of logging in to the computer took less than five minutes. Once there, she moved to a new place to reset a lost password, which took a little longer. In the middle of that, Chase returned with the water she requested.

The color had returned to his face, something she didn't realize he'd lost when he left the room.

"I'm in," she told him.

He set the water down and circled around and looked at the screen, one hand on the desk.

"That was fast."

"Like I said . . ." She clicked more keys. "Your dad constantly locked himself out."

She paused on the new-password screen and glanced at Chase. "What do you want the new password to be?"

Chase was hovering, his eyes narrowed.

Sensing his hesitation, she moved the keyboard slightly as if offering him to type it in. "You don't have to tell me what it is," she said with a grin.

"Like it matters, you just hacked through without my dad's." Chase pushed the keyboard back to her.

Piper set her fingers over the keys and waited. "Considering the indiscretions I have on your dad, I doubt there is anything in here that will shock me."

"You'd be surprised," Chase said, deadpan.

For some reason, the statement snagged one of her brain cells and didn't let go.

Chase rambled off a series of numbers, letters, and special characters.

Piper typed it in. "Do you want to write that down?"

"No. I got it."

What was random to her obviously meant something to him.

She typed it in a second time, set the password, and opened the computer.

Chase stood to his full height. "Wow. Remind me never to get on your bad side."

She leaned back in the chair. "Your dad did, but that didn't prompt me to do anything illegal."

"I'm not sure I could have held back if I were you."

She shrugged, somewhat over the drama caused by a dead man.

"My father always says that 'revenge digs two graves.' He's not wrong," Piper said.

Chase paused. "Wise man."

"He also hasn't spoken to his brother in twenty years."

Chase huffed out a laugh. "Do your parents live close by?"

"No." *Thank God!*

"You don't get along with them?"

"We get along fine. They're just very . . . different people. Very old school."

"What does that mean?"

It was Piper's turn to stare absently at a wall. The thought of her parents finding out she was pregnant without a husband would put her on the "do not call" list with her uncle. "I grew up in Ohio. My grandparents live three blocks away from where I was raised. My mom and dad haven't been more than fifty miles from where they grew up their entire lives."

"Not even on a vacation?"

She shook her head, focused on Chase, and lowered her voice to mimic her father. "You can fish and camp close to home . . . no need to spend the money on hotels and plane tickets."

"That sounds . . ."

"Ridiculous," she answered for him.

"Quaint," he said.

She rolled her eyes. "If you say so."

Chase leaned against the desk. "How did they feel about you moving to LA?"

"They hated it. They were certain I'd be on a milk carton for a missing person within six months."

"Not with that dog of yours."

"How do you think he came about?"

"Your parents?"

She nodded. "I graduated from college, Ohio State, and moved back home for the summer, knowing it was my last one there. I had to get my parents used to the idea of my move. They were relentless with fear tactics. Crime statistics became the topic of conversation over every dinner. Next thing I know, five-month-old Kit shows up, complete with a trainer to teach me how to control the dog."

Chase's lips were open in an *O*. "You have to give your folks some kudos. That's dedication to keeping you safe."

"On the surface . . . yeah. I can see how that looks. But do you know how hard it is to find an apartment that accepts dogs? Let alone a rottweiler? Not to mention, an apartment is no place for a big dog. By the time I left Ohio, Kit and I were a team, so it wasn't like I was going to leave him behind. I'm sure my parents thought of that obstacle."

"Trying to sabotage your move . . ."

"They'd never admit it, but yes."

"Shows they care."

That, Piper couldn't deny.

"Why move?" he asked. "Why not settle down close to home?"

Her eyes widened. "Have you ever been to Ohio?"

He started to nod, then shook his head. "No."

She lifted a hand and patted his forearm as if she were twice his age with a lesson that needed to be taught. "Once you've visited my hometown, you'll completely understand why I needed to get out as fast as I could, or risk never leaving."

His smile was warm. So unlike the expression he wore at the office. "I'm grateful you left, or I'd be on the phone with tech support for hours."

Chase Stone truly was a beautiful man. So much softer than his father. The random thought flashed in her head faster than she could stop it.

Piper's fingers warmed, and so did her cheeks when she realized she'd left her hand on his arm.

She snapped it away and cleared her throat. "Is there anything else I can do here?" she said, looking at the computer screen.

Chase shifted off the desk and took a step away. "Yes, actually. Can you identify any files that are affiliated with Stone Enterprises? Apps. Any passwords you might know. Open any bank links, business or personal."

"Didn't you get the personal bank logins when he died?"

"Not yet. Takes time. This will help us manage his life faster. Besides, Alex and I would like to know if any of the extra women in his life are being supported by him."

"Like a sugar daddy?" Piper cringed.

"Sadly, yes."

She turned back to the computer. At least she had something to focus on other than her good-looking boss. She pushed away and opened a drawer in the desk, looking for a pad of paper. "I can do that."

"You sure you don't want coffee? I could use some coffee."

She pointed to the water as he walked away. "I'm good with this."

Chase left the room, and Piper released a breath she didn't realize she was holding.

◦๑

Chase made it to the kitchen and placed both hands on the cool countertop, trying to get his shit together.

The whole time Piper shared her story about the efforts her parents went through to keep her close to home, Chase stared into her doe eyes and felt the need to protect her in her parents' absence. Then his thoughts shifted the second she touched him, and those doe eyes turned to sultry and seductive, and brought warmth to parts of his body that had no business heating up.

She was his assistant. A paid employee, and worse, his own father had hit on her. That thought made Chase want to punch a dead man.

He needed to shut this attraction down fast and hard.

Two words that quickly morphed into even more inappropriate images in his brain.

Chase crossed to the massive freezer and yanked the door open. And like a fifty-year-old menopausal woman, he shoved his head into the cold space, hoping to chill his body.

After several unsteady breaths, he closed the door and moved around the kitchen.

He eyed the built-in espresso machine with dread. The baristas of the world had no worries of Chase taking their jobs. Fancy coffee was beyond his skill set.

In the walk-in pantry, he found a traditional coffeepot and set it up on the counter. After more digging, he found coffee . . . the bean kind, and a grinder, which he managed.

While the coffee brewed, he rummaged around the kitchen to determine where things lived. Not that he planned on spending much time there, but it gave his mind something to think about other than the woman in the next room.

A good twenty minutes later, he mustered a stiff back with a hot cup of coffee and went back into the office.

Piper glanced his way briefly and went back to the computer screen before writing something down.

"Getting somewhere?"

She tapped a pen to the pad of paper. "Yeah. Your dad was not worried about someone getting in here. Most of his passwords are saved internally. All you have to do is click on the bank site and press 'Log in.' The passwords are hidden, but you can get around that by resetting using his email."

By now, Chase was beside her again, looking at the screen.

She pressed the email icon, and his father's email instantly opened.

"Is that a work email?"

"No," she said. A few clicks later, and Piper sat back. "That's the work email."

The private email was much more important when it came to finding the long-lost brother. "This is going to save some time."

"Full disclosure," she said. "I clicked on his bank site, fully expecting a need for a password, and it opened right up. I saw the balance."

Aaron Stone's net worth on the day of his death was front-page news, so Piper seeing the numbers wasn't that big of a concern.

"Well . . . let's see it," he said, hoping to put her at ease.

"You haven't?"

He shook his head. "Even with everything set up in a trust, the wheels spin slowly getting our names on accounts."

Piper shrugged and clicked into the banking account.

She sat back as they both looked at the number.

"One point two million in a personal bank account is obscene . . . right?" she asked.

Chase leaned over her, set his coffee down, and took control of the mouse. "That depends on your monthly nut."

He scrolled down, and they both took in the numbers of his father's monthly personal bills. Nearly everything was on autopilot. Utilities, groundskeepers, pool service . . .

Piper pointed at the screen. "Is that the mortgage payment?"

Chase skimmed past the entry she referred to, looking for the more personal entries. "Not high enough. It's probably an escrow account for the property taxes."

"Holy shit."

Chase looked at the number again. Yeah, it was *holy shit* worthy. "Crazy."

"I should have asked for a raise."

He twisted her way, their heads only inches apart.

Piper was glued to the monitor, and his coffee cup was in her hands as she sipped the brew.

Without looking at him, she pointed to the screen again. "Do you think that's the housekeeper?"

Turning back to the monitor, he kept refreshing the page until the woman's name showed up again. The amount was the same. "It could be."

She put his coffee down and wrote the woman's name on the pad of paper. "Here," she said, pushing away from the desk to stand. "You keep scrolling, I'll see if I can find any information on this person. You can't let a beautiful house like this grow dust."

Chase took her place, and she started to leave the room.

"Where are you going?"

"My work laptop is in my car. While I'm at it, I'll find the name of the gate system and see if there is a standard manual online with information on how it opens."

"That would be very helpful." And unexpected.

She smiled, narrowed her eyes. "We'll discuss that raise later."

He wasn't sure if she was teasing or not, but he liked her free attitude about spending his father's money.

Chapter Twelve

An hour later, Piper sat back from her computer, which was perched on the edge of the massive desk opposite Chase. "I have a phone number."

"For the housekeeper?"

"Yeah."

"Perfect. See if she'll come back."

Piper took the house phone with her as she stepped away from the desk.

The call was answered in two rings.

"Hello?"

Piper smiled, as she often did when she was on the phone with someone she needed something from. "Karina Skinner?"

"Yes? Who is this?"

Piper stepped out of the office and into the hall. "I'm Piper Maddox. I work with Chase Stone, Aaron Stone's son. I understand you used to work for Mr. and Mrs. Stone at their home."

"I did. Mrs. Stone fired me."

"I understand that. She wasn't really in a position to do that. Mr. Stone's children inherited the house. She should never have let you go."

"I don't really know them."

"Are you saying you've met them? Chase didn't let on," Piper said.

"I saw them at the funeral. I wouldn't expect them to remember me. They never came around when I was there."

That made more sense. "Be that as it may, they'd like you to come back."

Karina sighed. "I don't know. I dislike instability. Mrs. Stone wasn't an easy person to work for."

"I can promise you Chase and his sister, Alex, are nothing like their father or stepmother."

"I don't know . . ."

Not the answer Piper wanted. She poked her head back in the office, hand over the receiver, and asked Chase, "She wants a five percent raise."

"Fine."

Back on the phone and away from the office, Piper returned her attention to the call. "They're giving you a five percent raise."

"W-what?"

Her tone was much more hopeful. "Five percent, and can you come today? No one has been here since you were let go, and someone is bound to water a fake plant if left to themselves."

"Five percent?"

Shit, maybe Piper should have asked for more.

"Yes."

"I can be there in two hours," Karina spat out.

"Perfect."

"Except," Karina said.

"Except what?"

"My uniform isn't clean."

Piper winced. "Uniform? Does that help you keep a home clean?"

Karina laughed. "No."

"Skip the uniform. Just get here. Please."

"I'm on my way."

Piper hung up the phone with a spring in her step. "Housekeeper will be here in two hours," she announced as she walked back into the office.

"That's a relief."

It was, yet it sparked another thought. "I wonder if Melissa fired any of the other staff?"

"If she did, they're still getting paid. All the bills here are on autopilot."

Piper crossed to one of the windows overlooking the back of the house. Things didn't look out of place, but there wasn't anyone walking around doing any work. "Getting paid and not doing the work is a good gig if you can get it."

"Let's hope the housekeeper knows who works here and how to get ahold of them."

"In all the mystery movies, the housekeeper always knows everything."

Chase pulled his attention off the computer screen. "I bet she does."

"Eyes open, mouth shut . . . you learn a lot."

He unfolded from his chair and moved to the shelves. "I wonder if she knows where the safe is."

Piper's eyes lit up. "Safe?"

"Yeah. There has to be one."

"Your father kept more than a million dollars in his personal checking account. Why would he need a safe?"

"Cash, passport, legal documents, birth certificates . . . things you don't want lost to a fire."

All of those things were in the bottom drawer in her bedroom, completely surrounded by combustible materials. "Maybe he had a safety deposit box for that stuff."

"I'm sure he had those, too. But you wouldn't keep a passport and needed cash in a bank vault when you traveled as much as he did."

Piper couldn't help but think Chase was looking for something specific. Even with all the exploring he'd been doing on his father's computer, Chase seemed more frustrated an hour after getting into the thing than he had when he sat down.

"What are you looking for?"

He glanced at her briefly, then looked away. "I just want to know where everything is."

"Okay, sure!" She wasn't buying that and made certain her tone reflected her feelings.

"No, really."

She stopped him with a roll of her eyes. "You don't have to tell me, but don't pretend there's not something. You've been scrolling through emails and bank statements for over an hour, getting more frustrated as the minutes tick by. I just gave the housekeeper, who you don't know, a five percent raise, which could have been fifty percent for as much attention as you gave any of that. I've seen you rummage through this desk in the same manner you did at the office. You're looking for something and not finding it."

He opened his mouth, but Piper didn't give him room to deny it again.

"You don't have to tell me. But remember . . . I did my job. Head down, ears open."

Chase sucked in a breath and released it just as fast. "You're right."

Two of her favorite words. "Now we're getting somewhere."

"I'm . . . we're looking for a woman our father had an affair with."

"So, he *was* a sugar daddy."

Chase shook his head. "He could have been, but this one was a while ago."

"Your father had a lot of women."

"Somewhere around thirty years ago. Give or take," Chase added.

That news slapped Piper's confidence down. "That's a long time."

"I know."

"You think he was still seeing her? Your dad didn't keep things going for long, from what I could tell."

"No. But we believe he was sending her money."

Now the bank statements and email search made sense. "Sending her money after the affair was over? For how long?"

"Twenty years . . . give or take. Who knows, he might have still been sending her money."

"She must have had something really good on him. I'm guessing this is hush money."

"You could call it that."

"If it's hush money, no one knows about it, and you didn't want to tell me."

Chase shrugged. "I don't know you well enough . . . *yet*."

Fair. "Let me give you a clue. If I wanted to *out* your father, I would have done it while he was alive. And like I told you before, ratting out your boss is professional suicide unless you have a bigger boss in the wings. And since your last name is Stone, these rules still apply."

She walked around him and took the chair in front of Aaron Stone's computer.

Chase stood staring.

"Was this hush money for something illegal?"

Chase cleared his throat.

"Wait! Don't answer that. I don't want to know. Corporate espionage always results in the low men on the ladder doing time." Wouldn't that be her luck. Pregnant and in jail because of her shitty dead boss.

It had been two whole hours since Piper thought about her situation, and that removed the smile from her face.

She glanced up at Chase and forged a smile. He was staring at her, a half grin on his lips. The kind that warmed her body and made her wonder what he was thinking.

"I would never let you go to jail for something my father did."

Piper ignored her rising pulse and moved back to the most recent bank statement and hit the print button. "To use your own words, I don't know you well enough *yet* to believe that statement." But she was starting to want that to change.

"Let me give *you* a clue," he repeated her words as he removed the printed statement from the printer behind the desk and placed it in front of her. With one hand on the desk and the other on the back of the chair, he paused.

She looked up, found his face dangerously close to hers.

He smelled like spice and something else she couldn't name but wanted to bury herself in.

"I'm not the kind of man that says things I don't mean." He stood straight and released the trance he held her in.

Now *that* sounded like a promise she could believe.

⁓

"I feel like we're getting somewhere," Chase said into the phone as he stood in the backyard of his father's estate, far away from anyone who could hear him.

Piper had taken to the task of finding the mystery woman like she had when she completed the board meeting minutes before clocking out for the weekend.

"Did you find anything?" Alex asked.

"No, but Piper is eliminating names quicker than you and I can since she knows them."

"What did you tell her?"

"Only what she needed to know. That we're looking for a woman our father was having an affair with, and he was sending checks to. She concluded the money was to keep her quiet but didn't press for more answers."

"And you didn't elaborate."

"No." Chase looked up at the house behind him. "She's amazing. Maybe it's because she's not emotionally connected, but damn, she's smart. She all but hacked into the computer and pulled up almost all of Dad's sensitive information within minutes."

"How long do you think this is going to take?"

"No idea. But I know it will be faster with her working on it. She knew our father better than we did."

"The gardener knew him better."

Chase sighed. "Speaking of . . . Melissa fired the entire staff. Piper found the housekeeper's number, and I hired her back."

"Who cares, let the place rot."

His sister's bite had a sting. "That only hurts us, not him."

Alex growled.

"How are things there?"

"Not going to lie . . . I have a lot to learn."

It was nice to hear what he'd been feeling since the first day he walked into that office. "Your skill set is more equipped than mine."

"That talent is focusing on the vulnerability of this company, not profitability. I'm having a hard time seeing past the problems."

"That could be a good thing."

"Right now, it's frustrating."

Chase found himself pacing on a footpath surrounded by flower beds. "Don't let on to anyone watching."

"Oh, please. My poker face beats yours every day of the week."

He liked his sister's banter.

"Are you going to be okay without Piper for a couple of days? This is likely going to take a while."

"I got it here. Dee needs direction, but she's capable."

Chase kicked a pebble from the path. "Good. I have to get over to CMS. I had my own merger in the works before Dad died."

"Oh, that's right. Is it even needed now?" Alex asked.

The Beverly Hills house loomed over him; his father's personal bank balance flashed in his head. "Probably not."

"Want my advice?"

"Always."

"Keep as many hands out of your business as possible. If you want to buy out a competitor, do it. But avoid a merger. They're messy, people get fired, emotions run high. It's stressful for everyone."

Those had been his prevailing thoughts over the past week. "Thanks, Alex."

"Anytime."

"If it's all good on your end, I'll spend tomorrow at CMS and give a key to Piper so she can continue her search here."

"I'll call if something changes. Finding 'you know who' is our top priority."

After hanging up with Alex, Chase did a quick lap around the grounds and poked his head into the pool house, which doubled as a guest house. Two stories, two bedrooms, kitchen . . . an entire home that was likely used once a year at most.

Chase pushed his thoughts of massive homes and swimming pools that were never used away and walked back into the main house.

He heard Piper talking and followed her voice into the kitchen.

There, she and Karina were chatting.

Karina's arrival gave him and Piper the break they needed from his father's depressing office.

The mystery of the gate was revealed without any further research. Karina wrote down all the details, from how to open the thing to talking to someone at the gate who may not have pressed the button. She also showed them the monitor controls for the cameras around the estate. She dug through a catchall drawer in the kitchen to find a notebook with the names and phone numbers of everyone she would call to fix household problems. On that list were the groundskeepers and pool maintenance company.

Chase almost felt guilty when Karina and Piper launched into the list and called the household employees to get them to take their jobs back. A home was personal, and even though a third of the house he was standing in belonged to him, he felt no real connection to it. Yet Piper seemed determined to put into place everything needed to keep the home maintained. "You either maintain a house or fix big issues from neglect."

"The pool guy will be here tomorrow and then once a week on Thursdays. Said that if you have any big parties to let him know and he'll come the day after to treat the water," Piper told him.

"No risk of that happening anytime soon."

Karina finished her call and reported that the groundskeepers were more than happy to come back, but they'd filled their Friday slot since that was sought after. Chase quickly accepted whatever day that staff wanted to come.

Karina tapped the phone she still held in her hand after her last call and asked, "What about the cook? Should I call her back in?"

"A cook?" Chase asked.

"Yes. Mr. and Mrs. Stone had meals prepared for them four days a week, sometimes more."

Piper started to laugh. "My God, did they hire someone to change a light bulb for them?"

Karina, who was in her early fifties, all of five foot two and weighing under a hundred pounds, pointed to her chest. "Anything I can reach, I take care of. Otherwise, I have a handyman I call."

"I was joking," Piper told her.

Karina shrugged.

"We won't need a cook," Chase said.

"What about the handyman?" Karina asked.

"Keep his number handy." Chase didn't want to reveal to someone he just met that there was no intention of anyone living in the house. At least not at this point.

Piper moved around the giant kitchen island to retrieve her phone from where she'd left it. "We don't need a cook, but we do need food. Should we Uber something?"

Chase looked at the clock and cussed under his breath. It was after one thirty, and they'd skipped lunch. "I wasn't watching the time."

"It's all good," Piper told him.

Chase moved to the refrigerator and opened it. "Can we put something together?"

"I don't mind my assistant duties bringing me here, but I draw the line at cooking for my boss," Piper told him.

"I'm not my dad. I'm capable of putting a sandwich together for us."

Piper dropped her phone on the counter and lifted her hands in the air. "Well, now . . . that's a different story. If my boss wants to cook for me, I'm in," she teased.

Karina moved around them and started opening cupboards. "I'll do it. I know where things are. If you make a list, I'll order what you need through a delivery service."

Piper rolled her eyes. "Because rich people don't go to the grocery store."

Even though Chase agreed with Piper, he saw the practicality of what Karina offered. And considering he'd hardly had time to put a load of laundry in since his father's death, the domestic help she provided sounded very appealing.

Twenty minutes later, he and Piper sat on the massive back patio eating tuna wraps and slightly stale crackers and carrots that were salvageable from the refrigerator. Karina stayed back and was in the process of purging all the perishable goods from the kitchen.

"So, which one of you is moving into the house?" Piper asked him between bites.

"Neither. At least not at this point."

"Are you going to sell it?"

"Don't know yet. It's not a priority."

Piper looked around at a fully furnished outside patio, complete with a fireplace, a big-screen television, heat lamps for cold nights, and fans for the hot ones. "Seems a waste."

"This was his," Chase said as if there was no further reason needed for his decision.

"You really didn't care for him, did you?"

Chase washed his bite down with a gulp of water. "I didn't know him. He stopped being a father when he divorced my mother. His choice, not the court's."

"That sucks."

"Does it? What you told me alone proves he wasn't an honorable man. That's important."

"It is."

"Alex and I are both hoping that his lack of integrity in his personal life didn't morph into the company."

"It was his business to bleed into."

"True, but there're a lot of employees that depend on Stone Enterprises."

When she didn't respond, Chase glanced Piper's way, to find her staring at him. "You don't know any of those people. And you don't owe us anything."

"Are you suggesting we walk away?"

She shook her head slightly. "It's fascinating that you would jump into the company your father built with such conviction, given how little you thought of the man."

Chase considered her observation and tried to explain his actions. "Less than a month ago, I was happy running my own company. Building my own . . . enterprise. Alexandrea had a job she enjoyed and did well. Then you wake up one morning, and *this* is sitting in your lap. Overnight, you're thrust into someone else's world. Only this life is too big to just pass through and then go back to your own. Alex can't return to her world any more than I can ignore this one. While I feel no loyalty to my father, I do to my sister." And strangely, to a brother he had yet to meet.

"Wow."

"What?" Chase felt like he'd said too much, but at the same time, he knew Piper wasn't the kind of person to use his words against him.

"I didn't think it was possible to feel sorry for someone who turned into a gazillionaire overnight. I was wrong." She picked up her wrap and took a bite.

"You don't need to feel sorry for either of us. We'll be fine."

Piper dipped her head, wiped a drizzle of sauce from her lips. "Oh, I'm sure. Hard not to be with *gazillions*," she said around the food in her mouth.

The way she kept saying *gazillions* made him smile. "I don't think a *gazillion* is a thing."

"More money than I'll ever see."

"I don't know. You're a smart person."

She laughed. A single huff of a laugh that said she didn't agree. "Not as smart as you think."

"What does that mean?"

Piper shook her head. "Nothing. I, ah . . . as long as I'm in the assistant chair and not the corner office, I won't be packing away tons of money anytime soon."

"Perhaps. Your help has been vital. We appreciate it."

Piper picked up her glass of water and pointed it in his direction. "Feel free to appreciate it with any of those pesky gazillions you don't know what to do with."

Damn, she made him laugh. Her straight-up approach was refreshing. "I'll put that under advisement."

She rolled her eyes.

Chase laughed harder.

It was close to five in the evening when they called it quits.

Aaron Stone's home office was slowly being unearthed. Old paper files sat in stacks, most of which Chase had picked through.

Piper had traced several transactions out of his father's personal account. The amounts were small enough to not flag the IRS, but large enough to capture their attention. While neither of them was a forensic accountant, they were doing a slow but steady job of finding inconsistencies.

They still had a long way to go.

Chase sat back on the sofa, stretching his back and rubbing the back of his neck. "It's getting late," he announced.

Piper looked up from the computer. "This is not a fast process. You sure we can't hire an investigator?"

Chase shook his head. "We can't risk it."

Even without the whole truth, Piper nodded her agreement.

"I need you to come back tomorrow," he told her.

"This isn't in my job description, Stone."

He kind of liked how she bit his last name out at him.

"Everyone has a price."

"Fine," she huffed. "A gazillion will do."

"I'll get right on that."

Piper rolled her shoulders and pushed away from the desk. "If it's okay with you, I'll come at nine and avoid some of that traffic . . . stay a little later."

"This isn't the office, get here when you can. I have to spend time tomorrow with my staff. I'll try and come in the afternoon, if not, I'll call."

Piper's eyes lit up. "You want me here alone?"

"Is that okay?" he asked.

"Yeah . . . I just . . . Yeah, no. That's fine."

"Good."

"You don't mind me snooping in all of this without you?"

"We're combing through my father's files to find anything that might harm the company. That's not snooping, it's reverse filing."

Piper narrowed her gaze. "I didn't think of it that way."

Chase cleared his throat. "Your Honor, I wasn't looking for Aaron Stone's lifetime subscription to *Playboy*, I simply found it while purging his files after his death at the request of Chase Stone."

It was Piper's turn to smile. "Maybe your dad had a fetish."

"I'm not looking to find sex toys."

Piper sucked her lips in and bit them. "That would be funny, though."

"I don't want to know."

She chuckled and grabbed her purse. Before walking away from the desk, she powered down the computer.

Leaving everything in chaos, they left the office and backtracked through the house.

In the kitchen, Chase handed Piper a remote control for the gate and keys to the front door, along with the code for the house alarm. "Make yourself at home."

She palmed the keys. "Great, I'll bring my swimsuit."

And just like that, Chase found himself envisioning her in a bikini. The thought alone made his mouth dry.

"Kidding, Stone."

Chase closed his eyes, knowing they betrayed him. "Right. Sorry."

"But I'm not dressing for the office."

"I wouldn't expect you to."

Piper lifted her chin to look up at him. "Okay. I'll see you tomorrow."

"We'll talk at the very least."

He walked her to the front door and watched as she got into her car. Chase tore his gaze away only when her taillights faded from his sight.

He needed to nip this attraction in the bud, he just wasn't sure how.

Chapter Thirteen

Finding herself face down in a toilet two days in a row put a serious damper on Piper's mood.

There'd been moments the previous day that she'd completely forgotten she was pregnant. She loved that. Ignoring what was going on in her body was exactly what she intended to do for as long as humanly possible.

Only Mother Nature had other plans.

Ones that involved emptying an already empty stomach every morning.

Kit sat on his haunches, whining at the bathroom door and tilting his head in concern.

When the worst seemed to subside, Piper flushed the toilet and slowly stumbled to her feet. Over the sink, she turned the water on cold and looked at her pale reflection in the mirror. "This sucks," she said to herself.

Kit let out a husky bark.

"I'm not sure why anyone would choose to do this." Piper washed her hands and splashed water on her face.

Saved by a late-start day and the fact her boss wasn't going to be in, Piper moved slowly throughout her morning and packed the crackers that had saved her the day before. Wearing jeans, sneakers, and a simple button-up top, she glanced down at her feet at her companion. Either Kit knew what was happening to her, or he'd just become spoiled when she was out of work. The dog hadn't left her side since that first night the double lines on the pregnancy tests showed up. Truth was, Piper appreciated his concern. Even if Kit was a dog.

Kit walked to the front door and looked back at her.

"I gotta go to work, Kitty."

She'd unlatched the doggie door that led to the backyard and knew she could count on Mr. Armstrong to check on him throughout the day if needed. Kit loved their elderly neighbor and was often found on Mr. Armstrong's couch when she came home late from work.

Piper opened the front door, and Kit darted out before she could give the command for him to stay.

Moving quickly added to her nausea, so Piper took her time following her dog.

"Kit? What are you doing?"

He sat by her car, panting.

"I have to work."

Maybe the casual clothes gave off a *walk in the park* vibe.

"Kit?"

He barked and stared at the car.

Piper sighed and thought about what her plans were for the day.

She was going to be at the Stone Estate by herself for many hours. She'd agreed to meet with the grounds staff, who she didn't know . . . not that they gave off an untrustworthy vibe, but it wouldn't hurt to be safe. Karina was going to come in for a few hours, but . . .

Piper turned around and walked back into the house. She grabbed a couple of dog essentials and returned to her car. "Okay. You win." She opened the door, and Kit jumped into the passenger seat with what could only be described as a smile.

After settling behind the wheel, she sent a quick text to her neighbor, letting him know it was "take your dog to work day."

The drive was easier than it had been the day before. With the window half-rolled-down for Kit to sniff every passing scent along the way, the cool air seemed to settle her stomach.

She couldn't help but feel like she'd somehow elevated in life when she pressed the button on the remote to open the estate gates. She parked her car behind the closed garage doors to give space for the staff in the circular drive.

Piper rubbed the top of Kit's head. "This is a fancy place, Kitty. Stay off the furniture."

Kit stopped panting briefly, as if understanding her and not liking her words . . . but then quickly went back to panting.

Piper opened the door, and Kit bounded out behind her and immediately ran to a patch of green to sniff and relieve himself.

She grabbed what she needed from her car, especially the crackers that were saving her life, and called Kit to follow.

The alarm beeped the moment she opened the front door. Using the keypad, she turned it off and proceeded deeper into the house. Everything looked exactly as it had the night before, except for the absence of the broad shoulders of the man who'd been with her all day.

Kit quickly moved around the house, his sniffer working overtime.

Piper set her purse, dog treats, leash, and crackers on the massive island in the kitchen and took a good look around. This space alone rivaled that of her living room, kitchen, and eating space combined. If you added the walk-in pantry and the nook for casual dining, that would be her entire house.

She heard Kit's metal tag clink against his collar as he jogged around the kitchen and then out into a hall.

Piper let him explore as she followed behind. Truth was, she wanted to look around a bit herself.

She and Chase had pretty much isolated themselves in Aaron's office, with an occasional visit to the kitchen, a bathroom, and the back patio space for their late lunch.

While Chase didn't seem to want to look around, Piper's curiosity was piqued.

Following Kit, as if the dog offered an excuse for looking around the house, Piper walked past the doors of Aaron's office and down a hall she'd not been in. She found a home theater, complete with sofas and recliners, along with tiered levels so everyone in the room had a perfect seat. A spotless popcorn machine sat on a bar, along with a caddy filled with supersize candy that you would expect at a theater.

Another bathroom, this one without a shower or tub, but complete with a commode and a bidet. Down the wide hall from the home theater, she found a guest room with a masculine flair of dark colors and big wooden furniture. This entire wing felt filled with testosterone. Like a space where the man of the house would go when he'd been told to sleep on the couch. The thought of a billionaire sleeping on the couch made Piper laugh. Down another smaller hall, she found a laundry room and a back door. Instead of going outside, she followed Kit back through the way they'd come and spilled into the kitchen. A formal dining room, with seating for ten, that she'd seen passing through, and the bathroom she'd used the previous day. The columned great room with massive ceilings and windows that took up most of the back wall was the only part of the house she'd been in repeatedly.

When Aaron Stone had been alive and she'd needed to come there, she set up shop on a small seating area with a table that had a height she could work on. It was somewhat tucked in a corner, which helped Piper blend into the space. She looked at the table now with a passing thought that the man who'd bought it, or the woman, for that matter, no longer was here, and yet she was.

Kit scrambled out of the oversize room and up the stairs.

Now was when Piper felt the hairs on her neck tingling. She had no need to be on the second floor of the house, but up she went anyway.

An open balcony looked down on the great room below and wrapped around in both directions. Following her dog, she found bedroom after bedroom. Each slightly different in style than the last, each having its own bathroom.

She found what had to be Melissa's bedroom, based on the size and décor of the room. If the tone-on-tone white everything with a dash of light blue wasn't enough of a giveaway, the fact that the room appeared stripped sealed Piper's assumption. The walk-in closet was breathtaking. Floor to ceiling built-in cabinets with glass doors . . . nearly all empty. Only a few forgotten articles of clothing hung from the bars were left, along with scuff marks on the walls, which had likely been hidden by the clothing that once hung there. The bathroom was ridiculous. A tub surrounded by windows, a vanity mirror and separate makeup area that rivaled what you'd expect in a greenroom in a Broadway theater . . . all granite, or marble, or whatever the stone was. Piper didn't know the difference. The shower, again, fit for a small dinner party, opened to the room without a door. One entire wall of the bathroom was a rough horizontal stone in off-white, with a few pieces that stuck out with candles perched on them.

Kit had already tired of Melissa's bedroom and had moved on to the next.

The tone changed in Aaron's space. Where Melissa had tone-on-tone white, Aaron's was shades of dark blue. And nothing had been touched. At least not that she could see. This room was larger than Melissa's, with a fireplace directly in front of the bed. French doors led out on a patio with a view of the backyard. The bathroom was similar to Melissa's, but instead of a makeup station, there were two sinks. Piper couldn't help but wonder if Melissa and Aaron ever shared that bathroom.

Aaron's closet was a darker version of the other. This one was filled.

Suits, ties . . . more shoes than Piper knew a man could have. She itched to open drawers and snoop deeper but refrained.

Kit continued out of the room and paused at the doors to yet more guest rooms, another smaller media room with an oversize sofa and big-screen TV. A back staircase emptied her into a billiard and game room. This also had access to outside and onto the grounds. She hadn't opened every door, and was pretty sure she'd missed an entire hall, but her curiosity about what the rest of the house looked like was sated. At least for now.

Piper eventually stopped Kit from roaming any longer and made her way to her former boss's office to start her day.

As she made herself comfortable at Stone's desk and turned on the computer, she let out a big sigh at the same time Kit settled close by. "I never thought I'd be here doing this," she said to her dog.

Only Kit wasn't listening.

He'd already closed his eyes to take a morning nap.

∽

It was Busa popping his head into Chase's office at CMS to say good night when he realized the day had gotten away from him. For the first time in weeks, he'd managed to bury his head in his world and forget about his father's. It felt good.

"Are you back in tomorrow?" Busa asked as he shrugged into a leather jacket.

"No. I'm meeting with the estate attorney in the morning, then back to Stone Enterprises . . . probably end the day at the estate."

Busa lifted his chin. "This commute is going to get old before long."

"About that."

"What are you thinking?"

"There's an entire floor at Stone Enterprises that's vacant. Three times more room than we'll need right now but enough to give CMS the ability to expand. We can rent the space from Stone, add profit to the bottom line there, and give me the opportunity to be in two places at one time."

"We can afford a fancy place like that?"

Chase laughed. "I know some people. I'll get us a good deal."

Busa folded his hands over his chest and cracked a smile. "Is that your father's bank account talking?"

"Technically, it's mine now, so . . . yes."

"Can you do all this before you find *you know who*?"

"I need to speak with the attorney, but yes . . . I think so. We'll be able to grow faster. That's good for all of us."

Busa slowly started to nod. "We'll get some pushback from employees that won't want the commute."

"Let's consider the added cost for the average employee and try and make this profitable for them. Flextime in and out of the office to offset heavy freeway traffic. The Stone building is secured, from parking to entrance into the offices. If you can crunch the numbers so we can minimize any exodus of employee loss in this move, that would be great."

"I'll get on it." Busa tapped his hand on the wall he was standing by. "All right, then. I'll call if anything comes up."

"I appreciate it. I couldn't juggle everything without you here."

"Yeah, yeah." Busa waved him off and walked away.

Chase looked at his inbox and knew he had at least another hour before he could call the day done. He hadn't spoken to Piper all day and wondered if she'd gotten any further in finding the mystery mama.

Using his cell phone, he dialed her number and put the phone on speaker.

"Piper Maddox, private investigator, how can I direct your call?"

Chase tilted his head back and laughed. "That has a great ring to it. Are you changing professions on me?"

"Depends on how big my bonus is."

Chase appreciated how freely Piper talked to him. "How did it go today?"

"Tedious. But I did find something."

"I'm listening."

"Your father had an unaccounted-for checking account that he closed out about five years ago."

"What do you mean, *unaccounted for*?"

"I found the files with his personal taxes over the last ten years. Once the oxygen returned to my brain from the sheer shock of those numbers, I double-checked the bank accounts he accounted for on his taxes and found this one missing, so it made me dig deeper."

"If the account wasn't accruing interest, I'm not sure it would be on a personal tax return."

"I don't pretend to know tax law. It felt off to me, so I followed the numbers. A recurring amount just under ten thousand dollars a pop was transferred into this account on a fairly regular basis. The deposits were from him to him but at a different bank."

"That definitely sounds like what we're looking for."

"Right. If you're going to send someone hush money, you're going to do it from an account that isn't traced by the tax man. We need to get into that account. See who was taking the money from it."

"How hard can that be?"

Piper laughed. "I haven't done my PI in-service on hacking into a bank, but my guess is, the estate attorney can request old records. You might even be able to do that yourself since you inherited everything from Aaron Stone."

"Excellent. I'm meeting with the attorney in the morning. If you can send me the account and routing numbers, we'll get on it." Chase tapped a pen on his desk as he talked.

"I also found a locked box in the back of a file cabinet."

Chase felt his heart skip with that information. "What was inside?"

"No idea. I searched the office for a key, didn't find one. Rummaged through the catchall drawer in the kitchen . . . nothing. I was going to dig around in his bedroom but thought I should check with you first."

"Feel free."

"You sure?"

"Absolutely. And let me know if you find a safe."

"Isn't that what I found?" she asked.

Chase shook his head and tossed the pen in his hand on his desk. "A locked drawer in an office . . . no. A safe will have a combination or a biometric lock. It will be too heavy to drag away and bulky enough to withstand a fire."

"Ahhh, a rich-person thing."

Chase ran a hand down his face and felt the tired seep in. "A smart-person thing."

"I'm smart, but I don't have one."

"Where do you put your passport, birth certificate . . . bank cards you're not using?"

Piper laughed. "That gazillionaire thing is showing again. First, I don't have a passport. I got out of Ohio, not the States. The only bank cards I have, I use. And my birth certificate is in the bottom drawer of my desk."

With everything she just said, the thing that stuck out was the lack of a passport. "You really don't have a passport?"

"Where am I going?"

"What if you wanted to go on vacation to Europe?"

She snorted. "How big is that bonus going to be, Mr. Stone?"

The woman made him smile. "We need to get you a passport."

"Is that so?"

"Of course. My dad has holdings all over the world."

"*You* have holdings all over the world."

The enormity of it all hadn't settled in. "Right. Alex and I and . . ." Chase tripped on his words, nearly blurting out confirmation on the mystery brother. "And you're our assistant. I'm surprised you never accompanied my father abroad."

"I wasn't about to get on a private jet with your father."

"Oh, right." He closed his eyes, then opened them when her words sunk in. "Private jet?"

"Yeah. Technically, the company owns it, but yes. Wait, you didn't know about that?"

"Of course I did." He had no idea. Or maybe a hint of an idea but hadn't put two brain cells on the subject since his father's death.

Piper started to laugh. "You're a terrible liar."

"You just called your boss a liar."

"Fine," she said. "You're challenged at relaying inaccurate information in a convincing way so as to make someone believe it's the truth."

Chase's belly started to shake with a laugh that wanted to erupt. "Oh, that's corporate speak if I've ever heard it."

"Thank you." She sounded proud of herself.

"There is no way you talked to my father like that and kept your job."

"Technically, I lost my job. And since I did while I was corporate speaking out of my eyeballs, I figured it was time for me to change it up. Hope you don't mind."

He adored it. "I'll let you know if it goes too far."

"Good plan. And do so before you hand me a pink slip."

He didn't see that happening. "Now . . . about that passport."

Chapter Fourteen

The next day was a wash and repeat of the previous one. Only with rain.

Piper parked as close to the front door as possible, not expecting anyone to show up. Karina wouldn't be back until after the weekend. The groundskeepers and pool maintenance guy had come the day before and would resume a schedule the following week.

It was Piper, Kit, and a box of saltine crackers as she jogged up the steps to the house and let herself in.

Kit cleared the door in front of her and proceeded to spray the foyer with rainwater as he shook from nose to tail.

"Oh, crap."

Piper told the dog to sit and stay before dropping her purse and keys off on an entryway table and rushing around the dog, first to disable the house alarm and then to the nearest bathroom. There, she found a towel that didn't look like it had ever been used and returned to dry off Kit's paws and as much of his fur as she could before allowing him to go any farther into the house. Then it was another trip into the bathroom for a second towel that she used to clean the puddle off the floor that Kit left behind.

She tossed the towels into the laundry room, considered running them in the washing machine, but decided to wait in case she needed to add more to the mix.

Once that was settled, she went in search of replacement towels.

A linen closet upstairs uncovered what she was looking for. Once the domestic chores were done, she headed into the office space and turned on a light.

For a moment, she stood in front of the windows overlooking the backyard and nibbled on a cracker. The cool air from the massive pane of glass put a shiver down her spine. Not that the room was cold at all, only the space in front of the window. She twisted around and realized that the temperature was consistently comfortable. What did it cost to heat a place like this? She tried to remember the line item on the bank statements, but they all blurred.

Everything on those spreadsheets was an enormous number. Yes, the rich made money, but they sure spent it, too.

Piper knew from all the times she'd sent flowers and gifts to Aaron's liaisons that he thought nothing of dropping five hundred bucks on something that would die in a week. Then there were the first-class plane tickets for these women. Piper often wondered how he introduced these ladies to the management of the hotels he took them to. Not that he needed to excuse his behavior. Seems when you had that many zeros attached to your name, no one gave a second look when you showed up with someone who wasn't your wife.

Her mind shifted to Chase.

He was nothing like his father. Even though he had a stern expression when walking the halls of Stone Enterprises, the man took off that mask with her. It made her wonder which was the real man. The one who laughed at her snarky comments and encouraged her to say what she wanted to, regardless of the fact he was her boss.

Chase didn't feel like a boss. And she didn't feel like she was truly working. More like helping a friend out after the death of his father. And unlike any man she'd dated or worked for, she didn't find herself tongue-tied and worried that she'd say the wrong things.

When he'd shrugged out of his jacket and rolled up his sleeves, she'd had a hard time looking away. Broad shoulders and tapered to his waist.

Biceps . . . the man had the kind of arms that could pick you up and make you feel light as a feather.

And damn it, she shouldn't be thinking about the muscles on the man's body . . . or his lips and eyes, which made you stop and listen to your own breath.

Piper shook off her thoughts and opened the computer to continue where she'd left off.

"He's your boss, Piper," she whispered to herself. "And even if he wasn't, you're pregnant." There wasn't a man on the planet that jumped into that mess on purpose.

She flexed her fingers as if flicking away where her mind had roamed and opened Aaron's inbox.

His email was filled with notifications of bills, advertisements from places he'd likely frequented in the past . . . the usual suspects. It was a bank notification that had her thinking.

She opened the email, this one from a bank she'd yet to discover, and followed the ball. It was a notification of an available bank statement. She clicked over, found the expected password protection, but the username popped up on its own. After following the prompts to change a forgotten password, and using Aaron Stone's personal email to do it, she was in the bank account in less than five minutes.

It was too easy.

Once in, she quickly concluded that this was the account that Melissa had access to. There were deposits from Chase Enterprises and expenses that painted the image of a very privileged woman. The credit card associated with the account was filled with charges from restaurants, beauty salons, spas, high-end department stores, and ATM withdrawals. The balance in the account was just over three hundred thousand, which had an abrupt stop of all activity dating back to the day after Aaron Stone's funeral. Even the credit card was canceled.

It felt harsh, even to her, that Melissa was stripped of her life with the death of her husband. Sure, a bank account north of a quarter of a million dollars used for incidentals was insane, but to have the money one day and not the next had to hurt.

Piper printed out the last several statements to show Chase and exited out of the bank site.

She absently reached for a cracker and stopped it just short of her mouth. A surge of nausea rose like a tidal wave and had her bolting out of her seat and to the closest bathroom.

Her upset stomach had plagued her most of the previous day, but after the first few hours in the morning, she'd been able to hold down the crackers. Something told her that wasn't going to be the case today.

Piper washed her hands and rinsed out her mouth. Her color wasn't its normal rosy shade, which she suspected was caused not only by the nausea but also by her lack of sleep. Even though she felt exhausted, she wasn't getting through the night without bad dreams waking her at least twice. She ran a hand over her flat stomach and wondered how long it would be that way. Truth was, the jeans she was wearing seemed looser than normal. How was she going to gain twenty-five to thirty-five pounds if she couldn't keep down a cracker? Was the lack of food hurting the kid? Just because she wasn't going to keep it didn't mean she wasn't going to do what she could to give it a healthy start.

Her mind raced back to the bank account that paid for pedicures and facials and wondered if things would be different if she had that kind of money. It wasn't that she didn't want kids.

Piper shook her head, tried to clear the thoughts away.

The best chance this kid had was a family that had the financial security she didn't. Not to mention two people that wanted a child more than anything. Or even one person . . . so long as they could do all the things a parent needed to do to care for it. A single mom with the kind of resources in that bank account Melissa had control of. Only even she had that yanked out from under her. What if Piper kept the baby and then lost her job . . . again?

She buried her head in her hands and reminded herself that adoption was the best solution.

The sound of Kit panting at the open bathroom door brought her thoughts back to where she was and what she was doing there.

It was close to noon when Piper needed to get away from the desk.

Lunch was still not going to happen, not with her stomach on edge. The steady headache that came midday and didn't leave until she kept a decent amount of food down was firmly nestled between her temples.

After a brief pause outside, watching Kit water the already overwatered lawn, she went upstairs to search Aaron's bedroom for the missing keys and maybe a hidden safe.

She started in what she thought were the obvious places, bedside tables and containers sitting on shelves. All she found was ChapStick and pocket change.

In the closet, she found Aaron Stone's stash of expensive watches . . . an entire drawer full of brands she'd only heard about. She recalled noticing them on his wrist from time to time but didn't put much thought to it. Here, with at least two dozen of them pampered in a crush of black velvet, they were hard to ignore. Only one space seemed to have a missing watch. She wondered if that was the one he'd been wearing when he died.

She pushed the morbid thought away and kept poking around. Plenty of dress shoes and several casual pairs as well. Golf shoes and snow boots, which she found funny since it didn't snow in Beverly Hills. Probably for skiing in Aspen or at a chalet in Switzerland.

It was nuts.

Designer suits that wouldn't be worn again. At least not by the man who bought them.

Chase had to be a good three inches taller than his father, not that Chase would ever wear something his father once owned.

Maybe the watches, though . . .

She shook her head. "I doubt it."

Piper found a drawer filled with wallets, and another with sunglasses.

But no keys.

And no safe.

Kit, who had jumped up on the bed, something Piper recognized she shouldn't allow but did anyway . . . snapped his head off his paws and let out a low growl.

Piper immediately looked in the direction of the door and held her breath. "What is it, Kitty?"

She heard noise from downstairs and followed it. "Chase?"

Kit scrambled off the bed and stayed at her side on full alert.

"Chase?" She lifted her voice a little higher.

When no one answered, Piper walked with a little more caution. Someone was in the house and not answering her.

At the top of the stairs, movement from below had Kit barking.

"What in the hell?"

Piper let out a breath when she recognized the person. "Melissa."

"What are you doing in *my* house and with *that* . . . thing!" Melissa Stone stood looking up at Piper, hands on hips and venom in her voice.

Piper signaled for Kit to stay at her side as she walked down the stairs. "I'm here at the request of Chase and Alex. What are you doing here?" Just asking the question felt wrong. This was the woman's home . . . or had been.

Melissa looked between Kit and Piper and back to Kit.

When Piper made it to ground level, Melissa took a step back, eye on Kit. "Does it bite?"

"Yes."

Melissa took another step back.

Kit, sensing the retreat, barked.

"You better be able to control that thing."

"Melissa, I don't think you're supposed to be here."

She glared now, eyes fixed on Piper. "I forgot a few things, not that I need to explain myself to you."

Melissa sidestepped, indicating she wanted to go upstairs.

Kit growled again.

"Get that thing out of my way."

Piper weighed her options. Let Melissa do whatever she was there to do. As long as it didn't involve a gas can and a match . . . or demand she leave. Not that Piper knew if she had any authority to do that.

Piper took the first approach and stepped away from the staircase and brought Kit with her.

As soon as Melissa was out of sight, Piper told Kit to stay before running to the office to retrieve her cell phone.

On her way back to the foyer, she typed in a quick message to Chase. Melissa is here.

Chase didn't respond right away. She considered calling him but decided against it. How earth-shattering could Melissa's presence in the house be?

Piper glanced outside through the windows framing the front door and saw a Range Rover parked behind her car.

She debated checking on Melissa to see what it was that she'd forgotten.

With one foot on the stairs, Piper's phone buzzed.

Chase responded with, Why?

She said she forgot something.

Three dots blinked on her screen for over a minute. Did she bring a moving truck?

Piper smiled. No. Should I watch her? She's ticked that I'm here.

No. Chase's response was instant. Leave her alone. I'm on my way now. 20 minutes out.

Piper replied with a thumbs-up and left the foyer to take up residence in the living room, where she could see the stairs and the front door.

Kit sat at her feet, eyes intent on the foyer.

While she waited for either Melissa to leave or Chase to show up, Piper googled locksmiths and made a call. She spent some of Chase's money and requested an emergency call, and yes, they knew how to change the coding on electric gates. They'd be there in two hours.

Fifteen minutes later, Melissa hustled down the stairs with an oversize bag, like one you'd bring on an airplane as a personal item, in her hands.

Kit growled.

Piper made a point of staring at her phone, her legs crossed, as if she was uninterested in whatever Melissa was doing.

"Are you watching me?" Melissa asked.

Piper didn't bother looking her way when she answered. "Crossword puzzle. Name a country in Europe with five letters."

"This should have been my house."

Piper glanced up. "You won't get an argument out of me." The words should have deflated Melissa's anger. Instead, they fueled them.

"You were one of them . . . weren't you?"

Piper sighed as if she was bored with the questions, even though her heart rate started to climb. "One of what?"

"Them? The extra women. I knew about his affairs."

That hurt. "I'm sure you're not alone in the club of rich men's wives that ignore their husband's indiscretions."

"You did screw him."

Piper's stomach churned. "Don't make me sick."

"And now what? You're going after his son?"

Piper turned her head away and focused on her phone even though every nerve in her body was on high alert. This woman wanted a fight, and Piper didn't want to play. "Italy! A country in Europe with five letters."

"If there's something I know about Chase Stone, it's that he won't take sloppy seconds after his father. He hated the man."

Seriously, her stomach was churning.

The back of her neck started to sweat, and her palms grew clammy.

Piper dropped her phone on the couch and lurched off the sofa to the nearest bathroom.

Melissa chased after her. "You can't screw the boss and have a job for long."

Piper only heard her heart pounding and her brain telling her to hurry.

She got there in time for the cold water and crackers to come up.

With short gasps of air, Piper wiped her mouth with tissue once her stomach was empty.

Kit was glued to her side, facing the door.

Sure enough, Melissa stood there watching her with disgust. "What is wrong with you?"

"Leave me alone."

Kit let out a bark.

"I know . . . the memory of him touching me makes me sick, too."

"I swear to God, Melissa." Piper had held her cool but was about to unleash her inner bitch if the woman didn't stop.

Kit lunged forward, barking, his lips pulled back.

Melissa squealed and jumped. Her back hit the wall in the hallway.

"Get out!" Chase's voice boomed.

Piper quickly flushed the toilet and gave a command to Kit to hold back.

Kit walked backward until his hind end bumped Piper's leg, all the while barking at what he saw as a threat.

Maybe it was the dog, or Chase looming over Melissa, but the woman couldn't hide the scare in her eyes.

"That dog tried to kill me."

It took everything in Piper to hold Kit back.

Chase moved in front of the bathroom door, his back to Piper. "Leave. Or I'll call the police."

"Kit, quiet," Piper said as quietly as she could and still be heard.

With a whimper, Kit did as he was told.

The sound of Melissa's heavy footsteps filled the hall as she marched away.

Chase followed.

Piper used the privacy to rinse her mouth and splash water on her face.

By the time she walked into the foyer, Melissa was gone. Chase stood in the doorway, looking out as his stepmother drove away.

"That was ugly."

Chase turned around, slammed the door behind him, and was at her side in a heartbeat. "Are you okay?"

Kit once again took up position in front of her, the hair on his back on end.

"Kit, back."

He listened and sat.

"I'm fine." She was far from fine.

Chase moved closer, reached out, and put his palm on her face. "You don't look okay." His voice was soft.

Piper found it difficult to breathe. The desire to lean into him and accept his concern collided with the things Melissa had said. "I'll be okay," she whispered.

"You're shaking." His hand moved from her face to her shoulder.

Their eyes caught.

Piper swayed in his direction as if her body had a mind of its own and needed to move closer.

Melissa's words circled in her head. *Sloppy seconds.* Had Chase heard that? Would he believe any of her accusations? Piper's stomach rolled, and every beat of her heart was a loud thud in her head that brought along a hammer against her temples.

Piper took a step back and lowered her eyes. "I could use some cold water," she managed to say.

Chase dropped his hand. "I'll get it."

When he disappeared in the direction of the kitchen, Piper slid onto the couch and put her head in her hands.

Chapter Fifteen

It wasn't Piper who was shaking, it was him. He'd walked into the house expecting to confront Melissa, and instead heard raised voices with nasty accusations and a dog barking in a way that you'd only expect when they were about to rip someone in half.

When he realized that Melissa had cornered Piper in the bathroom, an unexpected rage filled his entire being.

That red-hot anger soothed the moment his eyes landed on Piper after Melissa was gone. All he wanted to do was gather her in his arms. He felt her head lean into his palm and saw her eyes fall for a half a second longer than a blink. There was no mistaking the look in her eye or the feeling it gave him when he saw it.

This attraction went both ways. He knew it as much as he understood the sun would rise in the morning.

Chase filled a glass with chilled water from the refrigerator and brought it back into the living room.

He found Piper sitting on the sofa, Kit curled at her feet.

Chase sat on the coffee table opposite her and handed over the water. "Here."

"Thanks."

She brought the water to her lips and took the smallest sip of water he'd ever seen.

"Your color is coming back."

"She's a real winner, that one," Piper said, laughing off his words.

"She had no right to even be here."

"It wasn't my place to tell her to leave."

No, it wasn't. But a confrontation with his dead father's wife wasn't in Piper's job description either. "I'll get someone in here to change the locks."

Piper shook her head. "Already done. They should be here . . ." She glanced at her watch. "In an hour and a half."

Chase sat back, his hands on his knees. This woman never ceased to amaze him. "When did you manage that?"

"When she was upstairs collecting whatever it was she forgot."

"You're incredible, you know that?"

Piper closed her eyes, her lips in a straight line. She placed a palm to her forehead. "I don't feel so incredible right now. My head is pounding."

He stood. "I'm sure there is something in this house for a headache."

She started to protest, but he left her side in search of pills.

The first place he looked was the kitchen. Opening and closing cupboards like a man on a mission. Which he was. When he didn't find what he was looking for, he double-timed his steps up the stairs and down the hall into his father's bedroom.

Chase had been avoiding that room since he stepped into the house. He'd glanced into it briefly during the funeral but dove in headfirst now. It was hard to slam doors and drawers when they had soft-close features, but he tried. Sure enough, he found a bottle of ibuprofen and jogged down the stairs. "This should work," he said to Piper, handing her the bottle.

Her eyes narrowed, as if the light was making her headache worse. "I can't take this."

Chase accepted the bottle when she handed it back. "You're allergic."

"No . . . yes."

"Which is it?"

"Tylenol. I can take acetaminophen."

Back up the stairs he went. He searched more drawers in his father's bathroom. Nothing. Melissa's bedroom.

More ibuprofen.

He moved down the hall to a guest bedroom. One of the bigger ones. He was about to give up and drive to a store when he found what he was looking for in the third guest room he checked.

Kit looked up at him as he approached Piper. By now, she was lying on the couch, a hand draped over her eyes.

"Piper?" he said her name quietly.

She held out her hand without looking at him.

Chase opened the bottle and dropped two pills into her palm. She propped herself up long enough to swallow the pills. "There're some crackers on your dad's desk. Can you—"

"Got it."

He found the saltines on the desk and brought them to her.

"Sorry," she said. "I need to keep the pills down."

"Is this a migraine?" Chase didn't have them, but his mother had on occasion, and he recognized the behavior.

"I'm not . . . I don't know."

"You don't have migraines?"

Piper pulled a cracker out of the packaging without opening her eyes and nibbled on one.

"I just need a few minutes."

Kit took that moment to nudge Chase out of the way, climb up on the couch, and wedge himself to Piper's side.

Her hand fell on the dog.

Chase grabbed a pillow from another sofa. "Here."

She opened her eyes briefly and lifted her head when she saw the pillow. "Thanks."

"Better?"

"Uh-huh."

Kit let out a huge sigh and laid his head on Piper's stomach and closed his eyes.

As much as Chase wanted to stay close if she needed anything, he knew if she opened her eyes to find him staring, that would only add a layer of stress to whatever she was dealing with.

Chase quietly pulled himself away and left her in the silence.

He called Stuart the second he was out of earshot. "What do we need to do to keep Melissa from showing up at the house or the office?"

∽

Piper pulled the blanket up around her shoulders and burrowed into the warmth it provided. The slow snoring of Kit encouraged her to go back to sleep. She felt rested and comfortable for the first time in what felt like forever.

And hungry.

Not nauseated, which was a huge relief.

The low whispering of voices made her open her eyes.

She was on a couch. Not her couch.

Stone's.

She'd fallen asleep.

At work.

The memory of Melissa and Chase . . . and all the graphic detail flooded back.

Her eyes drifted open. The light from outside wasn't as bright as it had been when she'd fallen asleep. It didn't feel late, but she'd done more than take a short nap.

She'd slept.

Piper pushed herself into a sitting position, dislodging Kit's head from her thigh.

She stretched her arms over her head and felt at least one vertebra in her back snap, thanking her.

"We woke you." Chase walked into the room from the foyer. "The locksmiths are here."

"What? I slept for an hour?" She glanced at her watch.

"Closer to three."

She blinked, her eyes finally focusing on the time. It was nearly five. "How did that happen?"

"It's okay."

"I'm so sorry."

Chase had shed the suit jacket and tie. His sleeves were rolled up, his shirt unbuttoned a couple of notches. After-work casual. "Don't be. How are you feeling?"

She covered a yawn and blinked away the sleep. "Embarrassed . . . and hungry."

"That's a good sign. The hungry part." Chase motioned toward the front door. "They're on the last door."

"How long have they been here?"

"Turns out there are a lot of keyed doors in this house. We saved this one for last since you were asleep."

"Mr. Stone?"

Chase smiled at her. "I'll be right back."

Piper pushed the blanket away and realized that Chase must have put it on her. This was not the kind of living room that had a throw on the back of a sofa for curling up on. She'd be surprised if anyone had napped in the room before her. She all but rolled off the sofa and then folded the blanket. Kit stretched beside her and shook off the sandman.

"You have to be hungry," she said to her pet.

She started toward the kitchen, where she'd left Kit's food, and realized she didn't have shoes on.

Glancing back at Chase, she wasn't sure what emotion was stronger . . . embarrassed or grateful. The sleep was desperately needed and not something she'd gotten a lot of in the past several weeks. Even though a headache of monstrous proportions had triggered the slumber, she was grateful for it.

Piper opened a can of organic dog food and mixed in a small portion of pumpkin, a few peas, and his kibble. She hunched down to Kit's side and patted his head as he dug in. "You took care of business today, buddy." She kissed the top of his head and left him to eat in peace.

"All done," Chase announced when he walked into the kitchen. "Melissa will have to hop a fence if she wants to come in here."

"She doesn't seem like the fence-hopping sort."

Chase looked down at Kit.

Piper followed his gaze and wiggled her bare toes. "You took my shoes off and covered me with a blanket."

He cleared his throat. "Yeah, you didn't look comfortable."

She leaned against the island and crossed her arms over her chest. "That isn't exactly boss behavior."

"Today hasn't exactly been a boss–employee kind of day."

"I suppose that's true."

Chase's smile put a flutter in her belly. The kind she welcomed even though she shouldn't.

"You said you were hungry."

"Yeah. I should get going."

"I owe you dinner."

She tilted her head. "How did you conclude that?"

"Today was above and beyond. It's the least I can do." He shoved his hands into his pockets. "C'mon, Piper, let me get you some food. There's a lot of choices just down the hill. We'll leave Kit here, pick him back up when we're done."

The day had been about pushing envelopes. Besides food within the hour versus the drive home and then cooking . . . "Let me put my shoes on."

A few minutes later, they were climbing into Chase's truck, with Kit's nose stuck to the glass framing the front door of the house.

Within twenty minutes, they were being seated in a steakhouse that Piper was entirely underdressed for.

Chase encouraged her to walk in front of him and then pulled her chair out for her before taking a seat.

"This place is fancy."

"Fits the neighborhood." Chase disappeared behind a menu. "I could use a drink. What about you?"

Her mouth literally watered. "That sounds great, but . . ." *There's a fetus growing inside of me, and that's a big no can do.* "I don't want that headache coming back. I'll stick with water."

Chase looked at her over his menu. "You sure?"

No! "Positive."

Piper studied the menu, searching out the chicken options. Or as she was used to doing, picking the least-expensive thing on the menu.

Only there was a fundamental problem with her proven date-night strategy. "Is it me, or are there not prices on this menu?"

"I'm paying for dinner."

She nudged her menu toward him. "But there are no prices."

He glanced at her menu and went back to his own. "There are prices on mine."

It took a second for that to register. "They assume you're paying?"

Chase lowered his menu and made a point of looking around the dining room. "This isn't the kind of place where a woman pays the bill."

"What?" Piper looked to her left and right. "That's sexist."

"Don't blame me, I didn't make the rules."

"How am I supposed to figure out what to order?"

"What are you hungry for?"

"That's not how it works. You tell me what you're ordering, then I pick something on the menu that's cheaper . . . since you're paying."

His smile went all the way to his eyes. "Are those the rules?"

"Of course they are."

"What if I only order a salad?"

Her shoulders slumped.

The waiter arrived and asked what they were drinking.

Chase ordered a bourbon, Piper stuck with water, and the suit-wearing waiter retreated.

"Order whatever you want, Piper. I'm a gazillionaire, remember?"

Yeah, she remembered, but still. It wasn't how she was raised and went against her grain.

She studied the menu and debated her options in silence.

The waiter returned with Chase's drink and asked them what they wanted.

"You first," she said to Chase.

"Oh, no. Ladies first."

Piper glared at him. "I'll go with the chicken." Boring baked chicken put on a fancy menu like this to satisfy the dieting Beverly Hills housewives that were afraid to put on a pound for fear their husbands would leave them for their secretaries.

Chase cleared his throat.

"Anything to go with that? A starter, perhaps? Caesar salad?"

She could always hit a fast-food place on the way home if she was still hungry. "Whatever it comes with is fine."

The waiter turned to Chase. "And you, sir?"

Chase looked directly into her eyes as he ordered. "The New York, medium rare. Loaded baked potato. Start with a shrimp cocktail."

Piper literally felt like Pavlov's dogs with how much her mouth was watering.

"Probably dessert, but I'll figure that out later."

The man was goading her. Daring her to eat the chicken when he picked what was likely the most expensive thing on the menu except the lobster.

He's a gazillionaire, Piper.

"I changed my mind," she said without breaking eye contact with Chase.

"Okay," the waiter replied.

"Eight-ounce filet mignon, medium rare, with that peppercorn sauce on it. Garlic mashed potatoes. Does that come with vegetables?"

"Grilled asparagus."

"Perfect."

Chase raised an eyebrow.

"And a Caesar salad."

"Will that be all?"

What else could she make Chase buy? "Fancy water," she said.

"Miss?"

"The bubbly kind."

"Pellegrino?"

"Sure." She was thinking of the kind from a can at the local super-market, but what the hell. "In a wineglass with lemon."

The waiter collected the menus and left them alone.

Chase leaned forward. "Did you just break the rules?"

"All of them," she replied.

He rubbed his hands together. "Good."

The waiter arrived with her water and fresh sourdough bread while Chase was telling her about his plans to move his business to the Stone building. "Seems a waste to have a completely empty floor in a building that size."

"How do your employees feel about the move?"

"We haven't told them yet. I need to make sure there are no obstacles."

Piper put a generous portion of butter on the bread. "Do I need to remind you again that you own the building?"

"Probably."

The bread literally melted in her mouth. She let out a moan and closed her eyes.

"That good?"

"Divine."

Chase reached for a section and followed her example. He took a bite. "It is good."

"Have your assistant at CMS call me. We'll get a design team to reconfigure the floor to your needs."

"We have a design team?"

"Of course. It's a hotel empire. Design teams are a phone call away."

"I didn't think of that."

"That's why you pay me the big bucks, boss." She washed the bread down with the bubbly water. "Will you use that floor as your primary office space?"

"I haven't thought that far yet. Alex and I sharing an office upstairs will eventually get uncomfortable."

"That's fixable, too."

"Oh?"

"If you can handle a slightly smaller office on the top floor, we can shift everyone over one space, remove the meeting space in the middle . . . it really doesn't need to be there. The larger meeting room, the one where we hold the board meetings, is plenty of space." She visualized the finished project within the blink of an eye.

"You sure you're not part of the design team?"

"Design is kind of a hobby."

"A hobby is reading or gardening."

"Or losing yourself for hours in a design program," she argued.

The first course arrived and interrupted their conversation.

Piper had to remind herself to slow down. Now that her body was accepting food, she realized just how famished she was.

"Did you want to be an architect?"

"Those are two different skill sets," she said between bites. "I like to point and suggest a wall go here, a window go there, and not worry about if the load-bearing wall will carry the weight."

"That sounds architectural to me."

She shrugged. "It's fun. And even better when you're spending someone else's money to make it happen."

He smiled. "I bet you do that well."

"Oh, don't worry. You'll get a chance to see me in action."

They moved from office design to what she'd accomplished in the day before Melissa had shown up and put a stop to everything. "The thing is, I'd have been happy to commiserate with her if she'd given me a chance. Seeing the size of the bank account she was used to having and knowing that was all stripped away must be a part of her anger."

"Don't feel too sorry for her. She got a very big check."

"He took her house away."

"Five million and then some."

Piper's jaw dropped. "Oh." That was a lot of money.

"Cars, jewelry . . . lots of things."

"Oh."

"The things I heard her saying to you were inexcusable."

"She caught me off guard, it won't happen again."

Chase pushed the empty martini glass that held the shrimp to the side. "You're right, it won't. Not if I can help it. The attorneys are talking, and if she so much as shows her face again, we'll find a reason to file a restraining order."

"That's a bit extreme."

"I don't think so. She had you cornered in a bathroom and was harassing you. In a house she was told not to come back to. Do you have any idea what she left with?"

"None. There didn't seem to be that much left in her bedroom, but I didn't sift through any of the drawers. Maybe she wanted the bed linens."

Chase shook his head. "I doubt that."

"Did you go up there and look?"

"No."

"Have you been up there at all?"

He looked to the side, picked up his drink. "No."

There was something to unpack in that. "I have. I didn't find any keys. I did find your dad's watch collection. He has . . . *had* a lot of them."

Chase nodded but didn't comment.

"That got me thinking, though."

"About?"

"Well, you carry keys with you, right?"

He nodded.

"Keys, your cell phone, a wallet. Your dad drove himself to the hospital, right?" She didn't spell out the facts she knew. Aaron Stone drove himself to the hospital and, within seconds of getting there, went into full cardiac arrest and died before they could get a heart surgeon scrubbed for surgery.

"That's what we were told."

"So where is his stuff? From that day? You go into the hospital, and they shove all your things into a bag. A man as rich as your father likely had a wallet, a watch . . . car keys, at the very least, on him. Maybe the keys we're looking for are in that stash."

Chase looked directly at her. "It's a good place to look."

"Where are those things?"

"Melissa would know."

Piper rolled her eyes. "She isn't helpful."

"In his car, maybe."

"Where is that?" Piper asked.

"The garage?"

"Have you looked?"

"No."

"When we go back, we should look."

The waiter arrived with their dinners and ended the conversation about a dead man's personal possessions on the day of his death.

Piper thanked the waiter and picked up her knife and fork and found Chase staring at her.

"When we get back, we're going to collect your dog, set the alarm, and leave the search for tomorrow."

Chase's way of changing the subject was noted. "Okay."

He cut into his steak and brought a bite to his lips. "Can you come in at noon?"

She followed his lead and sliced into the filet. "Doesn't my day start at eight?"

"Not tomorrow. I'm keeping you late tonight."

"Yeah, this is such a hardship." Sarcasm dripped from her lips. One bite, and she was in heaven. Exactly what her body needed. "God, this is good."

"Better than the chicken," he teased.

She sliced into the tender beef a second time. "With the right bank account, I could be a very high-maintenance girl."

"You're not now?"

"Oh yeah, I clean out Target every chance I get."

Chase was smiling again now that they'd gotten off the topic of his father.

Piper really liked his smile.

Chapter Sixteen

Chase arrived before Piper for the sole purpose of braving his father's personal space by himself.

Dinner with her the night before had been the highlight of his month, probably longer. Once they put to bed the subject of his father, he found conversation with her both delightful and entertaining. She did not have a filter and had no problem saying whatever she was thinking. Somewhere in the middle of their dinner, he thought about how much his mother would like her. Their deep dislike for his father would be the glue to bond them for life.

The only subject she didn't press was Chase's unease in his father's home.

She saw it, though. He could tell by the way she softened her gaze and dropped the subject when he didn't respond to her questions. But she didn't press.

Chase appreciated that.

The thought of digging through the clothes his father was wearing on his last day alive left a bad taste in his mouth. Truth was, Piper's conclusion that the keys they were looking for were probably in that pile was likely correct.

Somewhere close to midnight, long after he'd followed Piper down and out of the Beverly Hills driveway, he chided himself on not paying the locksmith to break the lock in question. He'd been so hyperaware of the house locks and letting Piper sleep as long as she needed to, he didn't even consider that option.

Today they'd get into the drawer one way or another. Both would require a trip to the garage. One to find the keys his father carried with him on a daily basis, and if that failed to manifest . . . a sledgehammer would do.

But first, Chase climbed the stairs and wandered into his father's bedroom. The bed was perfectly made. The number of pillows was just enough to be attractive but not overdone, as so many women liked to do. The knickknacks were less personal and more out of a magazine. No pictures of fond memories. Then again, what could the man be proud of? The wife he knew was there for the money he gave her? His children that he all but ignored growing up and didn't know as adults? No, Aaron Stone could take a selfie with himself and a handful of hundred-dollar bills. He spent his whole life building an empire and not cultivating one meaningful relationship in the process.

Chase walked around the room and into the closet.

He found the drawer with several watches, another with belts, ties . . . wallets and sunglasses. And tens of thousands of dollars in suits. Everything had a brand name and was likely tailored to fit him perfectly.

Chase was staring at his father's shoes when his phone rang.

It was Alex.

"Hey."

"How are you doing?"

She knew he was going to dig deeper today at the estate and had thanked him repeatedly for taking one for the team. "Our father had a lot of stuff."

"I'm sure he did."

He put the phone on speaker and set it on the island in the closet. "What do you want to do with it?"

"Is arson out of the question?" she asked.

"We'd have to cancel the insurance and make sure the fire didn't spread. Even then, it's still risky."

Alex moaned. "Any sign of Melissa today?"

"No."

"That's a plus."

Chase moved hangers and looked at the suits. His father did have good taste in clothing.

"How is everything there?" Chase asked.

"Definitely getting the icy shoulder from Gatlin. Anytime I ask a question, he seems annoyed I don't already know the answer," Alex said.

Chase paused his inspection of the clothes as a memory crept in. "Do you remember that guy that came to the funeral?"

"Could you be more specific?"

"The hotel one . . . Morrison?"

"I didn't meet him, you did," Alex reminded him.

"He opened the door for us to call him. I bet he could help us navigate this transition. Without an ulterior motive."

"What are we waiting for?"

"I'll give him a call."

Alex let out a huge sigh. "How hard would it have been for our dad to mentor us for this?"

"Too hard, apparently."

"If I ever have kids, they're going to grow up in this building."

Chase knew her frustration. "One thing at a time, Alex. What do you want to do with Dad's clothes? You don't think this mystery brother of ours would want them, do you?"

"Considering this man was even further removed from our soulless father, I doubt it."

"Some fresh-out-of-college kids would bend over backwards for these suits. I say we donate all of it. Stuart said we couldn't sell anything until we find the brother, he didn't say anything about personal donations. Sadly, Armani suits aren't considered an asset." Chase lifted a pair of shoes, realized how little wear appeared on the sole.

"Perfect. Want me to look into that?"

He dropped his hands to his side. "No. Piper has a knack for that kind of thing."

Chase's words fell out of his mouth as movement out of the corner of his eye caught his attention.

Piper stood there staring, arms crossed over her chest, a scowl on her face.

"Even better," Alex said.

How much had Piper heard? "Listen, I've got to go."

"I'll check in tonight if I don't hear from you."

"Sounds good."

Chase ended the call. "Hi."

Eyes lifted in accusation. "Brother?"

One word, and Chase knew exactly how much she'd heard. "Yeah," he said on a sigh.

"You were going to tell me . . . when exactly?"

"Eventually."

She pointed toward the door. "I've been busting my ass looking for a woman, not a man. This information would have been helpful."

"We are looking for a woman. The mother . . . which should lead us to the brother."

"The brother. Aaron had another son?"

"Apparently. We just learned about it . . . him. We can't let this get out. Not until we find him."

Piper moved into the closet and stood on the opposite end of the room. "The hush money was *I don't want to be bothered with a kid, so here's money and go away* money."

"Essentially."

Why did she look so stricken with the news? Surely, she couldn't think this was out of the realm of possibilities when it came to his father. "Makes me sick."

"I would have told you sooner, but I didn't know if I could trust you."

"You didn't tell me now."

All right, that was true. "I'm explaining things to you now. No one knows about this person outside of the lawyer, Alex, me, and our mother. We think that whoever this guy is, he has no idea about who his father was, or he would have come forward by now. But the mother must know about our dad."

"Yet she hasn't come forward."

"Or she's waiting."

"For what?"

"No idea. Either way, we need to find her and him. We can't even sell this house until we do."

Piper lifted her arms to the room. "This house, or *that* hotel . . . or *that* resort." Their eyes met. "Or shares in the company."

"That's not our intention."

"Your collective stock split three ways . . . if this brother wanted to sell, that could throw controlling interest over the line, depending on who buys it."

Chase waved a hand in the air. "Barely."

"There are some sharks on the board that would find a way to push that line. Yarros comes to mind."

"That's tomorrow's problem."

"It's a huge problem if someone finds him first and talks him into selling. Why are you being so casual about this? It's a big deal."

"We know that, Piper. That's why we're here digging into everything of Aaron Stone's so we can remain in control of the situation. Alex and I know what's at stake." Chase tried to keep his voice even but found it elevating to match Piper's.

"Damn." Piper sucked in a breath. "Wait . . . can you even take a vote on the board without this guy?"

Well, hell, that didn't take long for her to catch. "It's questionable."

Piper shook her head. "You can't vote with someone else's shares. You need to find this guy before the board catches on that you're stalling."

"And so we can sell things like these." Chase picked up one of the many watches sitting in their own drawer in an effort to change the subject.

Piper started to nod, then narrowed her gaze at the drawer. "Where are they?"

"Where are what?"

She walked to his side and opened the watch drawer farther. "The watches."

"These are watches."

She ran a finger over each one. "There were over two dozen of them yesterday. One had diamonds all over it. God-awful gaudy, but probably worth a small fortune."

Chase looked back in the drawer. "Are you sure?"

"Positive." She lined the watches up close together. "This was completely stuffed with only one unfilled spot. That's what made me think about what your dad was wearing the day he died. He probably had one on."

He ran a hand over his jaw. "Melissa."

"You think—"

"Who else? There're security cameras, but I doubt we're going to see anyone coming and going in this house other than us and Karina."

"Karina wouldn't. Besides, she wasn't here yesterday."

"But Melissa would."

"Do you want me to call the police?"

Chase shook his head. "No. I'll call Stuart. We'll handle this a different way. Truth is, I don't even care. Nothing in this house is of value to me. But this brother of ours . . . who knows. Alex and I need to manage this estate as if we did care, and we wouldn't be doing that if we ignored someone stealing right before our eyes."

"Wow, your dad did a number on you."

That sounded like Piper thought he needed therapy. And maybe he did, but not today. "I want to minimize that number by getting through as much of this crap as possible as quickly as possible."

"What are we waiting for, then? Let's check out his car, the garage is a space we haven't overturned. Or smash open the file cabinet with the locked box." She started walking out of the closet. "That might be therapeutic. Beating up something your father owned. Like the car scene from *Ferris Bueller's Day Off*."

He hadn't seen the movie. "What did the car do?"

"Nothing. The dad loved and spent more time with his car than he did his kid. So, the kid beat it up."

"What kind of car was it?"

"I don't know. Something old and vintage. Jaguar, Ferrari? I'm not a car buff."

"Was the dad pissed?"

Piper stopped halfway down the stairs and turned to look at him. "You haven't seen the movie?"

He shrugged. "Is it recent?"

"You're kidding, right? It's an eighties classic. One of the best films ever made." She started back down the stairs. "Teenager coming of age."

Chase went back to trying not to watch the sway of her hips as she led the way.

He failed miserably, but he was trying.

"I'm not a teenager."

"You don't have to be a kid to enjoy it. I think it reminds all of us about the joy of living. You need to put that film on your bucket list."

Piper headed for the front door since it was faster to get to the freestanding garage from there.

"I'll make you a deal, I'll watch the movie as soon as you get your passport."

By now, he was at her side.

She looked up at him. "How much does it cost to get a passport?"

"I don't know . . . a hundred bucks, maybe."

She pointed to her chest. "You pay for my passport, and I'll pay for your movie rental, Mr. Gazillionaire."

"Deal."

She lifted her hand, extended her pinky.

"What's that for?"

"Pinky promise."

He laughed. "How old are we?"

"Young enough to know the power of a pinky promise. Handshakes are for business professionals that have no intention of making good on their deals without a lawyer tweaking them. So how good are they?"

He went ahead and looped his pinky to hers and enjoyed the spark that rolled up his arm with that brief, innocent touch. She let go way too soon.

"No Kit today?" he asked.

She shook her head. "I can't let him get used to coming to work with me. He doesn't fit at the office."

"He could. As long as he doesn't eat anyone."

"Too much of a distraction."

He didn't have a problem with dogs in the office so long as they were behaved.

They walked around to the side door of the garage and walked in.

Chase flipped on the overhead lights as a line of cars came into view.

Piper blew out a slow breath. "Wow."

He pressed several buttons and opened the individual doors to each bay. Only one slot was empty. The one Melissa had used, presumably. There were still five cars lined up.

Chase rubbed his hands together. "Which one should I beat up?"

Piper started shaking her head. "Not that one, or that one." She pointed to the Aston Martin DB9 Volante convertible and a Porsche 911. The Aston had been Melissa's, and Chase assumed the red Porsche had been his father's.

"You have good taste in cars."

Piper walked in a trancelike state to the DB9 and opened the door. "What does something like this cost?" she asked as she moved to sit in the driver's seat.

"That one . . . probably about three hundred and fifty thousand."

Piper jumped up and out of the seat before she could swing her legs in. "Holy crap."

He laughed. "It won't bite."

"You sure? I don't want to scratch it."

Chase opened the door wider.

She lowered herself in . . . slower this time. "It still smells new."

"Rich people don't drive old cars. They collect them. My dad wasn't a collector."

On the passenger seat sat a large-brimmed hat.

That she had no problem grabbing and plopping on her head.

"I take it this was Melissa's."

"She drove it, but it belonged to the estate. Like the house."

Piper sighed and ran a hand over the steering wheel. "Your dad had billions, why did he care if his wife got the car after his death?"

"According to my mother, it was because he didn't value women. Only what they could give him."

Piper looked up at him. "Then why did he leave a portion of everything to his daughter?"

"My best guess is that he knew how close Alex and I are. I'd have given her half anyway. Or a third, as it stands. This way, he doesn't look like the ass after his death."

"And taking the house and the cars away from the wife makes him look good?" Piper asked.

Chase shrugged. "Melissa signed a prenup. On top of what she was promised, she was allowed to keep any gifts he gave her. He gave her a lot. Any more and who knows . . . she might have been motivated to end his life prematurely."

"I admit, when the news came about your dad, my first thought was someone had killed him."

"We wondered that, too."

Piper pushed out of the car, which was a bit of a chore considering how low to the ground it was. "Such a soap opera."

"Don't forget the missing brother."

"Any other craziness that your dad did that we don't know about?"

They walked behind the other cars. Piper pulled the hat farther down her head. It was over the top and didn't look like her at all, but it made him smile. "He hasn't been gone a month. Who knows what we'll find."

"Seems longer than that," she said.

He agreed but left the words unsaid. "Which car did he drive to work?"

Piper nodded toward a black sedan. "The BMW."

Chase moved around to the driver's side, opened the door, and peered around inside. No bags, nothing personal.

A single smart key had been tossed into the cup holder, probably by whoever had picked it up from the hospital and driven it back to the house. There weren't any other keys attached to the ring, suggesting that this was a spare.

Using the key, he popped the trunk.

Piper was standing a few feet away, looking out over the driveway.

"Is someone coming?"

"I thought I heard something."

Not seeing anything, Chase lifted the lid of the trunk and saw two white bags with the words *Patient Belongings* on them. "Found it." Finally, a break in finding what they were looking for.

Piper turned, a smile on her face, and moved to his side.

Instead of removing the bags, he picked up the ends and dumped them right there.

A suit jacket, shirt, and pants . . . all wadded up, came out first.

Chase heard Piper moan. "Oh, yuck."

He looked at the clothes to see what it was she was referring to. "What is it?"

"His cologne," was all she got out before she darted away.

Outside the garage, Piper had one hand on the wall, another holding her stomach as she doubled over as if she were going to be sick.

Chase came up behind her. "Are you okay?"

She coughed a couple of times and gulped in air as if she was fighting the urge to be ill. He looked at the ground, nothing was there.

Piper stood sharply and pivoted his way.

Her face was stone white, and she wavered on her feet.

Chase reached out to steady her. "Whoa."

She stumbled a step in his direction.

"Do you need to sit down?"

Her breathing started to slow, her eyes closed. "I'm okay."

"You don't look okay." He was a half a second away from picking her up and finding a bench to sit her on.

Her color started to return.

"It passed." She tried to smile. "I'm sensitive to strong smells."

"Or maybe the man who the scent reminds you of?" Her reaction made him wonder if there was something his father had done to elicit such a strong response. He rubbed his hands over her arms.

"That could be it."

She tilted her head back, the ridiculous hat making her exaggerate the move to look at him with how close they stood to each other. "There you are."

"Oh," she whispered.

God, she was beautiful, dusty rose lips and such innocent eyes.

Piper placed a palm on his chest, and they both froze. The only sound was that of their breathing, and the beating of his heart, which, from the pace of it, should have been heard over the birds in the trees.

How bad could one kiss be? Chase wanted nothing more than to brush his lips against hers.

The lift of her chin was so slight he almost missed it.

He leaned in.

She bit her bottom lip and shook her head. "I feel better now, thank you." One giant step back, and the spell was broken.

Chase dropped his hands, rocked back on his heels. "Right." He raised a thumb toward the garage. "I'll finish my search. Probably best if you stay away from the cologne."

"Ah-huh."

Fuck!

That had been close.

He wasn't sure if he was cussing that it almost happened or that it didn't.

Chapter Seventeen

Back in the estate office, Piper carried on as if nothing had happened outside. Occasionally, she'd see Chase watching her from the corner of his eyes, but she didn't call him on it.

Her previous boss's cologne had knocked her back. Never in her life had she responded so suddenly to a smell. She needed to make a call to her doctor, the nausea thing, the smell thing, and the dizzy thing were off the charts.

Now it seemed Chase was watching her more than ever. Was that because she damn near begged him to kiss her outside or because she'd been displaying damsel-in-distress behavior with the constant desire to puke or pass out?

Luckily, Chase found a bundle of keys in the second belongings bag, along with a wallet and cell phone.

They both sat around the locked box, hoping one of the keys worked. "Here goes nothing," he said with a wink.

He slid the key in . . . It turned. No hesitation.

"Yes!"

Piper didn't know who was more excited, him or her.

The first thing she saw was cash. American dollars, British pounds, and euros.

By now, she shouldn't be surprised by what the rich had just sitting around, but she was.

Chase waved a passport in her direction. "What did I tell you?"

"You thought that was going to be in a more secure place."

"True." He went back for more.

A small cloth bag held more keys, these ones smaller than the average house key.

"What do those go to?"

"Safety deposit boxes, maybe."

"People still use those?" she asked.

"I don't. But I also don't have thousands of dollars in different currencies in a locked file cabinet in my office."

"Do you have a home office?" she asked.

"No. I have a kitchen table and a laptop, like most people."

Piper found some of the humor that had vanished the moment they nearly kissed. "That sounds entirely too normal."

He reached in and pulled out several papers. "You're the one who has to remind me how rich I am, I haven't quite caught on yet."

"Do you have a safe?"

He poked through the papers. "I do." Chase lifted a single piece of torn paper with a triple set of two-digit numbers and waved it in the air for her to see. "And mine has a combination lock."

Piper lifted both hands in the air. "There has to be a safe."

Chase set the stack of papers to the side and stood. "I say we divide and conquer. Look behind books and paintings."

"Furniture?"

"My dad wasn't a big man, it won't be behind the heavy stuff."

Piper clapped her hands together. "Let's do this. You take that side of the room, I'll take this."

A rolling ladder gave access to the books on the top shelves of the office. When she'd poked around the room before, she hadn't done more than open the drawers and cabinets. Now she went at the search with a new sense of purpose.

A safe filled with a rich man's cash and a secret affair paled in comparison to a lost son who'd just inherited a multibillion-dollar portfolio.

She started up the ladder when Chase stopped her. "Hold up."

"What?"

"In the last two days, I've seen you white as a ghost and nearly passing out twice." He pointed toward the top shelf. "I'll take the upper half of the room; you take the lower."

"I'm not going to—"

"You're right. You're not going to. Get off the ladder."

"Chase!"

He stared at her.

"Fine." Back on two feet, she gave the rolling ladder a little shove in his direction.

"Thank you."

She attacked the reachable shelves, pulling large sections of books out, looking behind them and knocking on walls. Sliding books from left to right all down the line. Piper would finish one row, return the books, and move on to the next.

An hour later, they left the office, nearly everything out of place.

The common rooms went quicker. Nothing behind the paintings, which sounded a little too Hollywood for Piper to swallow, but it didn't stop them from looking.

Chase shoved furniture aside, and if it was too heavy, he didn't bother.

Upstairs, they started in Aaron's bedroom. The next most logical place for a safe.

She attacked the closet while Chase did the dance with the pictures and furniture in the bedroom. Like the books, she removed large sections of hanging clothes to knock on the walls behind. There were plenty of glass doors, closing in shelves of pricey-looking things. Cuff links and tie clips aside, the man had a ton of stuff. Even his belts were rolled up and displayed in a way you'd expect in a department store.

"I overheard your conversation with Alex about finding a home for these clothes," Piper called out to Chase, who was still in the other room.

"Can you do that?"

She picked up a jacket to put back on the rod, and something heavy from the pocket caught her attention. "What's it worth to ya?" Inside, she found a money clip with several bills folded together.

"I won't fire you for eavesdropping."

"That's fair."

Chase walked into the closet as she was tossing the money clip on the island. "Do we need to pinky promise again?"

"It's a corporate promise. Hey . . ." She pointed at the money. "You need to comb through each suit, or someone is going to get very lucky when they buy the discounted Armani. That was in the inside pocket of this one."

Chase winced. "I have zero desire to pick my father's pockets."

"I'll do it," she volunteered.

"Deal."

"For half of whatever I find," she teased.

"Okay."

He was serious.

"I'm joking."

"I'm not."

It was tempting. "No. That would be taking advantage."

"That was a deal. A quick negotiation, but a deal."

She hung another suit, patted down the pockets. "No pinkies were involved, so you need to call the lawyer."

Chase opened the glass doors that housed the belts, a grin on his face.

"I already looked in there," she told him.

He kept looking anyway and pulled out a couple of the belts.

Piper continued to pat pockets and hang clothing.

"Did you look hard?"

She jolted. "Did you find it?"

Chase was holding a belt as if it were something she needed to see. "Know what this is?"

"If you're asking what type of leather or brand, no."

He laid it on the counter, underside up, and peeled back a small section that housed a zipper.

Piper stopped what she was doing to watch as Chase pulled the hidden zipper open to reveal more money.

"A money belt? I didn't think they still made those."

"They're a pain in the ass to get into, but great when traveling. Pickpocket grabs your wallet, you still have cash."

Each bill had the face of Benjamin Franklin, and there were forty of them tucked in that tiny space. "That's crazy."

Chase waved one in the air. "Fifty percent."

She rolled her eyes. "You found that one."

"There are more in there."

"You're impossible."

The last jacket was back where she found it, and she turned to another section. This time patting down the pockets as she went.

Two more money clips . . . no safe.

She opened a drawer, immediately closed it. "I draw the line at your dad's underwear."

"I'll have Karina toss them in the trash."

"I'll go find a bag."

"You don't have to."

She walked away. "I need some water anyway. Want anything?"

"Water would be great."

Piper walked by the open door of Melissa's bedroom and paused. Something drew her into the room and had her looking around. An architectural inconsistency nagged at her sixth sense.

She walked into the closet. This one was larger, completely white, and stripped nearly bare. It sat on the same wall as Aaron's and should take up the same amount of space based on the bedroom design . . . only it didn't. The depth of the room was off by a good four feet.

Piper abandoned the trash bag and waters and walked back into Aaron's closet.

"That was fast," Chase said.

She walked to the wall in question and started taking the shoes off the shelves.

"What are you doing?"

"There's something behind this wall," she told him, tossing shoes to the floor.

"It's the patio."

"How much you wanna bet?" she asked, completely confident that there was a room behind the shoes.

She ran her fingers along the edges of the shoe shelves until she found what she was looking for. Every nerve in her body sparked to life when she pressed a hidden button and turned to watch Chase's expression.

His wide-open eyes were filled with excitement.

"Do I get fifty percent of whatever is behind here?" She batted her eyelashes, teasing him.

"Holy shit balls, Piper. You're kidding me."

She pushed open a small hidden door that swung into an even more hidden room.

Piper couldn't stop smiling.

Chase brushed past her to go inside. An automatic light clicked on with the motion.

She poked her head through the doorway. The room wasn't big enough for two people comfortably, so she stayed outside.

Chase stood in front of a five-by-four-foot safe.

"Damn, I'm good," she said.

"You got that right." Chase removed the paper with the numbers on it from his pocket and placed his hand on the dial. "Wish me luck."

He slowly moved the dial right, doubled back left and stopped, then right again. He placed his hand on the lever . . . and turned it.

The satisfying sound of solid locks clicking back made Piper squeal.

Chase looked at her . . . beaming.

He pulled the heavy door open.

Piper forgot to breathe. "I'll take you up on that fifty percent."

There were stacks and stacks of cash. Enough to make what they found in the office look like pocket change.

"Damn, Dad . . . what were you afraid of? The Great Depression?"

In addition to the cash, there was a shotgun leaning to one side of the safe and two handguns in the door.

"The only time I use cash anymore is at a drive-through burger joint," she told him. "How do you even spend that?"

"I don't think he did."

Chase ignored the money and went straight for the stacks of papers. He handed some to her and grabbed another handful for him.

Stepping over the mess of shoes, they took the bundles of papers out of the room and down into the living room.

Piper cleared books off the coffee table, and Chase pulled a chair closer.

"I'll get that water."

⌐◯

A half-eaten pepperoni pizza sat on one end of the coffee table. Piper was on the floor, her back against the couch, knees pulled up, with an open folder resting on them. In one hand she had the crust of the pizza she was nibbling on and in the other, a soda. Which wasn't on the pregnancy diet, but what the hell, she hadn't been sleeping, and the midday crash needed to be avoided. Thankfully, the pizza was hitting the spot, and the wooziness of earlier was gone.

So far, they'd uncovered many hard copies of deeds and mortgage statements for properties all over the world.

"This stuff can all be scanned into a document, uploaded to a server, and easily accessed from any computer. Why did he save this in a safe?" Piper questioned.

"Same reason he saved the cash, I think."

She stopped nibbling and looked up. "Why is that?"

Chase flipped the page of the pile he was working on and met her eyes. "I see him walking into that room, opening that safe, and visualizing his worth."

"This house . . . those cars, and the huge building with Stone Enterprises wasn't enough?"

"Maybe he was afraid someone was going to take it all away."

"That's not possible," she said.

"My father wasn't an open man. We may never know why he has Fort Knox behind his shoes. There are only two motivations I know that plagued him."

"Which are?"

"Money and women. And when you have enough money, you can get the arm candy that ignores the extras in your life."

"Your mom wasn't one of them."

Chase glanced up and then back to the papers. "No."

When he didn't elaborate, Piper went back to her pizza and the papers on her lap.

Deciding there wasn't any secret-son-worthy material in what she was looking at, she set it aside and grabbed a large legal envelope and opened it.

Pictures.

She pulled them out and shuffled through them. Some were old photographs, like the kind that were developed at a corner photo lab, a few Polaroid shots that couldn't be from the era when the camera came out, because of the cars in the background. "Do you know who these people are?"

Chase stopped studying his pile and took the pictures she handed him.

The first one he smiled at. "This is my grandfather." He twisted the image around for her to see. "That was his first hotel."

"That's cool."

Chase looked at it again before moving on to the next. "No idea, no idea . . ."

While he looked over the pictures, Piper removed a smaller, letter-size envelope from the larger one and opened it.

"None of these pictures are me or Alex."

"That has to suck," she told him. "You could hold the walls of my parents' house up with pictures of us kids."

"You have siblings?"

"I do, a sister and a brother, both never left the county."

She unfolded the paper in her hand and looked at it.

A chill went down her spine.

"Chase."

"Yeah?" He flipped another photograph over.

"I found it."

His eyes snapped to hers.

In her hand was a DNA paternity testing document.

She gave it to Chase, stood, and moved to his side.

Sitting on the armrest of the chair, they looked at it together.

There was a mother's name, a child's name . . . and *AS* in the section for the father.

Proof of parentage was stamped in red ink. Ninety-nine point nine percent was the final number on the paper.

Piper heard Chase take in a shaky breath.

He grew quiet.

She placed a hand on his shoulder. "You okay?"

He shook the paper. "She named him Maximillian Smith."

"Stone would have been too obvious."

Chase pointed to her name. "Lisa Davis. She could have used Davis. She chose Smith with an agenda. A million-dollar baby."

Piper slowly began to remove her hand from Chase's shoulder.

He reached up quickly and placed his fingers over hers, holding it in place.

For a moment, they both sat staring at the paper. Piper wanted to lean into him, comfort him.

They had a name.

"I need to call Alex," he said on a sigh.

"I'll clean this up."

Chase unfolded from the chair and walked out of the room.

An hour later, they were both in the driveway, the house put back in order, the hidden room once again hidden.

"I couldn't have found this without you," he told her as he stood in front of her car.

"All we have is a name. I don't think it will be as easy as googling him."

"We have two names we didn't have this morning."

True. "Don't forget all that money," she teased.

He laughed, looked up at the house. "I think we're done here for now."

"Back in the office tomorrow?"

"Yeah."

"I'm going to miss going to work in my jeans."

Chase looked up and down her frame with a grin. Then he squeezed his eyes shut. "Thank you, again," he said as he started to turn away.

"Anytime."

She opened her car door.

"Wait!" Chase pivoted, one hand raised in the air.

"Yes?"

He hesitated as if not knowing what words to use. "Earlier. Out here . . . with the cars."

Oh no. She was not ready for him to catch on to her condition.

"That wasn't just me, right? We had a . . . a moment."

Oh God, this is worse.

He tilted his head.

Did she lie, tell him she didn't know what he was talking about? Did she say it was only him?

Then the voice in her head, the one that told her to own her shit . . . the one that had stopped her from going to a clinic and getting on with her life, came out of nowhere and made her shake her head.

"It wasn't just you." Her heart was beating so fast she felt it against her rib cage.

Chase let a slow smile wash over his face.

"But we can't," she quickly added. "I need this job."

"Right." He was still smiling, as if her words didn't register.

"And people will talk."

"True."

"Good, we're on the same page."

He nodded several times and let his smile fall. "We are. I don't want to resemble my father."

"Ehh, no. Your dad was gross. You are—" She cleared her throat. "Far from that. But we can't."

"Of course not."

"Okay!" She was rambling. She hated it when she rambled. "I'm glad we got this out in the open. No elephant in the room."

"Right."

"We can get past it," she told him. And herself.

"Like adults."

"Yeah . . . okay. I'll see you tomorrow."

"Drive careful."

Piper cleared her throat and escaped into the interior of her car.

Chapter Eighteen

Piper was ready for the weekend. Even though she'd spent nearly all week out of the office, she needed to sleep in and nurse her nauseated body in the comfort of her own bed.

But it was Friday, so all that self-care time would have to wait.

She'd taken to getting up an hour earlier than she needed to in an attempt to get the discomfort out of her system before she had to see other people face to face. It seemed to have worked the day before, until the cologne incident.

Not eating anything substantial helped.

Not moving fast helped.

Crackers helped.

She had a call in to her doctor to see if there was anything she could do to make this better. Anything other than time off work.

Alex was in the office before Piper arrived.

Piper approached the office door with a soft knock. "Good morning."

Alex was all smiles. "Good morning. Welcome back."

"How did Dee do without me?"

"She did okay. She won't be taking your position anytime soon, but we managed. I think it helped that I'm learning the ropes around here."

"I have no doubt that you and your brother are going to be fine."

Alex paused and folded her hands together on the desk. "Chase told me how hard you worked on our . . . special project. How instrumental you've been."

"I'm the assistant, it's what I do."

She shook her head. "No. You've gone above and beyond."

"If there is something you need me to do on *that* subject, it's probably best that I do that away from here," Piper suggested, doing what she could to imply the missing brother without saying anything aloud.

"I couldn't agree more."

"If you can give me a few minutes, I'll come back in, and we can go over the schedule?"

"Perfect."

Twenty minutes and several splashes of cold water on the back of her neck later, Piper sat across from Alex, going over the agenda for the day and the following week.

"We need to leave Tuesday and Wednesday free."

Piper put a slash on those days on a duplicate calendar. "For both of you?"

"Yes. Jack Morrison agreed to meet with us . . . in Texas."

"That was quick. Didn't Chase just mention him yesterday?"

"Yeah, Chase called him last night. Morrison is clearing his schedule for us."

Piper typed in a note. "I'll call his secretary and collaborate."

"We'll need plane tickets, too."

Piper giggled. "Oh, you two. You're just like your brother."

"What?"

They really didn't have a clue what they had access to. "I'll call the secretary and get a timeline and then notify *our pilot* and have the plane ready to take you both to Texas. Do you have a preference for which hotel you want to stay in?"

Alex's wide-eyed stare was comical. "Uhm . . ."

Piper switched screens on her computer and pulled up Morrison's headquarters in Houston, then flipped screens again . . . "There is a

Grand Stone Resort and Conference Center and a Stone Residence Inn in the city. The Grand is a personal property, the Residence Inn is franchised. I'll book the Grand for you." Piper typed in a note on her to-do list. "I believe this hotel has two penthouse suites and four presidential ones. Will you and Chase want to share a penthouse, or require both? On the off chance they're booked, how big of a problem is it to take a presidential suite?"

Alex blinked several times. "I'm sorry, it's taking my brain a little time to catch up to your words. No, we don't need two penthouse suites."

"Okay. I'll let them know you're coming. And hire a car to get you around."

"We can rent a car," Alex suggested.

Piper stopped typing and looked up. "Let's try it the fancy way. If you guys don't like it, I'll contact rent-a-dent and hook you up the next time. Sound good?"

"I guess."

Piper went back to her computer. "Trust me, you can afford it, I saw the safe. Not that it matters, this is a business trip and a company expense. I assume the presidential suite is an acceptable alternative."

"More than acceptable."

Life was so much easier working for Alex and Chase. Their father had always demanded the best room, to the point of booting paying customers from time to time.

"Can I make a suggestion?" Piper asked.

"There's more?" Alex asked with a short laugh.

"It might be a good idea to meet with the on-site management team while you're there. Take the opportunity to connect faces to names. There doesn't have to be any earth-shattering conversation. It's good for morale."

"I don't see why that won't work."

Piper typed another note. "And do you have a list of names of people you want to grant access to? I don't think we've done that yet."

"Access to rooms?"

"Yes. Free of charge. Any more than two nights and we get a call, and that's only in place to accommodate weekends when we're not in the office."

"We do that?" Alex asked.

"*You* do that with the hotels that aren't franchised. We do have some deals with franchised establishments, but those are reserved for the executives and board members and require a reservation."

Alex scratched her head. "The only name I can think of right now is our mother. Vivian Stone."

"Consider it done. I'll pull up your father's list, and you can determine who stays and who goes."

"We really have a private plane?" Alex asked.

Piper leaned back, tickled at how refreshing it was to see the excitement on Alex's face at the thought. "I've never seen it, but I'm told it's nice."

"That's crazy."

"In a perfect world, the pilots like a twelve- to twenty-four-hour notice. There are FAA rules about how many hours they can fly in a twenty-four-hour period. They've gotten off the ground within two hours of a call, but they don't like it. Planning ahead is best."

The door to the office opened, and Chase waltzed in.

"Am I interrupting?"

Piper's heart skipped with the sight of him. His suit fit perfectly on his broad shoulders; his smile was full on his lips. And his eyes lit up when they looked at her.

"No," Piper choked out.

"Did you know we had a plane?"

Piper turned back to Alex and let loose a laugh.

"I've been told."

Alex's shoulders folded in. "This doesn't suck so much after all."

◦‿◦

She tried to sleep in.

Made sure the blinds were all the way closed before she lay down the night before, double-checked that the doggie door was unlatched so that Kit could make his way outside without her needing to get up and let him out . . . she'd done everything.

Twice, her bladder woke her up.

Then someone in the neighborhood thought it was the Fourth of July and let off a series of fireworks sometime close to midnight.

And if that wasn't enough, her phone jolted her awake just after six in the morning, making her miserable night's sleep one for the record books.

Piper dragged her phone to her ear. "Hello?"

"Oh, Piper . . . are you still in bed?"

It was her mother.

"It's six in the morning, Mom."

"But it's Friday. Aren't you working?"

Piper rolled over and ran a hand over her head. "It's Saturday." Her mother did this Saturday call at least once every three months. Every time thinking it was a Friday when it wasn't. Piper blamed it on retirement. Her mother had stopped working at fifty-five. Third graders were too energetic for her to keep up with, and she wanted to spend more time in the garden.

"No, it's . . . oh, honey, I'm so sorry. I'll call you back later."

"No. I'm up now." Considering how much tossing and turning she'd done all evening, there was no use in thinking any productive sleep was going to manifest now.

"It's so good to hear your voice. I haven't talked to you in a while."

Piper pushed up in bed and rested against the headboard. "I've been busy. Sorry."

"I'll bet. How is everyone at work? It must be awful with Mr. Stone's death."

Her parents had learned of Stone's death but knew nothing of how she'd been fired. Losing her job was a failure her parents would use against her living so far away for years to come, so Piper had kept it from them.

"He wasn't that nice of a man, Mom. People aren't as broken up as you'd think."

"Don't talk ill of the dead, Piper. That's bad—"

"Karma? I didn't think you believed in that."

"Taste," her mother corrected. "Bad taste."

"Death doesn't change how people lived their life."

Piper knew a lecture with Bible basics would ensue if she continued down the "my boss was a dick" path. "But I'll keep it to myself."

"Good. Now, how are you?"

Piper opened her mouth to reply, but her mother kept going.

"Are you dating anyone? When are you coming home?"

It was too early for this.

She swung her feet off the bed. Kit, who'd been at her side on the bed, lumbered off the other side and stretched with an audible sigh.

"I'm busy. Stone's adult children have taken over and have me running. No, I'm not dating anyone, and I don't know."

"You have to balance work with a personal life, honey."

"I do. Kit and I go for walks. I'm getting ready to plant my garden."

"It's too early for that."

"Not in California, it isn't."

"I guess that's true. It was thirty-eight degrees here this morning. They say it might even snow next week."

Her mother talked about the weather; her next-door neighbor, who happened to be her best friend; and her sister Kathy. "Can you believe it will be a year that Kathy and Phil have been dating? I bet they're engaged before the summer."

"I'm happy for them."

"Phil's a good man. He goes to our church, you know."

The kettle she'd put on the stove started to boil. "You've told me." Going to church was the bar for the definition of a "good man" for both her parents.

"When was the last time you went to church?"

"I was home for Christmas."

"That's a shame. You could find a good man—"

"Mom, I'm not looking." Piper glanced down at her still-flat stomach and cringed. "I'm happy single." Which was partially true. More so when she wasn't pregnant.

"No one is happily single forever."

"I never said forever. But for now, I'm good. How is Dad?" Piper changed the subject.

"Cranky. Two more years before he can retire with his full pension, and it can't come soon enough."

The topic moved off Piper's dating status and heathen lifestyle of not going to church and on to more gossip-worthy conversation. Thirty minutes later, her mother promised to never wake her early on a Saturday again, a promise Piper knew would be broken in four to six weeks, and they said their goodbyes.

Piper sat over a cup of herbal tea at her kitchen table.

Kit had gone outside and back in twice and was now curled up at her feet.

In that quiet moment, she realized she was hungry. But more importantly, she wasn't nauseated.

The nurse at the doctor's office had left a message the day before, giving her some ideas on how to combat the morning sickness and encouraging her to read the material she'd been given at the office that contained more suggestions. Material that Piper had shoved in a drawer in her bathroom and ignored.

Stepping over her dog, Piper retrieved the bag filled with information and returned to her kitchen.

She tossed aside the advertisements and coupons for prenatal vitamins and baby formula and opened a small pocket calendar that had each month spelled out with what was happening inside her uterus. Cutesy pictures of happy mothers-to-be filled the pages between the months with little blurbs of how they were feeling. Words like "upset belly" and "slight nausea" were used to describe morning sickness. Ginger tea and crackers, popsicles to stay hydrated. And the default, "Call your doctor if it persists." Warned baby mama on every page.

Piper flipped through the calendar to try and determine when she wasn't going to be able to hide her condition any longer. With all the variables explained, Piper figured she had a couple of months and might be able to limp that along for a third if she changed her wardrobe.

And then what?

The questions would come.

Who's the daddy?

That would be the first question she'd ask if one of her single coworkers announced she was pregnant. No boyfriend, no husband . . . then the judgment.

Piper liked to think of herself as a strong, confident woman who could care less what others thought, but she knew the whispering would get to her.

"Is it a boy or a girl?"

"I don't know. Don't care, I'm giving it up for adoption."

How would that judgment flow?

What did that say about her? It was one thing if she'd planned to be a surrogate for a couple, another to admit a night of bad decisions.

And the one question she knew would come was the one she had the hardest time with.

"Does the father know?"

Seeing the paternity testing paperwork found in Aaron Stone's safe hit her hard once she'd left the estate.

The woman he'd had an affair with had to prove he was the father. There was no way he was going to take responsibility without it. And even then, all he did was throw money. Even after his death, he threw money.

Piper was ninety-five percent sure her baby daddy didn't have money to throw. Happy hour drinks aside, they didn't even make it to his place since he had roommates, and Piper never brought anyone to hers.

Not that she wanted his money. This wasn't going to be a Maximillian Smith.

Then she heard the questions in her head she'd have to lie to answer. *"Does the father know? Did you try to find him and tell him? Did you give him the option to keep the baby?"*

Could she even go through the adoption process without the daddy's consent?

Now her mind was buzzing as worry started to worm its way into her brain.

Piper moved from the kitchen to her living room, opened her laptop, and googled.

It didn't take long to find her answer.

"Shit!"

Chapter Nineteen

Chase and Alex walked into the Morrison headquarters and were immediately escorted to the top floor. Unlike the clean lines of the Stone offices, this building displayed Texas pride in every corner. Heavy wood, iron accents, and leather were the palette of choice. The wall over the main reception desk had painted tiles with an image of an old western town and a sign saying, "Morrison Inn and Saloon established 1892."

Jack walked toward them as they stepped out of the elevator. He wore a suit jacket, no tie, and cowboy boots. "I'm glad you made it."

Chase extended his hand. "Thanks for having us."

"Anytime, anytime. And you must be Alexandrea." Jack shook Alex's hand next.

"Call me Alex."

"Okay, darlin', whatever you want." Jack stopped shaking her hand and quickly added, "I mean no disrespect or inappropriate advance when I say *darlin'*. My wife, Jessie, reminds me over and over that not everyone appreciates our Texas endearments. If it bothers you, I'll do my best to stop, but old habits are hard to break, so no guarantees."

Alex smiled. "You're fine. Thanks for the disclaimer."

"C'mon back." Jack started leading them out of the top-floor lobby. "How was the flight?"

"We can't complain," Chase told him.

It was nice to have their first private jet experience together. Chase and Alex both explored every inch of the plane, pushing buttons and lying down on the bed in the back. The only other person Chase knew that would absorb the joy they had in the flight would be Piper. Someone he wanted to see on the plane just to hear her call out his gazillionaire status for owning such a thing.

"Our thunderstorms are notorious for keeping you circling above the airport. I'm glad the weather cooperated."

Like Stone Enterprises, the Morrison headquarters was a series of wide halls and offices. The hum of a working office and chatter of employees were different only in the accents of those talking.

Jack led them into a corner office that doubled the size of the one they used in California. "I don't believe you've met my father."

Chase recognized Gaylord Morrison from the photographs in the articles he'd read up on while on the flight over. "We've not had the pleasure."

Gaylord pushed out of his chair when they walked in. "Hello, hello."

Gaylord's handshake was as strong as the man was tall. Or maybe his height had more to do with the boots on his feet and the Stetson on his head. "It's a pleasure to meet you."

"It's all mine." He turned to Alex. "Aren't you beautiful."

"Thank you, Mr. Morrison," Alex said. "Our mother speaks highly of you."

Gaylord's expression softened. "How is Vivian?"

Chase was instantly impressed that the man remembered her name. "She's doing well."

"Did she ever remarry?" he asked.

"No," Alex replied.

Gaylord let every emotion inside him show on his face. "That's too bad." He frowned. "Wait . . ." He smiled. "Maybe I should give her a call."

Chase and Alex looked at each other and started to laugh.

Jack moved to the other end of the room, where two leather sofas faced each other, with a giant distressed wood table in between. "Daddy . . . we've talked about boundaries."

Gaylord lifted a hand for Chase and Alex to take a seat. "I keep telling my son that there are only three types of boundaries when it comes to women. There's the invisible line . . . the one you know is there, but you cross over it anyway. Sometimes on accident, sometimes on purpose. Then there's the line with a wall and a door. You have to knock, sometimes it requires a key to unlock, or sometimes the person on the other side opens it up and lets you come right on in."

"And the third?" Alex asked.

"That's barbwire without a gate, darlin'. No matter how thick-skinned you are, it's gonna hurt going through it, and you'll aways come out on the other side bleedin'."

Chase couldn't hold back his laugh. The man had a point.

"Now the question is . . . which boundary would you classify your mama in?"

Jack met Chase's gaze and mouthed the words *I'm sorry* with a shake of his head.

After a solid hour of chatter, the kind that put Chase at ease and told him he came to the right place for a crash-course education on how to be the CEO of a billion-dollar hotel business, Gaylord spelled out the bottom line in what sounded like a fifteen-minute TED Talk.

"What can I help you with?" Gaylord asked once the small talk had ended.

"We don't know what we're doing or how to go about making the decisions that are best for the company," Alex admitted point-blank.

"You can't know . . . not without the right people. Listen here . . . some of the best advice I ever got from my granddaddy is something Jack and I use every day." He lifted a finger in the air. "You hire the absolute best person to do the job, whatever that job is, and get out of their way. Your job is not to do the tasks. That ended when you took over the corner office. Your job is to make the decisions, and you do that by hiring the right people. Do you see my theme here?"

Alex nodded, and Chase listened.

"Second"—Gaylord lifted another finger—"use your board. They're invested. Know those players, know what motivates them. This is where all those dinners and golf games come into play. You need to know who is padding whose pockets and weigh that into the information that comes across your desk. Corporate gossip almost always has a factual base to it. You worked in acquisitions and mergers and know this first-hand, I'm sure," he said to Alex.

"True."

"At the same time, don't ever discount your gut."

"What do you mean?" Chase asked.

Gaylord sat back and crossed one boot-clad ankle over a knee. "Let's say your numbers guy comes to you with something and *tells* you everything is green-light go on a project, but that gut of yours is making you hesitate. Listen to it. If something's too good to be true, it is. Something smells bad, you're right. This is a skill you will hone quicker than a snake strikes its prey when you know the players and what motivates them. Now . . . you really need to know your people, who to trust. There are a lot of wolves in sheep's clothing when you're playing with the numbers we have at our disposal."

Alex turned to look at Chase, a concerned look on her face.

"Who are you thinking about right now, little lady?" Gaylord asked Alex.

She smiled. "I think Arthur is a good man, our CFO. I don't know him well, but so far, he's been helpful in explaining things I'm unfamiliar with. Hasn't been pushy. A good feeling."

"Okay, who else?"

"Gatlin," Chase said for her. "Our VP."

Gaylord shifted his eyes between the two of them.

"He rubs me wrong," Alex said. "Not sure if we can trust him."

"You're listening to your gut, that's good."

"It might be that he thought he would take over after our father died and is ticked that he didn't," Alex explained.

For the first time, Jack spoke up. "Until he proves you right, or wrong . . . proceed with caution."

Gaylord smiled at his son. "And if he proves you right, and you can't trust him, get rid of him. You have to have confidence in your executive team. Otherwise, you won't sleep well at night."

Chase looked at his sister. "Time will tell."

"Don't rush anything. This business moves slow, or should. I always thought your daddy was growing way too quick for sustainability. I would double-check any new acquisitions that come across your desk and get second and third opinions if needed."

Chase felt Gaylord's advice seep in deep. "This has been extremely helpful. We can't thank you enough."

Gaylord shook his head. "I haven't done anything. And if you don't mind me saying—and even if you do mind—your daddy should have been mentoring you both to take over his company from the time you were knee-high to a grasshopper. None of us are getting off this floating rock alive, and he should have planned for this. But the fact that you've flown all the way here to seek advice from an old Texan innkeeper means you two are going to be just fine moving forward. That said, you need anything, we're only a phone call away."

Jack stood and clapped his hands together. "All right, who's ready for some barbeque?"

Chase and Alex stood at the same time. "We don't want to keep you," Alex said.

"What did I tell you?" Gaylord asked. "Dinners and golf. And I don't golf. Have no interest in chasing a tiny ball around a potholed field. Now if you ever want to go hunting, I'm your guy."

"I've never held a rifle," Chase admitted with a laugh.

Gaylord's smile fell, and he glanced at his son. "We need to fix this."

"One thing at a time, Dad. One thing at a time."

Chase leaned back in the back of the oversize black SUV that took them from the steakhouse to the hotel.

Alex held her stomach and moaned. "I ate too much."

"Gotta put some meat on your bones, little lady," Chase said with the worst accent he'd ever attempted.

Alex laughed. "Mom was right. Gaylord's a good man."

"Do you feel better about things?"

"Hard not to with all that energy. It's nice to know we have some-one to call if we need them."

Chase agreed.

Alex's phone rang. She pulled it out of her purse. "Hi, Mom . . . Yeah, we just left. Hold up, let me put you on speaker. Chase is in the car with me."

Alex placed the phone on her lap and pressed a button. "There we go. What were you saying?"

"Is Gaylord still a bigger-than-life personality?"

"Oh, yeah!" Chase said.

"He's got the hots for you, Mom. I wouldn't be shocked if he calls," Alex told her.

"Oh, please."

"We're serious," Chase added.

"That's ridiculous," Vivian said.

Chase could hear the fluster in her voice.

Alex nudged Chase's side with a huge smile.

"How did it go?"

"It was a good visit. Worth our time for sure," Alex said.

"Chase? What do you think?" Vivian asked.

Chase winked at his sister. "I think you should go out with him."

"Oh my God, stop it, you two."

It was fun to poke at her. For as long as Chase could remember, their mother didn't date, and whenever they mentioned she should, Vivian would blow them off and change the subject, much like she did now.

"Speaking of dating . . . who is the mystery woman, Chase?"

"The mystery what?"

"There's an article in *The Beat* with a picture of you and a woman."

Chase shook his head. "I don't know what you're talking about."

"Hold on, let me send you a link."

It took a minute, but his phone pinged in his pocket.

"I sent it to both of you."

Alex opened the link screen at the same time Chase did.

The gossip magazine had captured a picture of him and Piper standing in front of the garage the second he realized he was about to give in and kiss her. Chase's face was as clear as day, Piper's was hidden behind the large-brim hat covering her head. And if you didn't know her personally, you wouldn't recognize it was her.

Alex reached out and slapped his side and mouthed the question, *Is that Piper?*

"The article suggests she might be Melissa, but that's not Melissa," their mother said.

"Of course it's not Melissa, and it's not what you think."

"I know the expressions on my son's face, and that one is—"

Heated.

"Trick lighting, Photoshop. You can't believe everything you see captured from a zoom lens."

"Well, darn. I was hoping."

Alex hurried the conversation along. "Mom, I'll call you later. We're almost at the hotel."

They were nowhere near the hotel.

"Okay, honey."

The second Alex disconnected the call, she smacked Chase's shoulder with every word she spoke. "What. Are. You. Thinking?"

"Nothing happened." He rubbed his shoulder.

Alex zoomed in and shoved the image on her phone in his face. "You want to repeat that?"

"She was dizzy," he explained, which wasn't a lie.

"You're holding her."

"Not really," he denied. But yeah, he was.

"Other than you, there is only one person in that office I trust, and it's her. She's too valuable to lose, Chase." Alex was pissed.

"She's not going anywhere, Alex. You can trust me on this."

She grumbled and studied the image the rest of the way to the hotel.

What was it Gaylord had alluded to? *There's always a little truth in the gossip.*

Fuck!

ॐ

Piper stared at her phone in absolute horror.

Chase had sent her an article in a text message. They caught my bad side, was Chase's comment.

The picture of the two of them standing close together and Chase looking like he wanted to swallow her whole was going to keep the office gossip rolling for a very long time.

Everyone there knew she'd been at the Stone Estate working with Chase on collecting and putting Aaron Stone's personal office in order. But this picture painted a whole different idea of what was going on in that house.

The article didn't name her, but that didn't mean they wouldn't find out who she was eventually.

Piper blinked and imagined if that picture was taken a few months from now. She'd be obviously pregnant . . . and if her name popped up and her parents saw it . . .

This wasn't good.

This isn't funny, Piper texted back.

We're on the plane headed home now. I'll come by your place once we land, and we can strategize how to handle this.

Piper read his message, dropped her phone in her lap, and looked around to see if anyone was watching her.

Then she started typing.

Are you crazy? If the media follows you, they'll know exactly who the mystery woman is, and then what? How will we explain you coming to my house after hours?

Three dots flashed on her cell-phone screen.

Dee walked by Piper's desk.

Piper hid the screen of her phone against her chest, realized how suspicious that was, and then dropped it in her lap.

Once Dee had passed, Piper went back to her phone.

It's not like we're having an affair.

"That's what it will look like," she said as she typed the words.

One of us would have to be married for this to be an affair, he replied.

This? There is no THIS!

Instead of dots suggesting a text was coming in, Chase typed in three little dots.

... There is a little bit of THIS.

Piper wanted to throw her phone against the wall.

You don't want THIS, Chase. *For so many reasons.*

We'll talk about it when I'm back.

Do NOT come to my house. Piper looked at the time and pulled up Chase and Alex's schedule. They should be landing in a couple of hours, right about the time Piper made it home from work.

Fine. I'll call.

Fine.

Oh, no . . .

Her heart jumped. What?

When a woman says FINE it's never fine.

Was he flirting with her? In a text message?

Go away! Just because my BOSS isn't here doesn't mean I don't have work to do!

When he didn't text back right away, she put her phone on her desk, face down, and stared at her computer screen, at a loss for what she'd been doing before Chase's messages.

Her phone pinged.

Your boss understands and approves of this distraction.

Piper groaned out loud, opened the drawer of her desk, dropped her cell phone into her purse, and closed it with an audible shove.

He was flirting with her.

Chase Stone, gazillionaire and her *boss*, was flirting with her.

Chapter Twenty

Chase poured himself a drink and walked out to the crisp air on his patio before dialing Piper's number.

For the first time in weeks, his heart felt free.

The conversation with the Morrisons put the icing on his cake. Maybe it was false confidence, but Chase had a renewed sense of certainty that they could and would manage Stone Enterprises without causing the company to fail.

He and Alex had a name for their half brother, and a meeting with the estate attorney next week would put them on the path of finding him.

And then there was Piper.

Just hearing her name in his head made Chase smile. It had been a long time since he felt a connection with any woman on this level, and yeah, she was an invisible line that shouldn't be crossed, but damn, she felt good. How bad could flirting hurt? It wasn't like he had to worry about her boss firing her . . . or him.

Chase pulled up her number, smiled at the snapshot he'd pulled from the gossip magazine that he now used as her profile picture, and dialed.

"I'm glad you can take direction," she said when she answered the phone.

"Good evening, Piper. How are you?" he asked as if he didn't hear the snark in her voice.

He liked the snark in her voice.

"I thought when you said we could handle this like adults, you meant ignore it for the greater good of all. Not flirt with me over a text message."

So she'd caught that. "Was that what I was doing?"

"Isn't it?" she asked.

"If it sounds like flirting, and it tastes like flirting . . ."

She moaned. "One of us is going to have to be the adult here. I guess that's me."

Chase smiled, sipped his whiskey. "Did anyone mention the article today?"

"Only you. But you and I both know that there's a one hundred percent chance of that article circulating by morning. What are we going to say?"

"The truth."

"And what's that? That we were posing for the cover of a romance novel?" The aggravation dripped from her words.

"I like how you think, Piper."

"You're. Not. Helping."

Damn, she was getting pissed.

"Okay, okay. When Alex saw it, I told her—"

"Oh, God! Your sister knows?"

"Focus, Piper. I told her it was photoshopped and that nothing happened. Which we both know nothing happened. So essentially, we tell the gossip mill the truth."

She was silent.

Completely silent.

"You still there?" he asked.

"You think that's all we need to do?"

"Do you have a better suggestion?"

He heard her sigh.

"No. Nothing happened, so we're okay."

It was his turn to get quiet. "Not for lack of wanting."

"Chase . . . you don't want me. I'm complicated. So, so complicated."

He watched the ice swirl in his glass, the amber liquid sticking to the sides. "That may be, but it doesn't change the facts."

"Chase!"

"You're smart. You're beautiful. You're funny. You take zero shit from me, and I like that. Do you know how rare that is?"

He heard her laugh, and he knew he was opening the door to her locked boundary.

∽

The next morning, Julia slapped a physical copy of the mystery woman article on Piper's desk and folded her arms over her chest. "Someone has some explaining to do."

Piper's heart was in her throat as the practiced half lie, half truth came tumbling out. "Isn't that crazy? It's amazing what they can do with Photoshop . . . or maybe that's AI."

"Are you telling me he isn't holding you in this picture?"

"I tripped, and he kept me from going face-first into the planter. That's it." Her words sounded strong.

Her hands shook.

"But the way he's looking at you."

"Photoshop, Julia. Please!" Piper sat at her desk, pulled the crackers out of her purse, and set them aside.

"Well, damn. I was hoping for some juicy gossip."

"It's still good gossip, it's just not true." Piper hid her nerves by turning on her computer and pulling out the calendar for the day.

Walking down the hall, Chase came into view. He wore a dress shirt but hadn't bothered with a suit jacket or a tie. She liked the casual-Friday look . . . even if it was Thursday.

Julia snatched the article off the desk when she saw him coming.

Piper grabbed it from her and waved it in the air. "Hey, boss, did you see? We're a thing."

Their eyes met for one brief moment.

His jaw twitched.

"Good to know," he said, dismissing them as he walked by. "Oh, by the way, I need you to show Busa around the third floor when he shows up this afternoon."

"You're not going to be here?" she asked.

"I have lunch with a shipping executive and won't be back." He glanced at Julia. "Good morning, Julia."

"Morning, Mr. Stone."

And that was it.

Chase disappeared in the corner office and didn't offer one more word about the article.

By the time he left for the day, the rumor mill had been squashed from the first floor to the top.

And Piper felt she could breathe again.

⌒୨

"Chase Stone is on line two."

Stuart Cadry thanked his secretary and let his hand hover over the button to connect the call.

"Chase, how are you?"

"Good. We're good. I'm calling to see if you've gotten anywhere with the names I gave you?"

Stuart leaned back in his chair. "I'd love to tell you I have. But that would be a lie. I have two of my staff on the search, and so far they've come up with a lot of nothing. Smith and Davis are common names."

"I figured that out myself searching the internet."

"The mother may have taken him out of state. Hell, we don't even know if she was in California."

"Did my father ever suggest that?"

Stuart opened the bottom drawer of his desk and removed a leather-bound notebook from it. "Nope. Just my deduction. Have you found anything else out?"

"No. We've been overwhelmed at the office."

"I'm going to expand my search nationwide. If she left the country, we're going to need more to go on," Stuart said.

"What about the bank account? Any luck with that?"

"The secret one that was closed years ago . . . no."

"Damn."

"I know it's frustrating. We'll find him." Stuart opened the notebook.

"When do we consider a private investigator?"

"I must advise against it. You're making the headlines without a whisper of this. My staffers even ask what account they're billing their time to when they're searching. I trust my people, but you never know what can leak out."

Chase let out a sigh. "I'm impatient."

"These things take time, Chase. Leave the search to me. And if you stumble onto anything, let me know."

"We will."

Stuart disconnected the call and took a pen in his hand.

He wrote a note to himself, recapping what he'd told Chase so he could keep his story straight the next time they talked.

Two staffers searching nationwide.

Nothing on the bank account, didn't give hope to that thread.

He closed the notebook and put it back.

"You know, Aaron . . . you put me in a really shitty position with this one, and you're not even around for me to yell at."

Stuart opened the file on his desk he'd been working on and pushed all things Stone out of his head. Just as he'd been instructed to do as the executor of Aaron's will.

Dim lighting and loud music filled the club that had forever changed Piper's life. She'd come directly from work, but already the place was full. She'd met Jim—or was it Tim?—during happy hour, and they'd continued to drink long after the price of the drinks went up.

Piper felt this was the best time to try and find him.

She found a lone stool at the bar and took a seat as she scanned the room.

The bartender walked over and tossed a coaster in front of her. "What can I get ya?"

"Club soda," she said without hesitation.

He quickly returned with her carbonated water and moved to another customer.

Anytime a tall guy with broad shoulders and brown hair that was brushed to the side walked by, she did a double take.

A blond in a suit walked over to her after she'd been there for about an hour. "You look lonely. Can I join you?"

She smiled, looked around him. "Not tonight."

"What about tomorrow?"

Piper shook her head, and he walked away.

The bartender returned, a new club soda in his hands. "Let me know if you want something different."

She turned to him and smiled. "I'm actually looking for somebody," she said above the noise at the bar.

"Oh yeah?"

"He's about your height, little slimmer, brown hair. I think his name is Tim or Jim. Said he comes in here once in a while."

"You just described about half the guys that come in here."

"He splurges on tequila shots." Way too many tequila shots.

The bartender gave her a blank stare.

"He was with some friends. One was super blond, longish hair. And a short African American. I think they are all roommates."

The bartender wiped his hands on a bar towel and narrowed his eyes. "I'm not sure who you're talking about, but if anyone comes in with that description, I'll let you know."

"Thanks. It's kind of important."

"Oh? Did someone die or something?"

Piper shook her head and huffed out a laugh. "No. Quite the opposite, actually."

He looked her up and down, his gaze settled on her still-thin stomach.

She patted her abdomen one time and met his eyes. "Yeah."

"Oh, okay. I'll keep an eye out for him."

"Thanks. I appreciate it."

Three club sodas later, and she called it a night.

Piper repeated the entire thing on Saturday. This time taking up space at the bar where she had a view of the front door.

The same bartender smiled at her as she sat down and handed her a club soda without asking.

She wondered how many women had come in there before doing exactly what she was doing. She wasn't the first woman to find herself pregnant from a one-night stand and wouldn't be the last.

The bass of the music was provoking a headache, which made her call it a night after two hours.

She made her way to the bathroom before leaving since her bladder didn't seem to have the same capacity as it had two weeks prior.

In the bathroom, she stood at the sink, washing her hands, as two girls stumbled in, laughing at the top of their lungs. Both in short skirts and club-worthy tops that displayed their cleavage, Piper recognized the look.

One of them stepped over to the condom vending machine and started to dig into her purse.

"Those don't work," Piper said as she opened the door.

"Excuse me?"

She nodded to the machine and patted her stomach. "They don't work."

The girls stopped laughing, jaws dropped, and looked at each other.

Piper smiled as she left them behind, hoping her wise words saved them. She hiked her purse up on her shoulder and weaved her way through the crowd toward the door.

She smiled at the bartender, who was leaning in and talking with a man at the bar.

Piper froze.

The bartender nodded her way, and the man turned.

It was him.

Their eyes locked.

Her feet rooted in place, her smile fell, and Piper's hand moved to her stomach. She didn't mean for that to happen, it just did.

Tim or Jim turned stone white.

And then, as if flipping a switch, he turned to the bartender, shook his head, and shrugged.

And that pissed her off.

Tim/Jim kept his back to her as she approached him.

"Excuse me," she said, interrupting his conversation with his friends.

He turned and offered a half-baked smile. "Hey."

"Hi." She waited for him to say something . . . anything.

"Do I know you?"

Not the right words.

Yet perfectly right.

"I think we met." Piper was giving him a chance, even though she could see the sweat on his forehead. Even his friends slowly turned away, giving them space.

"I don't think so," he said, taking a long pull from his beer.

"Jim . . . isn't it?"

"No. Not me."

"Tim?"

"Sorry."

Asshole.

It didn't matter. This was all she needed to do.

He looked down her body, his eyes resting on her stomach as his Adam's apple bobbed up and down.

"I must be mistaken." Piper stepped back.

The bartender stood listening to the whole conversation while drying an already-dry glass.

She leaned toward the bar and said in a loud enough voice for Tim/Jim to hear, "If you ever see the guy I'm looking for, let him know I was here, but that I'm never coming back."

The bartender lifted his chin. "What's your name?"

Piper met Tim/Jim's eyes. "It doesn't matter."

Piper turned on her heel, shoulders squared, and walked out the door.

The cool air of the parking lot hit her, the music from inside followed her out. She'd given Tim/Jim a chance. And he, without question, fell into the category of an uninvolved father. Went so far as to deny ever knowing her.

Piper fisted both hands, tempted to walk back into the bar and punch the man.

Instead, she yanked open her car door and climbed behind the wheel.

Several deep breaths later, she felt her pulse slowing, and with it, clarity settled. She'd done the right thing by him.

Now she needed to do what was right for her.

Chapter
Twenty-One

After Piper confronted her sperm donor, she no longer referred to his name when she thought of him. The man didn't deserve a name in her memory book.

A routine at work had found a pace.

Alex was in the office every day, and Chase made his way in twice a week and didn't stay for long. He would say something flirty when no one was around but otherwise acted strictly professional . . . at work.

It was his occasional text messages that crossed the line.

Not that she minded.

The first one came the Monday after his and Alex's trip to Texas. He let her know that she'd been right about googling Max's name and coming up with too many to count.

They went back and forth a couple of times before he said good night.

Then he'd text her about something to do with work, usually a bullshit question that didn't need an after-hours answer. Then he'd tell her good night.

For the last couple of nights, he hadn't come up with an excuse at all. How is your evening? he asked.

I saw you three hours ago.

I thought that was yesterday.

She smiled into the conversation, against her better judgment. Don't you have dinner with the president or something tonight? she teased.

That was yesterday. Boring, and the chicken was dry.

And so it went.

Piper would toss a barb his way, he'd catch it, and then wish her good night.

Then, when he did come into the office, they'd exchange a smile, and that was it.

When Friday rolled around, Piper cut out early, saying she had a dentist appointment.

She sat on the exam table, covered in a paper gown and anticipation.

"You've lost three pounds." Dr. Resnik's words weren't an accusation, but they weren't approval either.

"I've thrown up every day, at least once a day, since I saw you last."

"You've tried all of our suggestions?" she asked.

Piper nodded. "The only thing that helps is crackers, but even that doesn't work some mornings."

"I'll give you a prescription today."

"Okay."

"How are you coping?"

Piper shrugged. "Fine, I guess."

"You're taking the vitamins . . . getting good sleep?"

"I take the vitamins at night so they stay down. Sleep is hit or miss. I've been busy."

"What about your support system?"

"You mean from people who know I'm pregnant?"

"Yes."

Piper laughed. The kind of unstable laugh that was a complete disconnect from what she was feeling. "I don't have that." She looked away, knowing how pathetic that sounded.

"A girlfriend? A sister?"

Piper shook her head.

"What about the adoption agency? Have they offered you help in that area?"

"I haven't contacted them. Like I said, I've been busy." Piper heard the defensiveness in her tone.

"No worries. Have you changed your mind?"

"No." Piper's response was quick.

Dr. Resnik smiled and changed the subject. "We have a lot to accomplish today. I'm going to do an ultrasound, see how the baby is doing . . . some more bloodwork." She removed the stethoscope from her neck and approached.

Piper sat still while the doctor listened to her heart and lungs and then asked her to lean back and pull up her paper gown. Making sure only her abdomen was exposed, the doctor rolled over a machine that had a monitor attached.

Next came the gel, which was thankfully warmed.

Then the camera.

Dr. Resnik pressed the wand low on her belly until she found what she was looking for. "There you are." She clicked a few buttons on the machine, and a rapid swishing noise filled the air. "That's the heartbeat."

Piper's eyes stayed glued to the monitor. The back of her throat constricted.

There was no mistaking the image on the screen.

The doctor froze the image and started typing.

"Can you tell what it is?"

The doctor stopped looking at the monitor and focused on Piper. "Do you want to know?"

Piper shook her head and then nodded. "I'm not sure."

The doctor changed the position of the camera and pushed a little harder. "It's a bit soon, and this little one is being shy. Your next visit, we should know."

For the rest of the exam, Piper stayed silent. Dr. Resnik told her she had entered her second trimester and that the baby looked healthy. Everything was exactly as she expected.

Piper sat with a tissue, removing the residual gel left on her stomach once the doctor finished with the ultrasound.

"I want you back in four weeks. If the nausea medication doesn't help and you're still not keeping food down, let me know. I want to see that three pounds back on you with a couple of her friends by your next visit."

"I eat a big meal in the evening."

"You are eating for two."

Piper hadn't really considered that.

"What you think is a big meal and what you need are probably different."

"I'll do my best."

Dr. Resnik wasn't done. "And I want you to find someone to confide in. It's very easy to slip into a depression when dealing with an unplanned pregnancy without a support system. Your body is going through a lot of changes, and I find that talking about it helps. There are support groups for women intending to give their child up for adoption. You might find those helpful."

Piper already didn't like that idea. But she nodded and smiled anyway.

"You cannot hide this pregnancy forever, Piper. Every month from here on out, you'll show more and more."

"Some women hide their pregnancies for five months."

The doctor nodded. "This is your first, so that could happen. But it's rare."

Piper's fake smile fell. "Got it."

"Okay, good. Go ahead and get dressed, the nurse will be back in to draw some blood."

Piper stood at the reception desk, making her appointment for the next month, when Dr. Resnik approached and handed her an envelope.

"A picture. In case you wanted it."

Piper barely made it to her car before breaking down.

～

Chase stood over a cutting board with a knife in his hand, his cell phone on the counter, when he decided a call instead of a text was in order.

Disappointment sat on the edge of his gut when Piper didn't pick up right away. After the fourth ring, he thought for sure he'd have to leave her a voice message.

She picked up. "Work is nine to five, Chase."

"Technically, it's eight to five with an hour for lunch."

"It's Friday night. I could have a life, you know."

He paused, knife midcut. "What's his name?"

He heard her make a tsk sound. "Kit . . . and he's very protective."

Chase went back to slicing the bell pepper. He could live with Kit.

"What are you doing next Saturday?"

She was silent for a breath or two. Then said, "No."

"I haven't asked you—"

"No."

Damn, this woman made him smile. "There's a charity dinner for the Regional Heart Association, and Alex and I think you should come."

Silence again.

"Alex will be there?"

"We have a table to fill."

"When did this all happen?"

He transferred the cut peppers into a bowl and moved on to the onion. "About an hour ago. I guess when a rich guy dies of a heart attack and a local organization that tries to prevent heart attacks learns of it, they tap into that company or family sooner or later."

"Uhmmm."

"The Regional Heart people have already reached out to several hotel associations, which are coming."

"Why hotels?"

"Because they are going to pay tribute to our father. Did you know that he donated to their organization?"

"No idea. They certainly weren't on the circuit of dinners and galas he went to."

The onion made Chase's eyes water.

"I think it's a damn smart way to guarantee big companies show up and their rivals join them."

"I think it's morbid curiosity. What better way for the competition to size up the fresh bait at Stone Enterprises," Piper said. "I wouldn't be surprised if another hotel chain was behind the tribute and the invitation."

"That's what Alex said. Either way, we're stuck going. We've asked Gatlin and Ripley and our mother."

"Why me?"

He turned on the water in the sink and washed the onion off his hands. "Have you ever seen *The Devil Wears Prada*?"

"W-what, wait . . . *you* watched *The Devil Wears Prada* but not *Ferris Bueller's Day Off*?"

Chase smiled. "I have a sister and a mother and yes . . . besides, Anne Hathaway is hot."

Piper started to laugh.

Hearing it put a spring in his step.

"We need someone who knows these people in our court. That's you."

"Are you suggesting I walk behind you and whisper who the people at the event are so you look good?"

He smiled. "Something tells me you'd never do that."

"You'd be right."

"How about walk beside us? The people at this event aren't going to expect that we know them all. But I'd guess they'd want us to make an effort. You know these players more than we do."

"I don't know as many of them as you think I do."

Chase wasn't about to let her get out of this. "Alex and I really need you there."

She moaned. "How fancy is this thing?"

"Black tie," he said.

"Well then, I can't. I don't have anything to—"

"Alex needs to go shopping, too. Company party, company expense. Free clothes on us." What woman said no to that?

"I don't—"

"Shoes and a handbag." Chase sweetened the pot.

Piper was silent.

He was getting used to her pauses in the conversation and simply waited.

"Can I drive the Aston over?"

He fist-bumped the air. "You could, but we're sending a limo to pick you up."

"Ha! This from the people that wanted to rent a car in Texas."

"What do you say, Piper? Help me spend some of my dad's money," Chase said.

"Well, damn . . . you should have started with that. I'm in."

"Perfect."

 ⁓

Piper knew she going to go shopping, what she didn't expect is that it would be a girl's day out.

Monday came, and she was sitting across from Alex, going over the schedule, when she told her to keep their schedule clear from eleven o'clock on.

Then, right before eleven, Chase showed up with an older woman walking beside him.

"Piper, I'd like you to meet my mother, Vivian."

Now she saw the resemblance. More in Alex than Chase, but he had her eyes.

Piper stood and reached out a hand. "It's lovely to meet you."

"I've heard a lot about you," Vivian said.

"Really?" Piper met Chase's gaze briefly. What was he telling his mother about her for?

"Alex and Chase have both been singing your praises since they took over."

Oh . . . okay. This was about work.

Of course, it was about work.

Just because Chase flirted with her on occasion didn't mean she was someone he told his mother about. In a flirting way, that is.

"Just doing my job," Piper said.

Alex walked out of the office, her purse in her hand. "I thought I heard you."

The two women hugged. "I'm glad we get to do this," Vivian said.

"Me too." Alex looked at Piper. "You ready?"

"I guess so."

Piper turned and addressed Dee. "If you have time today, get in touch with the Regional Heart Association and request a list of attendees. Then go to the corporate websites of the businesses named and gather bios and pictures that match the names on the guest list."

"I can do that," Dee said.

Piper opened the bottom drawer of her desk, pushed the crackers aside, and retrieved her purse. "Ready."

"Have fun," Chase told them.

"We will," Alex said.

Piper met Chase's eyes and held them.

Alex and Vivian started walking away.

"Piper?" Alex called her.

Shit. She shouldn't be staring at her boss.

He made a shooing motion with his hand.

Piper had a huge desire to smack it. Instead, she laughed and doubled her step to catch up.

Shopping started with lunch.

Thankfully, it was a four-cracker day, and the nausea had stopped before she got to work.

As soon as they sat, Alex suggested they drink champagne.

Damn, damn . . .

"You go ahead. If I start drinking now, I'll be asleep by two o'clock." Piper looked at the waiter. "Club soda for me. But bring it in a wineglass so I don't feel like I'm missing out."

"Suit yourself," Alex said. "Mom?"

"Bring on the champagne."

Disaster averted, Piper placed the napkin in her lap and looked around the fancy Rodeo Drive restaurant. "Have you been here before?" Piper asked.

"No," both mother and daughter said at the same time.

"Have you shopped here before?"

"A long time ago," Vivian told her.

"Never," Alex said.

Piper had questions. "Can I ask you ladies something?"

"Of course," Vivian said.

Piper narrowed her gaze. "If I'm out of line or . . ." She searched her words. "It's too personal, just tell me."

"Piper, right now I'm not your boss. We're having lunch on Rodeo Drive and are out to spend a ridiculous amount of money on Oscar-worthy gowns. Ask away."

Piper cleared her throat. "How is it that your father had billions, and yet you and Chase never saw the inside of his jet? I mean, the man lived only a few miles from here, and yet this is new to you? I'd think this would be an old stomping ground."

Vivian sighed. "I think I can answer that."

"Go ahead," Alex said.

"Aaron and I signed a prenuptial agreement when we married. Even though we were young, and he wasn't quite who he became, he had serious family money. His parents were adamant about protecting their son should we divorce. I didn't care, I wasn't in it for the money. Sadly, I loved the man. Fast-forward several years, he became obsessed with building his empire. A family wasn't part of that. When we divorced, I was given the predetermined settlement. There was even a cap on child support, which I now know was likely illegal and I could have fought it. But I didn't. The courts wanted to give him custody fifty percent of the time. When it became apparent that 'time with Dad' meant time with a nanny and never seeing Aaron, I threatened to take him back to court and make a scene if he didn't either spend time with his kids or leave them to me."

An absent stare rolled over Alex's face as her mother told the story.

"Obviously, they saw their father on occasion. Chase went through a phase in junior high where he thought he could force his father to have a relationship with him. My poor son."

"It wasn't your fault, Mom," Alex said.

"I know. I couldn't convince the man to step up when I was married to him, I certainly couldn't after the divorce. Aaron made sure there was enough money for a modest life . . . for college, but he didn't fly his children around on his jet. He saved that for the Melissas in his life."

"Wasn't there public pressure for him to do more for his kids?" Piper asked.

"I suppose there could have been, but I didn't want them exposed to that life. Yes, the last name was Stone, but people didn't know we were *those Stones*."

Alex leaned forward and lowered her voice. "We never even stayed in the hotels."

"Of course not!" Vivian exclaimed.

"Don't look so stricken, Piper. Chase and I had an amazing childhood. We took road trips, went camping. Went on a couple of cruises.

We didn't fly in a private jet or stay in the penthouse suite. No different than you, I'm sure."

Piper sat in deep thought. "You really weren't expecting him to leave you anything."

"Nobody was more surprised than us," Alex explained.

The waiter arrived with their drinks, and they ordered.

Alex lifted her glass. "To new experiences."

Piper lifted her club soda and chimed in.

After Alex set her glass down, she folded her hands on the table and looked Piper in the eye. "Now it's my turn."

Uh-oh.

"My parents live in Ohio. Pretty boring story."

Alex shook her head. "Not that."

An extra lub-dub in Piper's chest warned her that she wasn't going to like the next question.

"What?"

"What's the story with you and my brother?"

Piper wanted to pick up her water and hide behind the glass. But that nonverbal conversation would scream in a quiet room.

Vivian turned to Piper with a huge grin. "You and Chase?"

"She was the one in the photograph that ended up in *The Beat*," Alex informed her mother.

Vivian gasped and then giggled. Like a kid giggled.

"I tripped. He caught me." The practiced lie rolled off her tongue. Even she believed it at this point. "It was nothing."

"Huh . . . funny. He said you were dizzy."

Quick, Piper . . . quick. "I was dizzy and then tripped. I'm glad he was there. I would have had a fight with the pavement." Her hand inched toward her glass.

"Fascinating," Alex said.

Now it was time for that sip of water.

"We've laughed a lot about that article. Crazy what the media comes up with," Piper said.

She was never happier to see food than when their lunch arrived, forcing a shift in the conversation.

While Vivian voiced her disappointment and expressed a desire for her children to find partners in life . . . Piper kept her mouth full and did a lot of nodding.

Chapter Twenty-Two

Piper sat in bed, eyes open, on Saturday morning . . . hungry.

She tiptoed out of bed, moved slowly just in case, but the nausea never came. It was day three that the nausea fairy didn't make an appearance, and Piper was starting to think the worst was behind her.

After two bowls of oatmeal and toast, she piled Kit into her car and drove them to a park. Once there, she worked with him, giving commands and rewarding him on occasion with a treat. She liked early Saturday mornings when the park was nearly empty. There wasn't anyone around to complain to her that Kit needed to be on a leash.

She had one with her, but it was hanging around her neck like Dr. Resnik's stethoscope.

For the first time in a while, she thought of her obstetrician and didn't feel an ache in her chest. Maybe she was getting used to the idea that there was an actual human growing inside of her. Maybe it was because she didn't toss up her oatmeal that morning. Either way, Piper took the peace in her head and heart as a win.

After giving Kit some free time, the ability to run and play, they left the park so she could complete some chores.

First was a trip to the ATM to get some cash.

Kit was at her side, back to the wall, while she typed in her code and collected her money.

"That's impressive," the man behind her in line said as they walked away.

"Thank you."

Without more, they left the bank and went straight to her nail salon.

Kit walked into the place like he owned it.

Dao, the woman who worked on Piper's fingers and toes every couple of weeks, knelt and welcomed Kit's kisses. "My favorite dog."

"I thought it was me you liked."

Dao shrugged before walking behind a counter and pulling a treat out of a bag.

Kit instantly sat and waited.

After making Kit turn, sit, lie down, and bark, she gave him the treat.

Curled up beside the pedicure lounge chair, Kit made himself comfortable while Piper relaxed. The massage chair rolled up and down her spine while Dao painted her toes.

Her phone rang.

It was Chase.

She had him in her phone as Gazillionaire, but it was Chase. Not a fan of talking on her cell phone while in a public place, she let the call go to voice mail, intending to call or text him back after she was done.

He called a second time.

Dao looked at her and then the phone. "Must be important," she said to Piper.

Piper answered the phone. "I'm busy right now, can I call you back?"

"Oh, good. You are there."

"Is something wrong?"

"No. I'm calling to let you know that the car will be there at five thirty."

"You couldn't text that information?" she asked.

"And miss talking to you?"

Piper felt her cheeks heat up. "Well . . . get that out of your system now. We'll be surrounded by your family and work people all night."

"What are you doing?" Chase asked.

He wanted to chitchat.

Piper rolled her eyes. "I'm getting my nails painted."

"And I'm interrupting."

"Yes. You are!" she said sharply.

"Five thirty," he said again.

"Got it."

"And, Piper?"

"What?"

"Save me a dance." And he hung up.

Dance? There was dancing at this thing?

"Was that your boyfriend?" Dao asked.

Piper shook her head. "No."

"But he's picking you up at five thirty and dancing with you . . . and not a boyfriend?"

Piper looked at her phone. "You heard all that?"

"He was loud," the other technician said from across the room.

The woman who sat beside her spoke up. "And you're glowing. If he's not a boyfriend . . . maybe he should be."

"He's off-limits." Not that Piper needed to explain.

"Married?" Dao asked.

"No."

Dao looked at the customer next to Piper and shrugged. "Not so off-limits, then."

Piper scowled in a playful way. "That tip is getting smaller and smaller."

⁓

Chase had the limo driver park on the street since he knew from experience Piper's driveway was almost impossible to back out of.

He exited the back of the car and pulled at the cuffs of his tuxedo jacket as he approached her house.

Curtains from inside the second house on the lot moved. Proof that her neighbor was keeping tabs. Pretending not to notice, he stopped at her door and knocked.

Kit barked.

Chase heard Piper inside as she told the dog to quiet.

Then she yelled, "I'll be right there."

Chase stepped away from the door and looked up the driveway.

He heard the door open.

"You're a little e . . ."

Chase turned and ran face-first into heaven on earth.

Perfection . . . Piper was complete and utter perfection. Her dress was black. The top of it covered in lace, with straps and not sleeves holding it up. It dipped enough to show off the curve of her breasts and slimmed at the waist. There the fabric changed to something sleek and flowing . . . silk, maybe, with a slit that came up midthigh. Dainty high heels that had one hell of a sexy strap at her ankle covered her perfectly polished toes. Her hair was piled on her head, and glittery teardrop earrings hung from her lobes. Her gorgeous eyes were outlined in a heavier-than-normal kohl, and her kissable lips were a shade of red that Chase would dream of as soon as he closed his eyes. "Whoa."

"I thought you said you were sending a car."

"The car is . . ." He pointed behind him and lost his train of thought. "You're stunning."

Piper looked down at herself, lifted the dress slightly. "This old thing?"

"Wow."

"I need to grab my purse." She disappeared.

Chase started to follow her in.

Kit stopped him with a growl.

"Okay, buddy." Chase stayed on the porch.

Piper hurried back. "Be good, Kit."

Chase lifted his elbow in her direction.

She placed her hand in the crook of his arm and snickered. "I feel like we're on our way to prom."

"Without a curfew," he said.

She glanced up at him. "You clean up well, Stone."

"No one will be looking at me," he said.

At the limousine, the driver stood with the back door open.

Chase escorted her to one side, waited for her to get in, and then rounded the other to take his place beside her.

Piper took in the limo with a huge grin. "This is insane."

Chase couldn't stop staring.

"Not my normal mode of transportation, but I could get used to it."

Piper smiled and asked, "Won't people talk if we arrive together?"

He didn't care. Welcomed it, if he was being honest with himself. The itch inside of him to know Piper better, to see if she tasted as good as she looked, to smile at her in public and dare anyone to say a thing . . . was something he was ready to risk.

Alex's concerns rolled in his head, and yes, her worries weren't completely off the table. If he thought of Piper as a temporary person in his life, he'd heed Alex's warnings. But he didn't. Piper wasn't a date; she was a relationship. He felt that in his core. All he needed to do was get her on board with that.

"Let them," he said, meaning it.

"Chase . . ." His name was a word of caution in her voice.

"We've handled the gossip so far. Now put it out of your mind. We have some networking to do tonight."

Her smile wavered. "Right. Work . . . this is—"

"And dancing, cocktails . . . dinner. So . . . a little like prom."

Piper turned to gaze out the window, and Chase casually slid his hand over hers on the seat between them.

The only acknowledgment she gave him was her index finger wrapping around his instead of pulling away.

∽୭

Piper saw several media members lined up along the entrance to the event before it was their turn to be let out of the car.

"What is with all the cameras?" she asked.

"It's new for me. Must be a slow day in Hollywood."

Her heart was pounding.

The limousine pulled up next to the venue, and the driver jumped out to open their door.

Chase stepped out first and extended his hand to help her.

She placed her fingers in his palm and carefully climbed out of the car. The last thing she wanted to do was trip on her gown and do her best impression of a toddler learning to walk.

The second they were out of the car, someone called Chase's name.

"Mr. Stone, over here."

He didn't look at them. Instead, he leaned down and placed his lips close to her ear. "You're beautiful."

She squeezed his hand. "Don't let me fall."

"Never."

"Mr. Stone. Just a couple of pictures."

Instead of ignoring them a second time, Chase stopped, moved closer to Piper's side, and slid a hand to the small of her back.

"What are you doing?" she said under her breath.

"If we smile at them, they'll leave us alone," he told her.

Something told her this was a complete lie, but Piper smiled anyway.

Chase turned them in the other direction, and flashes of lights captured the moment.

With his hand still warming her back, he then urged her toward the venue door.

Inside was another cameraman, this one went about taking pictures without asking them to pose. The invited press, maybe? After all, in order to sell this event to others in the future, you'd want your own photo art.

"Good evening, Mr. Stone." An older man with a receding hairline and glasses met them at the door. "I'd like to welcome you and your guest on behalf of the Regional Heart Association. My name is Theodore Laughlin."

Chase extended a hand and turned to her. "This is Piper Maddox."

She, too, shook the man's hand.

The man smiled. "First, let me extend my deepest condolences with your father's passing."

Chase took a step back to be side by side with her. "Thank you."

"He was a fine and honorable man, and we will greatly miss his presence at our events."

Chase stiffened at her side.

"Mr. Laughlin," Piper interrupted. "Do you know if our other guests have arrived?"

Somewhat at a loss with her question, he stuttered, "I-I . . . Miss Stone is already inside."

"Perfect. If you'll excuse us," Piper said, ending the unneeded praise for the dead man.

Out of Theodore's orbit, Chase whispered in her ear, "Don't leave my side all night."

"You're going to hear that a lot."

And so it began.

Their feet barely crossed the reception area doors, and attendees descended upon them.

Occasionally she would recognize a guest and whisper the name in Chase's ear before they shook hands. Chase always introduced her as Piper Maddox. Not his assistant, his secretary . . . an employee of . . . just Piper Maddox.

Waiters circled the room with trays of champagne and wine. At one point, Chase stopped one of them and asked Piper if she wanted a glass. "I'll save it," she told him. *For about five months.*

She pushed those thoughts out of her head.

Chase excused the waiter without taking a glass for himself.

Piper saw Alex and Vivian standing in a circle of other guests. A man wearing a cowboy hat laughed loud enough to turn heads. Even without looking at his face, Piper knew who it was.

"Isn't that Gaylord Morrison?" she asked Chase.

A genuine smile warmed Chase's face when he saw him.

"If you'll excuse us," Chase said to the group they were talking to.

With Chase's hand once again taking up residence on her back, they walked over to Morrison, Alex, and Vivian.

Alex's gaze fell on the two of them as they approached.

She looked between them both and seemed to hold her breath.

Piper attempted to step out of Chase's personal space and nearly collided with a waiter walking by.

Chase tapped his fingers on her back but left them there. It was as if he knew how they looked and welcomed the questions that would erupt.

"Wow, Mom, you look fantastic." Chase let his hand drop and moved in to greet his mother with a hug and a kiss.

A slightly more conservative dresser, Vivian wore a cream mid-calf-length dress that had a black lace overlay with cap sleeves. Her hair was twisted up, with quite a bit hanging down her back.

"I told her she was the prettiest one here," Gaylord said with a wink.

"Stop," Vivian told him. Her rosy cheeks and perpetual smile said she liked the attention.

Chase moved to his sister. "Keep dressing like this, and I'll have to start calling you Alexandrea."

Alex wore gold, with plenty of glittery stones on the dress. Low cut, with sleeves that covered her shoulders but didn't fall down her arm. The full-length gown had a slit that made Piper's look like she was in sexy-dress training wheels.

It was simply stunning.

"Don't you dare," Alex told Chase.

Chase shook Gaylord's hand. "It's nice to see a trusted face in the crowd."

"Wouldn't miss it. Even though the invitation came late."

"Don't look at us. We just found out about it," Alex informed him.

"These organizations know how to bait the hook for big bucks."

Piper liked the Texas in his voice and the sheer presence of the man in the room.

"Gaylord, I don't know if you've met Piper Maddox."

"I'd remember that pretty face if I did."

She reached out to shake his hand. "I know all about you," Piper told him.

"That's downright unfair," he said, smiling.

Alex leaned forward. "Piper is our assistant. She worked with our father . . . before."

Piper felt a slight demotion in her right to be standing there in a three-thousand-dollar evening gown and equally expensive shoes and purse. Like Cinderella, she was at the ball, but she was going back to her one-bedroom guest house and family of animals.

Well . . . animal.

"Tell me, Piper . . . did Aaron have you keep tabs on me?"

"Corporate secrets, Mr. Morrison. I could tell you, but then . . . you know." Piper made a slicing motion at her neck.

Gaylord busted out laughing, turning heads as he did.

"I like you." He leaned in. "You ever get tired of working for these amateurs, you let me know."

"Hey!" Chase said. "Why don't you use that Texas charm on some-one closer to your own age." As soon as he finished talking, he turned to look at his mother.

"Best idea I've heard all day."

Vivian tapped her son's arm with her purse in a playful swipe. "Ignore him, Gaylord."

223

"Tell you what, Vivian. Why don't we let these young kids talk, and you and I can find a drink at the bar. They make you pay for the good wine at these things."

Vivian looked between her children and said, "Why not."

Gaylord beamed and stepped aside so Vivian could walk in front of him. "If you'll excuse us."

The second they turned away, Gaylord's hand was on Vivian's waist as they weaved through the crowd.

"Should we start calling him Daddy now?" Chase asked Alex.

"I think she's the reason he's here . . . not us." Alex moved closer.

"He's been single since his children's mother," Piper told them.

"How do you know that?" Alex asked.

"Your father did have me research the gossip that found us from the competition." She nodded toward the retreating man in question. "Morrison has two children, Jack and Katelyn. He was the one that took custody after his divorce. I forget the mother's name. It's been years. He never remarried."

"Girlfriends?" Alex asked.

Piper shrugged. "Anyone with a camera can snap a picture of you talking to a woman and make the story sound like you're headed to a church."

"He's a little old to be a player," Chase said.

Piper looked up at Chase and laughed. "Players play until they die."

"I don't get that vibe from him," Alex said.

Neither did Piper.

Alex suddenly shifted her gaze over Piper's shoulder. "Oh, shit."

"What?" Piper twisted around and cringed. Melissa Stone stood across the room, talking with the head of Regent Hotels.

"What's she doing here?" Chase asked.

"She is the widow," Piper reminded them.

"At least she's no longer our stepmother," Alex said.

Piper found a half smile on her face. "Have to give her props, though . . . I don't think the red spaghetti strap dress was an accidental choice."

"You think she's already looking for another husband?" By now, Alex had moved to Piper's side as they spoke in hushed tones and tried not to stare.

"You know she is," Chase said.

"Melissa's allergic to work and likes money. She'll find another one." Blonde, petite, and young. The woman had enough money to not look like she needed a man for more. But more was relative, and considering the wealth Melissa had been living with, Piper would bet a month's salary the woman would be married to a man that would keep her in the way she'd become accustomed to within the year.

With a better prenuptial.

"The good news is . . . she's not here to make a scene." Piper turned her back on the woman in question and stood so that Chase and Alex could look at her and watch Melissa without being completely obvious.

"We don't know that. She wasn't exactly Miss Manners when she showed up at the house and stole those watches," Chase reminded Piper.

"You could be right, but if she's here looking for the next Mr. to her Mrs., she'll keep the *Karen* attitude somewhere else. That doesn't mean she isn't talking crap. Just not to any potential husbands." Piper felt pretty solid in her convictions. "And she can't keep any corporate secrets because she doesn't know any of them."

"It's not the corporate secrets I worry about," Chase said.

"Oh . . . right." *The brother.* "You think she knows about . . . ?" Piper kept her voice as low as she could and still be heard.

"Never know," Alex whispered back.

The secret that, sooner or later, would be discovered.

Piper smoothed a hand over her dress . . . her stomach . . . and knew that eventually, all secrets had a way of revealing themselves.

Chapter
Twenty-Three

The cocktail reception soon moved to a dining room.

Floyd and Arthur both brought their wives, who Chase had yet to meet. Floyd's wife, Ann, sat between Floyd and Arthur and was content to talk only to them. Arthur's wife, Daniella, on the other hand, sat beside Vivian, and the two instantly found things to talk about.

"I wasn't expecting to see you here," Floyd said to Piper after they were seated and the first course was in front of them.

Chase felt Piper's unease with the question more than saw it.

"I don't see why not," Alex told him. "Piper is our right hand."

"Isn't your right hand my husband and Arthur?" Ann asked. "You didn't get demoted, did you, dear?" Ann turned to Floyd.

"No, honey. I'm still the vice president."

"Piper has been very instrumental in navigating the landscape of this transition," Alex told her.

"Not to mention she's become a trusted and important member of our team. There are reasons Stone Enterprises uses the word *assistant*. Alex and I now understand that more than ever," Chase explained.

Floyd squared his chin, his eyes level with Piper's.

The hair on Chase's neck started to spike.

"You're a first, Piper. I don't believe I've ever seen an *assistant* at one of these events."

The last thing Chase wanted was for Piper to feel out of place, and Floyd was doing just that. He was about to shut the man down, but Piper beat Chase to it.

"That's unfortunate, *Floyd*. Julia, for example, keeps an exceptional pace in managing your busy calendar. With the frequent shifting of your schedule for your long *family* weekends. It's not easy circumventing middle management when your boss isn't in the office." The smile on Piper's face had a hint of wicked behind it.

It was the shift in Floyd's gaze to his wife that clued Chase in to what Piper had just done.

Ann's next words solidified Chase's assumption.

"We don't take long family weekends very often. The last time was . . . back before Christmas." Ann's gaze turned to her husband.

"They're business weekends, Ann." Floyd's jaw tightened. "Piper is mistaken."

With one comment, Piper shut Floyd's commentary down on his obvious disapproval of her being at the event. And likely just caused the man a weekend of sleeping on the couch. Floyd and Aaron both had spent long weekends with their mistresses.

Chase rested one hand under the table and intentionally tapped Piper's knee. She tapped his toe with her foot in acknowledgment but didn't look his way.

The waiter arrived and refilled the glasses of champagne, and Alex changed the subject. "Mom, did Gaylord say why Jack isn't here tonight?"

"One of the grandchildren is sick."

"Nothing serious, I hope," Alex said.

"Didn't sound like it. They put their family first," Vivian told them.

Silence hovered over the table like a fog. No one there could say that about Stone Enterprises. Family was not a part of their mission statement, their values, their identity.

Chase was going to change that.

Dinner rolled on a little too slow for Chase's liking. Eventually, the head of the Regional Heart Association took up position at a podium at the front of the room and addressed the attendees.

Thank you all for coming . . . blah, blah, blah. It's your generous donations that save thousands of lives . . . blah, blah, blah.

Chase half listened and watched Piper's expressions while everyone else's attention was on the man on the microphone.

Even though this exclusive of an event had not been on Chase's calendar in the past, he identified corporate ass-kissing when he heard it. He was certain the Regional Heart Association did good things—most of the charities out there claiming to help the sick did. However, he was equally certain a big portion of their donations paid for people like Theodore to stand in front of them and tout their achievements.

From watching Piper's expressions . . . the slight roll of an eye, a closing of her eyes . . . a hand covering her lips as if hiding a grin . . . all these came at a time when Chase felt the same lack of sincerity spewed from the microphone.

Chase had nearly tuned out the man's voice completely when he heard the words *Stone Enterprises* in the middle of his speech.

". . . we are fortunate to have Alexandrea and Chase Stone join us tonight."

Alex turned and made eye contact with him as the room clapped politely.

"We at the Regional Heart Association see all too frequently the sudden and unexpected death brought on by heart disease and the devastating loss families feel when this occurs."

Chase felt the eyes of the room shift to their table.

Piper's expressions evened out.

Alex sat up taller.

And his mother shielded her face with a hand to her cheek.

"Please welcome Aaron Stone's surviving children to the podium."

He should have seen this coming.

The sound of clapping filled the room.

Alex turned to him and leaned forward. "If I go up there, my lack of *devastation* is going to show."

Damn!

Chase pushed his chair back and did what he had to do.

Piper smiled up at him and mouthed the words, *You got this!*

The clapping stilled once Chase stood at the front of the room. "Thank you. I guess this is my crash course in public speaking, and since I just picked the short straw at our table, you get me and not my beautiful sister."

Alex lifted her glass of champagne in the air at his words.

Chase paused and looked at the many nameless faces watching him. He met Gaylord's eyes.

The man offered a nod.

"Alex and I want to thank those of you who had no intention of coming to this event until our father was named in the program. It certainly has given us an opportunity to match faces and personalities, as I'm sure we have done the same for you. For most of you, this is the first time we've met. That is unfortunate." Chase took a breath. "When Mr. Laughlin speaks of the loss and devastation after an unexpected death in regard to our father, I can't help but wonder how that feels."

There were several audible noises from the room.

Chase continued. "There was nothing unexpected about our father's death. Not for Alex and I. When you spend more time building an empire for the sake of building it, and not for the family you will leave it to . . . what do you have? Heart disease, apparently. A family who doesn't know you. An empty house and cars that sit to rot. Let our father's death be a wake-up call to any of you who have not found balance in what is important. None of us are getting out of this thing we call life alive. How you live it will not solely be measured by the success of your companies. But by the love and memories you created while you were here. And perhaps by your generosity to organizations such as the Regional Heart Association who may very well help in saving the life of someone you love one day."

Chase's gaze met his mother, his sister, and landed on Piper.

She brushed at the moisture in her eyes.

The first to clap was Gaylord, and then the room erupted.

There really was nothing else to say.

Chase thanked the room and walked back to the table while everyone stood.

He accepted his mother's open arms. "I'm so proud of you."

He kissed her cheek and moved to Alex.

"You're doing all the speeches from now on," she whispered in his ear.

The clapping in the room eased, and music from the band playing for the after-party started.

Floyd and Arthur shook his hand, and Daniella offered a familiar hug. "I don't even know what to say."

Piper shook her head and wiped the corner of her eyes. "You're nothing like your father."

Chase moved in to hug her, taking advantage of the opportunity to pull her close with a room filled with people watching. Her arms circled his back, and for an all-too-brief moment, it was only the two of them.

All around them, people were moving away from their dinner tables. Several stood close by, anticipating an opportunity to talk to him.

Chase moved out of her arms, his lips close to her ear. "I won't repeat his mistakes."

They stared a moment too long.

A hand slapped Chase's back. "Damn fine speech, Stone."

Chase turned his attention to Gaylord, who pulled him into a man-hug. The kind that bordered on bruises from the pounding on the back . . . and Piper slipped away.

⁓

Piper made her way to the ladies' room while Chase addressed his new fan club.

His impromptu speech hit deep in her chest. Other than Vivian and Alex, Piper was probably the only one in the crowd that knew just how real his words had been. His carefully measured dis of his father's life choices was poignant and respectable. A combination not many people could pull off without sounding bitter or fake.

A woman exited the restroom as she walked in, said hello, and walked away.

At the mirror, Piper made sure her makeup wasn't a mess from the unexpected feels and tears. After a dash of powder and a fresh coat of lipstick, she turned to leave.

Right as Melissa opened the door.

"Fancy meeting you here," Melissa said.

Not again. "These bathroom encounters really do need to stop," Piper told her.

Melissa looked her up and down, her gaze landing on Piper's shoes. "There is no way you paid for that on your salary."

"Jealous?"

"That's absurd."

The woman had such a different personality when others weren't watching. "You can always sell your late husband's watches. I'm sure they will buy you a few things."

Melissa's smile didn't falter. "I don't know what you're talking about. If there's something missing from my late husband's personal belongings, perhaps the unsupervised, unpleasant secretary should be questioned. I mean, how else could she afford all this?" Melissa waved up and down Piper's frame.

Yeah, Piper could easily see how that would go. She stepped to the side. "Thank you again for the bathroom chitchat."

Another woman opened the restroom door, ending the scowl on Melissa's face.

"By the way . . . I love that dress," Piper said. "Red is definitely your color." The funny thing was, Piper meant every word. *Kill 'em with kindness.*

The scowl it provoked from Melissa was a bonus.

Piper left the widow with a light heart and a spring in her step. As Piper saw it, she'd managed to ping-pong Floyd's borderline insults into a "Don't start a pissing match with me that you can't win." And then there was the ongoing crap with Melissa that was bound to end soon since the two of them didn't run in the same circles.

Well, except for this night.

Piper knew this was a one-off. Floyd was right that assistants weren't a part of dinners where the table cost was ten thousand if you sat close to the podium and six if you sat in the back of the room. No matter how you spun that, the meal was stupid expensive. And the plus-one was not a well-titled secretary. It was a board member, or a family member. A perk for middle management. Not the Pipers in the world.

With all that in mind, she was determined to enjoy her time living the high life and not let Melissa or Floyd get under her skin.

The volume of the band had increased from the time she left the hall to when she returned. The lights were slightly dimmed, and several people were out on the dance floor.

The first couple Piper noticed were Gaylord and Vivian. Where most of the couples danced alongside each other, Gaylord looked as if he turned a current pop hit into something he could two-step to. In short, the two of them were holding each other as he moved her around the dance floor.

"They look cozy," Piper said as she came up behind Alex.

"Not sure how I feel about that," Alex said.

"What's the worst thing that could happen?"

Alex glanced at Piper, then back to the dance floor. "Let's see . . . they could start something up, it goes on for a while, or maybe it doesn't. Gaylord does something that isn't *kumbaya*, and a tiff between the Morrisons and the Stones begins. We have enough challenges. I hate to invite enemies this early in the game."

"Or . . . ," Piper started, "they start something and embark upon an amazing chapter in their lives that continues and unites both of your families. Or . . . if they do, in fact, find that they don't work, they act like adults and go their separate ways."

Alex seemed to chew on Piper's words for a minute. Then caught Piper out in left field. "Is that what you think is going to happen with you and Chase?"

A lump caught in Piper's throat, and it took a moment to respond. "There really isn't—"

"I see how he looks at you. There is no Photoshop to blame when you see what's obvious with your own eyes." Alex turned to face her. "My concern isn't you. I want to make that clear. I think you're lovely. Work aside . . . you've been a friend to us both and an advocate for what we've needed most since you appeared in our lives."

"But?" Piper needed to hear the rest of Alex's thoughts.

"If things don't work out . . . what happens then? Do you leave? Does Chase disappear from the day-to-day operations? Not to mention, you know more about us than anyone in this room." There was real concern in Alex's tone.

It wasn't what Alex was saying that got to Piper, it was that she had the exact same thoughts.

She could assure Alex that she wasn't leaving, but that didn't mean she wouldn't be asked to go.

"I'm not Melissa," was all Piper could say.

Alex reached out and placed a hand on Piper's arm. "I know that."

Tears welled in her eyes.

Alex squeezed the arm she was holding. "I shouldn't have said anything."

Pull it together, Piper. "No. You haven't said anything I haven't thought." She swallowed and said what needed to be said. "I've met the most wonderful person in my life, at the worst possible time."

"Piper?"

"Chase and I . . . we haven't. I need you to know that." Piper looked directly in Alex's eyes at that moment. When it was apparent Piper was pregnant, Alex needed to know that Chase wasn't responsible.

"I'm so sorry I brought this up."

Tears were seriously threatening to fall if she didn't exit this conversation. "Don't be. I need this job more than you can comprehend. I'm not going anywhere unless I'm told to." It was the only way Piper could ask that she not be fired for something she'd only dreamed about doing. "I need to go." And she did. Fast. Or make a scene.

"Piper, please."

Her eyes started to swell, and her nose filled with emotion.

Then she saw Chase working his way through the crowd toward them, completely oblivious to what they were talking about.

Piper was going to lose it.

"I'm not feeling well. I'm going to grab an Uber." And without anything more, Piper walked away.

"Piper!"

Chapter
Twenty-Four

All he wanted to do was dance with Piper and every damn person in the room wanted to talk to him.

One minute Chase was hugging her, savoring the feel of her . . . and the next, a nameless person was commanding his attention.

When he turned away, Piper was walking toward the ladies' room.

Finally, he caught sight of her standing with Alex.

At first glance, everything looked fine.

Then she was gone, and Alex was making a direct line in his direction.

The couple that had stopped him, names he would never remember, left off midsentence when Alex hurried to his side.

"Hello," Alex said with a smile. "I have to pull him away. My apologies."

An alarm in Chase's head went off.

They stepped aside.

"What?"

"It's Piper."

His head shot up, eyes roaming the room with her name. "What?"

"She's on her way out."

"Why?"

"I'll explain later. Go."

He turned to leave.

"I'm sorry," Alex's voice was weak.

It was never weak.

Chase hesitated, saw the pain in his sister's eyes.

He leaned forward, kissed her cheek, and ignored everyone on his way to the front door.

He found her standing just inside the venue's door, her head buried in her phone.

"Piper," he called out.

She looked up, tears streaking down her face.

His gut twisted.

What happened?

"Go back to your party," she told him when he was close enough to hear.

"Not on your life." And her life was all that mattered in that moment.

He saw the shift where she attempted to play off whatever was happening as if it was nothing. "I think I ate something wrong."

He was close enough now to see nothing but pain in her eyes. "Right."

"Really, Chase. Go. My ride will be here in ten minutes."

He signaled to the doorman and gave him the card for their driver.

"Chase."

She didn't want to tell him what was wrong . . . fine. Maybe a couple of dozen miles in LA traffic that never seemed to end would open her up. "They charge a couple of hundred bucks when you get sick in the back of an Uber."

She sucked in a slow breath and dropped her phone in her purse in surrender.

Chase kept silent. Much as it killed him to do so . . . his eyes focused on the front door and not on the woman he desperately wanted to hold in his arms and beg her to tell him what was wrong so he could fix it.

The driver pulled up.

Chase moved forward and waited for Piper to walk in front of him. All the while, his phone buzzed in his suit pocket.

The driver met Chase as Piper ducked into the car.

"Back to her place."

Chase followed Piper into the back of the limousine as the driver slid behind the wheel.

The car jolted forward in complete silence.

She would talk . . . when she was ready.

It killed Chase not to ask. Killed him to not look at his phone that buzzed no less than four times since he ran after her.

Silence.

Was it Floyd?

No . . . Alex was the one who apologized.

His forearm flexed with the need to check his phone.

Thirty long minutes later, they were pulling alongside the curb to her home, a whole lot less happy than when they'd left.

Piper pushed through the door before he could respond. "Thank you," she uttered.

Chase jumped out the other side, looked at the driver, who had barely stepped out of the car, and said, "Wait here."

Piper was already halfway down her driveway when he caught up to her.

His phone was out, a flashlight on.

"How do you run in those things?"

"I'm not running."

The light on her front porch greeted them. As did the bark of Kit from the inside.

She fumbled with her key until it made it into the lock. Then said, "Thank you for getting me home." Opened the door and closed it in his face.

He placed his hand on the door when he really wanted to slam it there. "I'm not leaving until we talk. Tomorrow morning, you'll see me sitting here in a rumpled tux with an aching back."

The only response was Kit, who whimpered at the door.

Twenty minutes later, he walked up the driveway and told the driver he could leave, then made good on his promise.

Thankfully, Piper had a single chair on her porch, which Chase thought for sure was his bed for the night.

"I'm still here," he said loud enough for her to hear if she wasn't already asleep. He pulled the collar up on his jacket to ward off the chill that seeped into the late-spring night.

His phone had stopped buzzing.

He hadn't looked at it.

Whatever was going on was between the two of them . . . and Chase didn't want anyone else's voice in his head all night long.

He'd long since undone his tie and unbuttoned the parts of his dress shirt that made it hard to breathe when the sound of the lock on her door made a clicking noise and the door opened an inch.

The sound was heaven to his ears.

A couple of bones Chase didn't know he had popped when he stood.

He walked into Piper's home and was met with Kit's narrow eyes.

Piper had already left the room.

"Hey, buddy."

Kit wasn't amused.

No playful panting.

No wagging of his partial tail.

Kit stood rooted in place as if commanded to do so.

Chase closed the door behind him.

Piper emerged from a hallway.

She wore a fluffy gray bathrobe, her hair still piled up on her head, the extra layer of makeup removed to reveal the natural beauty of her face.

"You should go home."

Chase shook his head several times and then sat on the arm of her sofa, which was right by her front door. The house couldn't be a thousand square feet. It reminded him of the doom room next to his in college. He and his buddies had made one room their living room and the other room their bedroom, giving the space a bigger feel, even though it was the same amount of square footage. "I don't doubt you're right, but I'm not leaving until we talk."

"Alex is right."

Chase really didn't want a wedge between him and his sister. Yet hearing her name told him that might not be an option at this point.

"Right about what?"

Piper leaned against the wall. "We can't. You shouldn't be here."

We can't and *you shouldn't* sounded very contradictory in his head. "Which one is it?"

"We can't." She slapped a hand to her chest. "I can't."

Piper was going to cry. He saw the shudder in her frame and the unease in her eyes.

Chase stood, and Kit warned him with a growl.

Piper said something to her dog in a different language that made him sit back down.

Chase moved to her and placed a hand on her face. "Talk to me."

Whatever was going on in her head was so painful he felt it to his core. Instead of repeating his demand again, he pulled her in his arms and held her until her body went limp.

Her shoulders shook while she took sharp, deep breaths as silent tears took over her body.

Chase wrapped his arms around her, held her tighter.

Much to his surprise, he felt her fingers crawl into his back as if asking that he never let go. Whatever this was, it was big.

Women as strong as Piper didn't fold like she was right now. Not without reason.

"It's okay," he whispered.

She shook her head in his shoulder.

He placed a hand on the back of her head. "I got you."

Piper lifted her head and slowly looked into his eyes.

The depth of the pain he saw pulled a deep desire inside of him to hurt whatever had caused the look in her eyes.

He rested a hand alongside her face.

Her lips parted, and Piper's eyes shifted to his lips.

A longing that had been growing inside of him since they met heated.

Piper's hand inched around to his chest, and when her fingertip brushed his neck, he leaned in.

Their lips touched with such tortured slowness that it felt like a dream. Warmth spread, and his gut twisted and fluttered in the way that first kisses did.

Her lips parted just enough to invite more, and then Piper broke away and pressed a hand to her lips. "I can't do this to you."

Why the hell did she keep saying that? "We both want this."

Piper squeezed her eyes as her body started to curve in on itself.

"What is it, Piper?"

She sucked in a breath . . . twice . . . and looked him in the eye. Twice she opened her mouth, then the words came. "I'm pregnant."

Two words he dreaded hearing when he was younger, and not anything he thought he'd hear until long after he was ready . . .

"What?"

Piper sat back, tears streaming down her cheeks. "I can't be with you. People will think . . . You don't deserve that."

Kit moved to her side.

"Who?" Chase regretted the question the second it passed his lips.

Her shoulders lifted; her head shook. And the words tore from her throat. "There was a nightclub and too many drinks. It wasn't . . . he wasn't . . ." She placed her hand under her nose and sucked in a cry. "It was a mistake."

Their eyes met until she covered her face with both her hands and a sob ripped from her lungs.

Chase felt a sucker punch to his gut.

But not in the way he expected.

He reached out and touched her shoulder.

Piper pulled away.

He took a breath and reached for her a second time . . . and she caved.

Crumbling into his arms, Chase held her as sobs racked her body and emotions he couldn't imagine poured from her lungs.

All he could do was hold her while she fell apart.

∽

Piper had finally fallen asleep.

She'd cried for what felt like hours. Her head buried deep in his shoulder, his hand brushing her hair.

The story he'd constructed by her broken sentences was put together.

A girls' night out at a club that ended with a guy and a mutual attraction.

How many times had Chase been that guy?

He had no problem using a condom, but clearly, they don't always do the job.

And now he held Piper, whose entire life was turned upside down because of one night, as she literally cried herself to sleep.

It all made sense now.

The crackers she always seemed to be nibbling on but never really eating.

The passing on the alcohol when they'd dined out together.

The midday doctor's appointments that were nothing serious but couldn't be avoided.

The denial of coffee, but the mistake of drinking his . . .

And the reason she refused to give in to the attraction they both felt.

Sometime after midnight, Chase carried her into her bedroom and laid her down.

The queen-size bed shoved between a closet and a dresser had barely enough room to walk around.

"I'm so tired," she mumbled in her sleep.

"Shh." Chase kissed her forehead and pulled the covers over her. Bathrobe and all.

Kit jumped up beside her and instantly took his rightful position at her side, his head resting on her outstretched arm . . . his eyes never leaving Chase.

"Good boy," Chase said as he tiptoed out of the room.

In Piper's kitchen, Chase splashed cold water on his face.

The thought of leaving was quickly replaced with the need to stay.

Piper had a couch . . . more of a love seat, but enough room to sleep on if you had a chiropractor on speed dial. Chase would make do with the unexpected accommodations.

He pulled the door to her refrigerator open, looking for a bottle of cold water.

Finding what he was looking for, he closed the door and twisted off the cap.

That's when he saw an envelope held on by a magnet on the surface of the refrigerator door.

A doctor's name followed by *OB-GYN* sat in the corner of a return address.

He probably shouldn't . . . but he did anyway.

Chase removed the envelope and pulled out what was inside.

He watched enough television to know what he was looking at.

It was an ultrasound picture of Piper's baby.

Chase rolled his thumb over the image, took a deep breath, and sighed.

Chapter
Twenty-Five

Piper opened her eyes to bright rays of sunlight streaming in her room.

Her bathrobe was crumpled up on the side of her bed. She vaguely remembered wiggling out of it in the middle of the night and wondered why she'd gone to bed in it.

A slow trickle of memories of the previous night played like scenes from a movie in her head.

Chase in a tux, the limo . . . the flash of media lights when they arrived, Chase's speech that made her cry, Alex's words . . .

And Chase's kiss. The desire to savor it and commit it to memory was something she didn't have time for before she told him her secret.

From that moment on, she dumped all her pent-up emotion on his shoulder and cried so much she didn't think it was going to stop. Next thing she remembered was kicking off her bathrobe and now waking up.

Her bedroom door was opened slightly, and Kit was nowhere to be seen.

The clock on her bedside table said it was after eight in the morning. She hadn't slept that long in weeks.

Piper placed a hand over her stomach and did a little inventory.

Nausea . . . no.

Full bladder . . . yes.

Flat-ish stomach . . . yes.

Still groggy from sleep that didn't want to let go, Piper forced herself out of bed and padded barefoot to her bathroom.

Once she was finished there, she drank some water and ran her fingers through her hair.

Two steps out of her tiny bathroom and around the corner into her living space, she stopped.

"Good morning." Chase sat on her love seat, his shirt half-open, hair rumpled, with the shadow of a day's worth of beard on his chin. How a man who obviously had a terrible night's sleep looked even sexier in the morning was beyond her.

"I thought you went home."

Kit bounced through the doggie door and straight to her side.

"I thought about it," he told her. "How did you sleep?"

"Surprisingly good. You're twice the size of my couch, is that where you slept?"

He bounced a couple of times and smiled. "It's not bad, actually."

Instead of calling him on it, she turned to her kitchen. "I'll make you some coffee."

Chase moved to his feet. "You do not need to wait on me. Point me in the right direction and I'll make it."

In her kitchen, she opened the cupboard that housed her coffee and filters. "I put the coffeepot away. It's on the top shelf," she said, pointing.

Chase moved around her to take it down.

Piper filled the kettle on her stove with water so she could have some herbal tea.

As she waited for the water to boil, she looked down at herself and realized that she wore only an oversize T-shirt since she hadn't bothered with putting her bathrobe back on.

"Be right back," she told him.

In her bedroom, she quickly pulled on a pair of yoga pants and a sweatshirt. One look in the mirror, and she tossed her hair up in a clip.

The mirror on her dresser let her know that she wouldn't be winning the "Sexiest Woman in the Morning" competition.

It didn't matter.

Chase had already seen her straight out of bed. There wouldn't be any unseeing of that anytime soon.

She heard her kettle start to whistle.

Back in the kitchen, Chase had poured her tea and set it on her small dining table.

She took a seat and lifted the string holding the tea bag and started to move it up and down in the cup.

Chase stood, leaning against the counter as his coffee dripped slowly.

"Why did you stay last night?" she asked quietly.

"It didn't feel right to leave. I don't think I've seen a woman more upset. Even in the early days of my mother's divorce, I never saw the emotion pouring out of her like you did last night."

"I'm usually so good at holding it together."

"I know. Which made it even more important that I was here when you woke up."

She had a hard time looking at him. Instead, she studied the water in her cup, which changed colors as her tea steeped.

"I'm not your responsibility." She pointed to her stomach. "*This* isn't your responsibility."

"I don't have it in me to disappear when someone I care about is aching."

She looked at him now and then quickly turned away. "I told you I was complicated."

He huffed a short laugh. "Yes, you did."

"Now you know just how wrong you and I are for each other."

Chase picked up the carafe of coffee and started to pour. "You lost me there."

Did he really need her to spell this out for him? "First of all, you're my boss."

"I don't see where that is relevant. You do the job of two people. I don't see that changing if we're dating."

"People will talk."

He took his coffee and sat opposite her. "Yeah, I'm sure they will. But I've come to the conclusion that I don't care. I don't care what people think, what they say. I've had a thing for you since we met, and as much as I tried to ignore it, it doesn't go away." He lifted the cup to his lips.

Piper stared at him like he was crazy. "I'm pregnant. Have you forgotten that part?"

He pointed to the refrigerator. "I saw the picture."

"Chase!"

He placed a hand over hers. "If we met a year from now, and you were a single mom, I'd still want to explore this attraction."

She paused, never once had she considered he'd feel that way. "If we're dating, people will think it's yours."

"That part is a little sticky."

"Sticky? Are you crazy? It's impossible."

He set his coffee down and gathered one of her hands in both of his. "When are you due?"

"November."

"That gives us a lot of time to get to know each other before diapers and midnight wake-up cries."

"There isn't going to be any of that," she told him. "I'm not keeping it."

The stunned look on Chase's face said he hadn't considered that option. "You're giving the baby up for adoption?"

She looked away. "I'm not financially able to support a baby. When I lost my job . . . right after I found out I was pregnant, it drove home how unprepared I am for this."

He leaned forward. "You're not going to lose your job."

"I don't have support, Chase. My parents live in Ohio. Not that it matters, they wouldn't condone this in a million years. The embarrassment I'd bring to our family—"

His voice softened. "Have you met the adoptive parents?"

"No. I haven't contacted the agency yet. I've barely come to grips that this is even happening. As it is, I've only seen the doctor twice. Even though I knew, it took getting sick every morning for the past couple weeks and an ultrasound picture to believe this wasn't just a bad dream."

He squeezed her hand. "Who else knows about this?"

Piper shook her head. "My doctor . . . and you."

For some reason, that put a smile on Chase's face.

He brought her hand up to his lips and kissed the back of it. He brushed her knuckles with a thumb and squeezed his eyes shut for a moment. "What about the father?"

She swallowed hard. "I seriously considered not telling him. This was one night. We both knew that. Bad sex in the back of a car with Jose Cuervo in the driver's seat is a bad combination." She tried to laugh at the situation. "Then I read what adoption agencies ask about when you're going through the process. Check a box. You can't find the father. Don't know who the father is. Father isn't involved. Father is willing to sign adoptive paperwork . . . those are the questions." Piper slipped her hand out of Chase's and picked up her mug. "I went to the club where we met. No guarantee that he'd show up again, but on the second night, he did. Even without me saying a word, he took one look at me and knew. Or the bartender told him. Either way . . ." It still stung how he dismissed her so easily.

"What happened?" Chase asked.

"He pretended like we'd never met. Pissed me off. It was right after you and I found the DNA test for your brother. What was I going to do, make this guy go through that just to wipe the smug *it's not me, lady* look off his face?"

"Asshole," Chase bit out.

"I called him that and more . . . in my head. Truth is, it makes it easier. I made sure he understood I was never going to look for him again and walked away. I bet by now, he and his buddies have switched clubs to ensure I can't find him. Not that I will ever look."

"He still should have owned up."

"There's a lot of men out there like your father."

Chase once again traced the hand she set on the table with one of his fingers. "This hasn't been easy on you."

"I can't imagine any unplanned pregnancy when you're single is. I doubt I'm unique."

"You've done a damn good job of not letting on."

"I don't do that kind of thing, Chase. The one-night thing. Obviously, I did . . ."

"Piper?"

She shifted her gaze to his.

"You'll get no judgment from me. I'd be an absolute hypocrite if I said *I never*. I thought about that a lot last night when I was watching the hours pass."

"That couch isn't meant for sleeping."

He shrugged. "My point is, it could just as easily have been me. It's been a while since I dated anyone for any length of time, but that doesn't mean I haven't had sex."

She set her cup down and sighed. "Thank you for that. Even though deep down, I know there is nothing wrong with what I did. I grew up being told *not* to."

"The perfect way to ensure your kids do *that* thing."

The heaviness of her condition felt lighter now that everything was out in the open. Well, at least with Chase. She didn't realize how much she needed to talk to another person about what she was going through. Having someone to tell her she wasn't a shitty person for getting pregnant in the first place wasn't something she wanted to need . . . but somehow was.

She pointed a thumb to the center of her kitchen. "I'm surprisingly hungry. Do you want to stay for breakfast?"

His smile went straight to his eyes. "I'd like that."

Piper pushed her chair back.

"Tell you what . . . I'm pretty good with eggs. Why don't you take a shower, or whatever you normally do in the morning, while I take on kitchen duty."

"You sure?"

"I have to prove I'm Sunday-morning worthy," he said with a sly smile.

"I think you've already done that."

He stood, and when he did, Kit, who had been lying on Piper's foot the whole time, jumped up.

"Is there a treat I can give that dog so he likes me a little more?" Chase asked.

"The cupboard above the fridge." She pushed to her feet and said to Kit, "Behave."

"Go," Chase said. "I got this."

"I could use a shower." Hot water and steam sounded perfect.

Piper had to step past Chase to exit the kitchen, and when she went to walk around him, he placed a gentle hand on her hip.

Their eyes met and held. The butterflies of firsts fluttered in her belly.

He gave her plenty of time to pull away as he bent down and touched his lips to hers.

Piper let all the sensations of his lips roll over her in soft waves of joy. She closed her eyes and let the kiss linger.

It wasn't a kiss that led to other discoveries, but one of commitment and promise.

Chase placed a hand on her cheek and ended their kiss. Then rested his forehead on hers and peered into her eyes. "Give me a chance, Piper."

"Are you sure?" she asked in a whisper.

"I wouldn't be holding you right now if I wasn't."

She searched his eyes and felt the honesty of his words.

"Alex isn't going to like it."

"Leave her to me."

"She needs to know about everything . . . before the news is spread."

Chase touched his lips to hers and talked around the kiss. "I'll tell her."

"You sure—"

Another brush of his lips against hers. "Positive."

One more kiss, and he put a few inches of space between them.

His words danced in her head. *"If we met a year from now, and you were a single mom, I'd still want to explore this attraction."*

"Okay."

He lifted an eyebrow. "Okay? Yes?"

She nodded several times. "And if it doesn't work out . . . we're adults about it."

His whole face lit up. "I can live with that."

"This isn't going to be easy. The baby, adoption . . . people's questions."

"I'm not letting fear get in the way of the joy you bring me."

She wanted to melt. *Okay . . . we're going to do this.* No more pretending she didn't feel anything for him. No more putting him off. Her heart started to crack open . . . which was scary, but exciting all the same. "Okay."

Chase reached for her again, his lips warm on hers. He pulled back, smiled, and kissed her again. She leaned into him for a few more seconds and drew away slowly. "Was that your pinky promise?"

"We're way past pinkies."

Way past! "Promise me we'll be adults if this doesn't work."

"I promise," he whispered.

Piper pulled in a breath, nodded, and turned to leave the room.

"Piper?"

"Yeah?" She glanced at him over her shoulder.

"What if it does work out?"

He was going to make her cry. "I don't know. I haven't considered that."

Chase paused. "Maybe we should."

Chapter
Twenty-Six

Chase walked into his house shortly after noon.

He dropped his keys and wallet on his kitchen island and stripped off his clothes on the way to his shower.

He was exhausted and emotionally hammered from the roller coaster of emotions he'd gone through in the last twenty-four hours. Sleeping on Piper's couch hadn't helped.

But damn, he was happy.

By the time he'd climbed into the back of an Uber to come home, he and Piper had secured their first official date for the following Saturday.

Now all he needed to do was come up with something epic.

After his shower, he tossed on a pair of sweatpants and grabbed his phone.

He'd put Alex off long enough.

She answered before the first ring had a chance to end. "I was about to call out search and rescue."

"My text last night said I'd call when I could. That's now."

Alex blew out a breath and paused. "I-I screwed up."

Understatement.

"I'm sorry."

"Good. Now we can get somewhere." Not that Chase doubted they would. He and his sister were tight, and he never wanted that to change.

"I shouldn't have said anything to Piper."

Chase pulled a bottle of water out of his refrigerator and took it to his sofa. He wasn't going to beat his sister up over the should haves and could haves. But he did need to set her straight on a few things. "I turn thirty-three this year. And at my age, I know the difference between someone I want to pass my time with and someone I might have a future with. Do you really believe that I would risk everything we're trying to do at Stone Enterprises with a fling?"

He heard her release a long-suffering sigh. "No. I couldn't see past the things that can go wrong."

"You and Piper are exactly the same in that. What if it doesn't work out? What if we ask her to leave? How will the other employees react to us dating? And believe me, she has a whole slew of *what-ifs* you haven't considered."

"Chase—"

"We've both fought this attraction, but that ends now. I care for her, Alex."

"I can hear that in your voice and see it in your eyes. I'm so sorry."

"Apology accepted. You don't need to say that again." Chase took a drink of his water and then pulled out the bigger news. "You trust me, right?"

"You know I do."

Should he beat around the bush? Make sure his sister was sitting down? Or just blurt it out?

"Piper's pregnant."

Blurting out won.

"Wh-what?"

"Four months ago, she met someone. Remember when you and Nick went to Vegas last year?" Chase remembered all the juicy tales that Alex and Nick talked about after their sinful weekend with name-less men.

"Yeah . . ."

"Kinda like that. Only the condom malfunctioned."

252

"Oh my God. The crackers. She's always eating crackers."

"She's had morning sickness for weeks. Piper told me last night. While I attempted to ignore my attraction, she was more concerned about what people would say and assume if we started dating when the news of her pregnancy couldn't be hidden any longer."

"Oh, damn."

"It does complicate things a little."

"A little?" Alex said with a laugh.

Maybe more than *a little*, but Chase wasn't going to concentrate on that now.

"She plans on giving it up for adoption."

"Wait, what?"

Yeah, he wasn't excited about that thought. But it wasn't his decision, and unlike Piper, he'd only had a few hours to wrap his mind around where she was at.

"She hasn't told anyone . . . except me. I'm not a woman, but I've lived in a house with them my whole life. If she's anything like you and Mom, she could use a nonjudgmental ear." Chase hoped his sister read between the lines.

"I can't imagine how she's feeling."

"You can a hell of a lot better than me. Due to the fact you both have a uterus."

"Suddenly, just dating you doesn't feel like that big of a deal," Alex said.

"I'm glad you see it that way. Right now, you and I are the only ones who know about this. I'll tell Mom. But other than that, Piper will let people know when she's ready."

"Wow," Alex said with a sigh. "Speaking of moms . . . ours didn't come home last night."

The water bottle stopped midway to Chase's lips. "Gaylord?"

"You have a better explanation?"

Chase felt the smile on his face grow. "Wait . . . is Mom through menopause?"

"Stop. That thought is not okay."

"It could happen."

"Stop," Alex said a second time.

"I'm sure she's fine."

He could tell by the way Alex groaned, she was concerned. "Do we have any news on Max?"

"Nothing. Stuart is painfully silent. I'm not sure he's doing much of anything."

"Why didn't he insist on knowing Max's name the second he ended up in the will?" Alex asked.

"If Dad didn't want to talk, he wouldn't. You know how he was."

"Aren't we getting the list of all Dad's assets and bank accounts soon?" Alex asked.

"Yeah," Chase said. "We need to go in this week and sign signature cards at the banks."

"Maybe we'll find something Piper missed in the bank statements."

"She searched them better than we could."

"True." Alex paused. "It's weird, isn't it? Knowing we're inheriting everything and actually having access to it . . . they're different things."

"Hell yeah." They were about to gain access to more money than they could count. And the responsibility that came with that wealth.

"Payroll is going to start cutting us checks. I told them to cut whatever Dad was making down the middle."

Seemed unnecessary, but Chase knew how companies worked. Even though you owned the company, you needed to make a salary for the tax benefits. "What do you want to do with what's in the safe?"

"Damn, I almost forgot about that."

"It's not easily forgotten once you see it."

"I don't need it sitting in my house, I don't have that kind of vault," she said.

"Seems wrong to just leave everything in that house to be picked off by the Melissas out there."

"I wonder if she knows about the safe room," Alex said.

"If she did, she wouldn't have lifted the watches that weren't even in a keyed drawer."

"You're right." Alex sighed. "I should probably see this thing."

"Yeah, it's impressive. Between the cash and the guns, I wouldn't be surprised if we found a kilo of cocaine buried in there."

Alex laughed, and then they both grew silent.

"You don't think—"

"No. Dad preyed upon women; a drug lord would have chewed him up," Chase said.

"All right, then. After the lawyer and the signature cards, we can go by the house."

Chase knew this wasn't as easy for Alex as it had been for him. "You're ready for that?"

"Need to pull the Band-Aid off sometime. Every day we're at the office, it feels less like his place and more like ours."

Chase knew what Alex was saying. "I think we should start implementing some of the stuff Piper has suggested. Bring up a design team and reconfigure the executive floor. Shift some parking spaces around."

Alex laughed. "Tired of parking your truck on the lowest level?"

"I'm bringing my entire staff over, and my management needs space. Might as well plan ahead. When we're done mixing things up, there won't be a lot of Dad left around to haunt us."

"Is it wrong that I like that idea?"

Chase heard the melancholy in her voice. "He's the one that missed out on our lives, not the other way around."

∽

Piper arrived to work early.

She knew from Chase's good-night text that he wasn't going to be in the office until Tuesday. He was informing his shipping business employees about the change in address and needed to hang around for the aftermath. Chase had also let her know that Alex had been told about the baby and their future dating status.

And because of that shift in their relationship, Piper was determined to work harder than anyone on the executive floor. No one would be able to accuse her of preferential treatment because she was kissing the boss.

When Alex rolled in just five minutes before the hour, Piper had already been there for thirty minutes.

"Good morning."

Alex paused at Piper's desk and smiled. "Morning." Alex looked around and then nodded toward her office. "Let's chat," she whispered.

Right.

Get any awkward conversation out of the way.

As soon as the door to the office was closed, Alex turned to Piper and grasped her hands in hers. "I am deeply sorry for what happened the other night."

"I understand where you were coming from, Alex. You don't need to apologize."

"Oh yeah, I do." Alex walked over to the couch and encouraged Piper to sit beside her. "I knew the second the words were out of my mouth that I messed up. My own insecurities do not need to be projected on you."

Piper offered her a free pass. "Our insecurities are a lot alike."

"Chase told me as much. Which makes me feel worse."

"Please don't. One of the things I like the most about both of you is the lack of bullshit. At least with me. You don't sugarcoat the crap and pretend the obvious isn't staring you in the face. You called me out, and that's fair."

"Still not my place. Your personal life is your own."

"Not when it involves the boss. And not when that boss is your brother and partner."

Alex shook her head. "I trust my brother, and I've learned that you're just as trustworthy. Which means I need to butt out."

Piper wasn't going to argue with her.

"If you feel my performance is waning or our relationship is interfering with my job, don't hesitate to tell me."

"You have my word on that."

"Good."

Alex placed a hand on the seat between them. "How are *you* feeling?" When she asked the question, she glanced at Piper's stomach.

"Better . . . actually. It's been a rough few weeks."

Alex tilted her head to the side. "Chase said you haven't told anyone about the baby."

She shook her head. "My closest friend here is Julia, and if I told her, the entire office would know by noon. I have a couple of friends back home, but if I told them, word would get back to my parents." Piper looked at her hands resting in her lap. "I can't have that."

"Are you scared?"

"Petrified!" The word came out with a laugh.

"Chase told me you're thinking about adoption."

Piper nodded and shrugged at the same time. "It's not like I don't want to be a mom one day. I just don't see how I can do this alone. Daycare costs would eat my paycheck, and I don't have much of a savings." Piper lifted a hand in the air and shook it in Alex's direction. "This isn't me looking for an 'I'm accidentally pregnant' pay raise. It's just the reality. Getting fired shortly after I realized I was pregnant really hit home how ill prepared I am to be a parent. Adoption makes the most sense." She'd crunched the parenting numbers and knew she could skim by with her salary, but that didn't change the fact that she had zero help and her parents would disown her.

Silence stretched for a moment.

"It doesn't sound like you're a hundred percent convinced."

Hearing Alex voice a thought that swam around inside Piper's mind brought a swell of tears.

She lifted her thumbs to her eyes and tried to hold back her emotions. "This is getting old." She attempted to laugh. "The hormones are awful."

Alex jumped up, moved to her desk, and returned with tissues.

"Thanks." Piper dabbed her eyes and nose. Took a deep breath.

"I thought I was pregnant once," Alex said as she sat back down. "Longest eight days of my life."

That helped lift the heaviness in Piper's chest. "It's been a little longer than that for me."

Alex reached out, touched Piper's hand. "I'm here to talk . . . or listen. Or eat ice cream," Alex mused.

Piper felt the control of her emotions returning. "I need that."

"Good. I'm sure my brother is going to dominate your weekends, but maybe we can grab a lunch now and then."

"I'd like that."

Alex nodded with a smile. "Actually, Thursday, Chase and I have appointments with the estate attorney and a couple of banks. Then we plan on going to *the house* to secure a few things."

"Secure?"

"Apparently, there's a very detailed list of my father's household assets. I guess some of the art on the walls is Christie's auction house–worthy. I've invited my friend Nick for moral support."

Piper leaned back. "Is Nick a boyfriend?"

"God no!" Alex exclaimed. "No. Nick and I play on the same team."

"Oh."

"We've been best friends since high school. You'll love him. Anyway . . . we're going to rifle through our dad's stuff, drink copious amounts of alcohol, and roast on the man. Wanna join us?"

Piper placed a hand on her belly. "I'm already a victim of tequila, but the rest of it sounds great."

"Perfect. Plan to break off early, around three thirty . . . and we'll meet you there."

"Sounds good to me."

Alex stood, opened her arms for a hug.

Piper accepted the gesture. "Thank you."

"For what?"

"Your acceptance."

Alex leaned back, looked her in the eye. "My brother is one of the good ones."

"I know."

Alex stepped back and clapped her hands together once. "Okay, let's get to work. We need to hire a design team. Change some things around here."

"I'm already interviewing people for the third floor."

Alex swirled a hand around in a circle. "I mean for up here. Out with the old, in with the new."

The corners of Piper's mouth lifted. "I'm on it."

Chapter Twenty-Seven

Chase and Alex both left the office at noon on Thursday. So far Piper and Chase had kept their attraction under the radar. As she saw it, they should probably have a first date before they admitted to anyone at Stone Enterprises that they were dating.

Something she still hadn't wrapped her mind around.

He would let his smile linger on her when no one was looking, let his hand graze over hers to let her know he wanted to be closer. But more than that . . . Chase would pass by her desk in the morning and drop off individually wrapped packages of crackers. "Just in case."

She nibbled on them even on days she felt completely fine. Truth was, she felt the worst part of that morning-sickness nonsense was behind her.

Thank God.

Now, while Chase and Alex were hammering out the details with the estate attorney, Piper was walking the third floor with the design team Chase wanted to hire and pointing out a few details.

"Lots of glass. Mr. Stone wants light spilling into the center of the room regardless of how many individual offices line the walls. But at the same time, he doesn't want the space to come off as cold."

There were three designers following her around the empty space. The clutter in the area was gone, giving the team a relatively clean slate.

"What about the corner offices?" one of the designers asked.

"Let's see what you can come up with to give the executive offices privacy and light and let the boss decide." She moved to where a small break room had been before. "An L-shaped kitchen with an island and a large space for staff. Range . . . two microwaves, perhaps one on top of the other. Dishwasher, sink, side-by-side refrigerator/freezer."

"Any brand preferences?"

Piper grinned. "It's an office, we don't need Wolf or Thermador. We want quality and efficiency. Warm colors. Gender-neutral bathroom stalls with a central area to wash your hands. Think of your favorite restaurant that has such a design and make it work here. Make sure every stall is big enough for a storage cupboard or cabinet to house the supplies for that bathroom. We have a lot of room in here, don't design tiny work areas. One locked cabinet in each space. We want an idea room, whiteboards. A media room for those who don't want to take a break in a kitchen. And a soundproof conference room." Piper smiled. "People can see you arguing but can't hear it."

One of the three of them laughed.

Piper kept walking, kept talking . . . and kept pointing.

She liked this.

Chase had given her the reins to fill the designers' heads with ideas. Piper had asked a few key questions that Chase answered, and now she was running with it. Being creative with an office design and leading the charge on this was giving her a distraction she desperately needed.

After giving the designers the must-haves for the space, Piper lingered behind after they all climbed into the elevator and left.

The current reception area was blocking off the rest of the floor and needed to be torn down. With a marker, she was in the process of putting a giant *X* on the wall to indicate it needed to go when the chime to the elevator told her someone was returning.

"Did you forget something?" Piper turned to find Floyd walking off the elevator. "Oh, hi."

Without saying hello, Floyd walked her way, staring up at the walls. "Looks like they have you doing a little bit of everything."

Piper walked to the opposite wall, put another *X*. "That's what you do when you're an assistant."

"I bet you do a lot more than most."

Piper wasn't sure where Floyd was going with this, but instead of giving him room to say more, she asked, "Is there something you needed?"

He walked farther into the area as he continued to look at the walls as if he was interested in the space.

Piper knew he wasn't.

"Yeah, there is."

She put the lid back on the marker and faced him.

He stopped moving around, looked at her, and his fake smile fell. "Don't talk to my wife ever . . . again."

Piper's knees started to knock. The last time she'd been cornered in a space alone with a man, it had been Aaron Stone, only his tone was an attempt at flirtation.

Floyd's was threatening.

"Excuse me?"

"Don't play dumb. Aaron sensed you were trouble and got rid of you."

Did he think he could make that happen again?

"I doubt I will see your wife in a social situation in the future." Not completely true. She could just as easily be a plus-one for Chase or the assistant for Alex. But Floyd didn't need to hear that. Not yet anyway.

"If she visits the office, I suggest you walk to the opposite side of the building."

"I'll take that under advisement."

"See that you do." Floyd rolled his gaze up and down her body, a scowl on his face. "I'm glad we had this little chat."

Once the elevator doors closed behind him, Piper let her disposition collapse.

Blowing out a breath, she glanced down and realized that her hands had gone to her abdomen and held on.

∽

Chase pulled into the Stone Estate driveway first, Alex and Nick followed behind.

The sight of Piper's car in the driveway put a smile on Chase's lips. He hadn't seen her outside of work since Sunday morning, and he couldn't wait to put his arms around her.

The second he exited his car, he heard Nick.

"Girl, we could have the best parties here."

"We just did," Alex told him.

"Please, funerals don't count."

Chase laughed. "Depends on who died."

Nick pointed his finger in Chase's direction. "Karma, Stone," he said in warning.

Piper walked through the front door. "How was traffic?"

"Stupid," Alex replied.

Chase jogged up the steps and pulled her in his arms. "Hi."

She grinned and placed her hands on his chest. "This is new."

"I can't touch you at work. I need to make up for it now."

He leaned down, brushed his lips to hers. "Hi."

"Hi," she replied softly.

Nick cleared his throat.

Keeping his arm around Piper's waist, Chase did the introductions. "Piper, this is Nick. Nick . . . be nice."

Nick slapped a hand to his chest with a gasp. "I'm always nice."

Alex rolled her eyes.

"A pleasure to meet you."

"It's nice to meet someone who has turned this one's head. He's picky," Nick told Piper. "And you're beautiful. I saw the spread from the gala. That dress was fabulous."

The gossip magazine had captured a small picture of the two of them, but the Regional Heart Association had filled its website with images from the dinner.

"I had help picking it out." Piper pointed to Alex.

"Well, that's to be expected. Alex gets all that from me."

"I am capable of picking out my own dress," Alex countered.

"Once upon a time . . . not so much . . ."

Chase pulled Piper closer. "They argue like an old married couple."

Inside the house, Alex let out a sigh. "It doesn't feel quite as oppressive without Dad and Melissa here."

Chase could beat that. Since he and Piper had spent more time in the house together than he'd ever done with his dad . . . all Chase felt in the place was Piper's presence.

"I took the liberty of putting together a little something to snack on, and I grabbed a few bottles of wine from the cellar to pick from. A Google search led me to the most expensive ones," Piper told them.

"I like how you think," Nick said.

Chase saw the "little something" Piper referred to on a buffet table in the living room. Meats and cheeses . . . crackers and fruit.

Nick half jogged to the table and started to inspect the wines Piper had pulled out.

"You didn't have to do that," Chase said at her side.

"It's completely selfish," she said where only he could hear. "I went from feeling sick to hungry all the time."

"Why are there only three glasses?" Nick called out.

"I'm not drinking," Piper said at the exact time that Chase and Alex both said, "Piper's not drinking."

Nick raised both hands. "Okay, okay."

Piper looked at Nick.

Chase looked at Alex.

Alex looked at Nick.

"Oh, for crying out loud," Piper started. "I'm pregnant."

Nick gasped and immediately looked at Chase.

"He's not . . ." Piper blew out a breath, sucked another one in.

"Oh . . ." Nick looked at all three of them. "This I want to hear."

"Loud music, tequila, and bad decisions. There's not much more to add," Piper told him.

Nick crossed his arms over his chest. "That sounds like the perfect night for me."

Alex moved beside her friend and pushed him out of the way. "That's because you can't get anyone you sleep with pregnant."

"I win," Nick boasted, hands in the air like he shot the winning field goal.

Chase saw Piper smile.

"It's getting easier to say out loud, isn't it?" he asked her.

She nodded. "You're going to get that look and question a lot, dating me."

"I know."

"You sure?" she asked him for the hundredth time.

"We're not having this conversation again," he teased.

"I don't know any of these wines." Nick was yanking a cork out of a bottle as he spoke.

"That's because we can't afford this stuff."

"You can now, Alex."

The cork came free with a loud pop.

"I'll grab some waters. Anyone want one?" Piper asked.

"I'll take one," Alex said.

Piper looked up at Chase. "That would be great," he told her.

As she headed to the kitchen, Chase walked back out to his truck, where he'd forgotten the files from the lawyer's office.

Thirty minutes later, they sat around the living room with the estate files spread out in front of them.

Alex held a paper in her hand. "You mean to tell me all these paintings have names? *Fulfillment* by O'Neil." She looked around the room. "Which one is that?"

"Start with the signatures?" Nick asked.

Piper looked up from her laptop, left . . . then right. "It's not in this room."

"You know who O'Neil is?"

She twisted her computer for all of them to see. "The Google does."

Chase sipped the wine Piper had picked out and once again was reminded how quick she was to solutions.

"Brilliant. She's brilliant," Nick said.

Piper made a *gimme* motion with her hands. "I'll take the list of paintings, print each one out, and you can go on a scavenger hunt."

Alex stood. "While you do that, Chase . . . why don't you show me this safe."

He patted Piper's arm before taking Alex up to their father's room.

⌒ʘ

Nick sat opposite Piper, legs crossed, foot bouncing in the air. He swirled the wine in his glass. "How much did this little bottle of lovely cost?" he asked.

Piper glanced up from the Google search. "Which one is that?"

"Rothschild. It's French. Quite good."

Piper had done a search before they arrived. "About a thousand bucks." She went back to Google.

Nick started coughing. "You've got to be joking."

Piper smiled and shook her head.

"And we're drinking it with Triscuits?"

"Don't knock my crackers. I've become quite the connoisseur since it's the only thing I've been able to keep down for most of the last month."

Piper sent another painting information page to the printer and went on to the next.

"How is it being pregnant?" he asked.

"It sucks. How is it being gay?" she asked with a grin.

Nick tossed his head back and laughed. "It's fantastic. Highly recommend."

It felt good to smile about her condition.

"Holy shit, Nick. You've got to see this!" Alex's voice called from upstairs.

He jumped to his feet, took his wine with him.

While they partied with a safe full of more money than Piper could even dream of, she printed out a dozen pages of paintings.

She was on her way back into the living room with the papers when the three of them returned from upstairs.

Alex pointed from the direction they came. "That shit is crazy!"

"Right?" Piper asked.

"I thought the safety deposit boxes were over the top." Alex refilled her glass, followed by Nick.

"What were in those?" Piper asked.

"A little bit of Fort Knox and more of what is upstairs."

"Gold?" she asked.

Chase nodded. "Coins."

"I guess we know now why he didn't give the house to Melissa," Piper pointed out.

"That bimbo would have sold the house without knowing about the hidden room," Nick said.

"We need more of this wine." Alex waved the empty bottle in the air.

Piper handed out the papers. "I'll get the wine, you guys work on finding these."

Alex and Nick headed off, wineglasses in hand.

Piper glanced up at Chase, his smile had mischief in his eyes.

"What are you—"

"I thought they'd never leave." He dropped his scavenger-hunt papers on the floor and reached for her.

Next thing she knew, his lips were on hers.

She sighed into his touch and wrapped her arms around his back. She went from *zero* to *hello there* in two seconds.

The kiss on the porch was soft and gentle, like *good morning*, or *have a nice day*.

And then there was this kind, where Chase damn near lifted her off her feet to get close, his tongue searching for hers. The kind of kiss that they hadn't explored all that much, but now that kissing was on the table . . . Piper wanted more.

Her body started to wake up the way hungry, open-mouth kisses made you do.

Her nails dug into his back, and Chase pulled her body so close she felt his arousal press against her belly.

She wanted that. Really, really wanted all of that.

Piper dropped one hand to his hip and pushed up against him the way a cat wraps around a leg of a table.

Alex's and Nick's voices drifted in from the other side of the house, reminding her that they weren't alone.

Chase clasped the back of her neck and moaned as he tore himself away.

Her heart beating fast and lips swollen, she uttered, "Wow."

He huffed out a breathy, staccato laugh. "Is it Saturday yet?"

"No," she whispered.

"Found one!" Alex called out.

"I should go get that wine," Piper said as she pulled out of Chase's orbit.

He looked down at himself, shifted his hips. "I should find a cold shower."

She tapped his shoulder. "There're ice packs in the freezer."

As she walked away, Chase gave her butt a playful slap.

"Careful, Stone. I kinda like that."

His head fell back, and he shook his hand with a balled fist. "Yes!"

Piper laughed all the way to the cellar.

Chapter Twenty-Eight

"Are you purposely staying out of the office?" Piper asked Chase Friday night on the phone as she climbed under the covers, her back against the headboard.

Kit jumped up on the bed, sighed, and put his head on Piper's lap.

"Yes and no."

"Which is it?"

"No . . . I had a lot to do at CMS, the attorney, banks, and until you're ready to let the office know we're dating, it's probably best I limit my time there."

"That's ridiculous. You're capable of holding back."

"Nope. I'm pretty sure we're going to get caught as I'm pushing you against the wall and finding all the places that make you squirm."

Piper fanned herself. The room warmed with only his words. The action was bound to get steamy. "When you put it like that."

She heard Chase chuckle. "How did Alex look when she came in today?"

"Like she drank too much wine and slept on a couch."

She and Nick took full advantage of the wine cellar and ended up sleeping at the estate. According to Alex, she all but passed out on the living room sofa while Nick happily took up residence in her father's bedroom.

"That good, huh?"

"She made it in by nine thirty. My bet was noon." Piper yawned.

"You're tired."

"I used to stay up and binge Netflix on Fridays. Now I can't keep my eyes open past ten."

"I won't keep you up. I get you from noon on tomorrow."

Piper rested a hand on her dog's head. "And what am I wearing for this all-day date?"

"Start out casual. Shoes you can walk in."

"What do you mean *start out*?"

"We'll have an opportunity to freshen up before dinner, a little less casual but nothing terribly fancy. Think slacks over jeans. And it might be chilly."

"Might be?"

"Bring a sweater," he told her.

She smiled into the phone. "Any other changes of clothing I might need?"

"This is our first date. I will have you home by midnight."

"Such a gentleman."

"Even if it kills me."

Piper laughed.

"And if I lock my door and don't let you leave?" she asked.

"That is an entirely different story . . . But no pressure."

The ball, as they say, was in her court.

"I'll see you tomorrow at noon, then."

"Get some sleep, hon."

Piper held her cell phone to her cheek after she ended the call.

She glanced at Kit, who was fast asleep beside her. "You need to get used to the floor, my friend."

Kit sighed but didn't open his eyes.

Her dog wouldn't be happy, but Piper felt like a promise of something fantastic was only a day away.

∽

Piper packed a bag, one she assumed she'd leave in Chase's truck until it was time for a wardrobe change.

The thought made her laugh.

Either way, she tried to plan ahead for anything and everything she'd need.

Starting with how she dried and curled her hair, then put it up with a loose clip so that it didn't crinkle in all the wrong places. With any luck, she'd be able to brush it out after a busy day, toss on some lip gloss, and go.

The day was on the cool side, so she opted for jeans, with the slacks packed for later. She realized as she was zipping up her most comfortable denim pants that they weren't as loose as they had been a week ago. She wasn't convinced that she was gaining any baby weight, but likely putting back on the pounds she'd lost tossing her cookies every morning . . . afternoon, and occasional evening. She grabbed a sleeveless shirt and layered it with a short-waisted jacket that she could use that evening as well.

With an eye on the clock, she found herself running around her house, picking things up. She'd spent most of the morning between the dog park and errands, as most of her Saturdays worked out to be, with Kit by her side. Mr. Armstrong was already scheduled to feed her dog later that day.

She realized the bin she stored the kibble she used in Kit's diet was nearly empty. The last thing she wanted was for Mr. Armstrong to have to lug the forty-pound bag from the storage room into her kitchen.

Piper looked at her watch. She had five minutes.

She double-timed her step, went around the back of her tiny house to the storage shed she and Mr. Armstrong shared to retrieve the dog food.

From the driveway, she heard Chase's truck pulling in.

She quickly grabbed the bag and hoisted it up in both arms, then attempted to shut the shed door with her foot.

The first kick didn't do the job, and the second closed it but not all the way so that the inside latch caught. She was seconds away from pushing her shoulder into the door when Chase called out, "What are you doing?"

"I need to refill the dog"—shoulder into door, the latch caught—"food!"

Before she could turn around, Chase was in front of her, grabbing the weighty bag from her arms. "Are you crazy?"

That felt better. "Hi." She smiled up at him.

He scowled.

"What?"

He shifted the bag to one side, dropped a quick kiss on her lips. "You're pregnant," he said.

"And?" She was genuinely confused.

"Let me lift the heavy things," he told her before walking toward her front door.

"I will take that as chivalry and not chauvinism and, at the same time, remind you that I live alone."

She could see the wheels in Chase's brain spinning.

"Then buy smaller bags of dog food."

Piper followed him inside. "They're more expensive that way."

Yeah, he didn't like that answer, but he didn't have a comeback.

"Where do you want this?"

She pointed to the kitchen and the large sealable bin that was open and empty. "In there."

Piper stood back and watched as Chase helped with the heavy bag.

Kit stood by with laser-focused eyes on the process, just hoping for a fallen piece of food he could jump on.

As the last bits of food were poured into the container, Chase grabbed a small handful and put it on the floor.

"It's not his dinnertime," she teased.

"Too bad. He didn't growl at me for the first time."

Kit gobbled the food in two bites and then looked up for more.

Chase reached back in.

Piper said a quick "No."

He pulled his hand back and put the lid on the container. "Sorry, buddy. Mom says no."

Piper turned. "I'm going to grab my things, and I'm ready to go."

By the time she walked back into the living room, Chase stood at the door, and Kit stood in the kitchen, chewing.

"What did you give him?"

Deer in the headlights. "Nothing. He must've found something on the floor." Chase took her bag from her and started to walk out.

Piper pointed in Chase's face as she walked ahead. "I'm onto you."

They left her house and headed toward the freeway. "Are you going to tell me what we're doing?"

"Nope. It's a surprise."

They talked a little about work and a lot about the design for the third-floor offices on the way to wherever they were going.

"We should be getting some preliminary sketches by the end of next week."

"That's fast."

"You said you wanted it done yesterday."

"I don't want to split myself in two directions. Different floors, fine. Different cities . . . not so fine."

"It's going to be nice."

They exited the freeway along with the traffic headed into LAX.

A tingle went down Piper's spine.

When Chase zipped around the bulk of cars, she released a sigh. Only to catch her breath a second time as he pulled into a private entrance.

"Chase?"

He rolled down his window and showed the man at the gate his driver's license and was let in.

"Chase?"

He glanced at her over the rim of his sunglasses. "What's the point of a fancy jet if you don't use it?"

Every nerve ending in her body went on high alert. "You're kidding."

They pulled up to a building where someone was there to open their doors.

"Good afternoon, Mr. Stone. Your pilots are here."

Piper smacked down on a girlie squeal but did a little shuffle when Chase walked around the truck and took her hand in his.

In front of them, someone carried their day bags as someone else drove Chase's truck away.

She grabbed onto Chase's arm. "I'm so excited," she said in a rough whisper.

They walked through a lobby and were immediately taken to a wide hall where someone checked their IDs. Then they were escorted out onto the runway and walked directly to a waiting airplane.

"That's it?" Piper asked. "No metal detectors, no X-rays?"

"Wild, isn't it?" Chase asked. His smile suggested he was just as excited about the process as she was.

The attendant with their bags walked up the ramp, and they stopped to talk to the pilot who was standing there.

"Good afternoon, Mr. Stone."

"Carson, right?" Chase asked.

"You remembered. Yes. And today my copilot is Megan. She'll come out and introduce herself once you're on board."

We have our own pilots. Piper was squealing inside her head.

"This is Piper Maddox," Chase told him.

Carson did a double take. "Maddox. Wait . . . we've talked on the phone."

"Oh my God, right." She put out her hand to shake his. "It's great to finally meet you in person."

Chase waved between the two of them. "You know each other?"

"No. Only through work. If there were weather delays or complications, Carson would tell me, and I'd break the news to your dad. Kept the stress level down while they were in the air."

"Piper was easier to talk to than the senior Mr. Stone."

"I hope you never have to say that about me," Chase said.

"I get the feeling I won't." He lifted a hand to the airplane. "Shall we?"

Chase held back. "Ladies first."

This was epic.

Piper walked up the stairs, feeling like a celebrity.

Inside, she turned toward what would have been the first-class seats and saw individual plush seats, a couch, a big-screen television. Everything in a bright white. The windows weren't even the same as on a commercial airplane. They were huge.

Chase came up behind her, placed his hands on her hips, his lips close to her ear. "Crazy, isn't it?"

She let out the squeal she'd been holding back, twisted around, and kissed Chase. "This is so unnecessary, I'm so glad you did it."

"I somehow knew you'd say that." Chase turned her around and started marching her forward.

"I'm guessing this is her first time," Carson said as he stopped to close the door of the aircraft.

"But not her last," Chase said.

Piper walked farther back in the plane and, without turning toward them, said, "Again, not necessary, but if you insist."

Both men laughed.

She opened the door in the back of the plane. "A bedroom?" she shouted out.

"With new bedding and a new mattress. Alex insisted."

Piper glanced over her shoulder at Chase. "Smart woman."

She continued her self-guided tour, found a bathroom and a kitchen . . . or galley. Is that what they called kitchens on airplanes? She'd look it up later.

Piper practically skipped back to Chase's side and placed both hands behind his neck. "It doesn't even matter where we're going. We could just fly around in circles and that would be great."

"I'll keep that in mind for next time. Today, however, we're going to San Francisco." His arms circled her waist.

And the squealing started again. "I've never been."

"Seriously?"

She pointed to her chest. "Broke." Then she pressed that same finger in his chest. "Gazillionaire."

"The gazillions just happened, but San Francisco is just up the coast."

She shrugged. "Stone Enterprises doesn't put assistants on the complimentary hotel list, and even with my discount, it is too expensive in big cities."

"Then we need to tell my assistant to put your name on the list."

"And wouldn't that be the very preferential treatment that the whole office would talk about?" They were going to be talked about enough once word got out, adding to that could cause all kinds of jealousy and issues.

"That's a *them* problem. If I want my girlfriend's name on a list and I own the company, my girl's name is on the list."

"Girlfriend?" she tested the word on her lips. "This is our first date."

His arms still circled her back, hers around his neck.

Chase swayed from side to side. "Technically, anytime I've picked you up, drove you somewhere, and brought you back, it was a date. I can count at least two other times that has happened. Steak dinner and the Heart Association gala. This is our third."

"When you put it that way . . ."

"Mr. Stone, Miss Maddox?"

They turned and met the copilot, who told them about their flight time to San Francisco and the expectation of smooth skies.

The sounds of the engines warming up prompted her and Chase to find a seat.

Chapter
Twenty-Nine

It took longer to drive from his house, pick up Piper, and drive to the airport than the flight to San Francisco.

The joy on Piper's face when she realized what he had planned wasn't something he'd forget anytime soon. The unbridled excitement of discovery was enough to thank his father for the opportunity to share this with her. It had been a long-ass time since he wanted to thank his father for anything.

Too bad the man had to be dead for it to happen.

A car was waiting for them at the airport, which quickly drove them down to Fisherman's Wharf, where, once again, Piper bounced around like a schoolgirl in excitement. Within minutes, they were sitting at an outside table, eating clam chowder out of a sourdough bread bowl and thanking their luck for a sunny day.

From there, they meandered through the open market, grazing their way with food from the small vendors and browsing through the various shops. They bypassed some of the more odiferous areas of the market since strong smells and pregnancy were not a combination Piper enjoyed. Not that it changed much.

Piper wanted to take home a loaf of sourdough bread and a magnet of the Golden Gate Bridge, and chocolates from the massive Ghirardelli store. Wine-tasting rooms were found on several blocks, which Piper said they'd have to try out once she could drink again.

Street performers entertained them, as well as a self-guided walk through a museum on the history of Fisherman's Wharf.

They stopped at a storefront that had a tank filled with clams. Inside were pearls, but you couldn't tell the size or color until you opened them up. Cheesy signs boasted about the person that bought a thirty-five-dollar clam and ended up with a pearl worth a thousand dollars.

"How does this work?" Chase asked the guy behind the counter.

"Pick one, and depending on what you find, you choose a setting you want me to put it in."

Chase glanced at Piper. "You want one?"

She shook her head. "No."

She hesitated.

Then reached for her purse. "Yeah, I do."

"I got it." Chase pointed to the tank that held the larger clams, and likely the larger pearls . . . and cost the most. Not that it was a lot. "Which one has your name on it?" he asked Piper.

"You don't have to keep buying me stuff," Piper said, pointing to the bag he held.

"A loaf of bread, a magnet, chocolate, and your weight in saltwater taffy won't break the bank."

"Not the point."

"Lady, when your boyfriend wants to buy you things . . . let him," the vendor told her.

"You heard the man."

Piper shook her head. "He flew me here on a private jet," she told him.

"Sure, lady," he scoffed, clearly not believing her story.

"He did."

Chase tossed his arm over her shoulder. "One day, babe. We'll have a jet with a bedroom in it."

"Let's start with a pearl. How about that? I'll even show you the real gold. I mean, if your aim is a jet, you might as well spring for the good stuff now."

Chase pulled her over to the tank. "Which one is worth thousands?"

"Okay, my *future* gazillionaire. Have it your way."

Piper peered into the tank, tilted her head left . . . then right. "What's under that one?" she asked the man.

With a small net, he pushed the large clam aside and revealed a much smaller one.

"I think this belongs in the other tank," he told them.

Piper shook her head. "That's the one I want."

"Ya sure, lady? It's gonna be small."

"I like the underdog. I want that one."

The vendor looked at Chase as if asking if that was okay. "You heard the lady."

"It's your money."

The man removed the clam and took it over to a table, where he used a tool to pry the thing open.

Around them, a crowd started to form, watching to see the unveiling.

The vendor looked bored as he pulled the flesh of the clam aside and dug for the gem.

For a minute, Chase wasn't sure there was a pearl to be found, then the vendor went back to the guts and squeezed out the round stone.

"Is that blue?" Piper asked.

The vendor stopped smiling at the crowd that stood behind them, arguably trying to make his next sale, and looked down.

Piper stared on like a kid at the county fair.

Chase could care less what the thing cost, watching Piper was a much greater prize.

In the sink at the counter, the vendor washed away the muck.

The pearl wasn't small.

And it was most definitely blue.

Nearly metallic blue.

"I didn't think they came in that color."

The vendor looked between the two of them, cleared his throat. "Yeah, lady. If you want a white one, I'll just toss this one and you can pick another clam."

"I like the blue."

So did the vendor. Chase saw it in his disappointment.

"You sure?"

"Yup."

The man sighed and directed them to the back of his store.

There, Piper picked out a necklace from the "real" gold section.

When it was all said and done, a couple hundred bucks and Piper had a chain around her neck with a shiny new pearl.

Once they walked out, Piper pulled the pearl away from her chest and looked at it. "What do you think this is really worth?"

"A lot more than that guy said . . ."

"Or he wouldn't have tried so hard to talk us out of keeping it."

"Exactly."

She shrugged. "I don't care if it's worth ten bucks or a thousand. I will wear it and always remember this day with you."

Chase texted the driver and told him they were ready for their next destination.

They stopped in Chinatown, made it a half a block, and the unfiltered aroma of the area drove them back to the car and pushed them on to Nob Hill. They crossed the Golden Gate Bridge . . . twice. And promised to visit Alcatraz the next time.

From there, the driver pulled up in front of a tower hotel with Chase's name on it so that they could freshen up and change for their seven-thirty dinner reservations.

The moment they drove up to the valet, Chase realized how much his life had changed.

The doorman opened the back door of the car, and Chase climbed out.

"Good evening, Mr. Stone. Miss Maddox. Your room is ready for you."

How did they know who he was?

Chase glanced over at the driver and remembered he was staff of the hotel.

They walked through the lobby, and while none of the guests gave them a second glance, the staff was arguably on high alert.

The bellman shouldering their bags led them to the elevator, up to their room, and opened the door to a presidential suite.

"I hope this is acceptable, sir. The penthouse was booked this evening."

"We're only here for a couple of hours." Why was the man apologizing?

"Still . . ."

Piper stepped forward; her assistant voice showed up. "This Mr. Stone isn't like the other Mr. Stone. Please let the manager know that we appreciate everyone's attention to detail."

"I'll pass that on. Thank you."

The man left.

Chase stood staring at the door.

"What was that?"

"It's your new life, Mr. Gazillionaire. Your assistant will be sure to send the manager a gift and a thank-you letter on Monday."

Chase turned to her. "How is it you're more comfortable with this than I am?"

She walked away. "That's easy. I've been in your father's world for five years. You've been in it for two and a half months." Piper moved to the window, gasped. "Holy shit, look at this view."

"How do you do that?"

"Do what?"

Chase joined her at the window.

The view was rather spectacular. The bay, the bridge . . . the wonder that was the city of San Francisco . . . "Be in complete amazement of jets, paparazzi, and views . . . and yet at ease with pilots and massive suites at hotels that you're only in for a few hours at most?"

Piper looked out at nothing, paused . . . "I've managed an incredibly rich man's life for five years. I'm arguably *teaching* that man's son just how rich his life has become and yet experiencing it for myself, for the first time."

He reached for her. Gathered her close. "You're perfect."

"Ha!" She laughed. "Pregnant . . . therefore not perfect."

Now it was his turn to teach her something. "That's insecurity talking."

"Perhaps . . ."

He placed a hand on her face. "We should get ready for dinner."

∾

With nothing more than a quick shower and a dusting of makeup, Piper emerged from the bathroom for whatever Chase planned next.

She entered the living room of the hotel suite and saw Chase standing at the window overlooking the city lights.

Piper eased up on him and slowly wrapped her arms around his waist.

How was it she was in this place, casually touching this man, and him leaning into her?

"Amazing, isn't it?" he asked.

Piper wasn't sure they were thinking the same thing. "Yeah."

Chase faced her and slowly smiled. "You're glowing."

She batted her eyelashes a few times. "Must be the new mascara."

"I don't think that's it."

Piper lifted her lips to his, expecting a brief moment, but when their kiss lingered, the world around them fell apart.

Chase ran his hand up her neck and captured the back of her head and kissed her deeper.

Piper pulled at his arms and moaned into his touch.

She gasped, or maybe it was him, and Chase eased her up against the wall, his body flush with hers. Fire deep in her belly sparked hot as he pressed one knee between her thighs.

Her hips buckled in shameless abandon from the feel of him.

Lips hot against hers, he murmured, "Dinner."

Piper pulled at his shirt, felt her fingers graze his skin. "Not hungry."

He grasped her hips and pulled her up his thigh, forcing every nerve between her legs to come alive.

Her head fell back, and Chase took advantage of her neck. "I'm hungry." His voice was rough.

One minute she was all but riding his thigh, and the next, Chase's hands were on her butt, lifting her off her feet. "Hold on."

Piper wrapped her legs around his waist and grazed her teeth against his jaw.

"Damn, Piper."

Chase walked them to the bedroom and fell with her onto the bed, coming just short of crushing her under him.

Not that she minded. The weight of him alone made her come to life. She clawed at his shirt. He fumbled with the buttons of hers.

Finally, she felt the span of his bare broad shoulders and ran her hands down his back to rest on his ass. Delicious and perfect, his lips captured hers again as his hands found her breasts and squeezed.

This was passion, the kind that would burn in her memory forever.

His lips broke away and trailed down her neck, her chest.

Piper arched so he could access the clasp of her bra and free her so he could touch and taste his fill.

And he did. So much so that sparks started behind her eyes. She felt her nipples pucker under his teeth.

Piper toed off her shoes and wrapped her free leg around his hip, needing to feel the heat of him where she desired it most.

The weight of his frame lifted from hers, and she wanted to cry. "Come back."

Chase looked up at her, his hooded eyes revealing the desire in his blood.

Their eyes locked, he ran a hand up her thigh until his thumb grazed her sex through her pants.

Her breath caught, her hips bucked.

"You want more?"

Mouth half-open, she didn't dare speak.

A single nod and Chase broke eye contact and lowered his mouth between her legs, his hot breath blew lava through the woven material of her pants.

One of her hands found the back of his head, the other pushed at her clothing to get everything off.

"Lift your hips," he demanded.

She did, and Chase removed everything.

Piper pulled her shirt from her arms, tossed her bra to the floor, and smiled up at Chase, who licked his lips and watched her squirm.

Free of her clothing and free of the weight of him, Piper bent one knee and lifted her hands above her head.

"Fuck," Chase said on a breath. His eyes drinking her in. The way he stared made her feel sexy and wanted. While she could tell the changes in her body, they weren't terribly obvious to a man who had never seen her naked before. There was comfort in him seeing her like this, knowing it was all changing rapidly.

"You're wearing too many clothes."

Chase reached for his belt, the movement made his cock twitch inside his pants.

She started to squirm. The need for him heavy in the air.

His pants hit the floor, and Piper stared with a smile. "Yes, please."

Chase retrieved his wallet from his pants and pulled a condom from it.

She almost laughed.

Instead, she sat up and plucked it from his fingertips. "Too late," she said, and tossed it away.

Chase laughed before capturing her lips and crawling on top of her until she was flush with the bed once again.

Damn, he felt divine. Better than she imagined anyone could.

His cock pressed against the warmest part of her body as if knocking on the door for permission.

She hiked a leg up on his hip, tilted her pelvis. "Please." She nearly begged.

Chase grasped her wrists and lifted her arms over her head and, with one hand, held them there while he leaned on the other elbow to keep from crushing her.

She was open and spread out for him like an offering.

Their eyes met as he slowly eased into her for the first time.

"You're so beautiful, Piper."

It was hard to breathe. The feel of him filling her up and making himself comfortable inside her body was like a homecoming.

"I want to hear you cry my name." He pulled back slightly and pushed back in.

"Keep that up and I will," she told him.

His hips started a slow dance, his lips lowered to hers, their kiss heated with the friction of their bodies.

A seed of passion started to build as they rose and fell in time with each other.

Chase released her hands and guided her hips with his.

He shifted his angle, or maybe she shifted hers . . . but yeah, this was perfect. "Yes. Right there."

The man followed directions, his hips moved, his pace didn't waver. Her body started to tighten from the inside out.

"You're like a vise grip."

She tightened those muscles again and saw pure pleasure ripple over Chase's face. The same pleasure pulsating through her body. With each push and pull, her body wound up and up, the perfect tension, the perfect pulse. Piper grabbed his ass and pulled him closer, deeper, until she couldn't breathe, and the sound of her orgasm filled the room. "Chase, yes. Oh, yes."

"Perfect . . . so damn perfect."

Her ears rang, and Chase changed his cadence, his hips moving faster.

Piper met his pulse. "Come in me, Chase. I want to feel all of you."

It was as if all she needed to do was ask.

"Fuck, Piper . . ." The ripple of his release splashed into her in hot waves.

Chase collapsed at her side, kept her body glued to his.

They held each other in silence as their breathing slowed.

Chase stroked her hair as she rested one arm on his hip. This tangled embrace and ease in his arms felt right on so many levels. "I feel so much better," she said into his chest. All that pent-up passion released into their lovemaking.

"We need to do that over and over." He kissed her shoulder and moved to her side just enough to keep from crushing her.

"And over again," she finished for him.

His breath warmed her ear as he spoke. "I feel like I just unwrapped the best gift in my life."

She shifted back enough to see his eyes. "Those words were so perfect, they almost sound like a line."

Chase pushed her hair back, his thumb traced her jaw. "You deserve nothing but truths. I won't lie to you, Piper."

She wanted to believe him. Men say things after sex they don't mean. Piper really wanted to believe Chase was different. And how would he feel when she looked different, and he knew the baby inside her wasn't his? She needed to get out of her head. Her gaze shifted away.

Chase lifted her chin and captured her eyes once more. "What are you thinking?"

"I want this. I want to hold on to this. But . . ." She closed her eyes, thought of the child growing in her womb.

"Talk to me, Piper."

She had nothing to lose by telling him her thoughts. And keeping them inside felt like a lie. Now that he knew everything, she was determined to say whatever she was thinking. "What if dating me becomes too much? My clothes are already getting tight. I can't keep this a secret much longer."

"Piper—"

"I've never . . . I mean, men don't stick around. Even when I wasn't pregnant."

"Piper—"

"All these emotions are swirling. That's not going to be easy." She wanted to cry. The most mind-blowing sex in her life hadn't even been washed from her body, and she wanted to cry.

"Piper—"

"Promise me you won't string me along. If your feelings change, you'll make a clean break. I can . . . I'll handle it." Yup, here came the tears. Because she already knew she wouldn't handle it well. Chase Stone was already seeping into her blood and rushing around her heart.

"Piper." He pressed a finger against her lips. "I'm not going anywhere. And I respect you too much to play games."

"Okay." She sniffled.

"Okay?"

She nodded and smiled when he smiled.

He kissed her, and then hugged her into his chest.

The need to stay there, exactly there, forever floated around in her head while Chase whispered all the right things and put her mind at ease.

⌒∽

Piper took a shower first while Chase canceled their dinner reservations and called room service.

Chase was exiting his shower when he heard Piper talking to the person that brought their food.

Her vulnerability gutted him. There was true terror in her eyes when she asked him not to string her along. How could she possibly think he would? Clearly, no one had cherished her the way she needed to be cherished.

He was going to change that.

If he were honest with himself, the sex alone would be worth him giving her anything and everything he could. It was like they were made for each other. Their bodies fit like a goddamn puzzle piece cliché. Watching her unravel in his arms, wearing nothing but a street-vendor pearl around her neck, gave him a sense of possession he knew was entirely too early to feel. It was primal and primitive, and he didn't care.

"It's getting cold," Piper yelled from the other room.

Chase pulled on his pants and draped a towel around a shoulder to capture the moisture from his hair.

He waltzed in and smiled when she looked up at him midbite.

"Couldn't wait," she said around her food. Her eyes grazed over his bare chest.

"The baby must be hungry."

"Mmm. So good." She took a chunk out of a potato.

Chase occupied the chair beside her and removed the cover from his food. "Not bad."

"Pretty sure this isn't the normal room-service food. The chef brought it up himself."

"Really?"

He cut into his steak.

"They know who you are even if you don't." She hummed again. "This peppercorn sauce is the shit."

"I love how you love food." His first bite proved she had a point. "This is good."

"See. I'll make sure the chef is mentioned when I send the manager the gift on Monday."

"I'm the one that was trying to take care of you, and here you are taking care of me," Chase mused.

"Oh . . . you took care of me. At the risk of pumping your ego too much . . . that was the best sex in my life. And as long as you're giving me access, I'm taking full advantage, so fuel up."

He slapped a palm to his chest. "Finally . . . a woman wants to use me for sex and isn't afraid to eat real food. You need to marry me." Where had those words come from?

"Ha." She chased her steak with a sip of water. "That would turn some heads."

Chase took another bite while she laughed off his suggestion.

"The peppercorn is amazing, right?"

"It is," he said.

"Is there a time that Carson is expecting us back on the plane?"

And just like that . . . his *marry me* comment was glossed over.

Chapter Thirty

Sometimes changes in life happen gradually, like growing out a bad haircut or saving the money to buy a home. While others slam into your world like an unexpected windstorm that carries you up in the air, and all you can do is look around and enjoy the view.

Chase was the windstorm.

They woke in her bed Sunday morning and spent the day together. It was after seven when she pushed him out her door so she could get to bed early for her work week.

On Monday, he called her twice from his other office to ask her about her day. And when she arrived home that night, on her porch were two large boxes. Written on both of them was a note that said, *Open the boxes outside and make a few trips.*

Piper nudged the boxes with her foot, determined they were rather heavy, and followed the instructions.

Inside one box were several smaller bags of Kit's food. In the second box was a similar theme, but this one carried small containers of the laundry detergent and fabric softener she preferred.

She didn't need a note to know who sent her the boxes.

On the phone that night, she told Chase that he didn't have to do those kinds of things. And his reply was a question. "What kinds of things?" And then he promptly changed the subject.

The next day, Piper was standing beside Dee's desk, going over a project she was working on, when Chase arrived in the office.

"Good morning, ladies." His smile was casual . . . his eyes, not so much.

"Good morning, Mr. Stone."

He lifted a single eyebrow.

Piper caught her smile by biting down on her lower lip.

Chase cleared his throat.

"Is my sister here?"

"No. I'm expecting her around ten."

He nodded toward the office. "If you have a few minutes, Miss Maddox. We need to go over my schedule."

"Of course."

He walked away.

Piper gave a final instruction to Dee and then grabbed the calendar.

Chase leaned against the desk and motioned for her to close the door once she was inside.

As soon as the door clicked, he was off the desk and had her pinned against the back of it, his lips on hers.

He swallowed her whole.

Piper couldn't get enough.

His hand reached for her hair, and she pulled it away. "Not the hair."

He nodded, kissed her again. Tongues dancing, breathing erratic.

One of them came to their senses and put space between them. "So, this is how it's going to be," she whispered.

"If I don't get that out of my system now, I won't make it through the day." He swiped a finger over her lips. "Soft colors when you know I'm coming to work."

Piper dabbed at his lips, too. Her lipstick leaving a mark. "Are you telling me what to wear, Mr. Stone?"

"Just a suggestion. I personally like the swollen lips and *just been ravaged* look on your face."

She pressed a hand against her warm cheek. "Soft color makes sense."

He kissed her again before letting her slip out of his arms. She used the office bathroom to fix her makeup and wash her hands.

Back in the office, Chase handed her the calendar that dropped to the floor the second he touched her. "We can go over this when Alex gets here."

"Okay."

He ran a hand down her blouse, tracing her breasts through her clothing and tugging her shirt in place. "Now . . . how much gas do you have in your car?"

She was still short-circuiting on his touch when his question registered. "That's random."

"How much?"

"About a quarter of a tank, I think."

He looked her in the eye. "I need your car keys."

"What?"

"It isn't safe for you to be pumping your own gas. For you or the baby. I need your car keys."

She rolled her eyes. "Oh, please."

Chase put a finger under her chin, his eyes pulled her in. "You can argue with me about many things and I'll likely cave. But when it comes to your health and safety, I won't budge. Car keys, Piper."

The seriousness of his tone captured her next words and kept them from coming out. "Okay."

"Good." He patted her ass before opening the office door.

༄

For two weeks they managed to keep their situation private until a picture of them holding hands and walking Kit in the park showed up in a gossip magazine.

Piper learned about it when Julia slapped it on her desk, arms folded over her body, toe tapping, waiting for an explanation.

"I suppose this is photoshopped, too."

Piper stared at the image in surprise. It was captioned . . . *Is the newest billionaire on the block already off the market?* "Dammit."

"I'm waiting."

Piper grabbed the paper and pulled Julia away from her work area and into a conference room that wasn't being used.

"Okay, fine. We're dating."

Julia went from annoyed to smiling in two seconds. "I knew it!" She grasped Piper's shoulders and hugged her hard. "Oh my God, Piper . . . I'm so happy for you."

"I am, too."

"No wonder you haven't been jumping on girls' night out."

That was for an entirely different reason. But one secret reveal at a time. "I'm worried about what people will say around here."

"Who cares. You're dating Chase Stone," Julia squealed. "Is he good in bed? I bet he's amazing in bed."

Yeah, that was not what Piper was ready to share. "We need to get you a boyfriend," Piper said instead of answering the question.

"Tell me about it. Let's grab lunch today and you can give me all the sexy details."

"I'm craving street tacos," Piper suggested.

"You're on."

Before Julia walked away, Piper said, "Do me a favor."

"Yeah?"

"Let me know what people are saying."

Julia rolled her eyes. "You can't date someone as important as Chase Stone and not have haters. Jealousy will be out there. Who cares?"

She didn't want to care. God knew, Piper wanted not to care.

But she did.

"I still want to know who the haters are. Lots of people smile in your face and stab you in the back."

"I got ya covered. Tacos and trash talk."

Back at her desk, Piper sent a text to Chase, who was working at the other office. Her text started with a picture of their images in the magazine. I came clean with Julia.

It took twenty minutes for Chase to respond. Why do they always get my bad side?

You don't have a bad side, she texted back with a devil-smiling emoji.

You good?

I am, actually.

If anyone gives you a hard time, I need you to tell me.

This was where things felt sticky. I'm not going to be responsible for someone getting fired.

Three dots flashed for some time.

Then her phone rang.

"Hello, Mr. Stone."

"We need to find a compromise," was how Chase opened the conversation.

"I'm listening."

"Your safety and happiness are my priority."

There really wasn't a downside to Chase repeating those words. Piper loved to hear them, but more . . . loved to feel them in his actions.

"If something feels unsafe, I'll tell you." The second the words were out of her mouth, she remembered Gatlin cornering her on the third floor. That was a while ago, and before she and Chase were officially dating, so she figured that was a pass.

Unless it happened again.

Then . . .

"I can't have you unhappy at work."

Okay, that made Piper giggle. "In that case, I need a new chair, this one is bugging my back . . . and an office with a view."

"Piper!"

"Do you see how impossible that is? Some people aren't going to like this, we know that. I can handle the water-cooler buzz. Besides"— she lowered her voice—"I'm not exactly a stable barometer on my emotions these days . . . considering." She found herself crying during commercials. It was annoying.

"Piper!"

"That voice isn't going to work this time. You said compromise. If something gets ugly, I'll deal with it. If it interferes with me doing my job, I'll bring you in. Fair?"

"Fine."

She smiled. That was not a "fine" voice.

"And you can't fire them," she said in conclusion.

"Now, wait up."

"Nope. You need to do all the things. Bring in HR, do the review . . . and no extra commentary on the back of a pink slip." They both knew what that referred to.

"I accept that with one exception."

"This is a negotiation . . . What?"

"If your safety is threatened. HR can fuck off, and I get what I want."

It wasn't often that Chase tossed out an f-bomb. It said this was a hard line.

"Your sister has to agree."

"Piper."

"Hear me out. Someone says something that feels threatening. It hits me the wrong way or at the wrong time, and I tell you. You kick them to the curb, and they take you to court. Cuz maybe it's an executive or a manager." She saw Floyd in her head. "They don't go out without a fight." Floyd would kick, scream, and call lawyers. "If you had another person looking at the situation that agreed it was threatening, you have a much better chance of beating them."

He blew out a breath.

"You know I'm right."

"Why do I feel like you took three points in this negotiation, and I only took one?"

Because that was how it turned out.

"Now that we have that out of the way, I've been told that the new striping on the first level of the garage is happening on Thursday." Piper changed the subject.

"Good."

"And I have my doctor's appointment on Thursday at four. I need to leave here by three thirty."

"The baby doctor?"

Piper looked around her. "Yes," she whispered.

"I want to come with you."

She paused.

"Are you still there?" he asked.

"Why?"

"What do you mean why? My girlfriend is pregnant, and I want to be with her when she goes to the baby doctor."

"But—"

"No, no buts."

"We can't negotiate?"

"Sure. We can drive *my* car. We can drive *your* car . . . or we can drive *separate* cars. I want to be there. You're not doing this alone, not as long as you want me in your life."

Cue the tears.

She sniffled.

"Please, Piper. Let me hold your hand."

She grabbed her chest and felt a flood of emotion roll over her. "Okay." She sniffled.

"Are you crying?"

"I'm just . . . I'm . . . I need chocolate."

Chase started to laugh.

An hour later, a delivery of Godiva chocolates arrived at her desk. It came with a card that said, *We'll take my car*. It was signed with a *C*.

Chapter
Thirty-One

Chase was completely out of his comfort zone, but he pressed through anyway.

He walked with Piper into the doctor's office, sat beside her in the waiting room with three other women. Two who were well into their pregnancies and one that either wasn't pregnant or wasn't showing.

He'd only just noticed the slightest change in Piper's body. If he didn't know she was pregnant, he would have missed it.

The door opened, and someone called Piper's name.

They stood at the same time.

"You sure you want to be here?" she asked for the tenth time since they'd left the office.

He gathered her hand in his with a smile.

He let go of her hand when they walked through the door, and he followed behind as the nurse, or assistant, or whoever she was, walked her down a hall.

The first place they stopped was a scale.

Chase immediately turned away and looked at the office wall art. Women and weight . . . he had yet to meet a woman who liked to share that information. Not that he cared, but he wasn't going to infringe on that unless invited to do so.

"Good. I'll put you in room four. We need a urine sample."

Chase was dropped off in the exam room while Piper found a bathroom.

So far, the office looked like any other, only this one had images of the female anatomy on the walls and several medical devices that he wasn't familiar with outside of a comedy bit on a social media reel.

Piper returned, and the nurse followed her in, took her blood pressure, and wrote it down. "No need to get undressed, you can pull what you're wearing down for what Dr. Resnik needs today."

Piper sat on the edge of the exam table while Chase sat in a chair. "Are you completely weirded out yet?" she asked.

"I haven't started playing with the speculum, so I think I'm doing okay."

"I'm impressed you even know what that is."

"I'm cultured."

Piper laughed. "Don't think being cultured falls into the OB-GYN category."

He leaned forward and placed a hand on her knee. "If you need me to walk out of the room, just nod at the door and I'll go."

She shook her head. "You know everything about this. I'd just tell you afterward anyway."

A knock sounded on the door right before it opened.

Chase sat back as the doctor walked in. "Hello, Piper . . ." The doctor's eyes landed on Chase. "Oh, hello." She smiled.

"Dr. Resnik, this is Chase."

Chase extended a hand. "Her boyfriend."

Dr. Resnik looked between Chase and Piper and back again.

For a moment, no one spoke.

"He's not the dad," Piper told her.

"All right." The doctor crossed to the opposite side of the room from the door and looked at Piper's chart. "How is the nausea?"

"Much better. My appetite has come back."

Chase laughed. The woman could eat. He liked that part.

"You put on the three pounds you lost and gave me one and a half. That's good."

"I've never gained weight and actually applauded it."

"If you're not gaining weight, there's reason for concern. I'll let you know if you're gaining out of what we like to see." The doctor looked at the chart again. "Your blood pressure is . . . okay. I'll have the nurse check it again before you leave."

"Is it too high?" Chase asked.

"Barely. Probably nerves." She turned back to Piper. "How are you feeling overall?"

"Better. Well, I cry at the cat videos on Instagram."

The doctor laughed. "A certain amount of that isn't avoidable. If you feel you're getting depressed—"

"No. I think I'm past any of that now."

Chase looked at Piper, a little surprised to hear that she ever felt depressed.

"Good. Let me know if it changes."

Dr. Resnik placed the chart down and moved to the sink and washed her hands. "How is your stress level?"

"Better. It helps that someone knows what's going on." Piper looked at Chase when she spoke.

The doctor listened to Piper's lungs and heart and asked her to lie back.

Chase stood and moved to Piper's side to give the doctor room in the tiny space. The doctor removed a measuring tape from a pocket and asked that Piper undo the button on her pants. As the doctor measured Piper's abdomen, she explained what she was doing. She tossed out words Chase hadn't heard before.

"My clothes are getting tight."

"Time to go shopping," the doctor said. "There are new-mom groups out there that sell their maternity clothes if money is tight."

"That's a good idea," Piper said.

Chase looked at her and shook his head. She was not going to wear another woman's clothes.

"What?"

The doctor wrote something down. "Excuse me?"

"Nothing," Piper responded.

"I'm going to do another ultrasound today. As long as everything looks good, we won't have to do another one."

"Okay."

"I'll be right back." The doctor left.

"Are ultrasounds safe?" Chase asked Piper.

"Yeah. She wouldn't do it if it wasn't."

When the doctor returned, she rolled in a machine. A few minutes later, and Chase viewed Piper's baby wiggling around. "There you are. Strong heartbeat."

A fast-whooshing sound put a huge smile on his face.

He reached down and grasped Piper's hand. "That's amazing."

"It is," the doctor said under her breath. "It doesn't get old. Are you feeling anything yet?"

"Like the baby moving?"

"Yeah."

"Not really. Is that bad?"

The doctor kept moving the wand over Piper's tiny belly as she spoke. "No. You will . . . any day now. Imagine a butterfly in your stomach. In a few months, it will be more like the baby is bouncing on your bladder."

"Oh, great." Piper wasn't amused.

"And do we want to know the sex today?"

Chase wanted to blurt out *yes*, but he looked at Piper instead.

She squeezed his hand. "You can tell?" Piper asked.

"I can."

Piper stared at Chase, he saw the indecision in her eyes. "Up to you." He lifted her hand to his lips and kissed it.

She gave a tiny nod, and he responded with an even bigger nod.

"What is it?" she asked.

The doctor pressed a final button on the machine and printed a picture. She turned and handed it to Piper. "You're having a girl."

Piper took the picture and started to cry. "I am?"

Chase didn't know what he wanted to hear, but hearing a mini Piper was headed into the world opened his heart in a way he wasn't expecting.

"Yes."

Chase dropped her a kiss. "A girl."

Piper swiped at her eyes as she sat up.

"I want to see you in four weeks."

"Doctor, is it okay if Piper flies?"

"Absolutely. You need to get up and move around later in your pregnancy, use compression stockings on long flights. Those tiny seats are a great place to form a blood clot when you're sitting for long periods of time."

"That won't be a problem," Chase told her.

The doctor narrowed her gaze.

Piper swiped at his arm. "Ignore him. Moneybags here has his own jet."

"Well, in that case . . . no, Piper needs medical supervision at all times. Where are we going?"

They laughed.

"Seriously, it's completely fine."

"Good."

The doctor watched them for a second. "Chase, I'm going to have you step out while I talk to Piper really quick."

"Of course." He leaned down, kissed Piper. "I'll be in the lobby."

Chase walked back to the lobby, all smiles.

She's having a girl.

Piper was having a baby girl.

∞

"He seems like a nice guy," Dr. Resnik said the moment Chase was gone.

"He is. I wish I'd met him before."

"Are you still considering adoption?"

She shifted on the table. "Uhm, yeah. I mean, Chase doesn't change that. Does he?" Why was she asking the doctor that?

"I can't answer that question."

"We're new, so . . . he's a great guy, but who knows. I did . . . let the biological father know. He denied knowing me. I read that adoption agencies ask those questions."

"I'm sure they do. Have you spoken with them yet?"

Piper shook her head. "I've been really busy."

"Flying on private jets, apparently," the doctor said, smiling.

"Yeah." Piper laughed. "I'll call them."

"Don't call them until you're ready. This is your choice."

Piper wiggled off the exam table. "Thank you."

"Stay here for a minute, I want another blood pressure on you."

Alone, Piper slid her hand over the smallest bump on her belly, smiled, and swallowed hard.

"I'll make sure you're born healthy," she promised.

∞

Piper had started making a Google search part of her weekly routine. In addition to Chase's and Alex's names, she had alerts placed on her name, Melissa Stone, and that of Stone Enterprises. Piper was getting tired of gossip magazines landing on her desk with pictures of her in them.

Even though there was a public relations team that watched out for the company, Piper was more interested in seeing where she landed. Twice she'd had a nightmare that her parents discovered she was pregnant because of a gossip magazine. Thankfully, their geography and lack of desire to keep up on the rich-and-famous chatter afforded Piper privacy in her relationship with Chase. Truth was, as the weeks were stretching longer into her pregnancy, she was growing more comfortable with it. Piper was also keenly aware that her dating Chase and being pregnant was going to make a headline.

It was only a matter of time.

Piper was combing through her personal email at lunch when she found an alert on Melissa. Of all the names Piper followed, Melissa's was the most active.

Expecting more of the "What is the widow wearing now?" crap, Piper was surprised to see this was "Who is the widow dating now?" crap. The dating part wasn't the shock, it was the man in the picture.

When Chase and Alex returned to the office after a lunch with a half a dozen members of the management team, Piper closed them off in the office and showed them what she'd found.

"In case you've forgotten, that is Paul Yarros. He's one of the more vocal members of the board."

Chase leaned against the desk while Alex sat behind it. Both scanning a copy of the picture and the article that came along with it.

"Melissa has a type," Alex said under her breath.

"Old and rich."

"I doubt Yarros has the zeros in his account to keep Melissa happy," Piper told them. "If you look at the picture objectively, they seem to be deep in conversation and not making kissing faces at each other."

Chase glanced over the paper in his hand and pursed his lips in her direction.

Piper smiled. "Yeah, there's none of that."

"If it isn't romantic . . ." Alex started.

"Then it's business," Chase finished.

"Yarros wants a bigger chunk of the company, that's not a secret," Alex said.

"He said as much during the board meeting. Even asked about Melissa, if I'm not mistaken," Piper reminded them. "Wanted her shares . . . if she ended up with any."

Chase put the paper down. "Which she didn't."

"I don't like it," Alex muttered. "All she needs to do is convince one of the board members to investigate the will."

"And if she does know about this brother, she's whispering into the ears of Yarros and those that think like him. You know damn well he'd try and buy those shares," Piper pointed out. "Time for one of you to spend some time with Yarros. Get-to-know-you lunch?"

Chase glanced at his sister. "You know what Gaylord said, dinners or golf."

"Dinner," both Chase and Alex said at the same time.

Piper laughed as she stood to leave.

Her hand immediately moved to her stomach as a small wave brushed against her skin. She sucked in a breath and held it . . . waiting for it to happen again.

Chase was at her side in two steps. "What is it?"

It happened again, a flutter, deep inside. Like wings of a tiny butterfly. "I feel her," she whispered.

"The baby?"

It happened again, and Piper grabbed Chase's hand and pressed it to her stomach. "There."

She looked up at Chase, waiting for it to happen again.

His eyes moved away as he concentrated.

When it happened a third time, Piper watched to see if Chase could feel anything. "Can you feel her?"

He frowned. "No."

By now, Alex was standing beside her, smiling. "Let me try."

They stood in the middle of the office, taking turns with their hands on Piper's stomach.

"How exciting," Alex said as she dropped her hand to her side.

"I guess it's only for me right now," Piper told them.

Chase kissed her forehead and patted her stomach. "I'm looking forward to it."

Chapter
Thirty-Two

Chase rolled out the office-remodel plans on Floyd's desk to bring the man up to speed on what the changes would entail.

"Instead of moving walls, we're going to create a new office space in place of the smaller conference room. It makes the most sense to move you to the new space, and I'll take over yours. Good news is, it will be bigger."

Floyd stared at the plans, his lips pressed together. "If it's bigger, why don't you take it?"

"Piper can't be in two places at once." Chase pointed to the space needed for Julia. "We'll shift this around to accommodate your assistants."

Floyd shrugged and moved away from his desk. "Piper . . . of course."

The hair on Chase's neck stood on end.

"There are rumors going around."

"I've heard." Chase had yet to speak with any of the staff about his relationship with Piper. The way he saw it, it wasn't their concern.

"You and Piper?"

Chase answered with a single nod. He wasn't about to give the man more.

Floyd huffed a laugh, looked away, and did it again. Standing at the window, he said, "You move fast, Stone."

Chase felt there was more. "If you have something to say, say it now. But tread lightly."

Floyd smiled like he had a secret. "Just be careful with that one."

A nerve in Chase's jaw twitched. "Why do you say that?"

"I can't help but think there was a reason your father fired her, now you're dating and rearranging the office to accommodate her. Bit much, don't you think?"

"You know damn well Piper isn't the reason for the remodel."

Floyd dropped his smile. "I do?" He shook his head. "I'm looking out for the best interest of this company."

Chase saw this for the pissing match it was. "It is in the best interest of the CEOs to have their assistant close to both of their offices and not running to opposite ends of the floor to do her job."

The fake smile returned to Floyd's face. "You're the boss."

"That I am." Chase rolled up the plans. "You'll be given the opportunity to weigh in on the new office space and a budget."

"Sounds appropriate."

Chase clapped the plans against his free palm. "And the subject of Piper is closed."

Floyd looked him directly in the eye and nodded.

Chase walked down the hall and passed the break room, where he noticed Piper out of the corner of his eye. She stood talking to Julia while three other employees were milling about.

He stepped into the break room and caught Piper's attention.

She smiled, as she did more openly since the news of their relationship got out, but instead of only smiling back, he moved to her side and immediately placed a hand on her hip. "These plans are good to go. Floyd has two weeks to offer input."

"Okay."

"I'll drop these on your desk." He brushed his lips against hers and dispelled any question of their situation to all who watched.

He smiled as he turned and left the room.

⁓

Piper sat poolside, under a cabana.

Kit went from lying down on the massive Baja step to shaking out and panting in the shade of one of the many trees surrounding the pool.

Even though Chase and Alex had no desire to live in the Beverly Hills estate, they had both found it easier to be there. When Piper suggested a few hours poolside since the weather was heating up, they agreed to make a day of it.

Piper's bikini felt a little off, considering the baby inside of her was making herself known. So far, she'd managed to buy a couple of larger pants and skirts and avoid anything maternity. But it was getting harder.

Chase pulled himself out of the pool and walked to her side.

The double lounge chair she occupied had his towel sitting beside her.

He crawled over to her and placed a cold hand on her leg. "You don't have to do that."

Piper held a section of Aaron's will with the many art pieces they had yet to identify in the inventory, which she found surprisingly relaxing to comb through. "I'm almost done."

Alex lay in the sun several feet away, her body lax in her sleep.

"We're here to relax and cool off."

Piper nodded toward Alex. "She got the memo."

Chase ran his hand up Piper's side and rested on her belly. "She's working too hard. Just like you."

"This doesn't feel like work."

Chase pushed the papers to the side and pressed his lips to Piper's belly. "What do you think, Baby Girl? Is Mom working too hard?"

Piper watched as Chase alternated between pressing his ear to her belly as if listening and talking to it. "I agree. What's that? You want to

309

go shopping?" Chase glanced at Piper. "She wants more wiggle room and thinks you need to buy the right clothes."

"You're not buying my clothes." They'd had this discussion before. Fancy dinners and carnival pearls. But maternity clothes were off-limits. Piper brought the paper in her hand in front of her again.

"Why not?"

"I can do it."

"But you're not."

"I will." Piper read the passage in the will a second time.

"When?"

"Soon." She read it a third time. Something felt off.

"If you don't want to go into a store, I can bring the store to you." Piper read it a fourth time. "Okay."

"Seriously?" Chase asked.

"Ah-huh . . ."

"I'll set something up this week."

"This is strange. Of all the things in the house, why would your dad think you'd want more of an artist's collection and even tell you where to go to buy it?" Piper asked.

"What does it say?"

"It says, 'To complete the set, contact L. Davis at Freedman Galleries.' Why would he . . ."

A shiver went up Piper's spine, she dropped the paper to her side and stared at Chase, who was still hovering over her abdomen. "L. Davis. Lisa Davis."

Chase pushed up on his forearms. "Holy shit."

"Freedman Galleries."

Chase reached around Piper, grabbed her computer, and started typing.

She looked over his shoulder.

"There's one in Palm Springs, Phoenix, and another in Dallas."

They looked each other in the eye.

"We need a phone."

⁓

A lazy Saturday by the pool ended up being a late flight to Phoenix with a morning appointment with the owner of Freedman Galleries.

The three of them rolled into a two-bedroom suite just after nine in the evening. Their phone calls had determined that Aaron Stone had purchased the artwork, this time bronze sculptures, from the Phoenix branch of the gallery. But since Lisa Davis was no longer employed by the gallery, a letdown for all of them, they requested an appointment with the owner.

It paid off to have the Stone name.

The three of them sat around the living room of the suite, going over the plan for the next day.

"I say we lie to the man, tell him your father left her something in the will," Piper suggested.

"Why would all three of us be there and not an attorney?" Alex asked.

That gave Piper pause. "The owner of the gallery doesn't know an attorney is the executor and not the two of you."

"True."

"The DNA test did say L. Davis," Chase pointed out.

"And maybe your ever-generous father left L. Davis one of the sculptures she sold to him all those years ago?" Piper suggested.

Alex pointed at her. "I like that idea."

"What better way to get as much personal information as we can out of the man?"

Chase smiled. "This can work." He placed a hand on Piper's thigh and gave it a soft squeeze.

"Should we tell Stuart we're here?" Alex asked.

Chase shook his head. "No. He knows that will better than we do, he should have picked up on L. Davis before we did once I gave him her name."

"I have to agree with that," Piper mused.

"You think he knows more than he's letting on?" Alex asked.

Chase let out a long-suffering sigh. "I think he's following whatever instructions our father gave him. Which may or may not be helping us find our brother."

"I suppose as executor, he sees all of the will, and we only see the parts that pertain to us." Alex stifled a yawn.

"We should get some sleep. Tomorrow could be a full day."

"It's strange to think we might meet our brother tomorrow." Alex's voice sounded distant. "I wonder what he's like?"

Piper hadn't even given the mystery man much thought. At least not about his personality or way of life.

"Just because he's blood doesn't make him family," Chase said.

"The gene pool would argue," Alex told her brother.

"That gene pool needs to be confirmed," Piper added.

Alex stretched her arms over her head and moaned. "We're getting closer. I feel it."

Chase stood and offered his hand to Piper. "Let's hope you're right."

⚬⚬

Walter Freedman was a tall, wiry man in his late sixties. From the first weak handshake to the paleness of his skin, Chase couldn't help but think the man spent way too much time looking at art and not being outside.

"Thank you for meeting us on such short notice," Alex said as they all sat in the man's office.

"When loyal clients ask for special attention, we do try and accommodate."

"Our father earned that title, not us, but we appreciate you seeing us regardless."

"I was sorry to hear of his passing," Walter said.

"That's why we're here, Mr. Freedman. We're hoping you can help us . . . with a couple of things."

He folded his hands together and placed them on his desk. "Anything I can assist you with, I will."

"Are you familiar with the Ziegler sculptures?" Chase asked.

"Of course. Ziegler has been one of our most requested artists through the years. And one your father collected. Such soulful pieces."

"I especially liked *Fire and Ice*," Piper said.

Walter's smile widened; his eyes lit like someone was speaking to him in a language only a few understood. "Some of his best work."

"Is that part of Dad's collection?" Alex asked.

"Oh, no. It belongs to a private collector . . ." Piper had read up on the artist during breakfast.

"Bauer," Freedman finished Piper's sentence.

Chase watched as Piper did her best to act like she was interested in the arts enough to motivate Freedman to keep them happy so they would return to buy more.

"Are you looking to add to your late father's collection?" Freedman asked.

"We haven't ruled that out," Alex said.

"Before we spend more money . . ." Chase looked at his sister and put a hand in the air, as if telling her to hold her purse closed. "We're here on a different mission. One you're in a unique position to help us with."

"I'm listening."

Chase sat forward. "Our father left an interesting request in his will."

"It was a bit cryptic," Piper offered.

"Took us a while to figure it out," Alex agreed.

"Ladies, we don't want to take up all of Mr. Freedman's time. Let me finish," Chase said.

"Fine," Alex said.

"Anyway, as I was saying. In the will, he bequeathed one of his Zieglers to Lisa Davis."

"L. Davis," Piper corrected him. "He wrote L. Davis in the will."

Chase placed a hand over Piper's. "It took us a while, but we determined that L., or Lisa, was the woman who sold this piece in question to our father many years ago. And we need to find her."

Freedman sat back. "I'd love to help you, but I don't know where Lisa is. She hasn't worked here in twenty . . . twenty-five years, maybe longer."

"But maybe you can tell us where she worked after here? Or maybe an address we can search out? Anything . . . did she have family here?"

Freedman rubbed his bare chin in thought. "I don't remember any family. Outside of her son."

Chase glanced at his sister and then Piper.

"Did she have a husband?" Piper asked.

"No. I remember that. She had her son while she was working here . . . actually went into labor in the middle of a show." The man nodded a few times. "That's right. It's coming back to me. No husband. But after the baby was born, she came into some money."

"Child support?" Piper asked.

"Maybe." Freedman pushed his chair closer to his computer. "Let me see if I still have anything on her. I won't have anything about the job after us. We don't keep reference information." He started typing and moving his computer mouse around . . . and typed some more.

Chase, Piper, and Alex sat in silence.

"Okay . . . yeah. I have her original résumé here." Freedman scooted a notepad in front of him and started writing down an address.

Chase felt his pulse rise and excitement follow.

"This is all I have. An address and two phone numbers. A landline and a cell phone. All the other hiring details, emergency contact, Social Security . . . all that is purged annually to help with identification fraud." He handed the paper to Chase.

"This is very helpful. Thank you."

"My pleasure. I'm sure Lisa won't mind me giving that information away when it means she'll acquire a Ziegler. Of course, I doubt she still lives at that address."

Chase removed one of his cards from his wallet and handed it to Freedman as they stood to leave. "If you think of anything else that might be helpful in finding Miss Davis, please contact me."

"Absolutely. And if you're ever interested in purchasing more . . . or considering selling your collection . . . they have gone up in value."

"We'll do that."

The three of them left the air-conditioned art studio and walked into the furnace that was Phoenix in the summer.

They sweltered inside the car until the air conditioner caught up.

"Should we just call?" Alex asked once they were in the car.

"Beats me," Chase said.

Piper shrugged.

Alex pulled her cell phone from her purse, dialed the number, and put the call on speaker.

The landline was disconnected. No shock there.

A male voice picked up when she called the cell number. "Hello?"

"Hi, uhm . . . I'm looking for Lisa Davis."

"You have the wrong number."

Disappointment crossed Alex's face. "Wait. Don't hang up. Is this . . ." Alex repeated the phone number.

"Yeah, but I'm not . . . whoever you're looking for."

"How long have you had this number?" Piper blurted out.

"Fifteen years . . . give or take."

Chase looked at his sister and Piper and shrugged.

"Okay, thank you." Alex disconnected the call. "Dammit."

"Who changes their cell phone number?" Chase asked.

"I've had mine since my first phone," Piper said.

"Me too." Alex sighed.

"Cell phones were new-ish back then," Chase said.

"I didn't think about that."

Piper pulled out her laptop. "You drive, I'll see if I can get any hits with the phone number and her name search."

Chase put the address they had into his navigation app and put the rental car in drive.

"You know she's not going to be there," Alex said from the back seat.

"I doubt it, but maybe someone knew her."

Chase pulled into traffic.

"I found more information," Piper said.

He glanced at her computer screen and saw a half a page listed under the name Lisa Davis. "We're bound to find something in all that."

Piper shrugged. "Only about a third of it will be accurate."

"What? How?"

"You've never googled your name?" she asked.

"No, he hasn't," Alex told her, laughing.

"I know who I am," Chase defended his lack of googling habits.

Piper smiled. "Let me show you. I'd type in yours, but there is too much information on you. We'll do me."

"You've googled me?"

Piper shook her head no but then said, "Yes."

"Ha. Told you," Alex exclaimed.

Chase looked at her through the rearview mirror. "Point taken."

"To be fair, I googled you before we met . . . and after."

"Women can't be too careful."

Piper turned her computer screen so he could see it. "This is me. I know it's me because this is my parents' address in Ohio. I got this by typing in my phone number and following the links. This shows possible relatives. This is my dad, but this guy . . . Ted Russo? Never heard of him." She pointed to another address. "No idea where this is. I don't know who this phone number is attached to, or this lady."

"I get the picture."

"But we have something to work from," Alex said.

"More than when we got here."

Piper jotted down notes and kept typing.

Chase pulled into an older neighborhood with mature trees and neglected yards and wound his way around until they found the house where Lisa Davis once lived. "It says 1536 B."

"That's a good thing," Piper said, opening her door. "I live in a B unit, and my landlord has been in the main house for forty years."

"What are we waiting for?" Alex pushed out of the car.

Chase opened the small chain-link gate and ignored the overgrown weeds. He noticed a back house more unkept than the front one.

Alex was already up the steps and knocking on the door before Chase could catch up.

He saw movement from the curtains framing a large window, only no one answered the door.

"Ring the bell," he told Alex.

She did . . . twice.

Nothing.

"Someone is home. I saw movement in the window."

Alex rang again.

Nothing.

"They probably think we're trying to sell them something," Piper whispered.

Alex rapped on the door again. "Hello?"

The door didn't open, but a voice from inside yelled out, "I don't need your Jesus. I have my own."

Alex smiled over her shoulder at Chase and Piper. "We're not here for that. We're looking for Lisa Davis. We think she was a tenant of yours."

A pause . . . and then the sound of a lock and a chain before the door opened.

An older, heavyset African American woman, salt-and-pepper hair, poked her head out the door and looked around. "You're looking for who?"

"Lisa Davis. She used to live in the back house."

The woman opened the door wide and stood in the threshold. Her eyes traveled to each of them as if measuring them up one at a time. "I haven't heard that name in a long time."

"You know her?" Piper asked.

"Knew. She hasn't been here for years."

"Oh, thank goodness," Alex said.

"Not sure what you're thankful for. She's not here."

"We really need to find her and haven't been very lucky in getting any information about where she might be or where to even start looking. Maybe you can help," Piper said. "Tell us what you know, what you remember about her."

The landlord peered between them. "She in some kind of trouble?"

"No," Chase told her. "I know this sounds like a spam call, only in person, but . . . our father recently passed away, and Lisa Davis was mentioned in his will."

"That woman always did seem to find money."

Piper leaned against the railing of the stairway, and the rotted wood squeaked against her weight. Chase caught her arm to keep her from losing her balance.

She thanked him and placed a hand on her stomach.

"You okay?" he asked.

"Just hot."

The landlord stepped out a little more. "Are you pregnant?"

Piper nodded with a faint smile. "I am. I'm not used to your Arizona heat."

"I'll get you a water from the car." Chase turned around.

"C'mon in. I have cool air and ice water."

Alex exchanged glances, her eyes wide with hope.

Piper and Chase walked up behind his sister.

"You sure you're okay?" he asked in a soft whisper.

"I'm just hot."

Chase closed the door behind him.

"My name is Abigale."

"Thank you, Abigale. We really appreciate your time. I'm Alex, and this is my brother, Chase, and our friend Piper."

She led them into a well-loved living room. A mismatch of furniture with quilted blankets tossed over the backs of chairs and a sofa. Old, spindled end tables and a TV that sat on a credenza that might have been as old as the owner. It was what Chase envisioned a widowed grandmother's house to look like. The outside showed neglect, but this space was cluttered and loved.

"Make yourself comfortable. I'll get some water."

Piper's hand ran along a quilt on the sofa before she sat down. "This is like stepping into my grandmother's house," she told them.

"I was just thinking that."

"Our grandmother's is nothing like this," Alex countered.

Chase took a seat beside Piper. "Our mother's mom lives in Florida. Single story, open floor plan, everything in its place. But this . . . this is what you think of when you hear *grandmother*. All it's missing is cookies."

Piper moaned a little. "We need to get lunch after this."

Footsteps stopped their chatter as Abigale entered the room, carrying a tray.

Alex popped up to help her by clearing a space on the coffee table.

Four ice waters and a plate of cookies stared back at them.

"Miss Abigale, you read my mind." Piper wasted no time in picking up a water and a cookie from the tray.

"You looked a little pale out there."

"Thank you," Chase said for all of them.

"Did you make these?" Piper asked as she lifted the corner of one of the quilts.

"I did."

"The hand stitching is beautiful."

Abigale eased her weight into a high-back chair. "I'm surprised someone as young as you noticed."

Piper took a sip of water and put down the glass. "I grew up in Ohio. My mother and grandmother are both quilters."

"Then you know how long it takes."

"I do. Never had the patience for it myself."

Chase saw their host visibly relax in her chair; a smile spread over her face. "Well . . . what can I help you with?"

"Honestly, anything you can tell us about Lisa Davis," Alex started.

"Let's see . . . she lived here for about five years. At first, I didn't think she'd stick around. She had a fancy job at some art gallery. This neighborhood isn't for that kind. It was better back then, but you know . . . people get old. Hard to push a mower around the yard with arthritis."

"You have a lovely home, Miss Abigale," Piper chimed in.

"You're sweet. Anyway, Lisa seemed to think she was too good for this place. She wasn't around much. Didn't have people over. Which was fine by me. What she saved on her cheap rent, she spent on a fancy car. She said it was a gift, but who does that?"

"No one I know," Piper said.

"Then she got pregnant. Didn't know of any boyfriend. Like I said, no one came over."

So far, everything was adding up in Chase's head.

"Then what happened?" Alex asked.

"She started engaging with me a little more. Asked me if I needed anything from the grocery store if she was going, brought in the mail from the street from time to time. I thought maybe becoming a mama was helping her grow up a little. She still had the fancy job, but she wasn't gone as much. Then Max came."

Hearing Max's name brushed away any doubt that they'd come to the right place.

"Her son," Alex said.

"Yeah. Cute as a button, that one." Abigale shook her head and lost her smile almost as quickly as she put it on when she mentioned Max's name. "Sad."

"What's sad?" Piper asked.

Chase's mind went immediately to the worst-case scenario. "He didn't get sick or anything, did he?"

"No. No . . . nothing like that. He just had a fatal case of a lousy mama."

It was Alex's and Piper's turn to physically relax in their seats.

"I became the babysitter. I was newly retired . . . was happy to do it. Lisa seemed to have more money coming in. She said she was selling a lot of that fancy art, so she paid me well. But . . ."

Piper moved to the edge of her seat; the uneaten cookie dangled from her fingertips.

Chase placed a hand on her knee.

"But what?" Alex asked.

"She worked . . . or so she said. Never home. Max would cry for his mama, but she was never around. And when she was, she didn't know how to care for her boy. I did what I could."

"I'm sure Max was grateful to have you."

Abigale had stopped smiling, and a mix of worry and regret crossed her face. "I couldn't keep him. He wasn't mine. I have real bad arthritis. Keeping up with a toddler was impossible."

Chase focused on the first part of her last sentence. "What do you mean you couldn't keep him? Did she ask you to take him . . . permanently?"

"Oh, she didn't ask." Abigale shook her head. "She just left."

Piper dropped her cookie on the floor. "What do you mean, left?"

"She brought Max over one morning before she went to work. Like normal . . . even though I'd been telling her he needed someone younger taking care of him . . . brought him over and went to work. Only she didn't come home. She was late a lot, and at first, I didn't think anything of it. I always let Max fall asleep in his own bed. I waited for Lisa . . . and waited. I left messages. I was about to call the police and hospitals. In the morning, I called her work. They said she hadn't been there in over a month. Then I went in her bedroom, and that's when I knew. Her closet was empty, and her flip phone was sitting in the bottom of the toilet."

Piper's hand crushed Chase's.

Alex's jaw dropped.

"She abandoned him," Chase whispered.

"That's why she hasn't come forward," Alex said.

"What happened to Max?" Piper asked.

There was visible pain in Abigale's eyes. "I waited through the weekend. Hoping she would come to her senses. When she didn't show up, I called the police. They asked me to keep Max for a few more days until they could find a foster family that would take him. Which I did. They tore that poor child away. He didn't want to go. I cried and I cried. I couldn't keep him. I knew the longer he was with me, the harder it would be for me to let him go."

"Of course not. That's understandable," Alex consoled the woman.

Piper wiped her eyes with the back of her hand.

Chase put an arm around her and pulled her close.

"Miss Abigale, do you know where Max ended up?"

"Not really. I wanted to keep in touch, but I knew it would be harder on the boy. And me."

"And he never tried to get ahold of you?" Chase asked.

"No. God willing, he forgot all about his mama and this place. He was young enough, barely two. Maybe someone adopted him."

Chase heard Piper gasp and stand up. "Can I use your restroom?"

"Of course, dear. It's right around the corner."

Chase had a strong desire to follow her but knew she needed a moment alone. He retrieved the forgotten cookie from the floor and placed it on the tray.

Alex fixed her gaze on something out the living room window.

"If your father left something to Lisa and it's worth anything, I hope you do the right thing and find her son and give it to him. That woman doesn't deserve anything but pain, as far as I'm concerned."

Alex stared directly in Chase's eyes and said, "Don't worry, Miss Abigale. That's exactly what we intend to do."

Chapter
Thirty-Three

Numb.

Piper was numb from head to toe. They all were, if the lack of conversation on the way to the airport was any indication.

Once on the plane, the shock had worn off Alex and Chase.

Piper, on the other hand, was still swimming in thick water.

If she gave her baby girl up for adoption, would she feel abandoned? And what if the adoptive parents divorced and gave up custody . . . could they do that? How could a mother do this to a two-year-old? How?

"Our father had a son, confirmed it was his, then sent a check to this woman for eighteen years but never bothered to check on his child." Alex looked up. "I hope you're burning in hell, Dad."

"Then the baby mama cashes the checks and abandons Max. It's so messed up."

Piper placed her hand on Chase's.

"It all makes sense now. Why he didn't come forward, why she didn't. It's illegal to abandon your child, right?" Alex asked.

"At two years old . . . yes."

"But who pursues that? A grandparent? The other parent? Without anyone driving that train, cases get lost. I'm sure she's changed her name. Looking for her is obviously a waste of our time, so we'll concentrate on

him. Then, once we find him, we'll hire whoever we need to find her."
Chase's angry tone matched Piper's mood.

"If Max was adopted, his last name might not be Smith," Piper
pointed out.

Alex moved from her seat in the plane to a server station and filled
the wine she'd started drinking the minute they were on board. Piper
hadn't craved alcohol much at all since she found out she was pregnant,
but man, she wanted something now.

She placed a hand on her belly. *Don't worry. I wouldn't do that to you.*

"It might be time to hire a team to find Max."

Chase started to nod. "It's risky. He owns twenty-one percent of
this company. That word gets out before we find him, and someone
else finds him first . . . there's no telling where his shares will fall. We
considered selling, what are the chances that Max will want that, too?"

Piper looked at Chase. "You wanted to sell?"

"It was a brief conversation. I can't speak for Alex, but it's not what
I want now."

Alex shook her head. "Me either."

That made Piper feel better.

"With forty-two percent of the company, there is no telling if
another shareholder will buy out enough to obtain controlling interest.
If that happens, we get booted out of the CEO position and have no
choice but to sit back and watch."

"Is that the end of the world?" Piper asked.

"It could be the fall of the company. Not to sound dramatic, but I
know a company at risk of a takeover, and we're awfully close. A couple
of board members were pushing for expansion, but according to what
I'm seeing, we need to cut some of that fat until the economy turns
around."

"Layoffs?" Piper asked Alex.

"I'm not saying that right now . . . but yeah."

"Let's not jump," Chase said.

"I'm not jumping, brother. Things aren't good. We need to try and keep it together for Max. I thought it was shitty to have an absentee father that I knew. I can't imagine what he's thinking." Alex sipped her wine.

Chase ran a hand over his face. "Clearly, Stuart isn't as efficient at finding Max as we are."

"Don't executors of wills get some kind of stipend for the work they need to do while the will is being settled?" Piper asked.

"They do. It's paid off the top from the estate," Alex told her.

"That's his motivation for moving slowly . . . if at all," Piper said.

"Or Dad told him to move slow," Alex said, lifting her glass in the air.

Chase cussed under his breath. "I'm calling Jack Morrison tomorrow. Going to tell him everything. See if he'll head up a team to find our brother. It'll be hard to link to us if it's done by someone else entirely. Jack has the resources, and we can settle up once we find Max." He looked up. "Unless you disagree."

Alex shook her head. "I think it's good."

Chase turned his attention to Piper. "You?"

"It's not my decision."

"I want your opinion."

"I like it." Not that hiring an investigative group was going to stop her from searching for Max herself. Knowing what happened to him was becoming a palpable need for her. As if agreeing with her, the baby started moving around.

Piper smiled and pressed her palm to her belly.

Chase reached over, as he often did, and snuck his fingers under Piper's.

He pulled in a breath. "Wait . . . is that her?"

Piper smiled when the baby moved again.

Chase twisted in his seat. "That's her."

"You feel that?"

He nodded, leaned over, and pressed his lips to Piper's.

"If you two are done, I need to get in there and feel."

Piper smiled under Chase's kiss as he pulled away, and Alex took her turn feeling the baby move.

∽

Chase told Jack everything.

He started with the mic drop of the will, continued to ending up in Miss Abigale's living room and learning that his brother was abandoned by both of his parents. "It's all kinds of fucked up, Jack," he said over the phone. "We need to find him before any of the board members start questioning our place in the company."

"Wow. My dad said Stone was an asshole, but I didn't think it could get this bad."

"Melissa was seen having lunch with Paul Yarros. He wants more shares of the company. I tried to book a dinner with him, but his secretary is stonewalling me."

"What does Melissa know?"

"We're not sure. But an investigation into our father's will needs to be avoided. And if it can't be, then it's even more important that we find Max before anyone else does."

"We need to work fast, then," Jack said.

"You'll help?" Chase stood, looking out the window at his backyard. He'd driven Piper home after flying in the day before and left late in the evening. Leaving her was a task that was getting harder and harder to do.

"Consider it done. Who knows about this?"

"It's a small list. Alex and I, our mother, Piper . . . my friend Busa, and Alex's friend Nick. And the attorney, of course."

"Piper is your girl?"

That made Chase smile. "Yeah. She's a big reason why I need help with this."

"Oh?"

"She's working way too many hours trying to find Max."

"Oh, I get that. Jessie gets a bee in her bonnet, and nothing is stopping her from getting what she's after." Jack's southernisms were a refreshing change.

"I can appreciate that, but she needs her rest. Especially now."

"Why now?" Jack asked.

Chase didn't hesitate. "She's pregnant."

"Well, hot damn, congratulations."

Chase felt the swell of pride and stomped it down. "Thanks, but, uh . . . it's not mine. Wish it was, if I'm honest. Piper was pregnant when we met."

"Well, that does put a little burr in the saddle. Not that it matters much in the long run."

"What do you mean?"

"When Jessie and I met, she was a single mom. I legally adopted Danny right after we got married. I couldn't love my son more."

"And the father?" Chase asked.

"Who knows. He didn't stick around. I love Jessie more than roaches love sticky buns. I wouldn't change her or Danny or any of it for the world."

Chase laughed. "That's funny."

"Yeah, Jessie still giggles when I compare our love to a roach. I love that woman's laugh."

It gave Chase hope to hear a man gush about his wife the way Jack did.

"My point, though . . . it doesn't matter that Piper's baby isn't from you. So long as you love her, it doesn't make a difference."

Chase blew out a breath. "How do you know when you're that far in?"

"Oh, that's easy. It isn't about the time you're with her, that part is always magical. It's about the empty you feel when you're not. The gaping hole in your soul you know would be there if she was gone forever. If she called you right now and said she wanted it to end, how would you take that? A shrug and delete her number? A bender in Vegas to get over her? Or with you sitting at her doorstep day and night with a guitar in your hands, singing off-key just to get her to talk things out with you?"

Chase instantly envisioned himself on Piper's porch, singing . . . with Kitty howling behind the door. "Oh, damn."

Jack laughed over the phone. "Hits ya like a ton of bricks when you figure it out, doesn't it?"

Chase sat back on the armrest of his sofa and felt the air rush out of his lungs.

"Want my advice?" Jack asked.

"Isn't that what you've been doing?"

Jack laughed. "Lock that in, buddy. If you know she's it, lock her in. Equally, if she's not the one, put space between that. You can't *maybe* about a child. That's not fair to the kid."

"Thanks, Jack. I appreciate your candor."

"Anytime. I'll get on the private eyes and find this needle in the haystack."

"Sounds good. Oh, and ah . . . you do know that my mother was with your father last weekend, right?"

Jack's staccato laugh was contagious. "Yeah, wouldn't that be something? Guess I'll be seeing you at the wedding, *brother*. Whichever one comes first."

Damn, Chase liked the sound of that. "Give your father a little grief for me. I need to know his intentions."

They were both laughing. "I'll be sure and pass that along."

Chase stared out the window, his phone dangling from his hand. His life was about to change in ways a gazillion dollars couldn't compare to.

∽

"I'm pregnant." Piper stood across from Julia in the break room with a cup of tea in her hands.

A slow smile spread over Julia's face. "I knew something was up. Holy shit." She looked down at Piper's stomach.

For the first time ever, Piper wore a dress to work that didn't exactly hide her condition. She was still small enough for people to question if she was gaining weight or if she was pregnant.

"How far along are you?"

"Far enough that I can't hide it anymore."

"How is Chase taking it?"

"He's been great, but—"

Julia moved closer and lowered her voice. "Are you guys getting married?"

"What?" For some reason, Piper hadn't expected that jump. "Julia, he's . . ." Piper looked toward the door. "I was pregnant when Aaron fired me."

Julia looked puzzled. "You met Chase before you were fired? Is that why you were canned?"

"No."

Two members of the accounting team walked into the room, ending their conversation. "We'll talk at lunch."

Julia kept smiling. "It's so exciting."

Piper put a finger over pursed lips as if asking Julia to keep quiet.

Not that Piper thought her friend would keep anything a secret.

Back at her desk, a catalog with office equipment stared at her. Two pages were flagged.

Office chairs and a note. *I looked it up, these two are recommended for pregnant women. Pick one.* It was signed with a *C*.

This was special treatment.

Special treatment from sleeping with her boss.

Special treatment that Gatlin would call out if she was the only one in the office being offered a new chair.

Piper put the catalog in the bottom of a desk drawer.

Construction had started on the third floor, where Chase was with his office manager of CMS, combing out a few details.

Piper shot him a quick text to let him know what Julia had said, and completely ignoring the new-chair idea.

The last thing Piper wanted was a rumor to get around about Chase being the father and anyone else jumping to the matrimony question.

I told Julia. She assumed the baby is yours and then asked when we're getting married. Crazy, right? I didn't expect that.

A few seconds later, her phone buzzed.

Are you proposing over a text message? He ended with a bride and groom emoji and a heart.

You're both crazy. I just thought you should know that was the second question out of her mouth.

Dots flashed on her screen for a minute. No comment.

Piper didn't get it. What do you mean?

More dots. When people ask the questions, answer "No Comment." We don't owe anyone an explanation.

And let everyone assume? Was he serious?

Lots of time with her screen flashing tiny dots. Then her phone rang. The sound of a hammer hitting something pounded behind Chase's voice. He didn't bother with hello or even a pause in their conversation. "The alternative would be for you to answer all the questions every time someone asks you about the baby and us. That sounds exhausting to me, and I'm not the one eating for two."

"But—"

"Babe, I don't care. I told Jack about the baby this morning. First thing he did was congratulate me. And you know what I did?"

Oh, God . . . "What?"

"I thanked him. Like, damn, that felt good to hear. I did set him straight, but after, I thought . . . shit. I don't want to spend my time answering questions that are going to come from people I don't care about. I like Jack, don't get me wrong. He's fine, but Julia or Floyd or Phillis in the mail room . . . No. I'm going to say *thank you* and smile and *no comment* to any of the detail questions that come up."

Piper felt the back of her throat choke up. "We can do that?"

Chase laughed. "Let's practice." He lifted his voice up an octave. *"You're pregnant? Congratulations . . ."*

Was he actually standing next to construction workers, role-playing over the phone with her?

"Chase—"

"No, I'm Julia, and you say 'thank you.'"

"Thank you," Piper said reluctantly.

"Is Chase happy about this?" Again, with the fake female voice.

"He seems more excited than me," Piper answered honestly.

"Are you getting married?"

Piper looked around to see if anyone could hear her. "We haven't talked about it."

"Perfect. Was that hard?"

A little. "No comment."

Chase laughed. "Now that we have that out of the way . . . I want you to take the furniture catalog out of the trash and pick out a chair."

Piper looked up at the ceiling and around the room. "Are you watching me?"

"No, I know you. Pick one or I'm buying both. Babe, I gotta go."

She wanted to cry. How was this man so amazing? "Chase?"

"Yeah?"

"There isn't a Phillis in the mail room."

He was laughing when he hung up the phone.

Chapter
Thirty-Four

Piper was ambushed twice in one week.

First by a Saturday brunch with Alex and Nick, which was supposed to be a girls' day.

Alex and Nick dragged her from brunch to a surprise, which happened to be in a Mommy To Be store. Chase and his mother were already there with racks of clothing set up.

Arguing was mute. Not with four against one.

When it was apparent that Piper wasn't picking anything over-the-top expensive, the attendant removed the price tags before handing the articles to Piper to try on.

When it was all said and done, Piper had more clothing to wear for the next three and a half months than she did to wear when this was all over.

It was silly and expensive and made her feel like Cinderella . . . without the evil stepsisters.

The second ambush happened after Piper revealed her pregnancy to everyone in the office. It happened at her home after returning from work on a Tuesday.

A man with a camera hanging from his neck stood in front of her car before she could pull into her driveway. He took several pictures of her and started shouting questions.

"Just a couple of questions, Miss Maddox."

She rolled down the window. "No comment. Now get out of the way."

"Is it true you're pregnant with Stone's baby?"

"No comment." She inched her car forward, but the guy didn't move.

"What do you say about the rumor that the baby is the late Aaron Stone's child?"

Her car lurched forward, and she slammed on the brakes. "What the hell?"

"Is that a yes?" he shouted.

"Where did you hear that?"

"So it's true?" the man asked.

"No, it's not true. Go away."

The man shot her a smile. "Makes for a great story, though."

"Fuck off. Get out of my driveway." Weren't there laws about paparazzi and personal property?

The man took another picture, and Piper laid on the horn.

"Are you and Chase Stone planning a wedding?" the man squeezed out when she stopped honking.

She really wanted to run the man over. Or at least make the man think she would.

Only her neighbor seemed to have a better idea.

Piper slammed her car in park and ripped off her seat belt when she saw Kit running up the driveway.

Mr. Armstrong had good intentions, but this wouldn't end well for her dog if this asshole was bitten on public property.

Seeing the dog, the jerk dropped the camera and jumped back.

Piper shouted a command to stop Kit mid-lunge.

The cameraman tripped on his own feet, and Kit stood over him barking.

Kit didn't bite him . . . thank God. Piper let the man panic before she called Kit off him completely.

Kit moved in front of her as the man scrambled to his feet.

The air around them stilled, except for the fast beating of her heart and the panting of Kit in all the excitement. He let out one more bark. "Chase is more protective than my dog. I suggest you don't come here again."

"It's a public street."

"My dog has the right to protect me against a threat. I find you threatening." She kicked the man's camera toward him.

He bent down to retrieve it.

Kit stood up and growled.

Piper made a motion with her hand, and Kit sat back down.

By now, a few neighbors had come out of their houses to watch, and Mr. Armstrong was walking up the drive. "I called the police."

The man put the camera back around his neck and ran a hand over his head. "Might want to learn the laws, Miss Maddox. You're having a billionaire's baby. That's always a good news story."

The man backed away, eyes on Kit, before getting into his car and driving off.

Once he was gone, she felt her pulse return to normal.

"Are you okay?" Mr. Armstrong asked.

She leaned against her car and released the breath she was holding. "Thank you."

Kit wagged his tail and nudged her knee.

It took the police fifteen minutes to get there.

By then, she had stopped shaking.

Without any real crime having been committed, they informed her about what she already knew.

The man could take pictures of her in public spaces. No, he wasn't allowed to block her car or her driveway, but prosecuting that was a waste of time. And yes, if Kit had actually attacked the man on a public street without an assault in progress, the dog would get the worst of it.

However . . .

And this was something Piper didn't know. "There is a reason why celebrities live behind gates. Those gates are often inset just enough on their property that anyone blocking it is on private property and subject to a different set of rules."

Piper thanked the officers for their time and advice. They would write a report but leave it alone unless the man returned and *threatened* her again.

She liked that they used her words and didn't completely disregard her situation. It helped that she was pregnant. The officers kept looking at her belly and asking if she was okay.

And that was refreshing.

By the time the officers were ready to leave, Chase was barreling down the driveway.

"I called him, too," Mr. Armstrong told her as they were saying goodbye to the police.

Damn near slamming into the police cruisers, Chase jumped out of his truck the second it was in park and ran over to her.

Kit stood up, saw it was him, and sat back down.

She was in a bear hug, his hand on her face, his eyes swimming in worry.

"I'm fine."

"What happened?"

The police stood there watching. Their radios filling the silent air.

"I need to go to the bathroom. She's jumping on my bladder."

Chase kissed her twice and let her walk away.

"What happened?" Chase asked again to the men standing around outside.

Piper took her time, knowing that someone would explain what had happened while she washed the stress from her hands. She took the opportunity to kick off her shoes and change into a comfortable pair of maternity pants and a simple T-shirt. She instantly felt better.

And hungry.

Kit was glued to her side as she walked around her house. Kit was given a hefty treat and a whole lotta love.

Noise outside told her the cars were shuffling around the driveway. Another look and the police were gone, and Chase stood talking to Mr. Armstrong.

Piper grabbed a bag of potato chips and finally relaxed into her sofa.

The second she sat down, the baby started to move. "Too much excitement, huh?" she said to her baby.

The salt on the chips tasted so good she almost moaned as she popped another one into her mouth.

Chase's heavy footfalls preceded him walking through her door.

"Sorry, I needed to get off my feet."

He dropped into a squat and nuzzled Kit's face first. "Can I buy you a pony? A girlfriend . . . what? What do you want, boy?"

Kit licked Chase's face.

Piper ate another piece of heaven.

Chase pushed the bag of chips off her lap and replaced them with his head. His arms circled her hips. "I aged five years on the drive over here."

"Mr. Armstrong shouldn't have called you."

He kissed her belly and went back to resting his head in her lap. "I'm going to pretend you didn't say that."

Piper ate another chip, talked around it. "I would have called once the police left."

"Driving into my girlfriend's driveway and seeing police cars here isn't something I ever want to experience again."

"It wasn't . . . It's over."

Chase finally lifted his head from her lap and paused. "How are you . . . really?"

She set her hand down that was holding a chip. "It was upsetting. I tried the 'no comment' thing, the guy wouldn't listen, then he said . . ." Piper thought about how best to say what he said.

"What?"

"He asked if it was your baby. I said *no comment.* Then he asked if it was your . . . father's baby." Just thinking about it again made her shake.

"What the fuck?"

She tossed the chip back in the bag. "Is that what people are saying? How can anyone think that? I literally wanted to run the man over with my car."

Chase moved from the floor to the couch and gathered her in his arms.

Piper felt the tears before she realized she was crying. "Where did that come from? Who is spreading this? What kind of monster do they think I am?"

"Shh. I got you."

Piper leaned back long enough for her to stare into Chase's eyes. "I swear on my parents' lives this is not—"

"Shh." Chase pressed a finger to her lips. "Don't even say it. Never think it again."

She nodded several times, pressed her head to his chest. "God, I hate these tears."

"You cry. I'll catch you."

Piper felt his words down in her soul, and the tears kept rolling. "Chase?" She sniffled and gathered the courage to say what came next.

"What, honey?"

Fearful of seeing rejection in his eyes, she stayed with her cheek pressed against his chest, his hand stroking her hair. "I'm falling in love with you."

Piper held her breath.

His hand stopped moving.

She heard him release a breath. His hand resumed the petting of her hair. "I can beat that," he finally spoke.

"Oh?"

He pressed a hand to her face and forced her to look at him. "I'm already in."

She bit her lip, the tears weren't going to stop. "What?"

"I love you, Piper."

She wiped her nose with the back of her hand and pressed her lips to his. She pulled away, searched his eyes, saw the love he spoke of, and moved in again. This is what love tasted like. It was warm and safe and surrounded her completely. "I love you, too."

Chase stopped her with his lips. Their kiss went from warm to passion in a heartbeat. There were teeth and tongues and promises of care and tomorrows.

Piper leaned back on the sofa as Chase yanked the blinds over the couch closed.

She fumbled with his pants and yanked the bag of chips from under her and tossed it to the floor.

They laughed together for only a moment before Chase was pinning her down on the sofa, her comfortable pants on the floor. He spread her legs with a knee and entered her slowly. "I love you, Piper. I'm going to love you as long as you let me."

It was as if his words and actions were seeping into her brain and taking over her body. He hadn't even moved yet, and she felt her orgasm tipping over the edge. She swallowed back her pleasure. "Never stop saying that."

"I love you." He pulled his hips away, pushed in again. "I love you." Oh, God.

She pulled his lips down to hers and whispered the words right back until their bodies couldn't physically talk and move at the same time.

∽

Chase had no idea how liberating three little words could be.

He made love to Piper with a whole new appreciation for the words and the act. And when they were sated enough to speak, he asked her to pack a bag. "The woman I love had the police in her front yard today. I'm never going to sleep if you're not with me."

She didn't argue. "What are we going to do with Kit when we're at work?"

"We'll bring him with us until we figure it out." Besides, there were days he couldn't be at Stone Enterprises, and if Kit was always with her, Chase would feel better about her safety.

And Chase knew, at the very center of his core, the moment she walked into his home, she wasn't leaving. He would find the right time and lock this in.

Liberating.

Knowing he'd found the one for him freed him in ways he never imagined.

An hour later they were at his house, Kit comfortable in the living room while Chase helped Piper unpack her bag.

"I have to be honest," she said when she was hanging her things inside his closet. "This feels a little caveman-ish."

"What does?"

She giggled. "You tell me you love me and then drag me to your cave."

He pumped his chest out. "I'd throw you over my shoulder, but someone would get crushed."

Piper pressed a palm to her belly. "I think she's used to you crushing me by now."

"I didn't hurt her, did I?"

Piper laughed. "No."

"Good. It would be hard not to touch you, but if I have to—"

"Bite your tongue. Pregnancy sex is the best. My orgasms are right there." Piper poked a finger in the air with a satisfied smile.

"Right where?" he asked as he walked up from behind and wrapped his arms around her.

"There." She poked the air again.

"You sure it's not here?" He pressed his fingers to the warmth between her legs.

She melted.

A puddle of goo in his hands. "Yup . . . there."

Piper dropped the clothes in her hands and rested the back of her head on his chest.

He found her spot, and did indeed confirm, her orgasm was right *there.*

Chapter Thirty-Five

For the first time, Chase saw the article resulting from the incident at Piper's house before she did.

It had him seeing red.

"I want to sue them," Chase told his sister in the office before letting Piper know about it.

"I don't think it's that easy."

"It can't be that hard."

Alex tossed the magazine on the desk. "It's amazing the lies they make up and put in print."

"I don't want her to see this." He turned around with his arms firmly crossed over his chest.

"She's tough. I know you want to protect her, but she's going to see this if she hasn't already."

"She'd tell me if she knew."

"The real question is, who came up with this? These yahoos aren't smart enough to spit out this big of a lie without someone whispering in their ear."

Chase crossed the room, sat on the sofa. "My first thought was Melissa."

"Yeah, but to serve what purpose? Jealousy? It's not like Piper is driving around the woman's car or living in her house. No. This feels more like a *stir up trouble here* kind of thing."

"Something Melissa would do," Chase said.

"If we're distracted by this nonsense, it gives someone else here room to invade. Pretty common tactic with takeovers. In war and business."

"Yeah, well, if I find out who is behind this, there's going to be a war."

Alex started toward the closed office door. "Let's let Piper in on this before someone brings it to her desk."

He knew his sister was right.

Alex poked her head out the door. "Piper, you have a minute?"

Piper walked in the office, and her smile instantly fell. "What's going on?"

Kit nudged his way past Piper and into the center of the room before lying down.

"Have a seat, hon."

She didn't sit. "What is it?"

Chase stood to stand by her. "That reporter wrote his article."

Piper's shoulders slumped. Paused.

"Let's see it."

"It's ugly," Alex warned.

Piper put her hand out, and Alex retrieved the gossip magazine from her desk.

She slowly backed into a chair as she read. The caption alone was all anyone needed to see. *Is Chase Stone Going to Raise His Father's Baby?*

Piper flipped through the pages of the article in complete silence.

Chase didn't like it when she went quiet.

She finished reading and stared at nothing for several breaths.

Chase pulled her hand into his and squeezed.

"Who started this?" Piper cracked out in a shaky breath. "And why?"

Alex blew out a breath. "I think this is all a distraction. Something to make the board nervous, give them a reason to ask questions."

"Who?" Piper asked again, her eyes kept looking at the article. "Melissa accused me of . . ."

Chase brought her hand to his lips. "This feels more like a corporate move than a jealous woman."

"To what? Break us up? If you believed this, then . . . my baby is being used as a pawn." Piper's blank stare scared him.

"We'll find who is spreading this. I promise," Chase said.

"Melissa hates me. Gatlin hates me."

"Gatlin?" Alex asked.

"He cornered me after that gala, told me never to talk to his wife again."

Chase had to stop himself from squeezing Piper's hand too hard. "What do you mean, cornered?"

"It was on the third floor after I met with the design people. He made sure I knew he wasn't happy about my words at the dinner table."

"Did he threaten you?" Alex asked.

She shook her head. "No. But I wouldn't put it past him to be behind this. Try to get me out of here."

Gatlin was gone. One way or another, the man was on his way out.

Piper tossed the magazine on the table and met Chase's eyes, the light in hers dimmed. "I need to call my parents. They can't find out this way."

"Of course." Chase wished he could shoulder the anguish of that call for her.

"They're going to ask about the father."

"Tell them it's me."

"Chase—"

Alex turned around. "I'm going to get some coffee."

His sister left them alone and closed the door behind her.

Chase took both of Piper's hands in his. "Tell them it's me."

"What if—"

"What if what?" Chase thought he knew what she was going to say, so he cut her off from the *worry* what-if questions and started in on the *what is* what-ifs. "*What if* we fall in love . . . oh, wait, that already happened. *What if* you move in with me . . . oh, wait, that is happening.

What if I fall in love with the baby growing inside the woman I love? *What if* all that?"

"What if . . ."

Chase saw her holding in all the emotions, which was impressive considering how quickly she cried these days.

"*What if* I told you I'm keeping her? *What if* I told you I want to go shopping for a crib and pink booties and I want to find the perfect name? And . . . *what if* I lose you for wanting that?" Piper choked on her last words.

He kissed her hands and then held them close to his lips. "You are not going to lose me, Piper."

"But—"

"Honey, what do you want me to do, get on one knee right now, without a ring or flowers or all the things you deserve?"

Her eyes opened wide, her questions stopped.

"Do you get it now? Do you understand?"

She nodded . . .

Cue the tears.

"Call your parents."

"Okay."

"Do you want me to stay?"

She shook her head. "I need to do this alone."

He kissed her and stood.

Kit looked up, sighed, and lay back down.

At the door, Piper stopped him. "Chase?"

He turned.

"I love you."

Chase found Alex pouring coffee and looking at the screen of her phone in the break room.

"Is she okay?" Alex asked quietly.

He nodded and started to smile. Piper's words coming back to him. "She's keeping the baby," he whispered.

Alex placed her cup on the counter. "That's the best news we've had all month."

Chase was going to be a father, if Piper would let him.

Someone walked past the break room.

He and Alex stopped talking.

"If she's right about Gatlin—"

"You don't even have to say it," Alex said, her voice low. "First, we find Max. Then we dive into Gatlin's life, find out who he's talking to. We can hire that private eye. We do this slowly and methodically."

"If he—"

Alex placed a hand on his arm. "I'll hold him while you take the swing."

Damn, Chase loved his sister.

His heart couldn't be fuller. "I need to find a jeweler."

"What?"

He scowled. "I don't know what Piper likes."

"You're serious." Alex was whispering, too. "You sure you're not rushing?"

Chase locked his sister down with a stare. "When the right man comes into your life, if he doesn't love you as fiercely as I love Piper, I'll personally run him out."

Chase accepted his sister's hug and told her exactly what he had in mind.

∽

"Is Texas as hot as everyone says it is?" Piper asked while she finished packing her bag.

"Honey, it's fall. Besides, I'm sure the Morrisons' ranch has air-conditioning."

Piper's third trimester was coming in hot. Literally. She couldn't wait for the warm California weather to shift.

Every month her body expanded to the point she thought she'd burst. And she wasn't even done cooking yet.

Her parents wanted to meet Chase. And since they hated flying almost as much as they hated the thought of their daughter pregnant and unmarried, Chase suggested meeting them halfway. Gaylord extended an invitation along with his private plane to pick her parents up.

In addition to a weekend on a ranch and the meeting of the parents, Jack had an update on Max.

Piper zipped up her suitcase and dragged it off the bed and to the floor.

"Stop doing that."

"Doing what?"

"Lifting heavy shit when I'm standing right here."

Piper placed both hands on her baby belly and said, "Okay, can you take this off my hands?"

Chase dropped a kiss to her belly. "I'll carry you the next nine months. I promise."

They had a driver take them to the private terminal of the airport, where they met with Alex and Vivian. Kit bounced up the steps to the jet like he owned it. He eyed the bed for him on the floor, then jumped up on the couch.

Alex sat beside the dog and rested her hand on his head. "It's hard to believe that less than a year ago, I didn't even spring for business class on a domestic flight," Alex said.

"Always remember that, honey," Vivian told her daughter.

"How does this compare to Gaylord's plane?" Piper asked.

"He has two, actually. One for those big family trips and another for cozy travel."

Chase took a seat next to Piper. "Define cozy."

"You know, smaller."

"Does it have a bedroom?" Alex asked.

"Of course."

"How cozy was that plane, Mom?" Alex teased.

Vivian's blush gave her away.

Piper laughed. "Is there a new member to the mile-high club?"

Vivian narrowed her eyes, but her smile contradicted her scorned expression. "I guess I have three of you teasing me now." It didn't seem like the woman minded.

The flight to Texas was painless, the air outside the plane was a bit sticky when they landed.

And the Morrison Ranch was out of this world. They drove along the boundary of the property for what felt like miles before pulling through the arched sign over the driveway. There were gates and cameras and trees lining the driveway that led to the front door.

Stone, pillars, and wood.

Piper saw a pasture with horses and another farther away from the house with long-horned cattle. It was exactly what she expected a Texas gazillionaire to own.

Gaylord stood on the porch with a couple at his side. "Is that Jack?"

"And his wife, Jessie," Vivian added.

"Exactly how many times have you been here, Mom?" Chase asked.

"A few more than it's none of your concern."

Piper laughed at the scowl on Chase's face.

Their driver dealt with their luggage as they made their way to their hosts.

Gaylord instantly slid his hand around Vivian's waist and kissed her.

"That puts an exclamation point on all of our assumptions," Piper whispered to Chase.

Hearty handshakes and introductions were made.

"You have a beautiful home," Piper said once they walked inside.

"Thank you, little mama. We have a rib roast and brisket smoking on the grill, and a slew of cooks making sure everyone is fed. If you're anything like Jessie, who could eat an entire steer by herself when she was pregnant, we have you covered."

"Thanks for throwing me under the bus, Dad," Jessie said to her father-in-law.

"We thought she was having triplets at one point," Jack added.

Jessie pushed her husband's arm and shook her head. "It wasn't that bad."

Gaylord cleared his throat.

"Your parents should be here in a couple of hours, Piper. Give you a chance to rest before they get here," Jessie said.

Piper didn't think resting was in the cards, she was much too nervous for this meeting for any of that. "The only thing I need right now is a bathroom. She uses my bladder as a trampoline."

"Oh, don't I remember that. Follow me. I'll show you your room."

Piper told Kit to stay with Chase before following Jessie.

"How was your flight?" Jessie asked as they walked up the stairs.

"It's a private plane, how hard could it be?"

Jessie laughed. "I remember thinking the same thing when Jack showed up in my life. I was a waitress when we met. I didn't go anywhere."

"It doesn't suck."

"No, it doesn't." They stepped into a guest room, where Piper and Chase's luggage already waited for them. "Here you go."

"When you're ready to join us, follow your nose. Gaylord has to feed people the minute they arrive."

Piper smiled. "I knew I liked that man."

Alone, Piper used the restroom and took a few minutes for herself.

An overstuffed chair with an ottoman sat in front of a huge window overlooking the Morrison land.

Meeting her parents here was the right move. Their dislike for big cities and masses of people would have complicated this event. Piper closed her eyes and leaned her head back. She ran through what she thought was going to happen when they arrived. Her mother would try and get her alone so she could talk, and her father would pull Chase aside and give him hell.

Chase could handle it. Or so he kept telling her. Not that their opinions truly mattered. Piper had come to the realization that seeking her parents' approval at the age of thirty was an absolute waste of time.

Piper rested her hand on her baby and chastised herself for letting that desire for their approval take away from her first few months of pregnancy. And in fact, almost caused her to give up her baby, just to avoid the shame of their disapproval. Never again. This was her life, and if they gave her or Chase any trouble, she intended to remind them of that.

Chapter Thirty-Six

"Babe . . . babe?"

Piper jolted awake.

Chase knelt down at her side, his hand on her shoulder.

"I fell asleep?"

She ran a hand over her eyes and sat up. "What time is it?"

"Your parents are pulling up the driveway now."

"What?" She shot up. "You let me sleep?"

"My mother threatened to disown me if I woke you up." Chase followed her into the en suite bathroom.

She went to grab a hairbrush and realized she hadn't unpacked her bag. "I can't look exhausted when they get here." Piper pushed past him and over to her suitcase.

Chase took it from her before she could lift it and set it on a rack, similar to one you'd see in a hotel. "You look fine."

"Fine isn't good." Piper grabbed her toiletry bag and rushed back to the bathroom mirror. She yanked the brush through her hair and then started digging through her bag for lip gloss. She applied the pink cosmetic while Chase watched her run around.

"You're beautiful."

She turned to the side, saw nothing but baby in the mirror.

Her shirt was over her head before she moved back to her suitcase. The dress she'd planned to wear sat on the top of her pile. A soft rose–colored short-sleeve dress that fell past her knees. It was pretty and sweet. Chase loved it because it pushed her ever-growing boobs up for him to feast on. She pulled the dress over her head and turned her back to Chase to zip her up. "I can't believe I slept for two hours."

"You needed it."

"It's rude. We just got here."

With the zipper up, she moved back to the bathroom and looked in the mirror again. She pushed her hair up, looked to the side, and let it fall back down.

Up, she decided, and then searched for a clip.

"Everyone understands."

With her hair up, she pulled a few strands down to fall around her face.

Piper blew out a breath.

Chase rested his hands on her shoulders and dropped a kiss to her shoulder. "You're glowing, love."

"Okay. Okay." Another look in the mirror. This was as good as it was going to get. "I'm ready."

Chase moved with her to the door.

"Hon?"

"What?" She patted down her sides, her back. "Is there something on the dress?"

"Shoes, maybe?"

"Shit."

Back in the room, she dug out the simple sandals she'd brought for the dress. Piper held on to Chase as she slipped them on.

Another deep breath. "How do I look?"

"Spectacular." He kissed her forehead, which she was grateful for since . . . lip gloss.

Chase held her hand as they walked down the oversize hall and to the grand staircase of the Morrison home.

She heard her parents' voices and squeezed Chase's hand.

"You got this."

Two steps down the stairs, she caught sight of her parents.

Her mother managed a soft smile.

Her father managed not to frown. His chin was elevated, his hands were folded in front of him.

"Somebody was tired," Vivian said when they approached.

"I didn't realize it. Sorry to keep everyone waiting."

"Don't give that a second thought, little mama. Sleep when you're tired and eat when you're hungry. We don't stand on ceremony in this house," Gaylord told her.

Piper broke away from Chase after the last step and moved to her mother first. "Hi, Mom."

Her mother wrapped her arms around her. "My sweet baby," she whispered in her ear.

Next was her father, whose embrace wasn't as endearing and bordered on cold. "Hi, Daddy."

They broke away, her father looked at her stomach and then directly to Chase.

"You must be the boyfriend."

Chase stepped forward and extended a hand. "I am, Mr. Maddox. Chase Stone."

They shook hands.

And shook.

And shook . . . tight hands, direct eye contact.

"Daddy!" Piper placed her hand over the two of theirs and broke up the polite tug-of-war.

Piper moved to her mother. "Chase, my mother, Margaret."

"It's a pleasure," Chase said, extended a hand to her as well.

Barely a handshake, and only a half a smile.

"I've heard a lot about you," Chase told them.

"We look forward to knowing you better," Margaret said. "Isn't that right, Darryl?"

Piper's father made a noncommittal noise.

"You've met everyone else, right?" Piper asked quickly to try and break any tension before it built.

"Yes, they have," Jack told her.

"Supper is ready when we are," Gaylord announced. "Darryl, how 'bout I get you a drink. You look like you can use one."

"I'm not much of a drinking man, but I could use a whiskey," her father said.

"I have you covered."

Piper watched as her father followed Gaylord.

Jack looked at Chase with a shrug.

Jessie and Alex walked together as they all funneled away from the hall.

Vivian moved beside Margaret. "We adore your daughter."

"She has a mind of her own, but she's always been a joy."

Piper glanced at Chase when he grabbed her hand.

They moved to an outside patio that was the size of an entire penthouse suite.

The smell of barbeque filled the air as country music wafted through speakers Piper couldn't see. The heat of the day was fading, and outdoor heaters took the place of the sun.

Chase leaned close and put his lips to Piper's ear. "I'm going to break the ice with your dad. If we walk away, don't panic."

She knew it had to happen, and since her dad wasn't big with crowds, it was probably best that Chase talk to him alone. Piper mouthed the words *I love you* before Chase left her side.

"That dress is beautiful," Alex said once Chase had joined the men with their whiskey. "I bet you can get it taken in after the baby is born."

"Or just keep it for the next one," Jessie said.

"One at a time, please. She's plenty already."

"I'm looking forward to being a grandmother," Vivian told her. "Gaylord adores his grandchildren. Can't stop talking about them."

"Where are your kids?" Piper asked Jessie.

"They're at home. We thought it was best for the adults to get to know each other without that chaos. Danny might bring them by later."

"You live on the ranch?" Piper asked.

Jessie pointed across the property. "We built on the east side of the ranch, Katie and Dean are north of us. But they're away right now."

"Jack's sister, right?" Alex asked.

"Yes. It gets rambunctious in this house when we're all together."

Jessie went on to tell them about the kids and the huge holiday gatherings.

As Piper expected, a few minutes into the small talk, her mother pulled her aside.

"Oh, baby," she said on a sigh as soon as they were alone.

"Mom, I'm okay."

"Are you, honey? You look tired."

"Of course I'm tired, I'm pregnant. And I've been fretting over seeing you two since I know you don't approve."

"No, dear—"

"Then you do approve?" Piper knew that wasn't the truth.

Her mother tilted her head to the side. "Well . . ."

"Right, well . . . I don't need your approval."

"Aren't you worried what people will say?"

"I did . . . for a long time. And what a waste of time that was. From the moment I found out I was pregnant, I worried what you and Daddy would say. What the people back home would talk about. How the people I work with would judge. I didn't see my doctor for ten weeks, and when I did, the first thing I considered was giving my baby up for adoption, not because I wanted that, but because I wanted to hide this from you forever."

"Oh, honey."

"I spent the first half of my pregnancy in agony and keeping it a secret to avoid hearing 'what people would say.' I convinced myself that I couldn't do this alone." Piper felt a wave of emotion swell up inside of her and, with it, the conviction she put into words she hoped her mother would hear. "To think I almost gave my baby girl away just so I wouldn't have to hear what people would say. So no, Mom. I don't care what anyone says anymore. When you're dating someone as well known as Chase . . . you end up getting talked about a lot. I never thought I'd be in the pages of a tabloid, but here I am, a weekly headline. And since the truth is boring, it's much better to tell outright lies. I am finally at the point where I don't care.

"I'm going to live my life on my terms with an even greater conviction than I had when I left Ohio. There isn't one person in this house tonight that has been anything less than supportive of me and Chase. Chase most of all. You should have seen his face when I told him I was keeping her." She took her mom's hands in hers. "I want you and Daddy to be a part of this. But if you're not going to be as proud of this grandchild as Gaylord is of his, then I won't have it. She deserves hugs and kisses, quilts and cookies, regardless of when she was conceived."

Her mom brushed away a tear that fell on her cheek and pulled her in for a hug. "Of course we'll love this child."

"I hope so, Mom." Piper lifted her chin and stepped out of her embrace.

Her mother tilted her head to the side and ran a hand down Piper's arm. "I can't believe my baby is having a baby."

Piper rested a hand on her belly and felt her little girl kick.

"Supper's ready."

Piper looked over at all the guests, heard laughter above the music, and knew in that moment that if her parents walked away and didn't look back, she'd be okay. The love and support from Chase alone would be more than enough to last a lifetime.

The two of them walked over to the outdoor dining table and searched for Chase.

He stood just outside the patio lights, talking to her father.

Her father made several gestures with his hands while Chase nodded the way he did when he was summing up a person's worth.

Gaylord came up behind her. "Your daddy hasn't asked me for a shotgun yet, I think he's safe."

Vivian was close enough to hear and started laughing. "Gaylord. Don't put thoughts in her head."

Jessie walked over. "Mrs. Maddox, would you care for some wine?"

"Yes, actually. That would be nice."

Piper took her seat, eyes glued to the men in her life.

Finally, after what felt like forever, Chase extended a hand to her father, and he shook it. Followed by a pat on the shoulder.

Alex leaned over. "They're both smiling."

Piper blew out a breath, smiled, and took a long drink of water.

"Where's Kitty?"

"You brought a cat?" Jessie asked. "I thought you only had the dog with you."

"No, my dog. Kit. I call him Kitty."

"That dog's name is Kitty?" Gaylord asked. "That's messed up, darlin'."

"He's playing in the barn with the dogs, Bear and Roxy," Jessie told her.

"You have a dog named Bear? That's messed up, Gaylord," Piper tossed back at their host.

Gaylord laughed loud enough to command attention. "I like your sass."

"She has a lot of it," Margaret told him.

Chase moved to his place beside Piper and pulled out his chair. "I missed the joke."

Piper looked at Chase, then her dad.

She hoped Chase's conversation with her dad was as conclusive as hers was with her mother. Either way, they were going to be just fine on their own.

Chase placed a hand over hers on the table and squeezed. She leaned into him and whispered, "I love you."

∽

Dinner was out of this world. Piper ate enough for her, the baby, and the next town over.

They assembled out under the stars. The glow of the patio lights and glass firepit was the perfect end to a wonderful night.

Her parents had visibly relaxed. Maybe it was the wine, but they didn't struggle with things to talk about. Gaylord would tell a story about Jack as a child, and her father would bounce something embarrassing about Piper's growing years. There was a little bit of laughter that gave Piper hope that everything was going to be okay.

Gaylord had walked away at one point and returned with a box. "I know this is a bit soon, but when I saw it, I couldn't stop myself."

He handed the box to Piper.

"What is this?"

"Just a little somethin'."

"You don't have to buy me gifts."

"Who says it's for you?"

Piper smiled, glanced at Chase, and untied the bow before lifting the lid.

Inside was a pint-size cowgirl hat, in dark purple and rhinestones. With baby cowboy boots to match. "Oh my God, these are so adorable."

Chase lifted the hat and popped it on Piper's belly. "It fits."

She pushed it away and stood to hug Gaylord. "Thank you."

"You're slipping, Dad . . . where's the pony?" Jack said with a wink.

"Shush, boy. We need to ease that in slowly." Gaylord patted Piper's back. "You're welcome, darlin'. Glad you like it."

"I love it."

"I have one more surprise." He walked her out, away from the lights.

Her heart started to pound. "You didn't really get a pony."

"Naw. I just like to celebrate life. And since you have one brewing inside of you, I thought we should celebrate hers." Gaylord looked over his shoulder. "Jack, tell them we're ready."

The patio lights dimmed, and Gaylord looked up at the sky.

Out of nowhere, lights started to dance. Not just any lights, but that of drones. Someone turned up the music around them, which synchronized with the show in the sky.

"Wow."

"Oh, Gaylord, that's amazing," Vivian cooed.

The drones outlined a baby's face with a single curl in her hair. The lights shifted and seemed to burst into colors like fireworks.

Everyone moved to their side, eyes on the sky.

Chase snaked a hand around her waist, she leaned into him. "This is nuts."

"Go big or go home, huh, Daddy?" Jessie said.

"No point in making money if you don't spend it."

Next came a purple-studded cowboy hat and boots that danced by themselves, then a baby was added. Then came the shape of a pony, with a baby on its back, wearing the purple hat.

"There's the pony!" Jack said with a laugh.

More bursts resembling fireworks.

Chase moved his hand to her shoulders and rubbed the chill from them.

Then, letter by letter, the drones spelled out *Piper* before going dark.

The next word flashed.

WILL.

Then . . .

YOU.

MARRY.

Piper's jaw dropped.

ME?

She sucked in a breath and turned around.

Behind her, on his knee, Chase held a box in his hand.

Piper sucked in a sharp breath.

"Piper, you are, without exception, the best thing that has ever happened to me. You make me laugh, and you take no shit from me."

Piper covered her smile and felt her eyes swell with happy tears.

"You make me a better man by being in my life. A life I want to live with you. I wake up thinking about you. I daydream about you when we're apart. I want you now, and I want you forever. I promise you all of my tomorrows. If you'll take them."

Piper was shaking, and crying, and smiling so hard her cheeks hurt.

"I love you with everything I am. Please say you'll marry me?"

She choked on a cry, nodding and reaching for him as tears rolled down her face. "You know I will. Yes. Yes . . . a gazillion yesses."

Chase stood and folded her into his arms. Their lips touched with sparks and love.

She heard clapping and the sound of her racing heartbeat.

She whispered in his ear, "This is a lot more than dinner and flowers."

"We're going to have the best life."

He pulled away enough to show her the ring in the box.

"Oh my God!" An oval diamond, large enough to mirror the drones in the sky, set in a whimsical setting with diamonds flowing down the band like ivy. It was way too much and oh-so perfect.

"Alex said you liked this shape."

"It's perfect."

He slipped it onto her finger and kissed her again.

Behind them, real fireworks took off, popping in the sky and filling the air with color and sound.

The drones flashed:

She Said Yes

Wedding bells and churches, and a three-tiered cake . . . all alongside fireworks that couldn't be a better fit to the joy in Piper's heart.

Not that they noticed much of any of it . . . they were in a sea of people, completely alone and staring into each other's future.

Chapter
Thirty-Seven

Jack pulled Chase, Piper, and Alex aside the next day while everyone else was out with Jack and Jessie's kids by the barn and the animals.

Jack handed each of them a photograph. Each of them different. "He goes by Max Smith."

"You found him," Alex said.

"I did."

Chase felt Piper's hand on his arm.

He tapped it as if to say he was okay with the news as he stared at a picture that looked a whole lot like he would if he grew a full beard.

"He's had a colorful life. It took some digging, but we found his records from foster care. The first family that had him lasted less than a year, then he was put back in the system. By the time he entered school, he had three semipermanent placements but ended up back at group homes for long stints in between."

"Oh, God." Piper whimpered.

"How does that happen?" Alex asked.

"I don't know, darlin'. When I saw the report, it made me sick." Jack took a breath and continued. "He has a not-so expertly sealed juvenile record."

Chase wasn't surprised. "Do we want to know how you obtained that?"

Jack shook his head. "Probably not."

"Deniability is important," Piper said.

"He ran away, dropped out of school, came back . . . and eventually aged out of the system."

"Damn," Piper said.

"What does that mean?" Alex asked.

"It means he was never adopted," Piper answered.

"How do you know that?" Chase asked.

"I went down the rabbit hole of what happens to children who end up in foster care and aren't adopted. If the foster parents don't adopt, and there isn't family who steps up, they 'age out' of the system at eighteen. Do we know what he was arrested for?" Piper asked Jack.

"Juvie record was all about theft, breaking and entering . . . assault."

"On women?" Chase asked.

Jack shook his head. "Other boys in the homes, from what I can tell. Good news is, we didn't find anything as an adult. He was on probation into his early twenties where he earned a GED. No college."

"What does he do for a living?"

"A little of everything. Trades mostly. Currently working with a concrete coring company. Whatever he was doing when he was younger doesn't seem to have followed him into adulthood," Jack said.

"That's a relief," Alex muttered.

"Where is he now?" Chase stopped looking at the picture and squeezed Piper's hand that had slipped into his.

"Palmdale, California. Not too far from you."

"Married, kids?"

"Nope."

Chase reached out and patted his sister's back.

"He looks like you." She tried to smile.

"I guess we have a road trip in our future."

"Everything you need to know about Max is in the file."

"Thank you, Jack," Alex said.

"Don't thank me yet, I got more."

Chase lifted his chin. "The mother?"

"No. Not her. Gatlin."

Chase's eyes widened. "You put a PI on Floyd?"

Jack tapped a pencil on his desk. "Yeah. I did that shortly after your visit. My dad and I didn't like how quickly his name came up when we asked you who you were concerned with. Hope you don't mind."

"Hell no, we don't mind," Alex said. "What did you find?"

"Snake in the grass, darlin'. He's met with Melissa twice and three of your board members in private."

"Do we know what was said?" Piper asked.

Jack sat forward. "There was a common thread. He is working on gaining board support to remove you both as CEOs."

"He can't do that, we have the majority of shares."

"He's not convinced you do. That was fed from Melissa."

"I knew she knew something," Alex muttered.

"She doesn't know everything, or she'd have played that card. She's putting suspicion out there to open an investigation. She is one bitter widow." Jack paused, took a breath. "And to add to that, Gatlin is telling the board members that the company has suffered since you've taken over. That the board needs to act to save their own investment."

"There isn't one person on the top floor that wasn't aware that the company has been struggling for a while. Long before Aaron Stone died," Piper told them.

"That's not how Gatlin is spinning it. He's added to the fire by suggesting that the bad media PR is bringing down the Stone name."

Chase and Alex exchanged glances. "Is he behind the press?" Chase asked.

"Don't have confirmation, but it sounds like it."

Alex let out a breath. "Then we fire him."

"Hold up there, spitfire. First, my report isn't going to make it into an HR file. I told my investigator to avoid doing anything illegal, like bugging phones or . . . places. But he doesn't always do as he's told.

Second, you've heard the saying 'keep your friends close and your enemies closer'?"

"Yeah," Chase said.

"You need him to bury himself. You fire him now, and the board
will believe his claims. When your board turns against you, you have
bigger problems on your hands, especially with a struggling company.
No, you keep Gatlin close. You catch him feeding gossip to the media
or fabricating untruths to make you look bad, the board will back you,
not him."

Alex looked at Chase. "He's right."

"I don't like it."

Piper squeezed her hand that held his. "You found your brother.
Let's concentrate on that. Make sure his shares don't make it into someone else's hands."

"Listen to your fiancée, Chase."

Chase found himself smiling on Piper's new title.

"Melissa and Gatlin are a tomorrow problem," Chase concluded
out loud. "We'll handle them. Max is first."

"I couldn't agree more," Jack said.

A collective sigh went over the room.

"This is above and beyond. Tell me what I owe you," Chase said.

Jack shook his head. "No, no . . . that's not how we do things."

"Jack."

"Don't worry, I'm not going to say you owe me one and then ask
you to break someone's legs. This isn't business. This is family. We don't
charge family for favors."

"We can't thank you enough," Alex told Jack.

They stood and started toward the closed door.

"I'll be waiting to hear how it turns out," Jack said.

"You'll be the first to know."

Alex hugged Jack, and then Piper took a turn.

"Congratulations again," Jack said.

"Thank you for everything. This weekend, finding Max. Warning us about Gatlin and Melissa. Calming my parents," Piper said.

Jack shook his head. "Parenting . . . it's the hardest and most rewarding job in the world. A job that never ends. Your mom and pop just want what's best for you . . . and they still think they know what that is. It will all work out."

Piper kissed Jack's cheek. "Thanks all the same."

Chase reached out, shook Jack's hand. "I'll never forget this."

"You'd do the same for us."

"I would." Chase felt the conviction of his words. His world may have expanded exponentially after his father died, but his friendships tightened into a small circle of trust and respect. Two things he had for the Morrisons.

Later that night, still buzzing from the excitement of slipping a ring on Piper's finger and learning where his brother was, Chase watched Piper as she brushed her hair out before they climbed into bed.

"It's strange to realize that it took my father dying to find the love of my life."

Piper dropped the brush onto the vanity of the guest room of the Morrison Ranch on their last night there and turned.

Chase sat on the edge of the bed.

Piper walked over and stood in front of him.

He traced the outline of her belly and dropped a kiss to their daughter.

"I sometimes wonder if one day you're going to break down," Piper told him.

"Because of my father?"

She nodded.

Chase shook his head. "I lost my father a long time ago. Peeling back the layers of his life reminds me every day why he wasn't in mine.

The only thing I'm grateful for is how he led me to you. Not the money, not the company . . . none of that. Only you."

Piper kissed the top of his head. "If the day ever comes where you need to mourn his loss, even if it's twenty years from now, I'll hold you."

Chase felt a strange twisting in his gut, as if Piper had given him permission to feel all the emotions he didn't want to feel.

He pulled her close. "I won't make my father's mistakes. I will never be like him, Piper. I will always put you—both of you—first."

"I know that."

"I want a home like this. Filled with love and laughter, kids and family."

"You won't have to wait long for that wish to come true. You're doubling your siblings, and she's going to be here before you know it," Piper said, patting her belly.

Chase pulled away enough to look at her. "And you. Forever."

She waved her left hand in front of him, his ring glistening on her finger. "I said yes. My tomorrows are all yours, Chase Stone. From here until my last breath."

Chase drew her close and lost himself in her arms.

Epilogue

They had the make and model of a Ford 110 pickup truck registered to Max Smith. It had Arizona plates. The motorcycle he drove was newer. According to the PI's report, Max drove the motorcycle more often than not on his way to and from work.

Palmdale was the last anything before reaching into the Mojave Desert. It was known more for its crime rate than its family-friendly communities, people lived there because they couldn't afford homes closer to their work. It wasn't that there weren't pockets of nice . . . it just didn't have many of them.

Max Smith rented a small home in one of those not-so-nice neighborhoods. Driving through it in Chase's truck had been a good call. Any one of their father's cars would have turned every head on the street.

Chase, Piper, and Alex sat in the truck, waiting for Max to show up. It was unnerving to have so many details about a man who knew nothing about them. The private investigators discovered when Max left work and when he was due home. They knew which bar he frequented on the weekends and which neighbor he didn't get along with.

Chase felt like he'd violated his brother's privacy before even meeting the man.

Since the Arizona-plated truck was in the driveway, they waited for the sight of a motorcycle before approaching the door.

"Maybe they got the time wrong," Alex said from the back seat.

"He's driving from Santa Clarita. There's traffic, even on a motorcycle."

"You think he's in there now?" Piper asked.

"No, I don't. I trust Jack's sources to be right."

Two minutes later, the sound of a bike queued Chase's hand to reach for the door.

In the rearview mirror, he saw what looked like the picture the PI had taken with a long-lens camera.

"That's him."

Max pulled into his driveway as the garage door was rolling up.

Chase jogged across the street in hopes of grabbing Max's attention before he closed the garage door.

The motorcycle turned off, and Max pulled the helmet from his head.

"Max Smith?" Chase called out from the edge of the driveway.

Piper and Alex walked up behind him.

Max looked over his shoulder and swung off his bike. He looked between the three of them. "I don't want whatever you're selling."

Piper laughed. "Miss Abigale all over again."

Max hesitated, looked at her.

"We're not here to sell you anything." Chase stepped closer but kept far enough away so as to not be seen as a threat.

"Still not interested." It looked like Max was going to walk away.

"We know who your father is."

That stopped him, eyes leveled with Chase.

"I don't have one of those."

Piper moved closer to Chase's side. "We know who your sperm donor is."

Doubt with a flash of hate filled Max's eyes. He stared at Piper's belly. "Not interested in knowing him."

"That's a good thing," Alex told him with a snort. "He died in April."

Max blinked several times in silence, then said, "Great. Thanks for stopping by and sharing the happy news." He turned away . . . again.

"Don't you want to know his name?" Alex stepped forward.

Exasperated, Max took a few steps closer and put Chase on edge. "Listen, lady. I don't give two shits about the man who fucked my mother." He stopped, looked at Piper. "No disrespect. So no, I don't care who the hell he was. I've had a long day. I'm tired, I need a shower and a beer. You guys have something to say . . . spit it out."

Chase held out a hand to stop Piper from walking up to the man.

"Your mother's name was Lisa Davis. You were born in Phoenix, Arizona, where you were cared for by a woman named Abigale until your mother abandoned you at the age of two," Piper rattled off the facts.

Max's gaze twitched, the anger in his face shifted after several silent seconds. "Abigale . . . was she a Black woman?"

Alex sighed. "Yes. Her house is filled with quilts and cookies."

"She isn't going to be happy that you remember her," Piper told him.

Max ran a hand over his beard. "This is fucking with my head."

Chase moved closer. "Take a good look at my face."

They had the same eyes, the same jawline. The same hair, minus the beard. Similar build.

"Fuck," Max said under his breath.

"I'm your half brother," Chase told him.

Max's nose flared; his fingers flexed.

Alex moved to Chase's side. "I'm your half sister."

Chase reached into his back pocket and handed Max a copy of the DNA testing paperwork. "The estate will need to confirm this is you. But . . . there's no reason to think it's not."

Max stared at the paper, ran a hand through his hair. "Estate? What estate?"

"Our father . . . your father . . . was Aaron Stone. Stone Enterprises . . . Stone Hotels and Resorts. You know what that is?" Chase asked.

"Yeah." The color in Max's face paled, the fight in his stance dropped as Chase's words registered. Max went from looking at the paper in his hands to Chase and Alex.

"Our father left his entire estate to his *three* children," Chase slowed down his words.

He pointed to Alex. "One."

Chase pointed to himself. "Two."

That finger moved to Max. "Three."

Acknowledgments

Now it's time to thank my team and leave a special message to those I'm dedicating this book to.

Thank you to my newest member of the fold, Lindsey Faber, your eye for details and cheerleading is greatly appreciated. Thank you for helping me make this book shine. It's a pleasure working with you.

As always, thank you to Amazon/Montlake Publishing and Maria Gomez for supporting me in all that I write.

Jane Dystel, my trusted agent and friend, thank you for everything you do.

Now to you ladies . . . the ones who prayed for a period and found two lines on a pregnancy test instead. An unexpected baby has been a romance trope for as long as I've been reading this genre. I felt it was time to put my spin on the difficult path a single woman has in front of her as she struggles with the decision to keep, terminate, or give her child up for adoption.

This decision is never easy, and it is often fueled by the judgment of others. I have had the unique experience of working in an ER for many years of my nursing career. In that time, I held a fifteen-year-old girl who hid her pregnancy well into her second trimester as her mother walked away from her when she found out her daughter was pregnant. The mother's parting words, "Your clothes will be on the porch. You're not welcome in my home."

I've watched a father berate his daughter, saying over and over . . . "But you're going to Harvard." When his daughter said she was keeping her baby, he begged her to terminate the pregnancy because it didn't fit in his plan.

I've witnessed parental judgment tear apart these young women who made a choice to keep their babies. And yes, this book was written with these young women in mind.

And we've all witnessed the judgment that rains down on women who make a choice to not continue an unplanned pregnancy.

I'd like to think that in 2023, we're past the point in our society norms that we villainize women with unplanned pregnancies. Unfortunately, we are not.

You will get no judgment from me.

With light and love . . .

Catherine

For Jack and Jessie Morrison's story, check out *Not Quite Dating*.

Chapter One

"This one's for the ball," Mike said, slurping down his tequila shot. "And this one's for the chain." He chased it with his beer. "Your turn."

Jack sat back as Mike pushed Dean to another round. Dean, the bachelor of the weekend, was well beyond three sheets but kept drinking anyway.

"W-what time is it?" Dean asked.

"You're not allowed to ask until Sunday," Tom reminded him.

"It's not Sunday?" Dean's gaze followed a cocktail waitress wearing a skintight miniskirt.

Jack, Tom, and Mike busted out laughing. "Damn, Moore, we might need to stay in your fine establishment for an entire week to work the bachelor out of this groom."

Jack Morrison's friends always called him Moore: more money, more women, and more time to do whatever he wanted due to his family's portfolio. His buddies at the table had known him since high school. If they ever wanted to stay at the Morrison Hotel and Casino on the Vegas strip for a week or a month or however long, for that matter, Jack would make it happen. They all held executive positions or owned their own businesses, making it nearly impossible for them to get together as it was. The weekend bachelor party would have to do.

Jack had insisted they drive instead of jet over the California desert. With Dean walking the plank—or aisle, as it were—they wouldn't have this golden opportunity again. Dean was the first of the four of them to get married, making this their last trip together as single men. The last time one of them didn't need to rush home to a wife or kids. The last time they could all get pissing drunk and not *have* to explain themselves to a woman. One last bash, complete with Vegas and a road trip . . . what could be better? Once Dean said "I do," it was all going to change. Deep inside Jack knew this . . . was ready for it. Life was a series of chapters, and this one would end in style if he had any say in the matter.

"Oh man, is that Heather?" Tom nudged Jack's arm and nodded toward the casino floor.

Jack followed Tom's gaze as it landed on the back of a woman he knew all too well. She had her platinum blonde hair piled high on her head; her shoulders were bare except for the spaghetti straps of the slim-fitting dress that hugged every surgically enhanced curve of her body. Just when Jack thought he could turn away without her noticing him, she shifted a glance over her shoulder and offered a painted-on smile.

"Well, hell, how did she know we'd be here?" If there was one woman Jack never wished to see again, it was probably Heather. As she swayed her hips while walking in his direction, Jack knew he wasn't going to get his wish.

"She probably heard through the grapevine it was Dean's bachelor party. And you do own the hotel, so where else would the party be," Tom reminded him.

"Jack, sweetheart, what a surprise finding you here." Heather's wispy tone was born of practice and not sincerity.

Unable to avoid her, Jack stood as she approached. She leaned in and kissed his cheek. He quickly stood back and motioned toward his friends. "You remember Tom, Mike, and Dean?"

"Of course." She offered them the fakest of smiles, her eyes narrowing on Dean momentarily before moving back to Jack.

"What brings you to Vegas?" Jack asked, as if he didn't know.

"You told me this was one of your nicer hotels. I thought it was past time for me to spend time in it."

"My father owns the casinos, Heather, not me." All Heather saw was money. Didn't matter where it came from so long as she could access it.

She waved a hand in the air. "You're splitting straws again, Jack."

"Hairs. Splitting hairs."

She placed her fingers on his arm and squeezed. "You know how I dislike being corrected," she reminded him.

You know how I hated you always showing up where I didn't want you. And that was when they were dating. Jack had broken up with her midsummer.

It was now November.

She leaned in and whispered in his ear. "Can we find a moment alone?"

He loosened his tie and tilted his Stetson back on his head. "We're in the middle of a bachelor party, Heather."

Dean tossed back another tequila and sucked on a lime.

"Won't take but a minute, darling."

It hurts to smile when you're gritting your teeth. Jack forced his jaw to unclench at her syrupy endearments. He remembered the day he put a halt to their brief affair. They were attending a fund-raiser at the club in Houston and Jack noticed a beautiful brunette across the room eyeing him. Heather had scolded him with her breathy voice. *"Jack, dear, please try and keep your eyes on me when we're together. I don't care what you do or who you might play with once we're married, but to be so obvious when we're standing next to each other, it's simply boorish, don't you think, darling?"*

Where Heather cooked up the idea she would ever be Mrs. Jack Morrison, he'd never know, but it was then Jack realized how superficial his arm candy was. In a way, he felt sorry for her.

"Well?" Heather pulled him into the present with her question.

Jack knew exactly how to get rid of her, for the last time.

He nodded toward Tom. "Out front in ten?"

Tom grinned. "We'll walk this one around, sober him up a little."

Mike helped Dean to his feet while Jack motioned Heather toward the door.

The two of them wiggled around the people hovering at the slot machines. Someone at a craps table yelled out and the crowd around him cheered. An older woman leaned back in her chair as Heather walked by and brushed against her. Heather scowled and muttered something ugly under her breath.

"Excuse me, miss."

Heather tilted her jaw higher, said nothing, and walked away.

The older woman looked genuinely sorry but at a loss for words.

Embarrassed, Jack took Heather by her arm and led her outside under the bright lights of the valet parking lot. The valet noticed him and snapped to attention. Before the valet moved a foot, Jack waved him off.

"So what are you *really* doing here, Heather?"

She angled her head to the side and painted on a smile. "I don't like where we've been lately, Jack. I miss you."

Jack held his ground when she moved forward. "There isn't a *we* any longer. I thought I made myself clear."

"I've given you a break. Now I want the break to be over." She slid her hand over his chest.

He stopped her by holding on to her wrist.

"I didn't ask for a break. I said we were over. We don't want the same things." He didn't want a trophy wife, and that was all Heather could offer.

The edges of her lips fell into a pout. "We know the same people, play in the same circles. We're perfect for each other."

"No, we're not. I want someone to be with me for more than my wallet. We both know that woman isn't you." Jack noticed the diamond-studded bracelet hanging off her wrist. They had been dating during her last birthday and Jack had given it to her. He regretted the gift now.

Heather's fake pout faded and a spark of anger flashed in her eyes. "Every woman with you is going to be there for the money, Jack. I just happened to be honest about it."

Her words stung, probably because they held some truth. It was hard to look past his father's billions and Jack's own millions. Still, the blonde in front of him had just made it clear she didn't care about him at all. Jack drew the line there.

He waved to the senior valet, who quickly ran over.

"Yes, Mr. Morrison?"

"Can you bring my car around?"

The valet glanced at Heather, then back at Jack. "A hotel car, sir?"

"No, my car. The one I arrived in."

"Yes, sir. Right away, sir."

Heather smiled up at him, probably assuming she'd won something.

"Is there somewhere I can have my driver take you?" Jack asked. "Or are you staying here?"

"I have a suite at the Bellagio. But I don't mind a move." Another sickening smile lifted her lips.

Jack's friends made their way out of the casino through the heavy glass doors.

"The Bellagio is perfect for you. I suggest you enjoy your time there."

Her facade fell and anger straightened her jaw. "You'll regret this someday, Jack. You're going to marry some woman thinking she loves you and in the end be brokenhearted because she wants your trust fund."

Out of the corner of his eye, he noticed his ride pull up. He walked to his twin cab, a well-past-its-prime pickup, dirty from the long drive, and opened the door.

"What is that?" she barked and stepped away as if the truck was a snake about to strike.

Finally, a real smile lifted Jack's lips. The look of absolute horror on Heather's face was worth her annoying presence. "It's your ride to the Bellagio."

"I'm not getting in that thing. What did you do, drive it from Texas?"

Actually, he'd had it shipped to California for his latest business venture, and that's when he and the boys had decided to drive it to Vegas. "Something like that. C'mon, get in."

"I will do no such thing."

"Suit yourself." Jack opened the door wide and waved his friends in. "C'mon, boys. We have a bachelor to send off." Jack turned to the kid who had jockeyed the truck around. "What's your name, buddy?"

"Russell, sir. I'm new here." The kid was maybe twenty-four.

"You know your way around Vegas, right?"

"Lived here all my life."

Jack patted him on the back while Mike helped Dean into the backseat. Tom loaded in behind them. "Well, Russell, my friends and I need a driver tonight. We have some serious drinking to do and could use someone sober with us. You game?"

"I'm working."

"And I'm paying you." Jack waved the head valet over. "It's Carrington, right?" he asked the senior valet.

"Yes, sir."

"Carrington, Russell is going to help us out for a few hours. I hope that's OK."

"Of course, Mr. Morrison. Whatever you want."

Jack winked at the man and turned toward the truck. When he lifted his foot into the cab, Heather called out.

"What about me?"

Jack spared her a glance. "I offered you my ride, darlin'. Maybe a Vegas cabbie would suit you better. Carrington, would you mind finding Miss Heather a ride?"

Carrington shifted his eyes from Heather to Jack a few times and then lifted his hand for one of the many cabs waiting in line to take guests to their next destination.

Heather lifted her arms over her shoulders. "Jack!" she yelled as he shut the door.

He tilted his hat as a good-bye while Russell shifted the truck in gear.

"Jack Morrison!" Jack could still hear her screaming as they pulled away.

"Ho boy, that is one ticked-off woman," Tom said, looking over his shoulder. "I don't know what you ever saw in her."

"She was a mistake." A huge one. Jack was thankful his heart never got involved.

"Jack Morrison. Hey, you wouldn't happen to be related to Gaylord Morrison, the owner of the hotel, would you?" Russell asked as he pulled out onto the strip.

Dean, Mike, and Tom started laughing.

"Did I say something funny?"

Jack buckled his belt and sat back. "That would be my dad."

~

"Overdue . . . overdue . . . oh great, a shut-off notice." Jessica Mann placed the highlighted water bill on the top of her pile with a grunt. Looking around the tiny break room of the twenty-four-hour diner she worked in proved just as bleak a view as her future. She really did need to make some changes in her life, and soon.

Leanne, the other graveyard shift waitress who worked with her, poked her head through the door and said, "You're up. A party of four just sat on twelve."

Jessie glanced at her watch and saw that it was twenty minutes past two in the morning. The after-bar crowd would soon start strolling in for black coffee and a place to sober up before their trek back home.

Like clockwork, Sunday mornings were the worst. The truly stupid actually thought they could grab a cup of joe and still manage to make it to work on time. After tucking her bills into her purse, Jessie stepped out of the break room, through the short hall separating the kitchens from the service counter, and proceeded to table twelve. With any luck, one of the four people in the party would be sober enough to remember to tip her before they left.

Hearty male laughter met her ears before she rounded the corner to greet her customers.

Two faces peeked over open menus while the other two caught her gaze as she approached.

"Whew, hey, darlin'. Are you our waitress tonight?" a dishwater blond sitting on the end of the booth asked. With his question, the other men at the table lowered their menus to look at her.

A quick assessment told Jessie that the yahoos at the table were definitely coming off a night of drinking. Maybe even a couple nights from the state of their five o'clock shadows.

Dishwater flashed his white teeth and a little-boy smile. The man to his left elbowed him in his side. "Pay no attention to Dean. He hasn't been sober for three days."

"You're one to talk, Mikey." These words came from a robust man wearing a baseball cap and at least two days of stubble on his chin.

"Jack is the only one remotely sober," Mikey said.

Yep, definitely a party crowd.

The one they called Jack took his time lowering his menu before acknowledging Jessie. His dark brown hair, topped with a Stetson, tilted as he moved his head. The stubble on his chin held the perfect amount of sexy. The slow, steady soaking in of his stare settled on her from the most unusual gray eyes Jessie had ever seen. Those smoky eyes took their ever-lovin' time as his gaze slid over her hair, her face. After looking his fill, he caught her eyes again and held them. As if calculated for effect, Jack allowed a slow and delicious smile, complete with dimples, to spread over his face. A smile meant only for her.

Smiles like that should come with a warning label. His staunch attention did a number on her belly and raised gooseflesh on her bare arms. She swallowed hard, and her skin tingled as if he'd caressed her.

Jessie blinked a few times, broke eye contact, and asked, "How about some coffee?"

"That would be great," Jack replied with an accent that matched his cowboy hat.

The Texan accent pulled a warm and fuzzy blanket over her insides. Southern California natives didn't have any discernible accent at all, so when she heard one, she remembered it.

Pivoting, Jessie shoved her notepad into her apron and walked to the coffeepot.

"Isn't she something to look at?" one of the party boys said.

Jessie knew she wasn't ugly, but she didn't see all that much when she looked into the mirror. Her light brown hair sat twisted into a knot at the base of her neck; her dull hazel eyes had dark smudges beneath them indicating a lack of sleep, and it was hard to be fat when all her money went to bills and care for her son, Danny.

The four men . . . no, make that boys . . . at table twelve probably didn't have one decent responsibility to scrape together if they combined them. They were all wearing jeans and T-shirts, and two of them smelled like beer.

Frat boys who never grew up. Heck, maybe they were all still in school. Jessie guessed their ages to all be about the same, around twenty-eight or so.

Returning to the table, Jessie set down coffee cups and filled them. "Thank you . . . Jessica," Jack with the mysterious gray eyes said after a quick glance at her name tag.

"Jessie, actually. Where are you boys coming from?" she asked, making conversation.

"Weekend in Vegas," the one named Mikey told her.

She should have guessed.

"Our buddy Dean here is tying the knot in a few weeks, so we decided to send him off in style."

"Vegas can be a dangerous place to have a bachelor party," she said.

"See, that's what I said," the man sitting next to Jack told them. "But does anyone listen to Tom? Heck no. You think everything went great and next thing you know your drunk ass is dancing naked on YouTube with some chick you don't even remember."

"I didn't dance naked with some chick . . . did I?" Dean rubbed the back of his neck and frowned.

Jack shot a dimpled grin at his friend. "You were pretty wasted."

"I still don't remember any naked dancing."

"Oh, chill," Mikey told him. "No one was *taping* you dancing naked."

Jessie had to smile. The boys were giving their friend a hard time, and it was fun to watch. From the look on Dean's face, he wasn't entirely sure he hadn't danced in the buff.

"You guys know what you want, or should I give you a few more minutes to decide?" Jessie asked.

"I know what I want," Tom said, setting his menu on the table.

The others chimed in the same. After taking their orders, Jessie left.

Leanne smiled her way once Jessie gave the cook the order. "Looks like a handful over there. Cute times four," she sighed with a smile.

"Two of 'em have accents, too."

"Lookie you, checking them out."

"I'm not checking anyone out. The last thing I need is another playboy messing up my life."

Jessie turned around and refilled the coffee cup of one of her night-owl customers sitting at the counter. "How are the pancakes, Mr. Richman?"

"Fine, just fine," he replied.

When Jessie turned back to Leanne, the other waitress continued talking. "Who's to say they're a bunch of playboys?"

"Frat boys who never grew up, most likely."

"Playboys, frat boys, whatever. One of 'em could be the rich guy of your dreams."

Jessie raised an eyebrow. "Right." Grabbing Leanne's hand, Jessie led her to a far window overlooking the parking lot. "Take a look, sister. See any crazy-expensive cars out there?" Actually, the only cars in the lot belonged to the employees and Mr. Richman. Except for one lone pickup that was new sometime in the mid-1990s. That seemed about the right speed for the cowboys at table twelve.

"That doesn't mean nothing." Leanne pulled away and frowned. "Besides, dating means free meals and a movie. Nothing wrong with that."

"Dinner and a movie in my world consist of McDonald's and *SpongeBob* on TV. Dating and Danny don't mix."

"Your sister will watch him for you."

"Yeah, but why waste my time on someone dreaming of the future instead of living it? You know my mom isn't the wisest woman in the bunch, but she told me once that it is just as easy to fall in love with a rich man as it is to fall in love with a poor one."

"Yeah, so?"

"So don't date poor men."

Across the restaurant, Jack with the gray eyes and the Stetson was watching her over his coffee cup. When he caught her gaze, his lips pulled into a grin, dimples and all. Then, without any provocation, he winked.

"Oh boy." Jessie lowered her eyes and tried to ignore the flirting frat playboy and the way his attention made her insides squirm.

"Mr. Cowboy is sexy." Leanne giggled when she spoke.

"I'll bet Mr. Cowboy mooches off one of his friends for the bill."

"Oh, come on, he can't be that bad."

"He's flirting with a waitress at Denny's, Leanne. His ambitions can't be all that high."

⁓

"Dissed!" Mike laughed, punching Jack in the arm. "Doesn't look like the waitress is taking a liking to you."

"Might have something to do with the way you're dressed, Moore."

"There's nothing wrong with the way I'm dressed." In fact, he liked the fact that Jessie, the sexy waitress wearing a god-awful brown skirt, had no idea who he was. Jack stayed out of the spotlight as often as he could. Here in California, people didn't know him by sight. In Houston, the story was entirely different. The thought of charming the waitress without waving his wallet felt like the right thing to do, especially after his recent encounter with Heather.

Jack removed his wallet and quickly handed Tom a twenty.

"What's this for?"

"Breakfast."

"Why are you giving it to me now?"

"Just hold on to it. If it comes up, I'm just a shit-kicker coming off a long binge of a weekend." Jack followed Jessie's movements until she disappeared around the corner.

Hell, he'd be in Ontario, California, for several weeks, overseeing the construction plans of a new hotel off the convention center. He might as well hook up with someone while he was there. He would love to burn the image of every Heather he ever knew out of his mind once and for all. Plastic *What can you do for me baby* women who flirted with his wallet more than him. There were times this kind of woman didn't bother him at all, but lately he'd been searching for someone he could talk to, someone to share his ideas and dreams with, maybe a down-to-earth waitress who wasn't ashamed to get her hands dirty and work for a living. Or ride in an old pickup truck.

Jack wasn't afraid of hard labor on the ranch or pushing papers at a desk. Ever since he'd finished college and his father put him in acquisitions and mergers, he'd gone out of his way to excel at his job. Unlike his sister, Katie, who probably did lunch with Paris Hilton, Jack actually wanted to work for a living. Living off his father's money didn't sit well with him. When the day came for Jack to take over for his father, no one could accuse him of being a slacker who was handed the job without any knowledge of how to do it.

"Hookay, I see what you're doing," Tom said.

"Do you?" Jack asked.

"Yeah, I do. I saw you this weekend, dodging the women at the hotel. For a while there I was wondering who was getting married next month, you or Dean," Mike said. "Tired of all the gold diggers, aren't you?"

"Tired of all the liars."

"That would suck," Tom agreed.

"My Maggie is the best th-thing that's ever happened to me," Dean told them.

"Lordy, now he's gonna go and get all emotional on us." Tom pushed Dean's coffee cup closer to him. "Drink up. Maggie, the fair maiden, isn't going to like it if you come home smelling like a bar."

Dean propped his elbows on the table and held his head up with his hands. "She's the best. And the sex."

"We've heard it, Dean."

"All friggin' weekend," Tom chimed in.

"You guys are just jealous."

Jack sipped his coffee and kept his mouth closed. He was happy for his friend, but not so sure Maggie was the right choice. Dean loved to play: motorcycles, camping, boating trips on the river. He wasn't afraid of hard work to pay his way, either. But ever since Maggie walked into his life, Dean gave up a little bit of himself daily.

"Maggie's worried that I'll get in an accident on the motorcycle."

"Maggie doesn't enjoy the river; boating makes her nauseous."

"Maggie would rather stay at one of your hotels instead of an RV."

Maggie might make Dean smile, but how long would it be before he blew his lid being molded into what she wanted him to be?

Jessie strolled around the corner with her arms stacked with plates. With choreographed ease, full breakfasts slid over the table and condiments emerged from the pockets of her dull, stiff uniform.

"It smells great, Jessie," Jack told her before she walked away.

"I'll let the cook know you're pleased."

Tom and Dean shoveled food into their greedy mouths.

Jessie disappeared long enough to grab a pot of coffee to refill their cups. "Are we missing anything?" she asked.

"I think we're good." Jack tried to capture her eyes, but she avoided them.

"Let me know if you need anything. You can see we're just swamped tonight."

Jack noted the one lone customer at the counter. "I'll bet you could tell some stories about working the graveyard shift at Denny's," Jack said, trying hard as hell to get her to reveal a thing or two about herself.

"It's hard to stay awake most nights. We start to pick up around four thirty."

"That's an ungodly hour," Tom said between bites.

"You'd be surprised at the number of suits that come in for a bite before heading into LA to work. They start early to avoid traffic."

"I'd heard that LA traffic was bad, but *that* bad?" Jack asked.

"The worst. You must not live here if you have to ask."

"I'm from Texas, mostly. My most recent job brought me here, near the airport." Ontario International Airport took some of the burden off LAX and Burbank, but the land around those airports was built out, without any ability to grow. Ontario provided plenty of room for new hotels.

Mike nudged him in the arm. "Bums off my place when he wants a decent night's sleep."

Which wasn't exactly a lie, Jack thought. Mike lived over in Claremont, and Jack sometimes stopped by to crash when he wanted a break from the hotel. The Morrison was a five-star luxury hotel filled with champagne and caviar. Sometimes Jack just wanted pizza, beer, and a ball game on the tube with a friend.

Jessie seemed to mull over the information a bit too long. She shrugged her shoulders with a flash of disappointment. "Well, enjoy your food." With that, she turned and walked away.

Dean laughed. "Not so easy, is it?"

"I'm not done yet," Jack told him as he picked up his fork. *Not by a long shot.*

By three, most of the food was gone and a few new customers had shown up at the counter, pulling Jessie away from their table.

An older man in his seventies turned in his chair to leave the counter and Jessie rushed to his side. "I told you to let me help you, Mr. Richman."

"I can do it," the older man said. But as he rose to his feet, he swayed against Jessie.

"It's the moisture in the air. Swells up my old bones," he explained.

Jessie wrapped her arm around his waist and helped him to the door, where he'd left his walker. Even then, she didn't turn away.

"I can make it from here," he told her.

"I'm sure you can, but I could use some air. All this bacon grease is getting to me. Walk me outside?" she asked him.

Mr. Richman offered a small smile as she opened the door and helped him to his car.

A couple minutes later, she walked back in with a contented grin on her lips.

"Hey, Jessie," the other waitress called from the cash register.

"Yeah?"

"Your buddy didn't leave enough money again."

Jack watched Jessie's eyes travel to the door. She shrugged and reached into her skirt pocket and pulled out her tips. "I've got it, Leanne."

Leanne shook her head. "I don't know why you cover him all the time."

"It's pancakes, Leanne. And he doesn't have anyone. Give the guy some slack."

Jessie covered the rest of the man's bill and walked away from the register.

Something inside Jack clicked into place. He absolutely needed to know more about Jessie.

Each time she returned to refill the coffee, Jack tried to engage her in some kind of conversation. She didn't bite. Jack started to think that maybe she wasn't interested, but the fact that she wouldn't look him in the eye, and how her cheeks took on an adorable rosy color when he paid her a compliment, proved she wasn't unaffected by his charms.

Jessie cleared their table and placed the bill in the middle. "I'll take this whenever you're ready," she told them.

For a minute Jack was tempted to toss his credit card on the table and cover the meal to see if Jessie would look him in the eye then. Tom saved him the trouble.

"Guess you want me to cover this one, too, huh, Jack?"

"Hey, I drove," he said.

"And we paid for gas." Which actually was the arrangement; staying at the Morrison Hotel and Casino in Vegas was on Jack.

Tom, Dean, and Mikey tossed bills on the table and handed them to Jessie. "Keep the change," Tom told her.

After Jessie walked away, Mike said, "Looks like you struck out with this one."

"Man, I can't believe my head is still spinning," Dean said.

Jack dug into his pocket for the keys to the truck. "Here, Mike. Why don't you see Tom off at the airport? Dean and I will stay for another cup of coffee."

"You know, that's a great idea. Getting in a car right now probably wouldn't sit well with my stomach." Dean looked a little green.

"When does your flight leave again?"

"Six," Tom said.

"We best get you there. Airport security takes forever to get through these days."

They all stood and shook hands.

"See you back home next month," Jack told his friend.

A strong pat on the back and Tom said, "Good luck, Moore."

Jack sat back down after Tom and Mike left. Dean laid his arms on the table and rested his head in them. "Why did you guys let me drink so damn much? Maggie hates it when I drink too much."

"We'll get you sober before we drag your sorry ass home."

Jessie did a double take when she noticed only two of their party leaving. Jack waved her over to the table.

"Your friends leaving without you?"

"Tom's flying back to Texas, and Dean is in need of more black coffee before we release him to his fiancée."

"Fair enough." Holding a pot in her hand, Jessie poured another splash for both of them.

Before she could walk away, Jack flashed his winning smile. "So, Jessie, could I interest you in a night out?"

She cocked her head to one side. "Was that a pickup line?"

Miffed, Jack shook his head. "If you have to ask, I must be losing my touch."

Dean laughed but kept his trap shut.

"I'm flattered, Jack. It is Jack, right?"

He nodded. "Why do I feel a *but* coming on?" Jack asked.

Jessie placed a free hand on the table and leveled her eyes with his. "*But* I'm a very busy woman. So unless you have a checkbook as big as your ego—and my guess is, since your friends spotted you for your meal and gas, you're probably broke—I'm not interested."

Dean blew out a whistle.

Jack was nearly too stunned to answer.

Jessie just kept on staring at him until he uttered, "Well, I'll be damned. I think that's the first time anyone has ever said that to me."

Jessie straightened her shoulders and lifted her eyebrows. "Well, at least I'm honest. You're cute, cowboy, I'll give you that. But cute doesn't buy you a cup of coffee in this town. Now maybe in Texas it does. You might try a waitress back home."

"I'm not in Texas. Besides, it's you I want to take out."

"Again, I'm flattered, but no thanks."

"You think I'm cute," he said, which wasn't the highest compliment he'd been given in recent years, but he'd work with it.

A smirk played on Jessie's face. "You don't give up, do you?"

"No. Not easily."

"OK then, how about this . . . I wait tables in this dive at night so I can spend more time with my five-year-old son at home."

Jack's gaze flicked to her left hand. No ring. "If you're married, why don't you just say so?"

She shook her head and rolled it back. "Married, as if. Honey, I don't even get child support. Not that any of this is your business."

Not married, raising a son on her own, and having to work grave-yard to do it. No wonder she was looking for a wallet and not love. Heather's words hovered in his mind. *Every woman is going to be with you for your money, Jack.* But this woman, Jessie, didn't have a clue about his wallet. And if she was so money hungry, why did she routinely foot the bill for her customers' pancakes? There was more to this beautiful woman than she was letting on. Suddenly the challenge of winning her over besieged him.

Jessie started to turn away.

He stopped her. "Kids love me."

Jessie's jaw dropped. "Does he ever give up?" she asked Dean.

"Nope."

"Do all the women fall for him?"

"Yep."

She mumbled something as she walked away.

"Dude, you're barking up the wrong skirt," Dean said after she left. "She's just not into you."

"No, she doesn't *want* to be into me."

"She has a kid, Jack. She's smart to not wanna date men who are posing as losers."

The gentle sway of her hips kept his attention as she walked away. In that moment he realized how long it had been since he had to pursue a woman. "*Posing* being the key word." Jack scratched the stubble on his jaw and smiled beneath his hand. *Posing as a loser.*

About the Author

Photo © 2022 Ellen Steinberg

New York Times, Wall Street Journal, and *USA Today* bestselling author Catherine Bybee has written thirty-eight books that have collectively sold more than ten million copies and have been translated into more than twenty languages. Raised in Washington State, Bybee moved to Southern California in the hope of becoming a movie star. After growing bored with waiting tables, she returned to school and became a registered nurse, spending most of her career in urban emergency rooms. She now writes full time and has penned the Not Quite series, The Weekday Brides series, the Most Likely To series, and the First Wives series.